ELENA
The Girl with the Piano

Veronica H. Hart

Uppity Women Press
Ormond Beach, Florida

Uppity Women Press

Elena-The Girl with the Piano
Copyright © 2015 Veronica H. Hart
ISBN # 978-0692492024

Author Photograph provided by Barbie Marland – used with permission

Cover Artwork: White Rabbit Graphix - Chris Holmes

This novel is a work of fiction. Names, characters, places, and incidents either are the product of the author's imagination or are used fictitiously.

Dedication

To Doris Grace Deare Hart, who sat under her dining room table reading to her little boy, Robert, while the bombs fell.

Also to all those survivors and their children who had to learn to live with the demons and nightmares

Acknowledgments

No book is written in a vacuum. The people who critiqued the book as I wrote helped keep me on track. I especially thank Joan King, Lois Gerber, Michael J. Carlson, Steven Smith, Jeff Boyle, and James Weiss. They are members of the Florida Writers Association who meet in different places here in Daytona. Several others, including Trisha Ruffino and Julie Eberhardt Painter, also reviewed the story and made helpful suggestions. My favorite amongst them all is my granddaughter, Lindsay Marie McIntyre, who acted as my beta reader. As a history buff, her suggestions and comments proved eminently helpful.

I also relied heavily on *The Second World War*, by John Keegan, published by Viking, *Encyclopedia of World War II*, edited by John Keegan, published by Great Pond Publishing as well as many interviews and letters on the internet with survivors of that time, including Russians, Germans, Poles, Austrians and Englishmen.

I thank Yana Maxwell, my young Russian friend, for her advice on Russian culture.

And last, but definitely not least, my husband, Bob, without whom I would be completely lost.

Foreword

I fell in love with the idea of Elena many years ago. Although this book is a work of fiction, I met several women who had survived extraordinary trials throughout WWII, including incarceration in concentration camps, and I have felt the need to memorialize them in some small way. One, a German who had been locked up with other Jewish prisoners, spoke very little about her ordeal, but wore her tattooed numbers without shame. One evening in the early 1960's her two teenaged daughters and I were playing with a new stereo sound system. I put on a sound effects record. We all laughed as a train ran through the house, dogs barked and cats meowed. My two friends and I laughed in amazement when fire alarms and ambulance sirens filled the room. To my astonishment, their mother rushed into the room, ran to her daughters, and slapped them both, hard, across their faces, and angrily spoke to them in German. When everyone had calmed down, she explained to us about the terror those noises held for her. She then told us a little about her experiences in the camps.

While I was studying Russian at college, the professor organized a bistro night of poetry reading and music where I met an opera singer from Leningrad, U.S.S.R. My new friend offered to help me with Russian if I would help her with English. She introduced me to her entire family and then told me how they walked from Leningrad to Germany.

I have used facts from their stories and from others, some who remember sitting under dining room tables while bombs rained over the countryside. I combined their stories to create the fictional Elena.

Elena

The Girl with the Piano

Veronica Helen Hart

PART I

LEAVING LENINGRAD

One

Leningrad, September 1942

Elena opened the lace handkerchief she had been using to filter the muddy water and found a pale, wrinkled finger curled inside.

She closed her eyes and shuddered as she threw it into the gutter. Just as quickly she opened her eyes and looked about for the body it came from. She saw only the rain-soaked pavement and puddles reflecting the burnt-out remnants of apartment buildings that mocked her from both sides of the broad avenue.

Her ears rang all the time from the shelling, bombing, and burning of Leningrad that had been going on forever. She did not want to see any more staring corpses or pick up more pieces of dead bodies. As she went on her daily rounds, she wanted only to find puddles large enough to scoop the water into a metal cup. If she could not find a good source of water, she had to strain the mud. Which is how she found the finger, a remnant of another starved, frozen body.

"Elena!" Her mother's voice echoed in the canyon of abandoned buildings.

Elena turned her head. At fourteen she ought to be preparing for a major recital. Instead she shared a corner in the basement with her parents and grandparents and played on a make-believe piano. She looked down the broad avenue, once lined with trees and remembered walking with her parents to the Winter Palace where the Imperial family had once lived. Now wounded soldiers covered the floor where the young grand duchesses grew up. Leningrad, the Venice of the north, a city once with a population of three million. Since the siege began, at least four hundred thousand had died. How many would die this winter?

"I'm coming, Mama. I'm almost finished," she shouted, tucking her handkerchief into her coat pocket. Tears burning her cheeks were from the smoke that drifted across the broad avenues. They're not from anything else, she told herself. They were not from finding fingers caught in lace handkerchiefs, nor from seeing corpses crudely wrapped in blankets and laid out in front of the buildings every day for the wagons to collect. The tears were not because she had not had enough to eat since her thirteenth birthday party; the day the shelling began over a year ago. It was also the day her best friend Tatiana disappeared.

She hunched her neck down into the fur collar of the red coat her mother and father had given her on her birthday last year. This year, on August 8, when she turned fourteen, Mama lowered the hem but she did not have to let it out.

She raised her face and opened her mouth to collect the liquid mist on her tongue. Maybe winter would forget to come this year and they could go straight to spring.

She picked up the half-filled bucket and nodded greetings to two other women who also collected water during the break in the shelling. An old man and a small child pulled a wagon down the center of the street. The wagon held a blanket wrapped body. Elena bowed her head.

Mama opened the door and snatched the bucket from her. "Why do you take so much time, Elena? If the soldiers see you, they might stop to question you. They can take you away for no reason."

Elena covered her ears, not wanting to hear it anymore. "The soldiers will kill you. The soldiers will hurt you. The soldiers will come and take your father away. They eat little girls for dinner." Soldiers, soldiers, soldiers. And those were the good soldiers, The Russians, the ones on their side. She threw herself down on her straw pallet in the corner. If that's what the good soldiers were like, she hated to think what the Germans would do if they found her family.

And then there was the KOMSOMOL[1]. She had refused to join, much to the annoyance of her father. He had belonged to the organization as a young man, and now was a loyal Communist Party member. He often pointed out that they would not have such a fine apartment, nor would he have his job as supervisor at the shoe factory if he hadn't been a member. His parents, her Grandpa and Grandmama, on the other hand, praised her for her independent thinking.

Mama further strained the murky water from the pail through layers of cheesecloth before dumping it into the big soup pot on the stove. This morning her grandmother had found two potatoes and a handful of burnt flour on her daily rounds, scavenging for food. They would have thickened soup for supper tonight.

"Why won't you call me Katya?" Elena complained as she set the bowls out on the metal table. Their elegant mahogany dining table had been sacrificed for firewood months ago. One beautifully carved antique chair remained of their fine furniture. Elena watched her father in the evenings as he sat in it and rubbed his hands along the polished curves of the arms. He would close his eyes and smile. She knew he was remembering the better days. As long as he had the chair, the family would be all right.

"Because your name is Elena. It's a fine name."

KOMSOMOL – Young Communist League, founded 1918, for youth aged 14 – 28. The party provided preferential treatment for jobs and education, amongst other things.

"But I want to be Katerina. I prefer that name. I only hear Elena when you're annoyed at me. 'Elena, you have not practiced enough today.'" She waited for her mother's sharp rebuke.

"I must sit down for a moment," Mama said instead. Even in the dimness of the candlelight, Elena could see her mother's face go pale. Father, who had been hovering next to the stove trying to read an American novel, hardly took notice. Without looking up from his book, he reached out and pulled a metal kitchen chair closer to the tile stove and put out a hand to help ease his wife into it.

Elena rolled her eyes. If she were the father in this family, she would be out killing Nazis or finding food, not hiding at home reading books. She longed for a fresh tomato or a bowl of real borscht. Today Grandmama said the authorities planned to reduce the food rations yet again. How little could a human being eat and still remain alive, she wanted to know. "When I go back to school, I shall be Katerina and my friends shall call me Katya," she grumbled as she ladled food into the bowls.

"Ah! Grigory Alexandrovich! What will we do with this child?" Mama groaned.

What could they do with her? The entire family was trapped in the remnants of the basement apartment which once belonged to the superintendent and his mean wife, a smart couple who left the city when the shelling first began. Elena had come downstairs one morning after a bad night of shelling to find only the gas mask the superintendent wore as he stood guard outside the building. The mask lay atop a low brick wall. Elena confiscated the mask and hid it in her room. Whenever her parents talked of the possibility of "Fritz" using chemical weapons, she wished she had remembered it and brought it with her when they evacuated to the basement. Now it was lost in the rubble.

Soup slopped over the edge of the last bowl as Elena set it down too hard. She cringed, fearing criticism from one of the adults, but no one even seemed to notice. Were they all too weakened with hunger to care? She carefully wiped up the spilled liquid, hoping they still wouldn't notice. Everyone's temper had been on edge lately, but not today.

Other families packed their things and headed for the countryside a long time ago. But Father had had his job at the factory. He was the supervisor so he could not leave. Mama would not go without him. And even if they wanted to leave now, where would they go? Everybody was dying either of starvation or from the cold. She heard Grandmama and Grandpa rustling about on their pallet as they gathered themselves together to come over to the table for supper.

With a big sigh, Mama got up and took the bread from the shelf above the stove. With the precision of a surgeon, she cut a portion for each member of the family. By some bureaucrat's fiendishly devised scheme they were down to two hundred fifty grams for children and four hundred for adults, which was twice as much as they had been receiving in January thanks to so many people dying during last winter's bitter cold.

"Tonight I'll play the Bach first," Elena said as Mama, apparently revived by the thin soup, tidied the makeshift kitchen following supper. Elena pulled her "piano" out from the cupboard and unrolled it onto the tabletop.

The "piano" she played was a strip of burgundy velvet on which her grandmother and mother had stitched black and white keys, using linens and dress fabric they'd rescued from the apartment.

Their building had been hit last June during the nightly shelling. They, along with the three other families who remained in the building, huddled in the basement hallway, listening to the bombs and shells raining down on their homes. When quiet returned near dawn, they'd worked their way out of the basement to find they'd lost their home. And she, her real piano. Even moving down into the cellar wasn't as bad as losing her music. On her birthday in August, her family had presented her with the new "piano."

She flexed her fingers before running them across the improvised keyboard.

Father came and sat next to her, watching closely as she began to play, humming the notes as she struck them. When she finished the piece, he said, "Excellent, little one. Now you must play a cheerful gypsy song for your parents. What shall it be?"

"That's easy." She laughed as she began "The Laughing Song." Her parents and grandparents joined in and by the time she reached the end they were all laughing.

She could almost pretend they were on the fifth floor sitting in the parlor with a fire blazing in the fireplace. Before bed, Sofia, the housekeeper, would bring in a pot of hot chocolate for them. The memory brought unexpected tears to her eyes. Sofia had been like another mother to them all, an old woman who came with the family to the city after the peasants had run Elena's grandparents from their home. She had died during the first round of bombings when a wall fell on her. Elena wiped the tears away before anyone could see them, then she made herself busy rolling her "piano" into a small bundle. "I'm tired. Do you mind if I go to bed?"

Her father hugged her. "Of course, you rest. Now say your prayers and I will give you a kiss."

Elena knelt next to the small straw pallet on which she slept. She blessed herself in the Orthodox manner before saying the ritual prayers. When she finished, she prayed silently. "And finally, Dear Jesus, I want all the Germans to die and I want Mama and Papa to call me Katya. Thank you. Amen." She said the last aloud so her father would know she was finished. After she crawled between the woolen blankets, Papa came over to her, knelt down beside her, said his own prayers and then kissed his daughter's forehead. Elena smiled, some things would never change as long as she was with her family.

She thought about her father for a moment and decided she would rather have a live coward father who worked in a shoe factory, than a dead hero father who shot people.

Two

A loud banging on the door jolted her awake.

"Over here quickly, Elena!"

She stumbled in the dark toward her mother's voice, dragging her blankets. The stove had been banked for the night and the room was cold. She felt her way onto her parent's bed, making sure to place her body on the raised lump. She drew the blankets around her shoulders careful to spread the edges over as much of the bed as she could cover. Her father's life would depend on her ability to remain calm while he hid, buried in the middle of the straw bed.

The banging continued. "Open the door immediately or we'll break it down!"

"You can wait out there until I make myself decent!" Mama shouted at them while she pushed and prodded at the straw around Elena. Once satisfied she struck a match and lit the lantern before going to the door to slide back the heavy bolt. The door crashed open and two uniformed soldiers pushed their way into the room bringing with them a blast of cold air.

Mama positioned herself between them and Elena, effectively blocking them from her view. But Elena already knew who they were. They weren't soldiers at all; they were her former schoolmates, Boris and Mikhail. She and Tatiana had had crushes on them at school. The boys were two years ahead of them and members of the KOMSOMOL. Tonight each wore tattered bits and pieces of military uniforms which made them appear menacing. While Elena and her family shriveled from starvation, these two seemed to have grown. The room felt smaller with them in it.

"Where is your husband, Citizen Federova?" Boris asked in a rough voice while Mikhail waved a flashlight around the room, lighting first one corner then another.

"You keep a civil tongue in your head, young man. You're frightening my daughter and the old people." She pointed to the other bed where Grandpa and Grandmama lay with their blankets drawn up to their chins. Elena knew Mama was trying to distract the intruders from her.

"Grigory Alexandrovich Federov lived in this building. Where is he?"

"How would I know?"

Elena silently cheered her mother on.

To her surprise, Mikhail, the taller of the two, pushed Anna Ivanovna aside and headed straight for Elena and the bed. Elena shrank back toward the wall. Her mouth went dry. She stared up at the face of her former friend and saw cold blue eyes.

"Mikhail?" she said.

"Move from the bed," he commanded as if she had not spoken. As if they had not played in the schoolyard when they were small children.

"I can't. I hurt my foot this morning."

Even in the shadows his white teeth glistened when he smiled. The same white teeth surrounded by ugly thin lips she and Tatiana had once thought sensual and exciting. They had giggled about kissing those lips. He handed the flashlight to Boris and then he raised the bayonet-equipped rifle and pointed it at her.

"Not my baby!" Mama screamed and rushed at him. Boris grabbed her and shoved her to the floor. Elena sucked in her breath, horrified. How could these boys act like this? Mikhail lunged and his bayonet pierced the blankets next to her thigh. Elena gasped. She felt her father's body twitch beneath her. She held her breath, waiting to hear his cry. Mikhail pulled the rifle back and plunged it in again, this time close to where her father's head should have been.

"Misha!" Elena screamed, using his nickname. "Stop it. You're scaring everybody! What's wrong with you? Don't you know who I am?"

Mikhail loomed over her with the rifle still stuck in the straw. He put his face within inches of hers. "And who are you? How would I know you?" he sneered.

"Misha. It is I, Elena Federova."

He stood up straight and pulled the rifle out of the straw, holding it with two hands across his chest. "That is not possible. Elena lived on the fifth floor. I have not seen her in over a year but, even so, you cannot be her. You are skinny! Elena was a pretty, rosy cheeked little girl."

She raised her chin and turned her head, offering her profile as Boris ran the light over her. Her eye caught the icon of the Virgin Mary in the corner of the room where Grandmother prayed. Now she closed her eyes and began her own prayer, "Dear Sweet Mother of God, protect these boys who assault their friends and make them nice again. Amen."

Mikhail bent over again to peer at her face. "Is it really you? Is Grigory Federov your father?"

"Of course it is. And yes, he is." She caught the look in her mother's eyes and understood she should say no more. "We have not seen him since the factory closed."

She felt her father breathing beneath her.

Mama covered her head with her hands as she lay on the floor. Her grandparents prayed aloud to all the saints. Elena's scalp prickled, her eyes watered. She feared she would wet herself.

Mikhail laughed. A cold angry sound. "I didn't realize it was your family that lived here like animals in the cellar, Elena. We were told to go find Citizen Federov."

Boris bent down and helped Anna Ivanovna to her feet. Then the two of them backed toward the door. As Mikhail exited, Boris paused. "I apologize to you and your family, Elena. We did not know it was your father. I am sorry for you. Your neighbor reported seeing a man here. We had to check. Every able-bodied man must be at the front. Perhaps your father is there. Records get mixed up. You understand." He saluted and closed the door gently as he left.

Elena reached out as her mother sank down on the bed next to her. Anna wrapped her arms around her daughter, afraid to speak. They waited to make sure the boys would not return. They sat for several minutes before Grandpa shuffled over to the door and latched it. "It is all right. They are gone. Grisha! Come out of there."

Elena rolled off the bed so they could all pull the straw from Grigory.

"I am going to sneeze!" he said, and then did. "That bayonet had to be millimeters from my face. Thank you, my darling daughter. You saved your father."

She looked at the icon but said nothing.

Everyone helped him remove the bits and pieces of straw from his clothing and hair.

"You know those boys, Elena?" her mother asked.

"They were at my school. They were nice boys, Mama, really. They used to be nice."

Her mother sighed as she picked straw from her husband's hair. "It is the war. It makes people do terrible things."

Elena did not bother to wipe the tears from her face as she helped her mother.

"That was too close," Elena's father said. "I have been forming a plan in my head and I believe it is time to talk about it. Anna, make tea."

They all laughed, with relief at Grigory's narrow escape, and at his attempt to make a joke by calling the hot water tea. In the past when there was to be a family conference her mother would have Sofia brew a samovar full of strong black tea and serve dainty cucumber sandwiches and strawberry ice cream. The men would drink vodka. Tonight they took turns sipping boiled muddy water as they huddled on the bed and waited to hear Father's idea.

Three

"I want to explain about your history, Elena. Before you hear my plan, you must know the reasons," Papa began. "During the Great War I was a boy. My father and my two oldest brothers fought for Russia and the czar. Your Uncle Peter was killed in that war. The two youngest, Alexander and Paul, left for America. But while that was going on, other events took place that changed Mother Russia forever. By nineteen twenty we were Soviet Russia. All comrades. All equal. But still, some were more equal than others."

"That's a funny thing to say, Papa." Elena giggled.

"Not so funny, Little Rabbit," Grandpa said. "Our family had been landowners for centuries. We had workers whom we treated fairly. But after we were told we were equal, the new communist government took our houses for the benefit of the 'people'. We were left a small gatehouse for our personal use."

"Yet, we were the lucky ones," Papa added. "Anyone who resisted was removed; they were never seen again. My brother Leo was twenty-one, only a year younger than I when he disappeared in nineteen seventeen. Hundreds of thousands of people starved and died. Your grandfather made sure I finished my education so I was able to secure the position at the factory."

Elena snuggled closer to Grandmama. She liked to hear her father talk about his work at the factory where he was the supervisor of everyone. At least, he had been until three weeks ago. Their factory supplies stopped coming in because of the German blockade of Leningrad and once they exhausted their existing stock, there was no more work. The employees, who had been exempt from the military service because they were making boots, had to join the army.

"On the day I was meant to report for duty, I walked home from the bakery carrying the family's bread ration. I felt torn. I didn't want to leave my wife and daughter, but knew it was my duty to go to war. I consoled myself with the fact that at least I'd been able to smuggle new pairs of boots from the factory for us. I had been thinking about my wedding to Anna and my joy at the birth of our first child, Elena, when I heard the sirens signal another attack."

Elena had heard him tell this story so many times in the last few weeks she could recite it herself. When he got to this part she wanted to sleep. Listening to her father complain about their plight was not productive. Her teachers at school would never get along with her father. Her mind drifted back to school while her father talked of love and marriage. She missed her best friend, Tatiana. Someday she hoped they would meet again. Someday, after this ugly war ended.

She and Tatiana liked to pretend they were sisters. Both had long blond hair which they wore in braids. Had anyone paid close attention, they would have realized Tatiana had a big gap between her two front teeth, and Elena's teeth were even. Where Elena had a smattering of freckles across her slightly turned up nose, Tatiana's nose was straight like a Greek goddess'. But when they wore their school uniforms, even the teachers got them mixed up. Tatiana suggested once that perhaps they were really twins, stolen by the gypsies and sold to their respective parents. As Elena wondered where Tatiana might be right now, something her father said brought her back to the present, to the dark basement room where they slept on straw pallets instead of soft feather beds.

He spoke quietly. She pictured his gaunt face, the ever lengthening beard and straggly hair and wondered again how her mother, whom he remembered as a soft and beautiful woman could have fallen in love with such a skinny little man who prayed to icons and believed in God. He was saying a prayer, but not one she had ever heard before. He spoke as if his god were right there in the room with them.

"And we are asking you now to bless our journey, provide us the strength we need in the days and months ahead. We ask this in the name of your son, our savior, Jesus Christ. Amen."

Grandfather, Grandmother and Mother all responded, "Amen."

Elena's heart sank. What are they up to now? She had lived in fear a neighbor would report her parents for keeping icons in the house. She knew she should have told authorities at the school about them, but in spite of their beliefs, she loved her grandparents dearly and would die if anything ever happened to them.

She held a grudging respect for their courage to have beliefs different from other parents. She had a hard time putting on the same uniform every day and marching in step with every other child in her class. She enjoyed the private piano lessons with Madame Uspenskaya and the French and English lessons from her grandparents. She often wished she could have lived on the country estate they used to own. She had learned in school that was bad thinking. She must think about the others. She was taught if she had something, she must share. And now, her father, who should be fighting with the army like other fathers, hid when soldiers came, and he sold the family silver to buy food on the black market.

She should have been paying attention. What could he have in mind? What journey was this imaginary god supposed to protect? Was he going to try to take them back to the old estate? She had never seen it, but she knew it was a long distance from Leningrad. Once her father had hired an automobile and taken them out into the country for a picnic by a lake. She asked him then if they were near her grandparents' old home, and he said the place was too far to ever visit again.

"I will cut Elena's hair in the morning," she heard her mother say.

Elena grabbed her braids with both hands. "Cut my hair? Why? You can't cut my hair!" She scrambled to get off the bed and away from them. She'd lost her piano, her home, her bed, her dolls, her clothes, everything, and now they were going to make her lose her hair! She threw herself onto her bed and pulled the blankets over her head. She wouldn't listen anymore. They could take whatever journey they wanted. She would stay right there until the war ended.

She felt her mother sit beside her. Her hand stroked her head through the blanket. Elena wanted to scream. Instead she cried softly, tasted the salt of her tears, and wished for real food. Her stomach hurt from hunger. She needed to sleep so she could dream of nice things. Food, warmth, and sunshine, that's what she wanted.

"My Little Rabbit. You can cry for now, but tomorrow we shall go on a long journey and you will have to be strong. In the morning we begin the preparations and by the following day we'll be gone from here. It is your father's wish." Mama squeezed her shoulders, gave her a gentle pat on her backside and then left.

"I'm not Little Rabbit anymore," Elena snuffled through the blankets. "I'll never be your Little Rabbit again."

It occurred to her she ought to be frightened but instead she felt calm. She thought about Tatiana and she dreamed about herself and Tatiana dancing in *The Nutcracker* at Christmas time. In her dream they lived together in Vienna and rode in a carriage drawn by two magnificent white horses. Boris and Mikhail were the coachman and the footman decked out in livery, wearing plumed hats. As she fell asleep, she knew she was truly saying goodbye to her mother's Little Rabbit and her own childhood.

Four

"I won't, I won't, I won't!" Elena protested.

Her mother stood, arms akimbo, scissors in hand. "Sit down!"

"Please, I don't want my hair cut."

"Your father will be back soon. I told him we would be ready to go."

Elena glared at her mother. She wished her eyes could burn right through her and make her go away. She looked at her grandparents sitting on the bench near the stove. Each one held a glass of the hot water and their morning's crust of bread. She hoped one of them would come to her defense, but they sat silently and watched. Their eyes moved from mother to daughter as if they were at a tennis match.

"If you come near me, I'll scream," she shouted. "Boris and Mikhail will come back and this time they'll find Father."

Her mother's face drained of color. She collapsed onto the chair.

Elena gasped. She knew she had gone too far. Instantly regretful, she rushed to fling her arms around her mother. "I'm sorry. I didn't mean it. I would never tell on Papa. But you can't cut my hair. Please," she begged.

"But your father said," her mother began helplessly.

"Let her keep her hair," Grandmama spoke. "We can tuck it under a cap. Who will ask her to remove it?"

"She's right, Mama. Who would look?" She immediately grabbed the ends of her braids and wound them around her head. "Look! Who could tell me from a boy? And I'll be a naughty boy and say bad words at the soldiers."

"You'll do no such thing! You're naughty enough as a girl. Go sit in your corner until your father returns. We'll see what he says."

Elena knew once her mother put the scissors down there would be no more discussion. Especially if Grandmama, Papa's own mother, agreed with her. She tucked herself into her blankets while her mother brought her breakfast over to her. Elena nibbled slowly on the small piece of dry black bread. It would be a long time until lunch.

She watched as her mother moved about the room, tidying the table, and putting things away like any ordinary housewife. Mama drew aside the curtain of their improvised clothes closet and pulled out Elena's dresses, then stacked them on the table before she dragged out the big old travel trunk. She held up a dress and looked at Elena as if remembering the last time she saw her wearing it. It was white with yellow roses on the bodice and along the sleeves. She had worn it to Tatiana's birthday party two years ago. She had grown so tall, it would never fit her anymore. Mother folded the dress and placed it in the trunk. She continued to check each piece of clothing in the same way, from time to time Mama consulted with Grandmama who sat on the good chair near the stove watching. Grandfather remained silent at the table nursing his hot cup in both hands.

Elena was finishing the last bit of bread when Mama snapped the trunk shut, took a key from her apron pocket, and locked it. She had only a few garments, stockings, her boots, and scarves left on the table.

There was a clatter on the outside concrete steps and for a brief moment she thought the soldiers might be coming, before her father pushed open the door. He entered with a bright smile on his face, glowing red from the exertion and chilled night air. He looked like Father Frost with an overstuffed duffel bag slung over his shoulder.

He dropped the heavy bag onto the table before hurrying to the stove. With his back to the room, he pulled off his thick gloves and rubbed his hands near the heat. "We leave at four o'clock tomorrow morning."

Five

Father addressed the family as they sat around the table. "We shall each have an egg and a sausage before we leave. It will give us strength to start our journey." He sorted the food into three bundles.

Elena wondered how he found food for their journey when Grandmama hadn't been able to find more than a couple of rotten potatoes and cabbages in the last two days. She looked at him with a bit more respect; he'd bought the food through the black market, something the rest of them feared doing.

Grandmama and Grandpa sat opposite her father lost in a game of cards as if nothing unusual was about to happen. Elena looked from them to the three bundles of food and realized for them, nothing unusual *was* about to happen.

Father's duffle bag held more than food. Stuffed in with the extra rations was a collection of winter clothing. He handed Elena a pair of heavy knickers and a gray woolen overcoat. She dropped them on her bed. *I am in control of how I dress. I can decide whether or not to wear them when the time comes.* She preferred to think she would wear her red coat as always.

Returning to the table, she looked at the bundles of food, wondering how long this mysterious journey would take. Perhaps the food would last a week; before the blockade it would have been enough for only two or three days.

People at the bakery talked about how others walked across the frozen Lake Ladoga to Finland and safety. Surely, that didn't take a week. But it probably wasn't frozen yet; maybe her family would be walking around the lake instead of across it.

Satisfied with his division of supplies, Papa smiled at her mother. "Now a cup of tea, if you please, Anna." He turned to his parents. "It breaks my heart that you will not come with us but I know you will survive. You have survived much worse and now you will have the extra ration cards after we are gone."

Elena heard his words but his voice sounded cold, like when he was the factory supervisor firing employees. He would tell them stories at supper about letting people go because there were not enough materials for making the boots. He never talked about how their families would get food without money. He never seemed to care. And now he was one of those without money.

She watched him as he moved to the stove and stood by his wife while she prepared tea.

Grandmama slapped her playing cards on the table with glee while Grandpa laid his on the table. "You owe me four thousand six hundred and seventy-five rubles, Sasha. Pay up!"

Grandpa sighed, reached into his pocket, took out a nub of a pencil and a piece of paper, and wrote out an IOU to his wife. She stuffed it into her apron pocket. "One day, my darling, I will pay you. Trust me on that."

Grandmama leaned over and gave her husband a kiss on his wrinkled cheek. "I'll be waiting, Old Man."

He laughed. "I'll show you who's an old man, Old Woman!"

She squealed like a schoolgirl and scrambled from the bench as he reached out for her.

"I think they'll be happy to have this little home to themselves when we are gone," Anna said as she brought the watery tea and hot food to the table. "Come, let us have our last meal together and be happy. Like they are." She smiled as she sat down, though Elena noticed her mother gripped the edge of the table to keep her balance.

"Not our last meal, Anna," Father said. "Only the last one for a while. When the war is over, we will be together again."

Her grandparents, now somber, returned to the table. Elena had never thought about their ages before. She studied their wrinkled faces and their rheumy blue eyes. Both had white hair, though Grandmama had quite a bit more than Grandpa. She wore hers in braids wrapped around her head like a crown. She always thought of Grandmama as beautiful and she especially loved her hands, fingers long, like Elena's, but the backs of Grandmama's were patterned with blue veins. Grandmama liked to work in the kitchen and while Mama had been away at work in the nursery school, Elena often helped her cook. They made sausages, borscht, potato pudding and coleslaw. Using a sharp knife Grandma would slice so rapidly through the vegetables and cabbages that Elena feared she would cut off her fingers. But it never happened. For holidays they made special bread with nuts and berries and delicate cookies sprinkled with fine powdered sugar. Elena smiled at the memory of the sweet fragrance of baking bread.

"Elena, bow your head!" her father's sharp reprimand brought her back to the present. He said a special grace before supper, thanking God for their bounteous meal and begging His blessing for their forthcoming journey. She looked at the table and realized the odor of fresh bread was not imaginary. Somehow, he had found two beautiful loaves of black bread. The table was laden with sausages, hardboiled eggs, and several boiled potatoes. Mama spooned out a bowl of broth for each of them. Elena winced from a stab of pain. Hunger. Would it never go away? As she eyed the food, she hoped that after tonight it would. There would be plenty of food in Finland.

"You mustn't cry, Little Rabbit," Grandmama said. "Even those mighty Germans can't fight forever. One day they will run out of ammunition. They will go home and you will be able to return."

Elena's eyes teared at the thought of real food again. She wiped them with the back of her hand and smiled at her grandmother. "I was thinking about making cookies with you, Grandmama. I'm going to miss you so much. I don't want to leave you." She clamped her lips together, but the tears rolled down her cheeks. She pushed her chair back, knelt beside the old woman and laid her head in Grandmama's lap. As she knelt beside the old woman, Grandmama patted her head.

"I wish I could travel with you. You make sure you take your piano. Grandfather and I will be right here waiting for you when you return."

"Humph," Grandpa snorted as he dipped his bread into the weak broth. "That's what you said to young Alexander and Paul when they ran off to America. Later we moved into the city. We never heard from them again. They disappeared as completely as Leo."

"Those days were terrible, the revolution, the Great War. Our sons had no choice but to leave."

"Grandmama," Elena looked up. "Do you think I could find my uncles in America? I could tell them all about you and about where you live and maybe they could write. And if they're rich, they can come visit you and Grandpa."

"If the old woman doesn't decide to move again."

"Sasha, you make it sound as if I had us moving every year since then. We moved twice. The gatehouse and then three years later to this building with Grisha. We have been here for twenty-two years. We are old now and we are not going to move again. Go with your parents, Little Rabbit, and grow into a happy woman in your new country."

What country will that be?" Elena asked. "How can I be happy anyplace without all of my family together?"

Suddenly Elena was filled with fear at the thought of leaving the only home she had ever known.

Grandmama helped her to her feet. "Go sit down and eat your supper. You have a long journey and a new life ahead of you."

Elena wiped her eyes again. "When I get to wherever we're going, I shall tell everybody that my name is Katya." She forced a smile as she picked up her spoon.

"Tonight I will write down everything I know about your uncles. Things to help you to find them if you go to America. And I will be praying for you all the time," Grandmama promised.

The only sound in the room for the next ten minutes was of the family eating. Elena savored the taste of the meat-flavored broth. When supper was finished, she helped her mother clear up.

Grandmama sat at the table and wrote on the back of an old letter, when she finished, she ripped open a seam in the piano and tucked the letter inside, then restitched the piano.

"Do you think we will go to America, Mama?"

"No, Elena," her father responded. "We are going to Germany."

Six

"Wait! Listen to me. I have a plan to keep us safe until the end of the war," Papa said.

"No! I will not listen to you anymore," Mama shouted at him. "Germany! Those people will be happy to have us there so they can murder us and take our daughter for their own pleasures. You fool!"

Elena stared in astonishment at her, Mama's own grandmother had been a German.

Father pulled himself to his full height and glared at his wife. "Do you think I could have been the manager at the factory all these years if I'd been a fool?"

"Yes! You were not a boot maker; you were a boot licker! A party toady. 'Yes, Comrade Mikhail Efimovich. No, Comrade Mikhail Efimovich. Let me kiss your backside, Comrade.' For weeks you have been hiding in that straw taking food from the mouths of your family. Your parents. Your child…"

Papa drew his hand back as if to hit Mama.

"No!"

Elena whirled about at the sound of her grandfather's voice. The old man who rarely spoke slammed his fist on the table. "You will not strike your wife! She is right. You are a fool."

"Such a fool that all these years you were happy to eat the food and drink the vodka I provided by playing their game. Who was the son who stayed behind when my brothers slithered away?" Father threw his hands in the air and then collapsed onto the one good chair. "I cannot stay here any longer and watch my family die because that is what surely will happen before this winter is out. We shall all die," he finished, his hands still.

For a long moment no one said anything.

"Peter was killed in the Great War," her grandmother whispered.

After a long silence, Papa spoke in a soft voice. "You understand this is not something I have suggested without considerable thought. Every day we walk out and see the bodies lying on the sidewalk waiting to be picked up by the trucks. One walks to the corner and trips over a neighbor's corpse. It is coming to all of us and I believe my way is the way to save us. I don't want to look at the bodies of my family lying stretched out on the sidewalk. Tomorrow we go."

Elena held the bowl she had been drying in one hand and a linen towel in the other. She shifted her weight, hardly daring to breathe. Every day she saw dead bodies, but until now, until tonight, she had never connected them to herself. She thought about the finger she had found in the handkerchief and looked down at her own hands. A small gold ring she had received on her twelfth birthday from Grandmama glinted in the dim light. "An heirloom," her grandmother had told her. "It was my grandmother's; now it is yours; and one day you will give it to your granddaughter." One day her body could be lying in the street and a stranger could come along and chop off her finger to get the ring.

Her stomach heaved. She dropped the bowl and towel on the table and lurched toward the back hallway and out into a narrow alley.

She returned to the room a few minutes later, disgusted at having thrown up her delicious dinner and making herself even more miserable. She saw her mother lying prostrate on her bed with her grandmother sitting beside her. Father remained slumped in the chair and Grandpa sat at the table with his back to everyone playing a game of cards by himself. No one took any notice of her.

She retrieved her piano from its cupboard and laid it out on the table. Sitting opposite her grandfather, she began fingering a light Bach piece. She hummed softly to the music in her head.

"He's a German, you know," Grandpa said.

"He is?" Elena continued playing. "That can't be true. Germans are bad people. He must be Austrian."

"Not all Germans are bad." Her grandfather spoke in a soft voice.

Elena thought for a moment. "I can't imagine Bach or Beethoven running around with a gun and shooting people. I just can't picture it."

"But then there was Mozart. Must not forget him. He was something of a scalawag." Grandpa chuckled as he scooped up his cards and shuffled them again.

"But he was only a menace to himself." She looked down at the keyboard and watched her fingers as they moved along creating the cheerful tune. "I don't speak German," Elena added.

"You are good with languages. You'll learn quickly. Just don't forget your Russian and French. And English will always be in style."

"Not if the Germans win the war."

"They will not. I knew an American once. If he was typical of the race, they will never let that housepainter, Corporal Schickelgruber, who fancies himself an emperor, win the war."

With a deafening explosion the shelling started again. The building shook and a light mist of dust rained from the ceiling. Elena stopped playing and swiped her keyboard from the tabletop. "They're doing an excellent job of working at it. My head hurts all the time from the shelling and bombing, Grandpa. I can't imagine going into the arms of the enemy willingly. Is Father right in what he wants us to do?"

Her grandfather set his cards on the table and folded his hands over them. "Your father is doing what he thinks is necessary to save your life. Your life and the life of your mother. He remained behind during the revolution when we tried to send him away with his brothers. Even then, at such a tender age, he felt his duty was to save his family. Your grandmother and I wanted him to leave with his brothers, but he refused. He fought off the peasants and they beat him until he nearly died, but he never gave up the manor house until the people swarmed over it like bees. They brought him to us bloodied and unconscious and told us we could live in the gatehouse until he recovered, then we would have to turn it over to the people." He absentmindedly picked up the deck of cards and began shuffling them.

"I don't understand my father," Elena said.

Grandpa pushed himself back from the table. "Take your piano with you, Little Rabbit. It will serve you well." He crossed over to his bed. She watched him go into the dark corner then looked over to where her mother and grandmother sat together speaking in hushed tones.

I'm nothing but a child to them, she thought. *They do what they like with my life. Like the governments to the people.* She picked up her piano from the floor. *The Germans couldn't produce such composers as Bach, Handel, Wagner, Liszt, Schumann, and the others and be a horrid race like we've been told. I wonder if it is even the Germans who are firing the shells and bombs at us.* The piano trailed behind her as she walked to her bed.

"You will leave that behind, Elena. Only food and clothing will be permitted."

She looked back at her father. If she had not recognized his voice, nothing in his demeanor suggested he had said a word. He sat, his head hanging, looking totally lost.

"Good night, Father." She crawled into her bed and pulled her piano under the covers with her. Vivid thoughts of her childhood mixed with excitement and fear fought against the solace of sleep.

They would leave for Germany in the morning. "Watch over us," she whispered to God.

Seven

During the night the weather changed. They stepped from the basement into a world of white. Papa pointed left. "We begin our journey this way. We will walk in a single line. Elena, walk behind your mother. Step in my footsteps. I shall watch for bodies and unexploded incendiaries. Come along."

She focused on what her father was saying instead of listening to her heart break at saying goodbye to Grandma and Grandpa. Grandma had crawled out of bed to light the fire for hot water before they left. A hug and a kiss on each cheek and they were out the door.

Elena, dressed in boy's clothing, kept her head down and carefully matched her footsteps to those of her parents'. The boots her father had brought for her were too big so she had added layers of woolen socks, grateful for the extra warmth they provided. She carried a pack, like a peasant, on her back. They turned the corner at the end of the street then her father led them across St. Isaac's Square.

"You see the cathedral?" He pointed to St. Isaac's Cathedral that dominated the square and withstood the shelling. "In the basement are hidden thousands of pieces of artwork from the Hermitage. You can't see them now, but the dirigibles, the big balloons that fly above, are here to protect the cathedral from enemy planes."

"I know about the dirigibles, Papa. It's too bad the government didn't make enough of them to protect the neighborhoods, too, instead of just the famous buildings and their artwork."

"Hush," Papa said. "That's no way to talk. So many of those paintings are hundreds of years old and worth more than one miserable life. At best we would live to be maybe seventy years old. The artwork will go on forever."

"Humph," Elena grunted as she shifted her pack and trudged along.

Papa continued down the street toward the river. Lines had already formed outside the bakery and she wondered where their own bread would come from when they ran out of their supplies.

At the concrete bridge over the Moika she paused to look back at the city she'd grown up in. Shelling continued in a distant sector. The fires created a silhouette of the skeletal buildings, but also glittered off the onion domes of the great cathedral. She hoped it would remain standing.

"Stop dawdling, Elena," her father whispered, although in the morning silence, his voice seemed to echo across the river.

She glanced back one more time. The water of the river gurgled beneath a thin layer of ice. Soon the river would be solid. Was it possible she had actually skated on this very river only three years ago? Someone carrying an electric torch stepped from a building, someone heading for the morning's bread distribution at the bakery. Where else was there to go? Except to Germany.

"Elena!"

She turned back to follow her parents. "These boots are too heavy," she grumbled.

She marched in their footsteps as she imagined herself the heroine of a story where she delivers a message to an exalted ruler who rescues Leningrad and restores it to its former glory. It would be the city her grandparents described with royal coaches and cabriolets drawn through the streets by magnificent horses. All the ladies would be beautiful, the men handsome. She would be presented at court wearing a hooped gown with twelve yards of fabric in the skirt alone to announce her engagement to the crown prince. A faraway barrage interrupted her fantasies. She wondered when they would get to the automobile, they would ride into Germany.

By the time they had picked their way through the rubble of the city Papa was practically carrying Mama. He had an arm around her waist and Anna clung to him as her feet dragged through the snow. Elena had no idea where they were as they passed through a silent residential street, narrower than where she lived–used to live–but equally devastated. Elena's ribs ached from shivering from the early morning damp. She had been cold in the past, but this morning was the worst she could remember. Between losing her dinner last night and then tossing and turning half the night with fear and anticipation, she had awakened at four o'clock already chilled to the bone and exhausted.

"It is six o'clock and we are not yet near the front lines. We have to pick up our pace." Father stopped to shift the weight of his pack so he could accommodate her mother's as well. With her burden lightened, Mama was able to walk more swiftly. Elena stumbled along behind.

At the rumble of a truck's engine her father hustled them into the darkness of a doorway. A truck entered the boulevard from a side street, its shaded headlights not reaching the little family. It stopped in front of a building across the way. Two men leapt down from the rear of the truck.

"Over here. Two more." One of the men pushed snow away from a lump on the pavement.

"Wait. I've got a little one with the mother."

"This one's wearing a gold cross."

The men continued to call to one another as they gathered up the blanket-wrapped bodies left out during the night. They tossed them onto the bed of the truck. When they finished, she could hear the driver shift the truck into gear as they pulled away, looking for the next lump of snow, the next body, the next piece of gold jewelry.

Shivering with cold and fear, she ran on ahead of her parents but within moments realized she didn't know where to turn next. While waiting for them to catch up to her, quick short puffs of steamy air escaped from her mouth and she pretended she was a sophisticated movie star with a cigarette in a delicately carved ivory holder.

"We'll be at the front soon. Remember, your name is Yuri."

"Yes, I remember, but I don't understand why I must be a boy. Boys are supposed to be *fighting* the Germans, not running to them."

"Not twelve-year-old boys."

"I'm a fourteen-year-old girl. I don't *want* to be a twelve-year-old boy," she said, beating her gloved hands against her body in an effort to warm herself. "How long do I have to pretend?"

"Until I tell you otherwise. And never remove your hat."

"Yes, Papa."

"Be quiet. I see something ahead."

Elena peered into the darkness seeing nothing but more snow. Perhaps Papa was seeing ghosts.

"Where are you going?" a disembodied voice spoke.

They stopped.

"Who is there?" Papa asked. Mama grabbed Elena so strongly by the wrist she feared it would break.

"Josef Stalin. Who do you think?"

"Where are you?"

A small man wearing a shabby raincoat, far too light for the weather, stepped out of the shadows, startling all three of them. The man held out two rag wrapped hands. "Have you any vodka? A kopek, perhaps?"

"You mock Stalin in front of the wrong people and your family will never hear of you again. Go away. We are leaving the city. We have no money."

The man hesitated before shrinking back into the shadow. "The patrol has gone by. They will be warming themselves and drinking in the alley two blocks south." He spoke from the darkness.

"Many thanks, old man. Here is a cigarette for your help."

They walked in silence, the sound of their footsteps muffled by fresh snow. In the distance, the rumble of the death truck announced its gruesome morning rounds.

It seemed hours later when dawn lightened the sky. They were in a cleared area. Buildings had been razed to create a gap between the lines. Russians on this side; Germans on the other.

Elena put one foot in front of the other, hardly aware she walked or was even awake.

"This is it. Silence. Neither of you speak," Papa ordered in a hoarse whisper. She didn't think there was much chance of Mama speaking. Anna leaned on her husband, too weak to stand alone.

Ahead of them massive rolls of barbed wire created an impenetrable barrier. Beyond the vicious fence she saw a soldier reclined on top of a tank track. He leaned against the giant machine and appeared to be asleep.

"Walk to the right. It won't be far to an opening," Mama whispered, her voice barely audible.

"How can you know that?" Elena asked.

"In the summer I worked for several days with the other women digging the trenches."

Elena remembered when her mother would come home from her holiday 'volunteer' work looking tired and exhausted. The women who weren't otherwise working in defense of Mother Russia were required to report for duty. Mama had never said just what she had been doing those days. Apparently, she'd been digging trenches around the city.

Elena looked across the vast expanse of the trench. It seemed to run on endlessly. "How deep is it?"

"Three meters. And six meters across. Enough to keep the German tanks from getting to the city. We did well, didn't we?" Mama said with a trace of pride in her voice.

"Hush. Both of you! Come along. I want to cross both lines before daybreak. We're falling behind schedule."

"But where's the car, Papa?" Elena whispered.

"What car?"

"The car that's taking us to Germany."

"There is no car, Elena. And if you keep talking, they'll hear you and shoot you."

"These are our soldiers. They're Russian." As soon as she said the words she remembered the boys who had been her friends. She clamped her mouth shut. Maybe her father knew more than she realized.

When they reached the opening in the barricade, Father led them to the edge of the ditch. A group of soldiers sat huddled around a smoldering fire, warming themselves, a couple nodding in sleep, others talking in soft voices. None watched for approaching civilians.

"Good morning, Comrade soldiers," Father said.

Two men jumped to their feet and pointed their rifles directly at the family. "Who goes there?" The speaker was tall and even in the dim light Elena thought he was quite handsome.

"I am Citizen Grigory Alexandrovich Federov," Father said. "I am with my wife and son."

Another soldier stood. His rifle pointed toward the ground. The others remained seated and watched. No one spoke for a moment then the first soldier said, "And so?"

Father grasped Elena by the shoulder and pulled her to his side. "I want to cross the trench. To go to the other side."

"You can't do that, Comrade. The Germans are over there. You can see the tanks. You can see their fires. Look!" The man sneered as he spoke and Elena sensed the patronizing tone in his voice. Embarrassed, she tried to pull away from her father's grasp, but he held her tightly against him.

"I understand, Comrade, but I still wish to go. I am taking my family to Germany. We'll die here. I'm doing what I believe will save their lives."

She felt her father stand taller and straighter and thought he was making a fool of himself. At the moment she preferred to die.

The two soldiers exchanged glances. One shrugged. They lowered their rifles. "Do you have any cigarettes?"

Father immediately let go of Elena and fumbled inside his coat. He pulled out a packet and extended it to the men. The handsome one took it.

"It isn't full. There are five of us here. Don't you have more?"

"No," Father lied. She had watched him stuff his inside pockets with at least ten packets of cigarettes this morning.

She waited while they considered Father's answer. *We can't die because Father won't give them cigarettes. Maybe I should tell them.*

Without another word the three soldiers turned their backs on her and her family. Father took a step toward them, but Mother grabbed his jacket and pulled him back. In silence they worked their way down the slope of the trench and walked to the German front line.

Only barely begun, the day already felt like they had been traveling for a year. Elena looked over her shoulder expecting to see the rifles ready to be fired when they reached the bottom of the trench, but the soldiers appeared to have already forgotten them. They sat hunched around their fire and ignored the Federovs. Too tired to cry, Elena grasped the edge of her father's sleeve as she stepped carefully over the uneven ground. If Mother dug this trench, she could have made it more level, she thought.

"What's the boy's name?" a voice suddenly called out.

Father stopped and looked back. "Yuri," he shouted.

Laughter. "He walks like a girl." More laughter.

Dead. Dead. Dead. Her face burned with shame.

Eight

"*Schiesse nicht! Wir koennen uns nicht verteidegen!*"

Elena's head jerked up at the words coming from her mother's lips. She'd fallen asleep—not sleepwalking, walking asleep. When did her mother learn to speak German? Could they have walked all the way to Germany already? She shook her head and wiped her gloved hands over her eyes forcing away the exhaustion. It was barely light and they were still in the trench. The sleep could not have lasted for more than a few minutes. Mama stood at the foot of the trench like a dark brown bear, her body wrapped in a fur coat up to her ears, her matching fur hat pulled down to meet it. Only a green woolen scarf divided them with a splash of color. Papa stood to one side sagging under the weight of their possessions on his back.

"I have told them we are helpless and asked them not to shoot us," Mama called over her shoulder.

The sentry signaled them to approach with his rifle.

"He wants to know what a German family is doing in Leningrad and why we didn't have the good sense to leave before the war." Mama's translation came in gasps as they climbed the steep rise from the bottom of the trench.

"What did you tell them?" Papa croaked. He climbed on all fours, bent under his load, each breath a harsh sucking effort.

"Not to worry, Grisha," Mama paused to speak to him. "I told them we are just like them, trying to survive."

Halfway up the side of the trench Elena began crawling. Her mother reached the top first and sank down onto the ground. As her father hauled himself over the edge, two soldiers grabbed him and dragged him out of Elena's sight. Her mother held out her hand to Elena, encouraging her to climb the last few feet. As Elena neared the top, she reached out to grasp the extended hand.

"Almost. Hold on!"

Elena clutched her mother's hand but then, without warning, tumbled down the embankment, still holding her mother's glove.

Fear abandoned her as she rolled and bounced along the frozen earth, replaced by relief when the world stopped spinning and she lay still, surrounded by soft, lovely, cold snow. Papa said if we stay in Leningrad we will surely die; but if we continue trying to walk to Germany we will also surely die. She closed her eyes. I can stay right here forever. It's so peaceful.

A beautiful girl in a blue gown floated into view, her hands caressing the keys of a lovely grand piano. Blonde hair was piled on top of her head, secured with a diamond clip. She was in a hall. A large hall. Thousands of people sat in the audience. She couldn't see them all as they faded away into the dark recesses of balconies and galleries. The image closed in on the face of the girl, Elena Federova, playing at a concert. She must be famous for so many people to be in attendance. She gave herself up to the dream.

"Yuri! Yuri!" the crowd chanted and applauded in approval. Elena wanted to stand up and take a bow but her legs wouldn't work. "It's not Yuri! It's me!"

"Yuri!" a woman's voice called. The voice seemed to come from high in the galleries. She wants me to stand. I must get up. Elena opened her eyes. Far above her she saw a group of people looking down on her. She moved her head from side to side and looked around. She was lying in a heap of snow. She thought about the images of herself playing in a concert hall. Her right hand automatically reached for her waist to make sure the padding was still where she put it. Wearily, she rolled over and pushed herself up to her knees. "If I get up this hill I will walk to America if I have to in order to play a real piano again. I will, if only there are not too many more trenches…" Dazed, she talked herself back up the slope. This time she crested the top unaided. She rested briefly, face down on the ground, panting.

Her mother grasped her by the elbow. Ten yards away her father stood on the verge of a heavily rutted road. "We have to hurry. We have many miles to cover today. No more time to waste!"

As if I rolled back down that slope on purpose. To collect bumps and bruises. She shrugged away from her mother and stumbled into step beside her. The last she knew her mother was chatting with these soldiers in their own language; now, unburdened by the weight of her pack, she could barely pause long enough for Elena to catch her breath.

They followed the road, nothing more than a farm path hardly suitable for horses and carts. The overnight cold had left a thin veneer of frozen mud covered by two or three inches of snow. From time to time one of her boots broke through the ice. When she tried to pull it free, the mud tried to suck the boot off her foot.

"We need a farmer in a cart right now to give us a ride to Germany," she said. A farmer and a cart. A truck would be better, but it didn't matter because whatever happened, she would get to America and play in a concert hall. She knew that. When they stopped for the night, she would take out her piano from under her clothes and practice every piece of music she ever learned. The thought kept her going through the rest of the day as one foot dragged in front of the other along the abandoned farm path, not a truck or cart in sight. At least the land was flat. Today they were the only people left in the world listening to the far-off sounds that told of the destruction of her home city.

By late in the day, those sounds had faded and still they saw no lights, no evidence of any human habitation, only the harsh road that led them onward. The snow continued, sometimes heavy and wet, other times only tiny, scattered flakes, but always snow as if winter could hardly wait to take hold. Trees glistening with ice dotted the landscape. They must be far from any town if no one had cut down these trees for their fires. On her street in the spring, pale green buds appeared first, then the green leaves and soon the whole avenue was shaded by summer's canopy of trees lining the avenue. They and their neighbors had long ago chopped them down for firewood.

Elena tried to focus on the end of their journey when she could once again be warm and safe and play her piano in a real concert hall. Imagined scales rose and fell urging her gloved hands, tucked warmly under her armpits, to practice fingering the keys.

As darkness overtook them her concert dreams vanished; bowls of hot borscht took their place.

"Papa, my legs don't want to move anymore. Please, can we stop for the night?" she begged.

"I know there is a village ahead. We will go there."

"Can I have some food, please?"

"We will eat when we rest. Not before."

She struggled to keep up with her parents, terrified if she faltered, they would leave her behind. She didn't know why she thought they would abandon her. Perhaps it was because her father walked away from his aged parents. She couldn't maintain any one thought for long in face of the bone-numbing cold. The pain had faded, so too the shivering. One foot then the other. Watch snowflakes flutter. She lifted her face to catch them on her tongue, misstepped, plunged her right foot in a rut and fell.

Already bruised from rolling down the side of the trench in the morning, she remained prone on the ground, hoping her parents would pick her up like they did when she was a little girl. Pick me up and carry me, please? She looked up for them, barely able to see through the snow and deepening gloom. They trudged on a dozen yards in the front. They hadn't noticed her fall. They really would abandon her!

"Mama! Papa! Help me." She rested her forehead on the back of her hand and wept with fatigue and relief as she heard them returning for her.

"Come child. Up you get." Papa wiped her tears away.

"I thought you would leave me. I'm so cold. Papa, I'm tired. Can't we stop someplace? Please?"

"There is no place to stop, yet. If you walk between your mother and me, we can all help each other keep warm. And we won't lose you in the dark."

They stumbled on with her in the middle, her parents' arms wrapped around her waist.

Papa relented about the food during the night and gave each of them a piece of sausage, a small chunk of bread and a piece of boiled potato. But he wouldn't let them stop; they ate as they walked. Elena imagined the food tasted good, but it was too cold to have much flavor. Each lump slid into her belly like lead balls and then rolled around sending shivers of pain up her throat.

Bowls of borscht returned to her mind. She could see them lined up in rows on a clean white linen cloth. She could smell the rich soup and felt like crying from the pleasure of the fragrance.

"It's a farmhouse, Elena," her mother said. "Come. Wake up. You've been sleeping for over an hour. We can't support you any longer."

Elena opened her eyes. Her parents' arms were locked together behind her. She disentangled herself from them, ashamed and embarrassed to have behaved like a little girl. Guilt overwhelmed her as she remembered how fragile her mother had become. Papa had had to help Mama to walk and now here, Mama had supported her while she slept. "I'm sorry," Elena said as she choked back tears, "I won't do that again. I should be the one carrying you."

"Come along," her father said. "It was only a little while. You fell asleep. Once you have eaten and slept in a warm house, you will feel strong again." He led them to the farmhouse. Smoke rose from the chimney of a cottage behind a stone wall. They stepped through a gate and down a path covered with a fresh layer of snow. Papa rapped on the wood door set into an arched entryway.

"Whoever might be in there is most likely asleep," he cautioned. "Stay to one side. They may choose to shoot us rather than open the door in the middle of the night."

Elena and her mother positioned themselves to one side where they would be protected by the thick stone walls of the cottage. Father leaned so his face was near the small window set in the ancient wood door.

Curtains in the window to the right of the door moved. Footsteps shuffled inside. Then a wizened old face peered out through the small window in the door. She couldn't tell whether it was a man or a woman. Father shone the flashlight on himself and then signaled her and Mama to step into the light. The face studied the three of them for a moment then disappeared. They waited.

Her father's face, the bottom part covered by his scraggly beard and mustache, the forehead hidden by his astrakhan, and with the light glinting upward showing it in relief, looked like a demon from hell. Elena would never open a door to him in the middle of the day much less in the middle of the night.

It was a few minutes before the latch was lifted, the door opened slightly and an ancient woman peered through the slit. A gray woolen shawl wrapped around her head and shoulders held it in place with gnarled fingers. It masked her face so Elena saw little more than her pale eyes. The warm air escaping through the opening carried the tantalizing fragrance of borscht. Involuntarily, she clutched her stomach barely able to restrain herself from forcing her way into the house.

Mama pushed in front of Papa. "I am Anna and this is my husband, Grigory Fedorov."

Elena was surprised at Mama's gentle tone, anxious as she was for food. Her father put his hand on her shoulder. "Mama does not wish to frighten her," he whispered.

"We only beg for a warm spot to sleep for the rest of the night," her mother said.

"I am called Grandmother Natasha Petrovna," the old woman said as she opened the door wider. "My sons are all away fighting. I have been left to care for their wives who are hiding upstairs, terrified of the Germans. When we heard your knocking, they scrambled away like rats. What do you think of that?" She cackled.

"We mean you and your daughters no harm, Old Grandmother," Anna said. "Just a little space in front of your stove."

"And perhaps a small bit of your soup." Elena added.

"Soup? You want to take my food? Oh, no!" She stepped back from the door as if to shut it in their faces but Grigory moved forward and put his booted foot in the way.

"Please. We are exhausted."

"Help! Help me, my daughters!" the old woman screeched as if being attacked.

Elena followed as her parents pushed into the little room lit only by a banked fireplace. Father focused the flashlight on the floor. Elena heard the scramble of footsteps from above and then someone in trousers thundered down the stairs to the left. "What is it? Who is it?" a woman's voice roared. The woman leapt over the last two steps and landed with a solid thud at the base of the stair.

Elena gaped at her as Papa's light washed over her. She was a model of the beautiful and strong woman on the posters plastered all over Leningrad, staring out at the world through large eyes surrounded by thick dark lashes. She wore dark gray long-sleeved overalls, but underneath those long sleeves, Elena was sure she had hardened muscles equal to any man's. When she stepped closer, she saw the small, peaked cap perched atop her swept-up hair. She even wore lipstick! She must be a model! Elena couldn't stop staring and wondering what she was doing up and dressed in the middle of the night.

"Close the door," the woman commanded. Elena, being the closest, reached behind and pushed the door shut. She heard the latch click. "You were letting all the warm air out. No need to heat all of the countryside." She leaned against the newel post. "So, what are you doing frightening an old woman?"

"They want our soup, Maria."

Maria straightened up and hooked her thumbs on her belt. "You want our soup? My mother-in-law dug through the frozen ground to find a couple of potatoes and frozen carrots to make our soup and you want to take it?"

"Not at all," Mother chimed in. "My…son was out of place to ask. We only wanted to sleep by your fire. We come from Leningrad." Elena hoped the women missed the hesitation before Mama said "son."

"From Leningrad? How did you get through the front lines? Past the Germans?"

Just then two more women appeared at the top of the steps. One of them carried a lantern. The two were clothed in long woolen nightdresses and heavy sweaters. Both had braids wrapped about their heads. Elena's first thought was neither of them had ever suffered a missed meal or any other deprivation. The fragrance of the soup combined with the sight of the two fat women made Elena angry.

"You need not fear them," Maria called up to the two women. "The boy has asked us for food and they want a place to sleep for a few hours. I have told them we have no food to spare." She turned to the Federovs. "Mother Petrovna worked out in the cold rain last week to dig up the few vegetables we have. The Germans have taken all the animals and we must keep our chickens for the eggs."

Something about the lengthy explanation seemed out of place to Elena but she was more concerned with trying to persuade the old woman to spare a little soup. She smiled feebly and looked from her to the large soup pot. Apparently, it worked a little because Grandmother Petrovna said, "Perhaps it won't hurt us to give each of them a small cup of soup, Maria. Then they might go to sleep in the barn."

Maria appeared to consider the idea then said, "A small cup for each."

"How can you give our food away to passing strangers, Maria? You have your nerve…" one of the fat women on the stairs complained, but before she could complete her sentence, Maria turned to confront her.

"I'm the one who provides the food for this family. I will decide who eats and how much. Is that clear?"

Surprisingly, the fat sister fell silent and sat on the top step. "Of course, you're right, Comrade. We must share what we have. Only a little bit, Mother," she cautioned the old woman.

Elena followed the grandmother to the stove and held the cups as the old woman scooped a rich broth into them. She was astonished to see bits of meat floating amongst the potatoes, cabbage, and carrots. Real borscht. Maria stood to one side of the stove and watched as the three Federovs drank their soup then spooned out the vegetables.

"You've been more than kind, Comrade. We thank you. Now, if we may sleep?" Papa pointed to the handwoven carpet on the floor near the fireplace.

"Sleep in the barn," Maria commanded. "It will be daylight in a few hours. You will leave at dawn."

"And don't steal any eggs while you're in there. We have a quota," piped up the shorter, stouter sister-in-law who'd come down into the room.

"You can't let them stay, Maria," the one on the steps whined.

"Why not?" Maria said.

"You know."

For a moment Elena thought Maria might dash back up the steps and strike her sister-in-law. Instead she took a step closer to the Federovs. "Comrade citizens, you may sleep in the barn."

Bolstered by the soup, Elena said, "My father and I can chop wood in exchange for a small meal!"

"You are a greedy little wretch. I told you we have no food to spare," Maria said. She then whirled on Grigory. "You said you left Leningrad. Why are you traveling in this weather? Where do you think you're going?"

Elena was afraid for her father to tell this woman the truth. These women were too well fed to be true Party women. No real Communist would hoard food while others starved…would they?

"Away from Leningrad. I am taking my family out of harm's way."

Elena cringed.

The four women gasped in shock at his statement. Maria exclaimed, "You're taking your entire family directly into the arms of the enemy?"

One of the sisters-in-law snickered. Maria glared at her.

"As you have made clear, Comrade," Papa said, "there is no food to spare here and I doubt there is any more elsewhere. The Geneva Convention states that prisoners must be cared for. That includes food. As we are non-combatants, we will be fed."

"Traitors!"

"Capitalists!"

"Why don't you go to America and live in Chicago?"

Elena was sure that was supposed to be an insult but couldn't understand it.

The fat women sneered at the Federovs as Maria herded the family toward the door.

The old woman opened it and snow blew in as they stepped outside.

"We'll just go into the barn. We won't stay long," Father said meekly.

Elena half expected her father to doff his cap like a lackey. She turned on her heel and rushed across the garden, through the gate onto the rutted path.

She beat furiously at her body to keep warm wishing they'd let her take charge. They wouldn't be in this ugly frozen wilderness if her father had only gone to the front like the other men. She could have gone out and found more food except her parents insisted on treating her like a child. And now, instead of arguing with each other, they remained behind and argued with Maria. Sure, they could sleep in the barn. They could put Papa under the straw just in case any soldiers appeared in the night. She was so angry and ashamed of her father she wouldn't stay in this place even if those ugly fat women begged. And like a light turning on in her brain, she recalled what bothered her about these women. Maria told them her old mother-in-law had dug in the mud to find vegetables, but later silenced her sister-in-law by saying she was the one who provided for the family. How could both be true? Did Maria work in the Army?

She watched through the open door to the cottage as her father pushed Maria into the room and her mother backed away onto the path. Voices raised in the cottage.

She heard snippets of words.

"Malingerer!" from one of the women.

"Whore!" from her father.

The door slammed shut with Papa still inside. She could hear raised voices but not the words.

Then she heard a woman's scream followed by two gunshots. She saw her mother hesitate before running out to find her on the path.

"Elena, I fear we may be on our own. Your father has angered a nest of hornets."

"But who shot who?"

"Whom," the schoolteacher in her mother answered automatically.

Nine

Anna and Elena clutched each other tightly and watched the house in horror as the door opened slowly. A slit of light streamed across the snow-covered yard. A shadow darkened the doorway as Father backed out briefly silhouetted in the entrance. He turned and stumbled toward them. His left hand hugged the top of his right arm that hung down by his side. A pistol dangled from his hand.

"We must leave. Hurry!" His voice wavered as he rushed past her, knocking her off the path in the process. She couldn't see his face in the darkness, but there was no doubt about the fear in his trembling voice.

"What happened? Did you shoot them? You didn't tell us you had a gun." Elena hurried to keep up with him.

"Come along. No time for talk." He sounded breathless as he rushed ahead of her.

"Did you kill one of them?" she called out.

"Be quiet," Anna ordered as they caught up to her.

"Anna, she hit me in the arm," Papa said.

"They shot you?" Elena's voice seemed to echo through the vast and silent night.

"Maria accused me of being a coward. She called me names, so I showed her my weapon and then the fat one on the stairs screamed. Maria pulled a gun. I shot above their heads. There was nothing else I could do. I – I wanted them to know I am not a coward."

"You pulled a gun because she insulted you?" Elena stopped, disbelieving what she had just heard. "Did you kill her?"

"No, I told you, I aimed above their heads. But she hit me. Come along. We have to keep moving." She could just make out a dark stain on his jacket where he clutched his arm. "They may be able to radio for help. We could be shot on sight."

Mama relieved Grigory of his pack and wrestled it onto her back. She set off, leading the way into the swirling snow.

Elena thought again about Maria. "She looked like a soldier, but she was beautiful, wasn't she?"

Her father grunted, "I had not noticed. We have to go. We'll lose track of your mother." Still holding his arm, Papa turned his back and began walking.

With no choice Elena forged ahead, following her mother's tracks. Her father was right, if they didn't hurry, they'd lose her mother altogether. Reluctantly, she grabbed hold of her father's coat and together they followed the footprints in the snow until they caught up with Anna. She rested on a low stone wall, tucked beneath a large tightly woven hedge now bare of leaves.

Elena climbed up beside Anna. Her father leaned against the wall. She still didn't understand what happened. "We were leaving. Why did you create trouble?"

"I told you. Maria accused me of being a deserter. When I tried to explain about the factory, she insulted me. When I showed her my gun, she pulled one from behind her. From her belt. We must continue walking. We have to create a great distance between us and that house." He staggered forward, stopped, and took a deep breath, then continued on.

"Grigory, you must let me have a look at your arm."

"It's nothing. You wouldn't be able to see anything now in any case. You can look at it at first light."

"Papa, I want to get warm and sleep," Elena said. "Can we stop at the next farmhouse? We could tell them we escaped from Leningrad and are going to family. Tell them we have plenty of our own food. We just want to be warm for a little while."

Father didn't respond.

They walked in silence for a few minutes. "How long will it take for us to reach Germany?"

"It's difficult to know," her father answered. "The war."

She hoped the war would be over and they would never have to worry about going all the way to Germany, but she wanted to stay alive until then. She worried if Father defended his presence to everyone they met, the rest of them would be shot before the day was out.

The wind picked up and snow swirled about them. Father led them into shelter beneath a hedge. For a little while as they sat huddled there, Elena felt nearly safe, like she was in a cave. Snug and almost comfortable. She nodded off to sleep leaning against her mother, who, in turn, slept with her head on her husband's shoulder.

Elena awoke to the sound of her mother's voice. Dawn light filtered through the trees creating a bleak gray and white landscape, but the snow had stopped and the weather had definitely turned warmer. Fall could be like that, one day warm and damp and the next freezing rain or snow. She began to perspire in the heavy clothing. She pulled her hat from her head and rubbed her eyes. "What is it, Mama?" she asked as she yawned.

"You have to help me fix your father's arm. Look at this!"

Elena peered around her mother and saw a huge purple swelling on her father's upper arm. Dried blood caked his torn shirt sleeve and fresh blood seeped from the center of the wound. Anna had been trying to stem the flow of blood with strips of fabric from her cotton slip.

When Elena saw her father's wound, she had to run behind a tree to avoid being sick in front of him. When she returned, she kept to one side, avoiding a direct view of the wound.

Anna tended to Grigory's arm, washing it with water from a stream and then wrapping it with the strips of fabric. Afterward Papa portioned out food.

As she nibbled on her meager portion, Elena considered the dark clouds. Today was a melancholy day, a day to play sad Russian gypsy songs in her head. Maybe the sun would shine later. The sun did shine in the autumn, she was sure she remembered that.

With only the stingy cup of soup she'd had during the night and now only a tiny piece of sausage and potato, she hardly felt refreshed enough to be able to go on.

"Is Papa going to be all right?"

"I cleaned the wound as best I could. Put your hat on," Anna said.

"It's too warm," Elena grumbled, but donned it anyway.

Papa took the lead as they set out. Elena followed behind Mama. The road, like the day, had turned mucky. They slogged through the mud and puddles the size of small ponds.

Their journey continued, slowly, painfully, each day like the last. They slept where they could in abandoned farmhouses, in skeletal remnants of buildings, or under the trees, barely sheltered from the ever-changing weather. Whenever they heard the sound of a car or truck, they left the road to let it pass. Elena lost count of the days it had been since they'd seen another living soul. Father's pace slowed. Elena knew he had been more seriously injured than he said. Since their encounter with the women in the farmhouse, Anna had withdrawn, echoing Papa's gradual decline.

Elena tried to remember what it felt like to be safe and secure, snuggling under her blankets on cold winter nights in Leningrad. She longed to be six years old again and in love with her teacher, Comrade Irina Ivanovna Uspenskaya. Comrade Irina, who insisted on being addressed as Madame Uspenskaya, was the one who told her parents that Elena had a talent for the piano. They already knew that and had been providing private piano lessons for her since she was four. She was enrolled in the special school for musically talented children.

While she still had to learn mathematics and literature, her lessons focused on music. Her friend, Tatiana, attended the same school.

In her second year she became friends with a new little girl, Dunya. At five years old, Little Dunya spent her time in wide eyed fear. She had a terrible cough and often had to stop practicing because of it. The instructors never scolded her, but their harsh glares could send Dunya crying from the room.

Dunya died. Tatiana disappeared. Boris and Misha turned into evil monsters, soldiers of the state, who threatened old women and children.

Who in their right mind would walk across Russia to join the enemy during a war? In her mind she drifted around in their old apartment, between the pieces of dark heavy furniture with crocheted antimacassars. A lace tablecloth covered the highly polished wood table in the dining room. Silver candlesticks flanked a bowl, which Mama kept full of whatever fruit was in season. Grandmama and Grandpa shared a bedroom at the back of the apartment beyond the small kitchen. Their room always smelled of eucalyptus. If Sofia stayed over for special occasions, she slept on a metal cot covered in a bright multicolored quilt in a room the size of a large closet. A short hallway led from the parlor to her bedroom where yellow curtains blew in the breeze through an open window. A fine old bed with a canopy and curtains filled most of the room. In one corner, beside the bureau for her clothes stood a hand carved rocking horse. This was a gift brought by Father Christmas when she was three, but really carved by her mother's father. Those grandparents died at the beginning of the siege when their building suffered a direct hit. Closing the door she wandered back into the kitchen where Grandmama stuffed sausages.

It seemed like they'd been walking forever. Elena itched all over and longed for a nice warm bath. Even a small bowl of water like she used in the basement for a sponge bath would be welcome. Perhaps the world really was flat and went on and on forever in a muddy hell. How long had it been since they had spoken with anybody?

"What did that woman mean about Chicago, Papa?" Elena asked.

"It's where the gangsters live in America. We mustn't go to Chicago," he said.

With the weather so humid, it was hard to decide if she was hot or cold. When Papa removed his overcoat, blood soaked through his sweaters. The wound stank; she could smell it from three feet away. Mama had checked it regularly and pronounced it "healing." If it was healing, why would it still be bleeding? She followed his example and removed her coat, still feeling uncomfortable.

"No, Papa. Not Chicago. Where shall we go once we get to Germany? Do you have a plan?"

"Elena! Do not question your father. It's taking all his energy to walk." Mama paused to look at the sky. "The weather will change tonight. We should stop at the first possible shelter, Grigory."

"Of course, Anna. The first shelter."

Elena looked up at the gray sky and felt the same gray mist soaking through every piece of her clothing. She put her coat on again.

Papa staggered, tripped over a fallen branch, stumbled, and fell. Anna and Elena rushed to his side. He was unconscious. Mama made the decision to remain where they were for the night.

Elena snuggled close to her father, hoping the warmth from her body would keep him going through the night.

PART II

THE GERMAN ENCAMPMENT

Ten

Early the following morning Elena watched her mother collapse, exhausted, beside her husband, her arms, like the wings of a black swan, covering his injured body. A light snow fell. The dark clouds overhead signaled yet another bitter, damp day. Black against white. Life against death. She dreamed of lying beside her parents and slowly fading into a dark peaceful sleep where there was no longer hunger, no longer cold. No longer life. She startled herself with the thought.

"Mama!" She must get her attention. They must not fall asleep in the snow. She squatted down and shook her mother's shoulder, terrified she wouldn't awaken. "Mama, remember the women in the farmhouse? How could they be so fat when there were no animals around? And they were cooking soup. Do you remember what was in the soup?" She must answer. She must stay awake. "They were vegetables, Mama. Potatoes and carrots and cabbage. And perhaps a rabbit. Can you catch rabbits in the winter? I bet hunters have tricks to make them come out of their holes. One, two, three, four, five," she began a nursery rhyme. "Little rabbit comes out alive. But, quick look, straight ahead. Bang, bang. Now it's done. Little rabbit of mine is dead."

She thought about the little dead rabbit for a minute before she realized she was thinking of herself. Of leaving the underground room to walk into the unknown and then to die. That would be the end of her. Who would know? Who would care? Without Papa, she had no idea which direction to take. How did he know? He kept telling them, "That way is west. We walk west."

"My uncles went to America. I'm glad they don't live in Chicago, Mama." She said, her voice rising in panic. She shook Mama again. "Maybe we could live in Washington where the president lives. I could play the piano for him. I have my piano with me. I didn't tell you. I'm sorry. I wanted to play for you while we were traveling. Mama, do you think Mr. Roosevelt likes the Minuet in G? I like it. It reminds me of the spring and of flowers. It's light and happy. Do you think we'll ever be light and happy again?"

Her mother made a noise, a croak like a door with stiff hinges.

"If we sit here, we'll get so cold we won't feel anything anymore. Perhaps then we can be happy. Not to be cold anymore, Mama."

"Elena."

Elena thought she heard her name spoken. Her mother still lay with her arms around Grigory's shoulders as if protecting him from the snow. In the cold stillness of the morning, the only sounds she heard were own breathing and the distant whine of an engine. Her skin prickled. A car? A truck? It had been days since they'd heard either. She listened carefully. Not an airplane. She looked again at her mother.

"Go away, Elena," her mother muttered through stiff lips. "Hide. They're coming. I'll call you when it's safe. Go!"

"Where, Mama? What do you think it is?"

"Don't argue. Get away. Anywhere. If they see us, they will leave us for dead.

"Oh, Mama."

"Sweep the ground behind you."

Elena dragged herself upright and looked around. Following the old farm path they had seen few houses, and those were abandoned. Any direction was as good as another. She dragged her knapsack behind, hoping the snow would quickly cover her footprints. When she'd gone about a dozen yards, she stepped behind a tree then glanced around it at her parents still curled in the snow. This is far enough, she thought. If no one knows I exist, then they won't be looking for me anyway. She leaned her back against the tree trunk then slid down to the ground to wait for the vehicle to pass.

She pulled a small piece of bread from her pack and chewed on it. If she portioned the bits out carefully, she would have enough for another day. Then what? What had her father been thinking when he bought the food on the black market? Did he really think it would last all the way to Germany? Well, at least her grandparents in Leningrad would have more to eat now they were gone.

The engine noises grew louder, the deep growl of the engine sounding more and more like a truck as it came closer. She twisted around to look toward the road. Perhaps a truck could take them…she slumped back as she realized it came from the direction they were heading, it could only take them back to where they came from.

She covered her ears with her gloved hands and closed her eyes. The engine roared. They had been walking in silence for so long she'd forgotten the sounds of internal combustion engines, automobiles driving down the avenues, trolley cars and trucks. They'd been scarce enough in the city, but out in the country they'd only heard a few, maybe four. The noise crescendoed and then receded as the vehicle moved on. Elena opened her eyes.

She stared into a pair of beady black eyes. She shrieked. The bird squawked but its cry of surprise was cut short by Elena's gloved hand. In a reflex movement she grabbed at its neck with her right hand, covered its head with her left, and then whipped it up over her head to smack it into the tree behind her. It fell into her lap - dead. She stared dumbly at the lifeless creature.

Her feeling of sadness at the sight of death fought with pride that she'd found food for her family. Holding onto the tree, she pulled herself up. Carrying the small bird over her head like a trophy, she staggered to her parents.

"Mama! Papa! Food! I've found food! Wake up." Still holding the bird, she shook her parents' snow-covered bodies. "Wake up! We have food. Please wake up."

She leaned close to her mother's face and pulled up on her eyebrow, opening her eyelid. Elena peered into the eyeball. "Mama? Can you cook a pheasant for dinner? I don't have any onions or carrots, but we can pretend."

Her mother didn't respond.

"Wake up, Mama." She shook her mother again, rolling her off her father's still form. "Mama! Come on!"

Setting her prize aside, she removed her right glove and forced her hand inside the collar of her mother's coat. Mama was still warm. She turned to her father and did the same. He, too, was warm. She watched them for several moments. They looked so peaceful lying there in the snow. And if she left them alone, they would be dead before nightfall. The fierce thumping in her chest made it hard to breathe. Holding her mother's shoulder, she rocked her backward and forward violently.

"I can't clean the damned thing myself!" she shouted, tears forming in her eyes. "You have to wake up and help me! You have to."

"Don't blaspheme, Elena." The croak was barely audible. "I will have to wash your mouth out with the snow."

"Oh, Mama." Elena wrapped her arms around her mother in relief.

She helped her mother to a sitting position, not the least bit worried about what her mother might do to her for swearing; Anna was so weak she could barely remain upright. "You can do that later, Mama, but tell me what to do with this bird."

"Elena." The voice grew stronger. "My husband, your father, is dying and you want to roast a bird. Go away," her mother moaned as she fell back against Grigory.

Elena threw the fowl at her. "I thought you were dead," she sobbed.

"Stop crying," her mother said wearily as if it was the last thing she'd ever do. "Go get wood for a fire."

Wiping tears from her eyes, Elena faced the trees, took a deep breath, and forced herself to collect dead wood. By the time she returned her mother was pulling at the feathers of the bird. Elena searched her father's duffel bag for matches then lit the small bundle of sticks. They flared up and were gone in seconds.

She stared at the dying embers. "I need bigger wood. I'll be back." She headed into the woods. This time she brought back small branches as well as sticks. The effort exhausted her and she had to stop to catch her breath every few yards. Once again, she built another pyramid of wood and tried again. This time it roared to life and burned like it intended to last, hissing and steaming from the wet snow. While she'd been working on the fire, her mother finished preparing the bird, scraping weakly at its innards with Grigory's poor excuse for a hunting knife.

Elena watched her mother drop the messy corpse into the cook pot her father had carried in his pack. "Aren't you supposed to drain the blood out?"

"We need everything we can get out of this bird. Throw plenty of snow in there to boil. We'll have soup to eat now and meat to carry with us."

The thought of fresh meat revived her. Leaving her mother to watch the pot, Elena staggered off to collect more wood to keep them warm for the next few hours. They would sleep after they ate and when they awoke all three of them would be stronger.

They took turns sipping the hot broth. She draped their blankets about them like a tent and they huddled in the warmth of the flames watching the food cook.

It hardly seemed to have cooked long enough when Mama said, "We can eat."

"In a minute," Elena said as she fished out the few scraps of potato she still held in her bag and then tossed them into the pot. "Chicken stew!"

Elena scooped out small pieces of meat with her metal spoon and fed it to her father.

They ate the meat sparingly and drank more broth. Elena settled herself, snug and warm between her parents. Grigory hadn't spoken much other than to complain about the pain in his arm and shoulder. Anna had fashioned a sling from a shirt, but any movement was clearly painful. She'd worry about him later after their rest. For the first time in her life she understood what exhaustion meant. When they had set out on their trek, she'd only been tired. She remembered her parents supporting her the first day. How strong they all were then and yet hadn't known it. The fire warmed her cheeks. Her eyes closed, her head dropped against her mother's shoulder.

Someone shook her. She didn't want to go to school today. She was too comfortable in her bed. "Go away, Sofia, I don't feel well. I'm…"

"Wake up. It's the Germans. They're going to help us."

Elena opened her eyes. Had she heard right? In front of her the wood had smoldered into ashes. Across the fire she saw boots, then the hem of a greatcoat and, as her gaze traveled upward, the rigid stare of a high-ranking German officer standing in front of a Mercedes-Benz. It carried small flags at the front of its long hood. She knew little of the military, but she sensed this man was no ordinary soldier like they had seen at the front lines.

"Your mother tells me you speak French, Yuri," he spoke in French.

Still groggy from sleep, it took her a moment to understand he was speaking to her. Her name was Yuri and she was a twelve-year-old boy from Leningrad. *"Oui,"* She said. "I am Yuri Federov."

"Colonel Hüber." He cleared his throat. He shifted as if pushed and it was then that Elena saw the woman standing half hidden behind him. "My lady friend pointed out your parents lying in the snow. We might have passed right by."

"She is no lady. Look at her." Anna said to Elena in Russian. "She is Maria, the whore from the farmhouse who shot your father. They drive in a car in one day the distance which took us almost a week to walk."

Elena could never forget the glamorous woman. She hated her, not only for shooting her father, but for being beautiful and well-fed. She lunged past her mother toward the woman. "You tried to kill him. He could still die!" she cried out in Russian.

The colonel stepped in front of Maria and grabbed Elena by the shoulders. "That will do, young man. Where did you get a chicken?"

Elena shrugged angrily away from him. "I found it in the woods. It's not a chicken; it's a pheasant. A wild bird."

The officer smiled and reached out as if to pat her on the head. She shrank back behind her mother. "I have a boy about your age. I don't know if he would be so clever to find a chicken in the middle of the forest."

"My husband, Sir. You said you would help him." Mama snapped.

Elena stared wide-eyed at her mother and held her breath, waiting to see how the officer would react to being spoken to like that.

The man briefly covered his mouth with his gloved hand before speaking again. "Never mind. If you can cook, madam, under these conditions, I would have you come to our camp to help. You and the boy can also do the laundry."

He turned and gave orders to the driver and another soldier who had been standing at attention near the automobile. The two men lifted Grigory, who never uttered a sound, and placed him in the back seat. Elena helped her mother to her feet but the officer quickly scooped her up in his arms. "You'll be all right, Little Mother. You!" he commanded to the other woman in German, "Sit in the front with the driver!"

Elena realized the woman hadn't understood. Leaning close to her mother, she whispered, "Mama, translate what he just said!"

Anna repeated the German's command to Maria in Russian.

"Ach. So. We have captured a group of linguists, have we?"

Elena reached for the pot of soup, the fragrance of the boiled fowl too good to leave behind.

"Leave it," the colonel said.

Reluctantly, Elena set the pot back on the fire but not before ladling out one more mouthful for herself. She climbed into the car and huddled beside her mother. The officer draped a bearskin rug over all three of them and then squeezed in next to Elena.

Eleven

Tuesday

"Yuri! Wake up!"

Elena's mother shook her shoulder. Elena turned her face away and moaned. "Go away. I'm tired."

"You must wake up. You've been sleeping for three days. Colonel Hüber is asking for you. He has been most patient."

Elena turned her head and opened her eyes.

"Here, I have bread and broth." Anna put an arm behind her daughter's shoulders and helped her to a sitting position. She started to spoon feed her but Elena grabbed the bowl and tried to drink the lukewarm liquid. "Not so fast. You'll get sick."

"I am sick, Mama. I'm starving." She reached for the bread and moistened it in the soup then sucked at the softened black bread.

"I have more bread and broth for you. You're lucky the colonel has a son your age or you might have been shot."

Elena's eyebrows rose in surprise and she asked through a mouthful of bread, "Shot for what?"

"For being alive. For being an extra mouth to feed. I don't know. Germans will shoot you without any reason if they choose. The doctor said you've had plenty of time to recover."

"I'm still sick," she mumbled as she continued spooning soup into her mouth.

"But while you slept, I've begun working. I've been doing the cooking for two days and now I must also work in the laundry."

"Who is the colonel? Is he the man who rescued us? The one with fat Maria?"

Anna nodded. "Get up. We have work to do."

Elena looked at her surroundings. She lay on a low wooden bunk in a large room. The room held at least fifty beds. They lined the walls in two tiers. Heavy burgundy velvet draperies covered several floor to ceiling windows. Her bed stood near an ornate marble fireplace that radiated warmth from dying embers.

She pulled herself up. Her head felt light and she had to sit back down. After a moment, she stood again, still a bit shaky, and put on her coat. She tightened the belt snugly about the middle. "It's gone! Mama, my piano is gone! Where is it?"

"Hush. It's under the bunk. The men wanted to undress you for the doctor to examine you, but I insisted it was my job as your mother to take care of you. We cannot let them know you're a girl. There are only a few women here and as far as I can tell you and I are the only ones who are prisoners." Anna secured Elena's cap as she spoke. "You should have let me cut your hair while we were still at home, Elena."

"Yuri," Elena corrected. She looked around the room again. "Who sleeps in all those beds? Where are we?"

"It's an estate the Germans are using for their camp. The soldiers sleep here. I have a space behind the kitchen. I haven't been permitted outside except to go to the toilet. I will say one good thing about them. They're very organized and they have food and medicine. I think this is a support unit for the front lines."

"What about Papa?" As she spoke Elena looked under the bed to confirm her piano was there. "Is he alive?"

"They said they took your father to the infirmary. That's across the compound in a cottage. We can only pray it is the truth. They are the enemy, after all."

"With food and medicine. Has it really been three days since we arrived?" Elena studied her mother's face. Her skin looked healthier and her eyes glowed more clearly since she'd last seen her. "I was so tired when the Germans found us. I do remember the hot broth and bread and even a little meat. That was you feeding me?" Elena was disturbed by the unusual show of tenderness. All her life she'd felt like a burden to her mother's existence. Mama always spoke of her children as the ones for whom she cared at the nursery school. It was her grandmother, Babushka, whom Elena went to when she was hurt and needed comfort.

"Yes, now come along." She took Elena by the hand and guided her through a large arched doorway that led into an entry hall with a curved staircase leading to a balconied landing. The furniture was missing but a massive crystal chandelier still hung incongruously from the domed ceiling.

The blast of cold air in the grand hall made her gasp for breath. Anna put an arm around her shoulder and pushed her along to the left, toward the back of the house. When they reached the end of a long hallway Anna opened a door to the outside where the air was even colder. A covered path took them a short distance to another, smaller, building. They pushed through the ancient wooden door and entered a magical place.

She was enveloped in warmth, flavored with the glorious fragrance of baking bread and frying bacon. Elena stood inside the doorway and took a deep breath. Anna shut the door behind them and removed her overcoat, placing it on a hook. Elena looked around the large room. A soldier stirred a large cauldron, another washed dishes, two others busied themselves at a butcher's block chopping potatoes and cabbages. The men glanced up at their entrance and waved to Anna, then returned immediately to work.

"Come along. See those large pots over there? It is the soup for lunch. We cook for the officers, but we make soup from the leftovers for the rest of the men. Remove your coat and we'll get to work."

"I don't want to," Elena said, feeling overwhelmed by the presence of the Germans and distressed at her mother's apparent familiarity with them.

Anna stopped and turned to look at her daughter. Elena stood stubbornly near the door. "I told you to remove your coat."

"I don't want to, Mama. I don't want to feed our enemy. Father said they would take care of us."

She'd hardly finished speaking before Mama was standing before her brandishing a large wooden spoon. "If you do not obey me, you'll have more than the German army to worry about."

Mama, who had seemed near death only three days ago now stood with the spoon raised, ready to strike. Elena decided not to test her any further. She could recall only three times when her mother had displayed anger, each time with the ferocity of a cornered wolf. She removed her coat and placed it on a hook next to her mother's as she glared resentfully at the German soldiers who watched her with amusement written all over their faces. "Tell me what I have to do," she said in a soft voice, fearing to anger her mother further.

"You can begin by helping Private Becker." She pointed to the man standing at a stone sink on the far side of the room. His shirtsleeves were rolled up to his elbows. He washed dishes and then placed them in a big rinsing basin. Elena had never seen a man washing dishes before. Anna spoke to him in German then explained to Elena in Russian, "I told him you are my son; you have learning problems so he must not try to speak with you, nor think he can befriend you in any way. Later when you're serving meals, you mustn't speak at all so the colonel won't catch on to our scheme. He will think you are being a polite little boy."

Elena looked at Private Becker's face. He was a blond-haired boy, not much older than she. He had nice eyes that brimmed with sympathy and a shy smile that creased a dimple on the right side of his face. "What kind of problems, Mama?" she asked without taking her eyes from the young soldier.

"That you are slow witted and you need your Mama to take you to the toilet.

"Mama!" Elena moaned, thoroughly humiliated. She turned her back on the private as she felt the sting of tears. "Why did you say such a stupid thing about me?"

Anna patted her as she might a small puppy. "There, there, my darling child. Please don't act up now. Imagine if you have to relieve yourself. Where do you suppose they will expect you to go? I will explain to Private Becker that you are overwhelmed and grateful to be here where it's warm. He can show you how to dry the dishes and where to put them away. I must get back to the stove and then later we will do the laundry." She leaned over and whispered to Elena, "There's a good girl."

And Mama left Elena in Private Becker's care.

Twelve

With downcast eyes, Elena wiped the dishes and set them on the countertop. If she looked Private Becker in the eyes again, he would surely know she wasn't slow witted. The plates she dried were beautiful even though several were chipped. She turned one over and read, *Limoges*. They must have been in the house when the Germans took it over. When she had a dozen of them piled up, she picked them up to put them in the cupboard. Before she could reach it, the private took the stack from her. He smiled.

After he'd put the plates away, he pointed to her, "Yuri." Then he pointed to himself. "Willie. *Ya?*"

She felt her face flush and quickly turned her attention to the tiled floor. "*Ya.* Willie," she replied. She glanced over at her mother, but Anna was busy supervising the removal of bread rolls from the brick oven. She was about to smooth her hair under her cap when she remembered who she was.

"Herman Werner, Ernst Zimmer, Walter Lauderbach," he said indicating the other three men in the kitchen. Herman was a huge, dark haired beast of a man and her first thought was to keep her distance from him. Ernst and Walter were both slightly taller than Willie but they had brown hair. They looked older than Willie and Herman, maybe even as old as thirty.

After they had cleaned up from the officers' dinner, she staggered, exhausted, back to the large room. Men clustered in groups around the stove. Mama spoke firmly to them. With good-natured respect they waved at Anna and Elena. Elena guessed they were saying "good night." Once Anna had Elena tucked securely into her bunk, she leaned over and whispered, "Tomorrow we shall have the men fill the tub for you and you shall have a bath. You're becoming quite ripe, young woman."

Elena smiled. This was the mother she'd always wanted, a caring, loving woman who saw to her needs. She reached up and hugged her. "It's not so bad here, is it, Mama? Papa was right, the Germans are taking care of us even though we have to work for our food. I hope he's getting better so he can come back to us soon."

Mama ignored her remark about Papa and said, "It's true it's better than it was in Leningrad, but still, you must be careful not to speak to any of the men here. When your father returns, he will figure a way for us to leave. Meanwhile, we have food and a warm place to stay. Now you sleep. We begin our work early."

The following afternoon during the lull between the mid-day meal and dinner Anna stood guard while Elena bathed in the tub in a room behind the kitchen. Anna explained the warmth of the small room, where she also slept, came from the great ovens on the kitchen side of the wall.

Elena was enjoying the cleansing soak, her first in nearly a year, when she sensed her mother standing close behind her. She thought she heard her whisper, "I'm sorry," before she turned and saw the big butcher's knife in her hand.

Anna grabbed a braid and began sawing at it.

"No! Don't! Please, don't! I'm not speaking to anyone. No one will know I'm a girl. Stop, Mama!" she screeched.

"Be quiet and be still, you stupid girl. You can't keep wearing a hat in such a hot kitchen, even if you are simple. And I've seen how the men look at you. You, smiling and flirting at them. This is a dangerous time for you. Stay still. I don't want to cut your neck."

"I don't flirt. I'm smiling like the stupid boy you want me to be. I'm trying to be simple."

"Well, you're far too pretty for your own good. I'm almost done." And with one last slice at the second braid, Elena's hair was shorn. Elena climbed out of the tub and dried herself, pulling away from her mother's offer of help. The filthy clothes she'd been wearing since they left Leningrad lay in a heap on the floor. She shuddered at the thought of having to put them on again. Her father promised the Germans would feed them, but would they ever issue new clothes?

Before they left, her mother trimmed the edges of her hair as best she could, not as short as a military haircut, but at least above the ears.

She worked all afternoon with a long face. Even Willie's smile didn't cheer her up.

Each morning for the next three days, Anna arrived at Elena's side to awaken her. But Elena, ashamed and angry about her hair, refused to speak to her. She pulled on her overcoat for the short walk to the kitchen, grateful the soldiers arrived even earlier to get the fires going for the day.

Every day Willie told her the German words for objects while they worked side by side, cleaning, sweeping, chopping vegetables, and serving meals in the dining room. She found a certain comfort in the routine of working next to him. She fetched the food from the pantry; cracked fresh eggs into the powdered egg mixture; chopped sausages to roll into biscuits and learned to like the strong drink concocted of burnt wheat and chicory to replace real coffee. She found it difficult to pretend to be simple, but she figured even a simple person would be able to repeat words like a parrot and it made her happy to be learning something new.

Her mother had easily moved into a position of authority in the kitchen and made sure Elena and the four soldiers kept busy every minute of the day.

Anna bossed the men and Elena about like a group of her personal servants. They seemed amused but responded as if she were their mother. The evening meal became a daily feast of no less than four courses. This not only pleased the officers, but also everyone in the kitchen, for in spite of the extra work, the food included more than enough leftovers to provide generous portions for the kitchen help.

On the fourth day when Anna arrived in the sleeping quarters, Elena was already up and prepared for work. She found she was eager to see Willie's smiling face. She wondered how he could always be so cheerful working as a dishwasher and doing all the menial tasks her mother demanded of him without complaint. The thought of him made her face burn and she didn't understand.

"I am glad you have come to your senses, Yuri. There's no need to pout. You have work to keep you busy and food for your belly. Now give your Mama a hug." Anna reached out and Elena reluctantly allowed herself to be embraced. She would have much preferred the hug be from Willie.

"We have to work, Mama. Those soldiers already think I'm an idiot; I don't want them to think I'm a baby, too." She moved gruffly away from her mother.

The moment they entered the kitchen, Elena knew something was wrong. Willie kept his head bent over the counter where he was slicing potatoes. Ernst, Herman and Walter, the other soldiers on kitchen duty, also kept their eyes averted. She removed her coat and placed it on the hook. Mama went straight to the pantry. Herman and Walter dropped their brooms and helped her turn out the dough she'd prepared the night before for the day's bread and rolls.

"Willie?" She stood near him and picked up a paring knife.

Willie's knife poised over a potato before he turned and pointed it at her. "*Du bist madchen?*"

He glowered at her. He'd asked her a question, but she had no idea what he wanted. "*Vass?* What?"

"*Du. Madchen?*" He outlined the form of a woman with his hands, the knife coming dangerously close to her face.

Elena backed away. "*Madchen?*" Her eyes widened with understanding. "Girl? I'm Yuri, Willie. Yuri." She looked around the room frantically. Her mother slapped gobs of dough around on the counter, too busy to see her daughter needed her. The other three men stopped work to watch her and Willie. Her parents' dire warnings left her in no doubt about what the Germans would do to her if they learned she was a girl. Her skin prickled with fear. Terrified, she looked into Willie's eyes. The eyes she'd thought so kind and sympathetic only a few days ago.

Willie grinned at her. *"Ach. So."* He put the knife on the counter and reached for the hem of her heavy woolen sweater. "I see it is true."

She leapt back and bumped into the butcher block behind her. In a panic she shouted at him in her newly learned German. She even tried English and French, hoping he'd understand something she said. *"Nicht madchen. Nicht. Not a girl! Je suis garçon."*

He threw his hands up. *"Ach!_*You are speaking English. That is good. I am speaking English as well. *Kommst du hier, Yuri.* We talk."

She looked in vain for her mother again, but she'd gone into the pantry. Ernst and Herman placed themselves between her and the pastry table. They were making sure Anna and Elena stayed apart. Elena turned to see where Walter had gone. He stood with his back to the main entrance into the kitchen. With his arms folded across his chest he grinned at Elena. She shivered despite the heat.

Willie repeated his request. "Come here, into the little room. We talk."

"The little room?" she managed to squeak. She wanted to scream but feared she might cause trouble for her mother.

"Where your mother sleeps. Come. I will not hurt you." He reached for her hand, which she quickly pulled away and put behind her back. Praying if she did what he said, he wouldn't hurt her, she followed him.

With a last hopeful glance for her mother, Elena stepped into the back room feeling like a prisoner going to her execution. It was the first time since she'd been at the camp that she fully realized her position – she *was* a prisoner, no matter how kindly she'd been treated up until now.

Thirteen

Willie closed the door and led Elena to the small bed where her mother slept. She squeezed her eyes shut to keep back her tears. She feared everything her parents had told her about what the enemy did to young girls was about to happen.

"Please, not to be frighten," Willie said. She felt him sit beside her, his body close. She didn't dare move.

"Frightened. There is an 'e-d' at the end of the word," she automatically corrected.

"*Ach, so.* Frightened. Do not be so. I will not hurt you. Ernst searched through your mother's things last night and found your hair-cut."

Before the words registered, he'd grabbed her cap and pulled it off. Her hands flew to her head in a feeble attempt to cover it, but by the look on his face, she realized he knew the truth. "You found my braids."

"Yuri?" he said softly.

"Elena Grigoryovna Federova," she said, sitting with her shoulders slumped, her arms hanging limp across her legs.

"That is a very long name." She heard the laughter in his voice and relaxed a little.

"You may call me Katya," she said.

"Katya is much more easy, but we must not seem to be friends. You understand what they expect me to do in here with you?"

She trembled at the memory of her mother's explanation about what bad men did to young girls. "You will rape me."

"It is what they expect. We will not tell them anything at all." He touched her shoulder. "You are crying. Good. Your eyes will be red."

She slid away and turned to face him. She saw only tenderness in his eyes. "You mean you will not rape me? You are the enemy. Mama says that is what Germans do to girls."

He smiled. "Only bad Germans. When we go into the kitchen you must let them think you are now my woman. I will tell them they cannot touch you."

She jumped up in alarm. "What do you mean? They can't touch me anyway. I'll scream if they do. And why would they listen to you? You're the dishwasher."

"Sit down again. I am also the boxing champion of this unit. It does not mean much in the rest of the world, but here I am respected. Your mother tried to protect you by making you a boy, though she does not know all the ways of men. In here, with us, you were safe as a boy, but that is not always true. Now they know you are a girl, they will want their way with you and your mother cannot protect you. The colonel might have something to say, as he is a kind man, but that would be after the fact."

"The fact of rape?"

"Yes. So, I will tell them when we go there, they must leave you alone. And now, we must play the act. You must scream."

"Scream?"

"Shout," he said. "I am hurting you. Shout!" He stood and kicked the bed so it banged loudly against the wall. He shouted at her in German.

She cringed and screamed. And screamed more as he continued to say German words she knew instinctively were ugly, demeaning words. She watched him thump down on the bed and bounce. A rhythmic sound she'd often heard from her parent's side of the room. She felt herself blush and covered her mouth with her hand as she smiled. Suppressing a giggle, she cried out, "*Nyet! Nyet!*"

Someone banged on the door. Mama called out her name. Elena froze. And then suddenly silence. Had the other men hurt her? Willie went to the door, unlocked, and opened it slightly. He peeked through the slit and then closed and relocked it.

When he returned to the bed he sat by Elena and reassured her. "They are keeping your mother quiet so she does not alarm anyone, though no one could hear her through the thick walls. They are not harming her. What do you do?" he asked, suddenly changing the subject.

"I help you in the kitchen."

"No, I mean before you came here? Do you live near here? Did you go to a special school for – for… "

"Morons? Fools?"

He grinned with embarrassment. "Of course, that was part of the deception. A simple boy. So?"

"So, we lived in Leningrad and I played the piano. I was in a special school for talented musicians. Someday I shall play before all the world. I want to share my music with everyone. They should know Chopin and Beethoven and…"

Willie held his hand up. "Hush. You must speak softly. They cannot think we are a nice conversation."

"*Having* a nice conversation," she whispered to him. "My friend Tatiana and I went to school before the blockade and bombardment began. We tried to continue, but Papa said it was not safe. What do you do?"

"I was a clerk in an insurance office. Not such an important job, but I have a sign on my desk, Wilhelm Günter, Clerk. It was my first job from school. I did not qualify for university."

"Did you like your work?"

He smiled. "I liked to put on a suit in the morning and walk with my hat on my head and a newspaper tucked under my arm. People would see me and think I was a businessman."

"But you were. And very young for a businessman."

"I am just turned to nineteen years," he said proudly. Then after a pause added, "And I pray to live to twenty years."

She explained about living in the basement and life in Leningrad under the siege. "In the beginning my parents did not tell me anything about the war. They protected me from all the news. Of course, my friends talked about it at school, but it was not real to me until it came to our city. Your airplanes bombed and burned so much. I had headaches from the noise, but then I became used to it. Until one day it was our building that caught fire. I thought my grandfather would have a heart attack as he tried to put out the fire. Everybody screamed and ran around beating at flames, but there was no use for it. Mama threw many things out the window which we later used to make our home in the cellar of the building."

"I am sorry," Willie said.

"Why? You did not send the bombs and the fire, did you?" She smiled at him.

"I am sorry it was so terrible for you. You are so thin."

"Food was difficult to find. We had rations and my father worked so he received extra tickets for food and shared with us. We didn't die."

They spoke for a while longer and he explained what it was like being a child during Hitler's rise to power. He was embarrassed when he told her about being forced to join the Hitler Youth party. His parents had strongly disapproved, but contrary to Nazi policy, he hadn't turned them in. He enlisted and was sent to the front, terrified he'd be killed the first day, but found he was mostly bored with having to wash dishes and clean up for the officers at this house.

"I enlisted because my father, who fought in the Great War, demanded I do my patriotic duty. I wish he had been more like your father and taken us out of the country when he knew what was coming. Now we are here for the winter. We are a support unit. We keep the supplies for the front lines and a field hospital for the wounded."

"Where my father is," Elena said hopefully.

"I do not know about your father. I have not heard of a Russian prisoner in the hospital." Her hands flew to her face in an attempt to hide her alarm. Willie quickly added, "But I am not in a position to know about those things. I only know we were told not to take prisoners!"

"But Colonel Hüber brought us here! Are we not prisoners?"

"I think Colonel Hüber was in need of a cook. The previous one was sent to the front last week and Ernst, Herman and I have been trying to make the food."

"My mother was a teacher. She had classes of babies, four and five years old. She's not much of a cook. Grandmother and our housekeeper, Sofia, did all the cooking and cleaning."

"Then your mother is a good faker. For this past week the colonel has been happy with the food. You can be proud of her cleverness."

"I suppose he had no use for my father, especially with such a bad wound to his arm." She sighed. She hoped Papa would have been pleased to learn not all the enemy soldiers wanted to rape young girls.

"Perhaps he is in the hospital." Willie patted her hand.

Elena looked down at his hand covering hers. "He's dead, isn't he?" Tears ran down her cheeks. "Poor Papa. He so wanted us to be safe."

"Please wipe your eyes."

She reached into her pocket and pulled out the lace handkerchief she'd been carrying since the day her family left Leningrad.

"That is a very beautiful handkerchief. Did your grandmother make it?" he asked.

"No. I have had it for many years. I carry it now with me because one day as I was searching for clean water and could not find any, I used this to strain water into a container from a muddy puddle. When I squeezed the water through and opened the handkerchief, I saw a finger. It looked like it belonged to a lady. There were two covered bodies in front of the building next to ours; I supposed a thief had cut it off to take a ring. I scrubbed it with my strained water, the handkerchief, not the finger. I threw the finger away." She slipped the piece of linen back into her pocket and wiped her face on the sleeve of her sweater. "I didn't cry when I found the finger, Willie. It was only a little part of a person. A whole person who died. There were so many bodies that I stopped crying. I thought, 'this person will never play the piano again, if she ever did.' And I worried about my own fingers. If I died, would somebody cut them off?" She sniffled.

Willie didn't respond. He sat quietly beside her while she cried and after a few minutes said, "I think we must go out now. Please, behave as if I treated you badly. Will you?"

"I should mess up my clothing."

Willie chuckled softly. "You are already a mess, Katya. A nice mess."

"You're very kind, Willie."

"Do not say such a thing in front of them!"

They exited into the kitchen where Ernst and Herman flanked Anna at the stove. Walter was not in the room.

As soon as she saw her daughter, Anna broke free of the two young men and rushed to embrace Elena. Elena felt suffocated by her mother's overwhelming grasp. "It's all right, Mama," she whispered in Russian. "Willie is a good person."

Anna's arms stiffened. She hissed into Elena's ear. "What are you saying to me? I heard you screaming. My heart was breaking for you and you tell me he is good? Look at me, Elena! Look at me and tell me that he did not touch you!"

Elena stumbled and fell against the work island. "He did, Mama, but only in kindness. Don't be angry with me. See them? They're laughing. Willie says the others should believe he did bad things to me. I should pretend to be his girlfriend."

She never saw it coming. The blow from her mother's hand across her cheek sent her crashing to the floor. "You foul, horrible girl!" And then her mother was kicking her.

Elena tried to protect herself from her mother's blows, confused and terrified by this turn of events. Anna's heavy boots caught her on the legs. In the end it took all three men to subdue Anna.

Willie helped her to her feet and led her to a stool near the ovens where he examined her stick-thin legs. Grateful that her mother's kicks hadn't broken any bones, and comforted by Willie's touch, she wanted to reach out and pat his head as he bent before her. Willie's body blocked her view of her mother, but she could hear her arguing with the others in German. Whatever was said, Anna returned to her work and the others continued theirs.

When Walter entered the room a few minutes later, Anna was furiously pounding and kneading the dough. Walter spoke rapidly to the other three men and then stood to attention as the colonel entered the room. Ernst kept turning to look at her and Willie. The knowing smirk on his face frightened her.

The colonel paused in the entryway. He looked deliberately from one person to another, slowly studying the tableau. His aide muttered something to him and he moved further into the room so the door could be closed. The aide made an announcement and the three young kitchen soldiers lined up in front of the colonel.

"Now we will see how good your German boyfriend is," Mama said in Russian.

"He is not my boyfriend; I only said he was kind to me."

The colonel shouted.

"He said we have to be quiet." Mama's hands automatically continued kneading while she listened and translated what he said. "He knows you are a girl and Willie has molested you."

"But he didn't! Tell the colonel that he didn't!" Elena shouted.

Colonel Hüber looked at them. Anna wiped her hands on her apron before she spoke to him. The only words Elena understood were, "Wilhelm Günter."

Then the colonel responded, gesticulating angrily.

"He disapproves of that kind of behavior and also disapproves that I kept a secret about you. He wants to know if Willie is the one who hurt you. I told him it is true."

Elena leapt up from the stool. "It's not true," she shouted in Russian. "Sir, colonel, sir. Willie isn't bad."

"He understands you are upset about the man's behavior and will have him shot." Anna stopped translating as the colonel continued speaking in a more subdued voice.

"Willie, my mother says the colonel is going to shoot you. Is that true?" Elena spoke in English.

She saw the back of Willie's ears turn bright red. He spoke briefly in German to the colonel then, without turning around, said in English, "No. He is saying we were bad and are not to – to do that thing again."

The colonel continued his dressing down for several more minutes.

Anna translated. "He is sending Private Günter to move your things into my room. He says you can share my bed. I will not share my bed with you. You can sleep on the floor."

Elena's eyes burned with shame that her mother thought so poorly of her. That her mother really thought she had done bad things with Willie. She knew she hadn't done anything to be ashamed of, yet she still felt that way. She was confused and afraid of her feelings. Meekly she asked, "Can you please ask Willie to bring my piano?"

Anna snorted and turned her back. Bewildered by her rejection and frightened of the men in the kitchen, Elena put on her heavy coat and struggled to the main house.

Fourteen

Elena fought against the wind to pull the large door shut behind her. The wind howled between the buildings. She rushed across the gap gripping her coat to her body and climbed the four steps to the covered stoop. Inside the house she paused and took several deep breaths before deciding where to go. She'd never been beyond the servants' entrance to the dining room during the course of the days. She went straight from her sleeping quarters to the back door in the mornings and then returned the same way at night. She hesitated. She wanted to get her piano but had no idea if there would be soldiers in the room during the day or if they knew her secret. Her heart thumped so loudly in her chest she was sure it would be heard echoing off her ribs.

Then she heard voices from above. Where the officers had their meetings. She decided to go upstairs and talk to the colonel. When he asked why she had come to him she would tell him she wanted to thank him for protecting her from the men. Then she would ask him if she could sleep in one of the rooms in the house, away from her mother. With her plan in mind, she turned toward the grand staircase at the front of the house. At the foot of the stairs she paused to look at the huge, curved wall. Large rectangular shapes patterned the staircase wall, faded memories of family portraits long ago looted. She assumed they'd been burned along with the other furniture to keep the men warm. Willie told her there was one entire unit of men who did nothing but go out into the countryside to cut down trees and chop the wood for the fireplaces. In this house, burning wood meant warmth. The thought comforted her and she ascended the steps. The voices grew louder.

It sounded like laughter. Believing the men to be in good spirits she rushed up the last few steps to the landing. She stopped for a moment using the sound of the voices to lead her in the right direction. They came from the right. She moved slowly. Now that she was almost there, she had second thoughts. Why should the colonel be kind to her? Just because he had children? He said so, but he hadn't done anything more for her than he had for her mother. She had been left with the soldiers in the big common room when they thought she was a boy, and then sent to live in the servants' room in the kitchen with her mother. She was stupid to think she could gain any special privileges. Maybe if she explained how her mother hated her for talking to Willie–Private Günter–maybe he would relent and let her live in the house.

A sudden movement caught her eye. She gasped and turned to see a filthy urchin standing beside her looking horrified at seeing her. She reached out to reassure the poor boy she meant him no harm. He reached out to her at the same time. She looked down at his hand. The same glove. She looked up at his eyes and realized she was staring at a mirror. She backed away until she bumped into the opposite wall. She continued to gape at her reflection. There'd been no mirrors in the cellar in Leningrad. The last time she'd seen herself in a real mirror she had plump rosy cheeks and long blonde hair. She lifted first one foot then the other and watched the urchin do the same. The heavy black boots looked far too big for such a skinny body. She pulled off her gloves, seeing for the first time the skeletal outline of her hands. How had she not noticed before? She slowly unbuttoned her coat still staring into the gaunt, haunting face and eyes. Suddenly, she threw her hands over her face.

"No. No. It's not me. It can't be me," she moaned as she turned and ran in the opposite direction, past the stairs and along the hall until she reached the end. She turned the handle of the last door and pushed through the opening. She didn't care if she'd found a closet or a sitting room. She needed to hide. She wanted to die, finally, to die as she'd been doing slowly but surely ever since the apartment burned.

Her eyes adjusted to the weak light leaking through the heavy draperies still covering the windows. A massive, canopied bed in the center of the far wall stood. A tiled stove heated the room. She listened, waiting to hear sounds that someone was there, but heard nothing more than the gentle crackling and hissing from the stove. With a sigh of relief she crossed to the bed and ran her fingers over the soft silken covers. Her roughened skin caught on the fine threads and she withdrew her hand. This room must have belonged to the mistress of the house. Everything was so feminine and pretty. At the window she slid back the draperies to expose the room to the daylight. Turkish carpets on the floor, paintings on the walls, even silver trays and perfume bottles on the bureaus.

Then she saw the German army jacket hung over the back of a chair in front of the vanity. Boots stood at attention under the chair. She went to the closet. It was filled with shirts and trousers.

"Colonel Hüber," she whispered. She touched his clean clothing, remembering how she and her mother helped to make them clean. His undergarments would be in one of the bureau drawers. Orderly. Like her father.

A large steamer trunk plastered with colorful labels from cities around the world caught her attention. Elena thought Russians could no longer travel because the rest of the world didn't like Communism and Russians. Her mother and her parents had traveled all through Europe before the revolution. She looked at the freshest label, pasted on top of others. It suggested this person was headed elsewhere. "Mme. Olga Lubichnaya, 1450 East 48th Street, Brooklyn, New York, U.S.A."

Forgetting her wish to die, she unlatched the trunk and lifted the lid, becoming enveloped in the scent of lavender. She'd been right. A woman *had* occupied this room. The trunk was filled with shoes and dresses. Little compartments contained handkerchiefs, stockings, and gloves. Pretty, delicate gloves for pretty, delicate hands. Elena smiled, imagining the woman or girl who was lucky enough to own these things. But wait, she thought. Where are you? Where did you go without all your pretty things? Could you be in New York without them? She must ask Willie what had happened to the family that owned this house.

She picked up a soft white flannel nightgown and held it to her cheek. She let it fall open and held it in front of her as she looked across the room at herself in the vanity mirror. The filthy urchin still needed a bath. She dropped the gown onto the bed and then searched the trunk for underclothing. Without waiting to sort through her finds, she hid a small bundle of camisoles and undergarments under her sweater inside her coat, lowered the lid and then made sure the latch fastened securely. She was about to leave when she saw the nightgown on the bed. She gasped at her carelessness. Grabbing it, she bundled it under her coat with the other clothes.

Beginning to tremble she tiptoed to a door set so cleverly in the wall to the left of the bed it was barely noticeable. She listened for a moment, then hearing nothing, she risked pressing the handle down. The door opened outward into a dark narrow hall. She peered to the right. In the dimness it looked like a staircase led down to the next level. To the left, the hall ran on into darkness. She guessed it continued to the other end of the house, a way to give servants access to the bedrooms. If her communist schoolteachers were to be believed, this hall wouldn't have been used for at least twenty-five years. She stepped back into the room and pulled the door shut.

"*Bonjour, ma petite.*" The colonel's voice erupted behind her.

She whirled about. "*Monsieur!*"

"You seem to duplicate yourself. Didn't I see you only a few moments ago in the kitchen? There was a question of fraternizing," he continued in French.

Elena took a step backward. She wrapped her arms about her middle to keep the clothes from falling out. "*Oui, Monsieur.* But I wasn't … I didn't. Sir."

"What are you doing in here? You know the upstairs is off limits."

"No, sir. I didn't know."

"How many rooms have you explored?" She watched his eyes. The eyes she considered kind earlier now appeared uncertain. Could he be frightened of something?

"Only this one. And I only arrived a moment ago. I opened the draperies to let in light so I could see. It's a beautiful room, isn't it, sir?"

"It's a girl's room. For a girl, I suppose it would be considered beautiful. It is now my room and I consider it far too feminine. My friend, Maria likes it." He crossed over to the bed and sat down.

Elena wondered how she would get out of the room without giving herself away as a thief. "Maria? The woman who shot my father?"

The colonel chuckled. "The story I heard is that there was an exchange of gunfire. Maria is a clever girl. She knows how to take care of herself and her family."

"My mother doesn't like her. She says she's a traitor."

Ignoring her comment he smiled and pointed to his boots. "Come, little one. Help me remove my boots. I must have a rest."

Elena lowered her arms as she stepped toward the colonel's outstretched leg. For a brief moment she felt terror as the stolen clothing shifted downward. She dropped to the floor in front of him and grabbed the heel of the boot. Propping her legs against the edge of the bed she tugged and pulled until the boot came off. She did the same with the other boot.

"You can take them with you when you leave and give them to my orderly, Klaus. Now, come sit beside me and tell me about your family." He fluffed the down pillows and leaned them against the ornate headboard, then stretched out on the bed and rested his head on them and closed his eyes.

She looked to where he patted. Just because Willie hadn't raped her didn't mean the colonel would be as kind. Would he save her life only to ruin it for her? She hesitated.

He opened his eyes. "What is the matter, child? You are not afraid to chat with Günter. Perhaps if you pretend, I am your father you can talk."

"How is my father, sir?" she asked, still not moving.

"I don't know. I sent him to a hospital. It is their business to deal with the sick and wounded. Even prisoners."

"Is he alive?"

"For God's sake, girl! I don't know. Will you come sit and talk with me or do I have to do all the talking myself?" His face turned red.

She wanted to cry.

"Ah," he said as he sat up. "You're afraid of me." He laughed. "Child, have you looked at yourself in the mirror?"

"Yes, sir. I did, just now, when I came into the room. And out in the hallway there is a large …"

"And what did you see?"

"A skinny boy with badly cropped hair. He looked lost in a bundle of heavy clothing. He looked dirty."

"I miss my family. Please, sit and talk with me."

Feeling like a traitor to her own family, Elena pushed herself up from the floor to sit on the edge of the bed, ready to spring away if the colonel even looked like he might touch her. "What should I say, sir?"

"Tell me what you did at home on Sundays. Did you have a large dinner on Sunday? Before the war, I mean."

"No more so than any other day, sir. On Sunday we are supposed to do community services. Grandmother told us how in the old days they used to spend Sunday in church and then all the family would come together for a feast. Every Sunday. It's difficult to believe, isn't it?"

"Ah, yes. You are a communist, yes?"

"I don't think so, sir. At least not a very good one. I don't like sharing everything with everybody. I had private piano lessons. Mother worked in a nursery school. She's angry with me right now. She thinks I did something bad."

She kept her back toward the colonel so she didn't see when he reached up to touch her head. She jumped as if she'd been burned.

"No, don't run. I meant to comfort you. Come back and sit again."

She eyed him carefully and decided he was being honest. She returned to the bed.

"Your mother has been protecting you all of your life. Your mother was frightened for you and that's how they react sometimes. She will forgive you." He kept his hands to himself.

Elena sighed. "Colonel Hüber, I have done nothing to forgive! I'm not like Maria. Mama says she is a bad woman. She called her a whore." Her body tensed when she realized what she'd just said. She waited for a blow or at least an explosive reprimand from the colonel.

Instead she felt him shift on the bed and then he was still. She turned to look at him. He'd rolled over on his side with his back to her. "Go back to your mother, child. Stay out of my quarters."

She slid off the edge of the bed, picked up his boots and then headed toward the door, relieved to be let off so easily.

"If you have removed anything, even one small item, from this room, you will be executed."

Elena's scalp prickled like a thousand bugs crawling over her head. She let go of the door handle. The beautiful clean undergarments burned her skin through her sweater. She slowly slid her feet sideways until she reached a straight-backed chair where she loosened her coat and let the soft clothes fall to the seat. The gentle fragrance of lavender floated up. She breathed it in, storing the delicate scent for the future.

"My mother will most likely kill me first," she muttered.

Fifteen

Sunday afternoon

Elena stood in the hall trembling with fear and relief. Where to go now? She could slip into the kitchen to see if Willie had brought her piano. Then she had another thought. In a house like this, one of the rooms must contain a piano. They wouldn't have chopped it for firewood. Or would they? If she could find a piano she could live here forever! At least until the war was over and she could move on to America. She looked down the long stretch of hallway. She huddled at the furthest end of one wing with the center hall and staircase between her and another wing. Plenty of rooms. If they were all furnished like the colonel's she could be like a princess. She wouldn't even mind being the stepdaughter who had to play the piano for her survival. "Not likely, *jeune fille,*" she told herself as she eyed the door next to the colonel's room, and then stepped back so she could count the doors in this end of the house. Four rooms. Surely the colonel didn't use all of them! She skipped the one immediately next to his and went to the next one. It opened easily. No one locked doors here. And it was no wonder as she'd just learned; justice was swift. You take things, you die. She entered another dark room.

No windows. She left the door open until she found a lamp and a match. This room was not a bedroom at all, but a sparsely furnished sitting room. It smelled cold and damp. The only furniture in the room was a tattered Victorian settee and the table on which the lamp stood. A worn Oriental carpet remained on the inlaid wood floor. A few books stood on the top shelves of a built-in floor-to-ceiling bookcase. Rodent droppings along the shelves and in the corners of the room suggested the room was not in use. She couldn't imagine the colonel in his fastidious pink bedroom ever tolerating a rat or a mouse in *his* room.

She sat on the edge of the sofa. Compared to the bunk bed, the horsehair cushions felt luxurious. It would certainly be far more comfortable than a bunch of blankets on the floor in her mother's room. After tying the colonel's boots together by their laces so she could sling them over her shoulder like a pair of ice skates, she picked up the lamp and went to examine the bookshelves. Within moments she found a secret entrance slightly to the left of the center of the wall, the same position as the one in the bedroom. Several attempts at prodding and pushing the shelves finally led to a three-foot section of bookshelves opening outward into the dark passage. She took the lamp and this time, unafraid, she stepped from the room and shut the bookcase behind her.

If it weren't for her mother hating her, she could be happy on this estate until the war was over. The Germans were not as bad as her parents had led her to believe. And Papa had certainly been right about them having more food than the Russians.

She smiled at her own boldness as she explored the back halls of the house. At first, she trod carefully, putting her weight on each foot slowly in case the floorboards creaked and gave her away. But the floor was firm, her movements hushed. No one would hear her. Listening for voices on the other side of the wall she tried to figure out how far she was from the room where the officers had met.

By the light of the lamp she could see the doors were clearly marked by empty light sockets above them.

She reached the stairs at the end of the hall without hearing any voices. Perhaps all the officers were resting as the colonel was. She grasped the rail and carefully descended the steep narrow stairs to find herself in another hallway similar to upstairs but far shorter; this one lit by small windows high on the outside wall. She doused the lamp and set it on the floor. She opened the door at the end a crack. It led into the main hall in front of the reception rooms. She dashed to a door in the opposite side. It opened into another hall like the one she just left except two long narrow tables stood outside one of the doors. She figured that would be the dining room. When there were real servants in the house, they were kept out of sight. What snobs, she thought. She wondered if her grandparents' estate had had these secret passages for the servants. She hoped not.

She opened the dining room door wide enough to peek into the room. Mama and Herman were setting the table for the midday meal. Mama paused to shout at Herman in rapid fire German, using her hands for emphasis, making what Elena considered an ugly language even uglier. Herman didn't raise his head; he stared at the table like a naughty schoolboy. She wondered what her mother was saying to him. She felt badly for Herman even though she didn't like him. She knew how humiliating Mama's angry words could be. She pulled the door closed and hurried back to the kitchen.

Willie caught her by the arm as soon as she entered the room. "Where you were?" he demanded.

"I went to talk to the colonel. About this morning." She shrugged away from him. "I must work now. And the colonel wants his boots polished." She dropped the boots, picked up a ladle and began spooning out thick vegetable soup and dumplings into bowls set out on the counter.

Willie passed the empty bowls to her. "Did you see him?"

"I did."

"What did he say?"

"He told me to go away. I found a secret passage is behind all the rooms. Upstairs and downstairs."

"Your mother is angry with you because you speak with me. She says you are a traitor and your father will be ashamed. I am sorry."

Elena's cheeks burned. "This kitchen is too hot!" Soup spilled onto the countertop. She threw the ladle into the pot and then ran from the kitchen to her mother's room. Someone, probably Willie, had arranged a pallet of blankets on the floor and propped her rolled up piano against the wall as a cushion.

She flung her body onto the bedding and hugged her piano to her chest. Tears dribbled down her cheeks.

"Katya. Come. We must serve the *Soupe.*"

Willie stood by the bed. He held out his hand and smiled. Her body shuddered as she drew a deep breath. "Soup. Soup. Soup. It is the same in every language," she grumbled. She could not look at him.

In the kitchen they found Anna and Walter loading the soup bowls onto the serving trays. At the stove Herman sliced meat from a side of roast pork while Ernst set roasted potatoes around the edge of the serving platter. A bowl of steamed carrots decorated with fresh parsley and dill stood on the back of the stove.

Without being told, Elena went to the larder, pulled out the butter and sour cream, placed them on serving dishes and loaded them on a tray. She stopped at the sound of her mother's voice, the first words directed at her since the beating this morning.

"We have agreed you will continue to be Yuri to the rest of the people in the camp. Keep your cap on. Continue to be simple. Is that clear?"

Elena sniffed and nodded. Her lips trembled as she passed through the door, into the cold and once again into the house with its secret passages. She wondered why she hadn't noticed them before. But then, they were made for the servants to use. Unobtrusive, unnoticed. Both the servants and the doors. She carried the dairy products into the empty dining room and set them on the table.

Mama would announce dinner to the colonel when all was ready.

She bumped into Willie in the doorway. He carried a tray of condiments. Mama marched in right behind him with bread rolls. He paused just long enough for her to see the kindness in his eyes, then he stepped by without saying a word. Mama scowled at her as she went past.

Feeling utterly miserable, Elena returned to the kitchen to put the enamel pot of ersatz coffee on the stove. The men drank it as if it were the real thing, even adding cream to it. But the

French wines Herman and Ernst fetched every day from the cellar were real. They were strictly for the officers.

After Mama had gone to call the officers in for their dinner, she asked Willie, "Are you sure we are in Russia?"

"*Ya*. Soviet Union and Joseph Stalin. This is the place." He laughed. "I am happy to see you back to being curious. You were very *traurig*–um–sad. Why do you believe we could be not in Soviet Union?"

"This house. So much is not right here. The food. The cows for milk and butter. The wine. People starve in Leningrad."

"*Ach, so.*" He wiped down the tray and then loaded it with the warmed dinner plates. "Do you know about the statue in the harbor of the United States? It has words on it. A poem. 'Give me your tired, your poor, your huddled masses yearning to breathe free. The wretched refuse of your teeming shore. Send these, the homeless, tempest-tost to me, I lift my lamp beside the golden door!' The words were written by a Jewess. I was made to learn them in school. And always I wanted to see the United States, but now they are our enemy."

"There are gangsters in Chicago," she stated solemnly. "I will go to New York and play my music at Carnegie Hall. My mother and my father say it is the best place. When you play there, you are important."

"The statue is called the Statue of Liberty. It means people who live there can work and be whatever they want to be. They can be rich or poor. It is their choice."

She laughed. "Father says people starve on the streets in America while the capitalists keep all the money for themselves. Communism is much better for all the people."

"Katya, are you hearing yourself? Come. We fix the coffee cups on the tray. The people who lived in this house no longer exist. We were fortunate to find it for our headquarters."

"Why did you tell me about the poem on the statue? And is it important that it was written by a Jewess? Are you telling me the people in America are Jews?"

"Not all of them. And they are allowed to live and work where they please and many of them are the biggest Capitalists and run the government. Mr. Roosevelt is a Jew."

She looked at him, bewildered by the turn of the conversation. "Is he? I learned that most people in the United States are Christians."

"That, too. And they are the good ones who will be on our side when we win this war. Then when you go to America and play at the Carnegie Hall, you will be able to play with pride. You will be free but there will be no Communists and no Jews to take over your job or force you to share what you honestly earn."

Elena cleared her throat. "Mama will be back for the main course soon. We should have it ready."

She kept busy and managed to avoid looking at him during the entire dinner service. He'd said so many new things to her. Things she never thought about or considered in her life. America meant Carnegie Hall to her, nothing more. And what was important about Jews? What did it matter? What she wanted to know was how could a Communist family live in such luxury while so many starved? How could the government permit it? If her mother ever spoke to her again, she would ask her.

The colonel didn't speak to her. The rest of the officers never did, so nothing was different. She still wanted to know what happened to Olga Lubichnaya who owned all those pretty clothes in the trunk. And now, she had so many more questions. She wondered if the colonel might know even more than her mother did about America.

Sixteen

Elena slept snugly on her pallet with her piano tucked under her arm like a favorite stuffed toy. The next day, Monday, she scurried about obeying orders, hoping to get back in the good graces of her mother.

Once everything was cleaned and tidied after the midday meal, Elena put on her coat and headed back into the main house. Her mother still hadn't spoken to her except to boss her around. She hadn't even scolded her when she dropped wine on the table when she poured for a young officer. Spilled because the man spoke to her in Russian. He'd invited her to nap with him after he was finished with dinner. Her ears burned with embarrassment as she scrambled to escape from the dining room. He wasn't supposed to know she was a girl.

After folding a thin blanket to hide under her coat, part of her plan to transfer bedding one piece at a time so she could have her own private retreat, she left the kitchen and headed back to the main house. She'd not been alone in over a year, always with her parents and grandparents, first in the apartment and then in the basement.

If she used the left side door she would be in the correct wing. The stairs were at the far end. She should arrive upstairs near the colonel's room. Next came the pretty little bedroom followed by "her" room. She reached the second floor when she realized she'd forgotten a lamp. Muttering at her own her stupidity, she turned to go back down and bumped into someone coming up the steps behind her.

"Hush! It is I," Willie said in a loud whisper before she could cry out.

"You are following me?"

"I think we must speak together for a better understanding."

She backed up the last step to the landing. "It is too dark here, Willie. And the colonel has his room right behind this wall. We cannot talk here."

His hand brushed along her body as he sought to take her arm. "We will go to where you were going. You have some place in mind. I saw you take the *Decke*."

"The *Decke*. Oh, yes, a blanket! I see. Come along. We must count the doors. It will be number three."

To her surprise, Willie struck a match and lit a candle. They moved stealthily to the third door. She pressed the latch. They slipped inside and pulled the door closed behind them.

"Now we can speak freely," she said. "But still softly. People can be in the hallway and possibly hear us. Where did you get the candle?"

Willie chuckled. "I collect the small pieces when we clear the table. When I have enough, I melt them and make one big candle. So. Tell me more about your plan to go to America," he said while he led her to the sofa and placed the candle in a holder on the table.

"That light won't last long, Willie," she said as she sat beside him.

"Then we shall snuff it until we need it again."

"We have to go back to the kitchen soon. I feel so ashamed that my mother is thinking such bad things about me. I am not a bad person, Willie." Elena rested her head against Willie's shoulder. He slipped his arm around her and drew her close. She liked the feel of his warm breath on her neck. He made her feel safe. She closed her eyes and dozed in the comfort of his arms.

She awoke with a start. Something had happened. The room was still dark, but Willie held her more tightly. She could feel his heart racing through his thick jacket. She tried to sit up but he restrained her. Then she heard them. Men giggling softly like young girls. They'd come in through the secret entrance. They must have, otherwise the light from the hallway would have disturbed her. She held her breath, terrified of what would happen next.

Willie gripped her arm and gently pushed her away from him while the men continued to make noises like two children playing. She prayed the newcomers wouldn't trip over the sofa. Willie slid from the sofa and led her to the front corner of the room and pushed her down to the floor. She huddled like a pile of rags. He touched his fingers to her lips to indicate she should be quiet. She didn't need to be told.

In the dim lighting she could just make out his feet as he walked back toward the sofa, then he disappeared into the dark recess of the room.

He shouted and the other men replied with startled shouts of their own. They were obviously startled to find someone else in the room with them. An argument ensued, followed by congenial sounding laughter. Eventually, she heard the secret door close and once again the room was quiet. She waited, praying for the sound of Willie's voice. Someone chuckled in the darkness.

"I shall light the candle, Elena Katya."

"Willie!" Her voice squeaked as she cried out in relief.

"Hush! We have only a little while. They will return."

Elena followed him back to the sofa. "What was that about?"

"They came here for the same reason we did. They are friends and they want some time alone. They live and sleep in the barn outside with the cows and pigs."

"Oh," Elena said, puzzled by the explanation. "It is difficult when there are too many people. I like to be alone with my friend, Tatiana. We could sit in my bedroom and talk. Not many girls had their own bedroom in Leningrad. I was fortunate."

"But your home was destroyed. When the war is over, our people will help yours to rebuild."

"You believe Germany will win?"

Willie laughed. "If we don't all freeze to death first."

"That is not funny. I saw too many bodies of my neighbors who had starved and frozen to death."

He patted her head as if she were a small child. "I am sorry. War is not funny. We fight with guns and die from frostbite. Perhaps I choose the wrong words."

"What happened to the people who lived in this house? Did they freeze to death?"

She felt him shrug as she leaned against him on the sofa. "Shot, I think."

"Shot? You mean shot with rifles? There was a girl named Olga. She was to send her trunk to New York in the United States. You shot a girl?"

"I did not shoot anybody. I came here three months ago when the camp was established. Others told me about the family. They refused entry to our men and so they were shot. Katya, we are in a war."

Elena eased herself away from Willie. "Why did the colonel not shoot my family?"

"The others say it is because the colonel did not like the cooking of Walter and Herman. Your mother recommended herself to be a fine chef."

Elena snickered. "Mama almost never cooked at home. My grandmother did the cooking for us."

"Then your mother is a clever lady and is to be admired for the saving of your life. I am happy she has done this thing for you because now I have a friend with whom I can speak."

Elena felt the same sadness wash over her as when her grandmother told her the story about the Grand Duchesses and how the soldiers shot all the Romanovs. One of them was named Olga, too. "And now the girl, Olga, is dead. She didn't do anything to anybody. Light the candle, Willie. I want to go back to the kitchen. I don't want to be here any longer. Your friends can come to use the room for their *tête-à-tête*."

"Yes," he responded as he fumbled for a match to light the candle. "That is a good word for their meeting. *Tête-à-tête*."

Seventeen

Elena kept her head bowed as she and Willie entered the kitchen. Willie's attitude about the Germans winning the war and his idea about the Jews troubled her. She wondered if he really believed everything he said. Papa had said the Soviet Union and the United States together would defeat evil in the world. Yet people starved in Leningrad; died in the streets. None of it made sense to her. She shrugged her coat off and draped it over a peg near the door.

Mama was already braiding bread for the next day's breakfast. Ernst and Walter stood at the butcher block cutting meat into small pieces while Herman leaned against the far wall smoking.

"Go prepare the table for dinner, Elena," Anna barked.

Elena shuddered and began loading a tray with silverware. She wanted to tell Mama about Olga and her family, but she didn't trust her voice. If she tried to speak, she knew she'd burst into tears. She wanted today to be yesterday.

She struggled alone through the doors into the house and the dining room. Setting the large tray on the sideboard, she found a lace tablecloth, shook it out and spread it over the beautifully polished table. Did Olga ever help with setting the table for meals? Perhaps not. Anyone who lived in a house like this had to have servants.

In an effort to forget about the war, her mother, and the dead family, she made a game out of counting the silverware. Sixteen men for dinner. Sixteen soup spoons. Sixteen butter knives. Round and round the table she went, pretending to be a princess on a carousel horse passing out favors to the princes.

She had set out all the knives and spoons and was working on the forks when she heard the door behind her open. She turned to see Herman leaning on the doorframe. She stopped prancing. "I'm almost finished," she said in Russian.

He grinned at her. "Yuri!"

With half a dozen forks still in her hand, she rushed away to the far corner of the dining room. Herman started down the right side of the table and she quickly dashed up the left toward the exit, but Herman was faster. Before she could reach the door, he grabbed her wrist and pulled her toward him. "Yuri, *nein. Madchen, ya?*" He pointed at himself with his free hand. "Herman. *Freund. Ya?*"

Elena knew those few words. Her heart raced. "*Nein. Freund.*"

"Willie *freund?*" He twisted her arm. She dropped the forks. They clattered onto the floor.

"Now I have to go wash those!" she said angrily in Russian as she tried to pull her arm free.

Herman pulled her close and wrapped his arms about her in a bear hug. Her arms were pinned to her sides. She tried to kick him, but her legs flew wide of the mark. He picked her up. His face leered close to hers. She smelled his stale cigarette breath and the sour stench of wine.

"Put me down!"

He pressed his mouth to hers. She clamped her lips together sucking them between her teeth, turning her head from side to side. He yanked her hair so hard she opened her mouth to scream. Before she could, he planted his mouth over her lips and jammed his tongue in her mouth. She gagged and bit his tongue.

He pulled back, wiped at his mouth with the back of his hand. She crumpled to the floor. With his other hand he grabbed her hair and yanked her back to her feet.

He laughed at her screams. She didn't understand the words, but she knew by his actions the rest of the soldiers and officers weren't in the building or within earshot. Mama and the others were busy in the kitchen. She was on her own. Her arms flailed as she tried to scratch at his face, but he held her frail body at arm's distance.

She already ached from her mother's brutal treatment this morning. What was he going to do now? She didn't think she could stand another beating. She prayed Willie would walk in.

Herman pulled her close again. So close she couldn't swing at him. He began to rip at her jacket. Angered by this insult, she cursed him with every swear word she knew in Russian, French and English. Her anger only energized him. She heard the buttons hitting the carpeted floor. Then he pulled at her trousers and she knew what he was doing. He wasn't beating her up; he was going to rape her.

She screamed again and again, but that earned a slap across her face. She saw stars. She spit at him, but now he was a wild animal. She continued fighting. Her kicking legs buckled as he threw her onto the floor and grabbed a sharp knife from the side table and pointed it at her throat.

She didn't need to understand the words. His motions were clear. He would slit her throat. She nodded to him. "I won't scream," she whispered.

Tears squeezing from her tightly shut eyes, she lay stiffly on the carpeted dining room floor as he forced her legs apart. Herman's body invaded hers. She cried out in pain, but he pressed a hand over her mouth. It hurt so much. How long could this take?

Carnegie Hall. Elena Katya at the piano. An orchestra with everyone dressed in black tie. Just for her. She played the Mozart. That always impressed her audiences. Her quick, nimble fingers dashed up and down the keyboard. But that vile, stinking body odor permeated the concert hall. Someone should clean the air. She couldn't work like this. Her chest heaved with sobs. All had gone quiet. She opened her eyes.

Herman stood with his back to her as he adjusted his clothing. To her left she saw the maze of table and chair legs; to the right she saw forks. Straight ahead he stood, still fixing his clothes. Without thought, she grabbed a fork, sat up, and tried to stand. Tripped by the clothing tangled about her ankles, she stumbled and fell back.

Then she saw her lower body exposed for anyone to see. She dropped the fork and began to pull up her clothing. Herman turned to look down on her.

He smiled. A sick, taunting smile. "Good morning, miss. How are you today?" He spoke in English. "You should know your enemy, Yuri, and be careful in front of whom you speak." Then he saluted before wheeling about and leaving the room. He whistled his way down the hall.

She sat with her arms wrapped around her legs, her head resting on her knees, eyes closed. This ugly thing couldn't have happened to her. She wanted to run to her mother, but when she opened her eyes, she saw the bruises on her legs, not from Herman but from her mother. She struggled into her clothes while still on the floor. Her heartbeat sobbed, "No good. No good. No good. No good."

Eighteen

Elena looked about the room. The elegantly set table shimmered through her tears as if viewed in a faulty mirror. The large double doors across the room that led into the main hall were closed. She didn't want to see anyone now. Not ever again. She grabbed the back of a chair and rested her head on her arm as she gasped for air through her sobs.

The room. A vision of the dark room upstairs swam into her thoughts as her mind instinctively sought sanctuary. Stumbling to the back wall she searched the wood panels for indications of the real servant's door she knew should be there; she'd seen it from the other side. Frantically running her hands over the panels, her scrappy fingernails caught on the release. She pressed it and slipped through the opening into the dark passageway. Her body hurt, and so, like a wounded animal, she sought refuge. A quiet place where she could die. That was the only peace she wanted.

In the fading light of the late afternoon, she found her way to the stairs and slowly climbed to the second floor. She stepped up into the darkness.

She wanted the dark room so strongly she could feel it beckon to her as she staggered painfully, using the walls for support and as a guide to the room.

The colonel's room. The first one. She continued moving, but a wrenching pain caused her to cry out as she fell to the floor. Moaning softly, she pushed herself up and as she did, she felt a rush of warm liquid run down her thighs. "Mama. Mama. Please help me," she cried.

"Hush!" a woman's voice whispered.

She felt someone's hands on her shoulders and tried to brush them away, but as she turned and saw the light from the small bedroom, she collapsed into Maria's arms.

"Make me die, please make me die."

"Oh my God! You're the boy…" Maria began.

"I'm the girl. The girl. Not the boy," Elena cried. "Not the boy. Mama and Papa told me. They warned me!" She twisted from Maria's grasp and started back to the passage. "I want to go die."

Maria pulled her by her collar into the room and shut the door. Elena tried to resist but had no energy left.

"Sit down here on this chair. Tell me what happened. Who are you? Aren't you the boy who came with the cook?" While she spoke, Maria locked the doors to her room and began unbuttoning Elena's sweater. "If you are the same child, then I'm the one who shot your father. I didn't mean to kill him, but he frightened my mother-in-law when he pulled his gun on us. How did we know he wouldn't hurt us?"

"My Papa couldn't hurt a worm. What are you going to do?" Elena watched as Maria poured water from a kettle on the tile stove into a washbasin.

"I'm going to clean you up and make sure you're all right."

Elena drew her knees up and wrapped her arms protectively around them. "I don't want your help. I told you what I want. Let me go."

"Where were you headed when I heard you in the passageway?"

"There's an empty room. I want to be in there. I want to stay in there until everyone goes away." She dropped her head onto her knees; her body shuddered with sobs.

"You can't do that. Now tell me what happened to you. Who did this thing?"

Elena covered her head with her hands. "Don't talk to me." She closed her eyes.

"Take deep breaths," Maria ordered, and then asked in a softer voice, "What shall I call you? Your name surely isn't Yuri."

Elena peeked out. Maria sat on the edge of the bed. She was dressed in a lovely green gown, ready for the dinner Elena was supposed to be serving. "I have to go." She dropped her feet to the floor and started to stand, but another sharp pain forced her to gasp aloud and once again, Maria rushed to her aid.

"You'll stay right here. I'll inform the colonel you're not well and then I'll get your mother—"

"No! You mustn't tell my mother about this! She already thinks I'm bad for being friends with Private Becker." Elena slumped back onto the chair. Her chest heaved as she tried to catch her breath and every pore of her body oozed moisture. She rubbed her eyes with the heels of her hands. "My name is Elena but they thought it would be better for me to be a boy." Her voice trembled.

Maria continued to speak to her in soothing tones and Elena remembered how her mother had spoken in that same manner when confronted with hysterical neighbors during the worst of the shelling. Mama always reminded the people they were still alive; it was only a house or a possession that was lost. As long as there is life, there is hope, she said. But Mama hadn't been . . . been hurt by an ugly man.

She closed her eyes again and focused on the tears running down to her chin and then dropping away into oblivion, where she wanted to be. Maria moved about in the room and Elena was relieved she hadn't gone to tell Mama. After a few minutes Maria came back to her and gently picked her head up. Elena looked into her green eyes and wondered how she could have felt so mean about her before.

"We must wash you and there is something else I must do. You have to trust me, Elena. I don't want to hurt you but it must be done."

Puzzled, Elena followed Maria across the room to a beautiful screen that separated the corner of the room. Behind it stood a washing table with towels and the bowl of water. "Sit on the stool here and I'll help you."

Still suspicious of what Maria might have in mind, Elena took a face cloth from her and began to wipe her face, head, and neck with the perfumed water. She waited for Maria to step out of sight before she removed her sweater and shirt. The sight of her body, reflected in the mirror, startled her almost as much as it had when she saw herself clothed the other day in the hallway. She found it difficult to recognize herself. Her ribs stood out much like a skeleton's might; her small breasts had rounded a little. She winced at the odor coming from her armpits and scrubbed feverishly to rid herself of the stench. When she finished with her upper body, she replaced the old clothes and then stood to remove the trousers. She froze. "I can't! Maria, I can't do it! I have to leave now. I have to . . ."

"Elena! You must and you must hurry. I have to go down to dinner shortly. The colonel expects me and won't start without me."

Elena knew only too well. How she had hated the beautiful Maria, a Russian woman, sitting at the German officers' table.

"Listen to me, you can't change what's been done. You have to go on with your life. My husband and my brother were hanged by the Germans after they were forced to watch the soldiers rape me and my sisters-in-law. Don't think you're the only one who suffers." Maria yanked open a bureau drawer and pulled out a piece of white linen. "Wash yourself, then put these on. You can't wear those awful bloody clothes. I'll wash your trousers and put them on the stove to dry. Now, come on, take off your pants so I can treat you."

Elena caught the silken underpants that Maria threw to her and then, overwhelmed by the woman's story, hurried to remove the rest of her clothing in order to clean herself. Her inner thighs already showed signs of bruising, and the lightest touch of the cloth to her private parts hurt horribly. She sloshed the water, wiped away all signs of blood and then dried herself while Maria did as she said and cleaned her trousers for her. The old underpants she threw into the stove.

Then Maria did something totally unexpected. She picked up the clean water pitcher, the one used for drinking water and poured the contents into a rubber hot water bottle with a long tube attached.

"Hold this." She handed it to Maria while she rummaged around in a drawer in the vanity. She pulled out a packet of powder, tore it open and poured the contents into the bag. "Now lie down on the floor and put your legs apart."

"No!" Elena pulled away from Maria. "What are you going to do with that?"

"It will clean that slime the bastard put into you!"

"No! You can't. You'll hurt me again." Elena covered herself with her hands.

"It might hurt," Maria conceded, "But it will hurt far less than having a baby nine months from now."

"A baby? That's what makes babies?" Elena thought she might faint. How could that be? Is that what her own parents did to get her? She and Tatiana always talked about love and making babies as if they were the same. They'd never considered the actual mechanics of the thing.

"Yes, you stupid girl. Hasn't your mother told you about men and women? Haven't you seen the animals mate?"

"What animals? I play the piano. I don't watch animals. You still haven't told me what that's for," Elena said, pointing to the rubber container.

"It's a powder my mother makes up from herbs to prevent pregnancy."

"You mean . . ."

"On the floor. Lie on the towel. This won't take long."

Elena found herself on the floor once again, her body invaded. Maria knelt beside her with a large sheet for an apron to protect her gown and spoke gently as she worked. Elena didn't hear the words. Her mind went back to the first time she successfully played *Für Elise*. It was written simply so a child could learn it.

"You have a lovely voice."

"What?" Elena hadn't realized she hummed the notes as she saw the music.

"A lovely voice. When I'm finished you can use my commode. Dry yourself, put on one of these and get dressed. You should be all right."

Elena rolled over and curled into a ball on the floor. "I don't feel all right. How can you talk about being raped and live with these people?"

"The colonel isn't the one who hurt me; he wasn't even there. It was others. They, hopefully, have been killed at the front lines by now. It happened several months ago. A lifetime. I'll leave you now. What do you want me to tell your mother?"

"Can you pretend you haven't seen me? Maybe they'll think I ran away."

"Your mother should know what happened to you."

"Don't tell her. Ever!" Elena felt anger burn in her chest; an anger that took away the pain in her body. She rolled over and sat up. Without looking directly at Maria she said, "I don't know how you can do what you do with the colonel; from now on I will make it my business to kill as many Germans as I can whenever and however I can."

"That's the way to speak. And if I can help you, I will. By keeping company with Colonel Hüber, I also learn of troop activities. Do you think I only do it for the food for my family?" Maria spoke as she repaired her hair. She finished pinning it back in place, brushed her skirt and checked herself one more time in the mirror. "When your trousers are dry, go back to your quarters. I'll keep your secret, but I still believe your mother should know."

Elena remained on the floor for several minutes after Maria left for dinner. The odor of the damp wool drying on the stove reminded her of the basement where she'd lived the last year. Babushka washed their clothes whenever there was enough water and laid them out on the stove to dry. In the winter the room became all warm and steamy and even felt cozy and snug. If only they'd had enough food none of this would have happened. One day her parents told her to stay away from soldiers, any soldiers because of what they would do to young girls; the next day it was how well the Germans treated their prisoners, fed them, kept them sheltered. But they still raped young girls. Now she knew her parents were right about everything. For days now she'd eaten more food than she had in the last six months and she had a warm place to sleep. And she'd been raped.

She pushed herself up, feeling weary. A hundred years old. Staggering to her feet, she put on the underpants and then lined them with wads of cotton from Maria's dressing table. After turning the trousers to dry on the other side, she lay on top of Maria's bed, closed her eyes, and played Chopin's Moonlight Sonata.

"Elena! Wake up! Get dressed. Revenge shall be yours. You can't believe the excitement."

Elena rolled over on the bed to see Maria dancing about the room as she pulled clothes from her closet and bureau drawers. She'd fallen into a deep, dreamless slumber. When she moved to sit up, she remembered what had happened. She fell back. "Go away."

"Stop that. Two hours ago you were ready to fight the Germans singlehandedly for what they did to you."

"What are you talking about?"

"Your boy, Private Becker, has called out Private Werner. There is going to be a fight tonight at eleven."

"I don't understand," Elena said, "What am I supposed to do?"

Maria whisked off the green dress and slipped on a pair of fatigues and a man's T shirt. "You are supposed to support Becker."

Elena sat up. "Support Willie?"

"Tonight, you'll be avenged. Becker knows about Werner. He'll kill him. Put your clothes on. We're going to a boxing match."

Nineteen

Monday night

"What do you mean, a boxing match? Who is Werner?"

"Herman Werner. The man who—"

"He knows? Everyone knows? What about my mother? What did she say?" Elena ran to Maria's side and grabbed her arm.

"Your mother knows nothing. You asked me not to tell and the men certainly didn't want to say anything to her. Now come on. Dress!"

"Please, tell me the truth. Didn't Mama wonder where I was? Didn't she ask about me?"

"I told her I required your assistance and you would no longer be available for kitchen work. You will be my personal maid and laundress." Maria pulled away from Elena to go sit on the vanity stool while she pulled on her combat boots.

"You…you helped me, but…but you're as bad as everybody else! Your maid and laundress? I won't. I won't do it. I'll go back to the kitchen—"

"And be treated like a dog? Don't be silly. I don't need you or anyone else as a maid. I made that up. It's easier for them to believe badly of me than to think I might be trying to do something good for Mother Russia. And you can help me."

Elena pulled on her own boots. "You're too confusing for me, Maria Petrovna. At your cottage you were mean and stingy with your food. You shot my father and turned us out into the cold. Now, you want to help me."

"This is a war, don't you understand? At my mother-in-law's cottage, your family, all of you, were a threat to us. Many others have been there begging food and the old woman gave it to them as if she had enough to feed the world when we, too, were starving. Someone had to take charge. I'm not sorry I defended our family. I'm sorry your father was hurt. Now you and I are both here. Do you think I had a choice any more than you?" She paused and stared at Elena. Her face appeared softer than Elena had seen before. She spoke again, a little quieter now. "We can work together. You have befriended Wilhelm as I have befriended the colonel. When I hear any snippets of news I report back to my late husband's colleague, who filters the information for its usefulness before passing it on to higher authorities."

"Wouldn't it be better if I stayed to work in the kitchen where I could be near Willie and learn more?"

"But I can get out and about. With me, you shall meet more people, more soldiers and hear more than you'll ever hear in the kitchen. You don't understand enough German to learn anything useful at the dinner table; I can and I do."

"How am I going to learn more walking around outside this house?"

"Have you not been outdoors?"

"Only to the kitchen and the latrines behind it."

"You have a lot to see then. Come, put on your sweater and coat. We're going out."

They stepped out the front door into the darkness together. Maria turned on a hooded flashlight to show the way through the snowy path. Elena couldn't see, but she sensed the houses around them as they walked. Once her eyes adjusted, she detected slender lines of light behind blackout curtains in small houses along the way. When they'd walked for about ten minutes, she heard voices that grew louder as they approached a large building. Maria switched off her flashlight in front of a small door. She slid it open. Elena found herself standing in a vestibule created from heavy canvas. After closing the outside door, Maria pulled the canvas back to reveal a barn full of German soldiers and Russian peasants surrounding an improvised boxing ring.

"Stay close to me. And remember, you're still a boy called Yuri."

Elena had no intention of arguing, in fact, she had no intention of ever trying to look like a girl again. Tense with the excitement of being in a crowd whose focus had nothing to do with finding food or fighting the war, she forgot her pain. She held on to the back of Maria's jacket as she pushed her way through the crowd to the opposite side of the old barn. Elena was surprised to see horses still in the stalls, pigs in pens, and hear cows mooing as if annoyed at the intrusion into their living space.

Maria settled on a front row rough-hewn bench, pulling Elena down beside her. "They've had the regular bouts already. Generally, it starts with the peasants against the soldiers, followed by the various military units competing, but Becker and Werner are an added feature tonight. It hasn't been announced officially the reason for their fight, but there is an undercurrent that Werner seriously insulted Becker."

Elena sat quietly, overwhelmed to be in a noisy crowd after so much time sitting alone with her family in the basement apartment. Even their trek into the wilderness of the countryside was isolated and lonely. For the past ten days she'd become somewhat adjusted to living as a boy, happy to have plenty of food and water without having to scavenge in the streets. Today so much changed.

Someone jostled her as he sat beside her. "Move over, boy!"

"Sorry, sir," she murmured as she shifted closer to Maria to make space for an old man. By his attire, she guessed him to be one of the habitants of the hamlet. At least he wasn't a German soldier.

Then everyone cheered as a middle-aged man leapt to the center of the ring and held up his hands for silence. He spoke first in German then in Russian. "Finish your bets quickly, my friends. This next match is a grudge match between Private Herman Werner and Private Wilhelm Becker, whom we all know is our number one boxing champion. But if you think this is going to be an easy bout, Werner tells us he was first in his hand-to-hand combat training class. This will be a fight to the finish, until one of them can't get up. Sergeant Braun will referee."

Several men booed at the mention of Braun's name. "Braun is a bastard; he'll let them kill each other. Nobody likes him," the old man whispered close to her ear. "He never heard of fair play."

Braun stepped into the makeshift ring and spoke to the announcer then signaled for the fighters to come forward. There was a shuffle of bodies in the dark recesses of the building as the contenders emerged into the light of the single bulb above the ring. They climbed in and, without acknowledging one another, went to separate corners.

Never having seen a boxing match, Elena wasn't sure what to expect next. She'd seen boys fighting in the streets, but their mothers usually broke up those skirmishes before there was much blood. She watched fascinated as Braun spoke privately to each of the men. Willie looked so small and skinny standing in the far corner dressed in his regulations trousers and a khaki colored undershirt.

She kept her eyes averted from Herman but couldn't help seeing he was dressed the same. He appeared twice as large as Willie. She grabbed Maria's hand. "I can't watch this, Maria Petrovna. Can't we go back?"

"Never." Maria said the word with such fury that Elena clamped her mouth shut, turned her eyes straight ahead and tried to focus on what was about to happen. If there were a god as her grandmother promised, then Willie would beat Herman to a pulp and hurt him so badly he could never touch a girl again. However, as she thought she believed, not a god, then it looked like the larger man would undoubtedly kill the smaller.

Maybe it was better she was under Maria Petrovna's protection. Mama surely wouldn't take care of her in the kitchen. She folded her arms across her chest and waited for the bell to ring.

Twenty

Both men hopped out on the balls of their feet and skipped tentatively in circles, each jabbing at, but not hitting, his opponent. Then Herman lunged and Willie jumped out of reach. Willie lunged; Herman ducked. They did their circle dance again. Willie kept his gloved hands in front of his face when he wasn't jabbing. Herman kept his moving, one hand up when he danced right, the other one when he danced left. Elena sat entranced while the crowd began to murmur.

After a few more minutes of the dance, the crowd booed and shouted. The bell rang and each man stepped back into his original corners. Elena was getting the idea of the rules but didn't understand why no one hit anyone.

"They were feeling each other out, kid," the old man explained when she asked Maria. "You haven't come here before?"

She shook her head. "What happens now?"

"Next round they'll begin bashing each other. You wait and see."

The bell rang again. The old man had been right. Immediately, Herman nearly ran across the ring before Willie could even think about it, and clipped him on the jaw, sending him staggering into the rope. Willie shook his head; the referee signaled him to carry on. Willie managed to step sideways so he stood in the center of the ring. He waited for Herman to attack again but when he did, Willie was ready with a strong right cross to the jaw. It was Herman's turn to stagger. Only he didn't wait for a referee to tell him to continue, he lunged back at Willie and grabbed him in a bear hug.

Elena held her breath, remembering how terrifying that had felt. Then with one arm around Willie, he began pummeling him in the back. The crowd booed, but Braun did nothing to stop him. She missed what Willie did next, but suddenly he was free of the hold, gasping for air and Herman was clasping his stomach. Herman was still staggering back when Willie rushed forward and struck him with a left and a right low in the chest. Herman tried to cover up to fend off the blows and made the mistake of dropping his head. Willie brought his right fist up in an uppercut, catching him on the jaw and snapping his head back. Herman grappled with him, spinning around to the side, and wrapping his left arm tightly around Willie's neck while he tried to beat his face with his right. Held tight in the headlock, Willie brought his elbow back sharply and at the same time stamped on his foot. Herman let go, but as he stepped away, he swung wildly at Willie's head. He caught him high on the left cheekbone. Elena was sure she heard a bone crack.

The bell rang.

Willie's friends tended to him while others helped Herman. She couldn't imagine how anyone could be a friend of Herman's. She winced as the old man nudged her in the ribs, "Told you, didn't I? One of 'em's going to get killed tonight. My money's on the little guy."

"Willie?" she squeaked. "Why? He's a good boxer. He told me."

Rounds three and four went much the same way. Elena found herself so caught up in the fight, she forgot where she was. All she saw was her friend Willie being beat up. Herman reminded her of Boris and Mikhail. Bullies.

Round five started. The men didn't dance so lightly on their feet now. Willie bent over, hands high and stalked Herman. Herman laughed aloud and taunted Willie. The audience joined him in laughter. Elena felt embarrassed for Willie. Then they were at it again. Trading punches, but with a new urgency. As if they were both tired of entertaining the crowd and were now ready to get down to business. Herman caught Willie on the nose. Blood flowed freely. Willie responded with a rapid tattoo of blows to Herman's middle until Herman backed off. In a rage, Herman rushed Willie, caught him on the shoulder and knocked him down. While Willie was on the ground, Herman took the opportunity to kick him in the ribs. Braun took no notice. The crowd cheered.

During the break before the sixth round Elena asked Maria, "Can't we make them stop? Willie's hurt!"

"Don't be stupid. If you were to try that, your Private Becker could never hold his head up amongst his friends again."

"It's better than being dead!"

"For him it isn't. Say something to him. Just remember you're still Yuri to everyone else." Maria gave her a shove. "Go on. You've got enough time to run over and say a word of support."

"I can't."

Maria yanked her arm and forced her upright. "Go!"

Elena looked down at Maria, who glared at her fiercely. She turned back to see Willie's friends swarming around him and moved quickly, edging herself around the ring to his corner. When she arrived, no one paid any attention to her. She cleared her throat.

"Willie!" she shouted.

He looked at her. His face was swollen around his left eye. Bloody cotton balls clogged his nostrils. Sweat soaked his shirt. "What are you doing here?" he asked in surprise. The men stopped working on him.

"Maria Petrovna brought me."

"Are you all right?" He leaned toward her, his gloved hands reached out.

With his friends blocking the view, she was able to kiss her fingertips and touch his gloves. "I will be now. Thank you."

His face reddened and she turned away.

The sixth and seventh rounds exhausted her and by the ninth she was sure the men in the crowd would kill each other long before the two boxers did each other in. Both men were now bloodied and in obvious pain. Herman kept going at Willie's lower back, Willie to Herman's stomach and head.

Then Herman gave a war cry and lunged. Willie screamed. Elena couldn't see what happened but Braun actually stopped the round and called for the assistants to come help Willie. Willie covered his face with his gloves, yelling in pain as he was led to his corner. There was a lot of discussion while Herman pranced around the ring, declaring himself the victor. Braun sent him to his corner with a warning. The crowd leaned as one toward Willie's corner wondering what had happened.

After several minutes, Braun declared the fight would go on. The bell rang. The crowd roared.

When the bell rang and the group surrounding Willie stepped aside, Elena gasped to see his head swathed in bandages, his left eye completely covered. Herman puffed up his chest, grinned and sauntered to the center of the ring. Elena wanted to cover her face but she stared fascinated by the horror going on before her. She heard Willie's voice and didn't need to understand the words to know he was daring Herman to come close. Herman made chicken noises as the crowd laughed. Enjoying the moment, Herman tucked his gloves under his armpits and cackled at Willie while dancing around him. Willie could barely lift his arms. He continued to talk to Herman. Finally, he said something that caught the man's attention because Herman stopped frolicking about and glared at him. Before he could raise his defense, Willie lurched forward and caught him with a one two uppercut. First the right then the left. Herman staggered into the ropes while Willie followed continuing to punch, finding strength in his frenzy. Left. Right. Left. Again and again into his belly.

The crowd noise was deafening.

"Kill him! Kill him!"

Elena looked around and realized it was her screaming. She stood, hands flailing the air as if she were the one striking Herman.

Twenty-one

Someone carried her. Maria's voice chattered breathlessly nearby as if she ran beside them. "I'm sorry. I thought you would want to see Herman get beaten. I wanted to help you. I know how you feel. I tried to talk to your mother but she won't listen to me. You'll be safe with me. I'll make sure of that. I'm sorry I took you to the fight."

Part of Elena wanted to thank Maria; another part wanted to scream at her to go away, leave her alone. Most of her wanted to sleep. Forever.

"Hier, danke."

The arms released her onto a soft mattress. A door closed. Elena tried to bury herself in the covers but Maria insisted on removing her boots and coat first. Once she was done, Elena covered her face with her hands and let the tears slip through her fingers. Maria pulled a quilt over her body. She heard her leave the room.

In her mind Elena saw the door open and the two badly dressed soldiers enter the room. Boris and Misha! She remembered the terror of being in their control. She could do nothing but sit on the straw mattress and hope Papa didn't sneeze. She couldn't cry then. The gunshot from the cottage on their first night outside the city pierced her heart as surely as if the bullet had hit her. Her relief when Papa came staggering out was short lived; they had to get away. No time to cry. Never time to cry. Except now.

Her mind raced over the events of the past few weeks, finding the finger, killing the chicken, talking to Willie, and watching the fight. It looked to Elena like Willie killed Herman. What would happen to him? What would Boris and Misha have done if they had found Papa under the straw? Would they have killed him? Oh, Papa, where are you? You must come back and take me to a place where I can play the piano again and make Mama love me again. Come back, Papa.

She rocked herself to sleep snuggled deeply in the comfort of the feather mattress, the warmth of a layer of quilts over her body.

"Get up, you lazy girl! You're supposed to be helping me, not the other way round!"

Elena opened her eyes. Maria peered at her over a tray, a smile on her face in contradiction to the tone of her voice. It took Elena a moment to realize Maria joked with her. The door to the next bedroom stood open letting the morning light stream across the bed. Maria was dressed in the military fatigues like the first time she'd seen her. Beautiful and fierce at the same time. The sight of her took Elena's breath away.

"Breakfast has been finished for an hour and you sleep on. Come, eat. This is the last time I'm bringing your food to you. You collect your own after this."

Elena rubbed her eyes and started to sit up, but pain stopped her. She gasped. She must have hurt herself somehow last night when she and Maria went out. "What do you mean, 'the last time?' When did you bring me food before?"

"Never, and I don't intend to continue. If you're going to get well, you have to take care of yourself."

"I'm not sick, so there's no need to get well. What did you bring?" She wasn't curious, but it would be interesting to know what Mama fixed for her.

"Fresh rolls, butter, coffee and a boiled egg. It's probably cold." She set the tray on the vanity. "Come on, hurry up. Your job will be to keep the stoves going in these two rooms."

"An egg!" she gasped. "I haven't seen an egg for so long."

Elena pushed herself off the bed and bent to retrieve her boots. She groaned as she tried to lift her foot to pull one on. "What happened? My whole body is killing me. My eyes feel swollen as if I've been crying all night."

"The pain will go away in a few days. I'm going home today, but I'll be back soon. You stay up here, except to collect your meals when the others have finished eating and to empty the chamber pot. You'll be safe here."

"What are you talking about? Going home?"

"Yes. Well, the cottage isn't really my home, but I'll never be able to go back to Leningrad even when the war is over. For now, my husband's mother and his sisters depend on me for food." Maria tapped at the soft-boiled egg with a silver spoon, preparing it for Elena as she spoke. "Once a week, if conditions allow, the colonel lets me take a small supply of food to them. I spend the night; tell them how well the war is going and how terrible the Germans are, then I come back." She lowered her eyes. "They don't really understand. In many ways I have made the war too easy for them."

"You come back to the German colonel. I don't understand either." Elena shook her head.

"The night you and your family came to our house, I had arrived the same day with fresh food." Maria paused and studied Elena's face for a moment as if gauging how much to tell her. Something in her eyes told Elena she was satisfied with what she saw. "When you arrived, I was on the radio to Leningrad."

"A radio?"

Maria nodded and sat next to her on the vanity bench. She looked at her in the mirror. "You heard me, a radio. The others were afraid you would steal their food. Of course, you saw Mother was willing to share, but not the others. I again must apologize to you for shooting your father, but it was a situation in which we might have killed each other. It is better how it turned out."

Elena felt a fresh flow of tears. "Maybe for you; you didn't get shot like Papa or..."

Maria sighed. "I do and say so many stupid things. When you are older and the war is finished, you will perhaps understand."

"I don't need to be older to understand." Elena dug her spoon into the egg and for the first time in two years, savored the flavor and texture of a soft-boiled egg. She closed her eyes and waited a moment before taking another spoonful. "I must thank my mother for this food."

"You must thank me for this food," Maria grumbled. "Your mother is still angry with you."

Elena's eyes met Maria's in the mirror. Elena decided she wouldn't want to make Maria angry; her father had and she'd shot him. "Thank you. But I must go to my mother."

Maria put her hand over Elena's. "Wait for a while. Give her time to realize what has happened. She'll soften. She must; she's a mother. For now, be kind to yourself while you have the chance. Things will get worse before they get better. Somebody has to win this war and it's not going to be you or me. I do my part to survive, I know, but who should I want to win this? The Russians? And then we're still stuck with Stalin. Or the Germans and have Hitler marching us all over the place?"

Maria stood and began donning her overcoat.

"You sound like an old woman, Maria Petrovna. My grandmother talks just like that. She wants the 'good old days' to come back." Elena broke off a piece of the roll and used it to scrape up the remnants of the egg.

"Older than you anyway. I'm twenty-three. And you?"

"Fourteen."

Maria looked at her in the mirror. Their eyes met briefly. "Poor child."

"Is it all right if Willie comes to visit me while you're away? He can help me carry the wood."

"I don't think Willie will be carrying anything for a long time."

"Why not?"

"Didn't you see what happened to him last night?"

Elena puzzled for a moment. Last night? Last night she and Maria went out…to a fight. "But Willie won the fight, didn't he? He told me he was the champion of his unit. I've never seen a boxing match before."

"Finish your breakfast. Willie was hurt so the colonel is sending him home."

Sending Willie home? Elena didn't believe what she heard. Willie was her only friend in the world. "How can he do that? Just because he was hurt in a fight?"

Maria hesitated before speaking. "I really have to go now. Please make sure to stay out of sight as much as possible while I'm away. I told your mother you're working up here. She knows to prepare a plate for you after each meal and leave it in the dining room. You pick it up there. Yes?"

Elena nodded. "Can I find a book to read, at least?"

"If you can find one. The troops have burned everything possible. Perhaps you can write a letter to your Willie. If you can find paper, there is ink in that drawer."

"It still doesn't make any sense to send him home. All the way back to Germany?" And it wasn't fair.

"If that's where he's from."

"He worked for an insurance company. He liked his work. Maybe he can go back to that."

"Perhaps. Goodbye. And remember to be Yuri!"

Elena looked at her own glowering face in the mirror. "That won't be a problem."

Maria left and Elena returned to her image. Her red eyes, splotchy skin and short, chopped hair the color of straw seemed to belong to a stranger. Compared to the healthy, glowing Maria, she looked like a pathetic bag of bones. As she studied the gaunt features, hollowed cheeks, scrawny neck, a shadow passed across the mirror. She let out a short scream and whirled around on the stool.

No one was there. She clutched her hands to her chest and called out weakly, "Who's there?"

The curtains at the open window in the next room billowed with a gentle breeze. Silence. And in the silence, she remembered everything that had happened yesterday from her mother's brutal treatment to Willie's kindness and then Herman. Herman in the dining room. Her teeth began to chatter and still she sat with her hands gripping her sweater. "Is someone there?" she whimpered.

"I want my piano. Where has my piano gone?" She slid from the bench to the floor, her entire body shivered as she curled into a ball on the Persian carpet. "I want my piano. I want my piano."

Hours passed as she lay there, sometimes sleeping, sometimes counting the flowers in the carpet. She yawned and rolled over. From her vantage point she could look under the bed, through the open doorway into the colonel's room, the one that used to be Olga's. Someone had shut the windows and drawn the curtains. The heavy draperies remained open so a soft evening light filtered in. She pushed herself up.

Food. Maria told her to get her food. Maria, the woman who had shot Papa and now cared for her like a kind aunt. The little ticking clock on the bedside table said it was three thirty. She'd missed dinner. Or perhaps not. She waited for the dizziness from standing too quickly to pass, and then picked up her breakfast tray and stepped out into the hallway. No one was about.

That was fine with her. The trip down the stairs and around to the dining room entrance went unnoticed. No one saw the pains in her legs or felt the lump on the back of her head. When did she hurt her head? When she fell on the carpet? No witness shared her rapidly beating heart.

She stepped onto the broad expanse of the hardwood floor and turned to her right. Opposite her, the large double doors into the dormitory stood open. No need to keep them closed during the day; soldiers didn't need the stoves operating while they were out. A few more steps and she faced the dining room doors. Those remained closed so the heat would stay in for the officers. Mustn't let the gentlemen of the Third Reich get chilled while they ate their *Soupe*. Soup, soup, soup. It is the same in every language. When did she say that? Only yesterday she said it to Willie.

Two feet from the doors she stopped. They looked the same yet somehow larger. The brass handles curved upward in a split grin, daring her to enter the room. Above the handles the white wooden panels became eyes that mocked her.

"Come into my parlor, little girl. Come and see what we have inside for you."

She stood mute before the doors, the tray still in her hands.

"We have a large ugly soldier, that's what we have."

Those last words screamed in her head and she dropped her tray as she staggered back away from the door. She whirled around and slid on the floor as she grabbed the newel post and struggled up the stairs, back to the security of Maria's room. As her legs scrambled to keep up with her mind, she remembered every instant of what happened before dinner last night. Like a motion picture running too fast.

She didn't cry this time. As she gasped for air and fought to regain control, she felt feverish. That room. She couldn't go into that room ever again, she told herself. Yes, you can. Herman's dead. Didn't you hear them talking last night? Didn't you see the fight with your own eyes? Private Wilhelm Becker killed him in a boxing ring. And now Private Wilhelm Becker, my Willie, is going home to be an insurance clerk.

She slid off the bed and paced between the two rooms. From the window around the bed, to the vanity in the small room, back around the bed across the room. She didn't know how long she paced as her thoughts tried to unscramble themselves.

Then the body in the mirror caught her eye. She braced herself and leaned over to study the face. It looked like the same splotchy, undernourished girl who'd been there this morning, but Elena didn't recognize the eyes. She studied them more closely. They were blue with dark circles surrounding the pupils, the same as hers used to be, but these eyes looked older – sadder.

She eased herself onto the stool and continued to confront herself.

"I see you in there, Elena."

She pressed her right hand to the glass, like a prisoner in a gangster movie saying goodbye to a visitor.

"We will always share the same name, but I must say goodbye to you, little girl."

She turned away, stood, and went back down the stairs to the dining room to collect her lunch. The breakfast tray she'd dropped was gone.

Confronting the doors, she squared her shoulders and stepped into the dining room. Her lunch tray waited for her on the massive sideboard.

The *Soupe* was cold.

Twenty-two

By the time dinner was over and Elena should have gone down to retrieve her own meal, Maria still hadn't returned. The stoves warmed the rooms; Elena had done her job, but with nothing else to do and no one to talk to, she was at a loss.

In her travels to and from the wood pile this afternoon, she hoped she'd see Willie at least one last time, but she didn't see anyone she knew, not even her mother.

She wandered listlessly down the stairs to the dining room to collect her supper. Even through her resolve not to be frightened of this room, her body trembled as she picked up her tray. When she pushed the door open with her shoulder, she heard footsteps in the hallway. Frozen with fear, she waited for them to pass by. The footsteps slowed as they neared her. She dared not breathe.

The pressure of the heavy door moved from her shoulder. She stepped back and turned. An officer held the door with one hand, and with the other signaled her to come through. She kept a wary eye on him as she passed by and headed for the stairs, but he ignored her and went on into the dining room. From the top of the staircase she saw he had retrieved his cap. He went out the front doors without looking up.

"This can't be my life forever. I'll go mad."

She wished Willie would come, but he never would. Maybe she ought to go to see her mother. She couldn't still be angry at her. She couldn't think those bad things of her. Not really. Mama had had nearly two days to think about it; by now she was probably sorry for the way she treated her daughter, Elena reasoned. *If I go see her, she'll hold her arms out and we'll laugh together.*

With that comforting thought, Elena wolfed down the chicken and dumplings, more dumplings than chicken, and carried the tray down the stairs and out the back door to the kitchen, looking forward to the warmth, already thinking of it as her home.

She pulled open the door and stepped inside. Mama stood with her back to her, stirring something on the stove. Ernst and Walter were at the sink, finishing the dinner clean up. A stranger swabbed the floor with a rag mop. No one took any notice when she first entered.

"Mama, can I talk with you?" she asked in a timid voice as she approached her from behind.

Ernst and Walter snickered, making her face burn with shame. Lowering her eyes, she turned her back on them as she moved to her mother's side so she could see her profile.

Anna's lips were compressed, disappearing in a stern grimace. She appeared to be angry at the stew she stirred. Elena focused on the gray woolen sweater that hung so loosely on her mother. She willed her to turn her face and look at her. Anna continued to ignore her.

With her eyes downcast, she turned and placed her empty bowl next to the other dirty dishes. Walter bumped her as he reached for more dishes to wash. She staggered and caught her balance but didn't look up at him. Instead she turned back to her mother, hoping to see a glimpse of the woman who bathed her such a short time ago, the woman who worried over her.

Anna moved her head only far enough to acknowledge Elena's presence in the room. Elena stood frozen in place, waiting for a signal, a flicker of encouragement, so she could fling her body into her mother's arms. Anna shifted the large wooden spoon from one hand to the other before returning her focus to the bubbling liquid in the pot.

Elena felt the tears well in her eyes and heard the chuckling behind her from Ernst and Walter. Her right hand raised, almost involuntarily to touch the rough wool of her mother's sweater, but it stopped short before reaching it. Letting her hand drop to her side, Elena turned and left the kitchen.

Twenty-three

January 1943

Elena worked with Maria Petrovna, helping her to maintain her façade as friend to the colonel and covering for her when she was late returning from her secret missions. Elena didn't know exactly what Maria did, but she knew she was the bravest woman she'd ever met. In her role as Maria's servant, Elena watched her come and go from the German encampment. On Sundays she was permitted to visit her family at the cottage and always returned with chickens and eggs as well as a few vegetables for the week. It was the other nights, following no discernable schedule, that made Elena's heart race as she watched from her cot while Maria dressed in her military fatigues and crept out the secret door while the colonel snored in Olga's feather bed. She often caught Maria listening at the closed door to the room where the officers met. Had a German caught Maria, there would be no question—she'd be shot.

Working for an officer, Elena was privileged to have sufficient food to keep from starving, enough even to gain a little weight and grow taller. With this growth came a more womanly form and she and Maria giggled over how to bind her breasts so she could remain Yuri. So far, the news hadn't been good for either side. The Soviet Union and Germany both claimed victories every other day.

Part of Elena longed for the comfort of Babushka's arms, but she missed the friendship she had developed with Willie more. Mama's coldness and seeming indifference in September had evolved to anger and antagonism. Elena now felt nervous whenever she had to enter the kitchen, fearing a tirade from her mother. She knew Anna blamed her for her father's injuries, as if somehow Elena caused Maria to shoot him, forgetting Papa had drawn his weapon first. When she wasn't blaming her for her father's absence, then she was accusing her of conspiring with the enemy by working for Maria and the colonel.

Working for Maria and the colonel also provided Elena with a new sense of identity, a security almost like having a family again. Every morning she carried breakfast up to Maria and the colonel. Maria and Elena had established a secret code of facial expressions so Elena knew the moment she entered the bedroom whether the colonel would be in a bad or pleasant mood. Eyes rolling up to the right and lips pinched meant she should watch out, he was likely to throw his tray across the room or begin a tirade of abuse about Russian harlots running his life. Eyes left and down with a small smile, meant he would begin telling stories about his family and reminiscing about the old days.

One of Elena's jobs was to collect the colonel and Maria's laundry and haul it out to the yard where soldiers were assigned to do the washing. She was charged with handling the women's clothing. Maria was expected to dress for dinner in the fancy dresses and gowns left behind by former residents of the house, so it fell to Elena to starch and iron the petticoats worn under those garments.

In the kitchen, Herman had been replaced by Freidrich, another fair-haired man but with a dreadful complexion, pockmarked and greasy. Elena could hardly bear to look at him. But he didn't pay any attention to her and that was fine with her.

Elena didn't like being in the kitchen in the role of handmaiden to a traitor, her mother's words, but she did like the warmth of the kitchen. Even with the fireplaces and stoves operating at full blast, the big house was drafty and cold.

Elena pulled a petticoat off the ironing board while Mama ranted. "It's four months since we left our home and now look at you! A traitor. As bad as that whore you serve!"

But it's all right for you to cook for them, Elena thought. What's the difference? If you only knew how brave and strong Maria is. She is going to help Russia to win this war. Elena thought those things but her heart clenched every time her mother spoke that way.

Maria had made it clear they each had to fight the war their own way. Maria worked in the underground; Elena was her support. Elena closed her eyes, as if she could shut out her mother's strident voice.

"Whores and sluts! Prostitutes. Those are the only women who survive. You think I don't know about that kind of women? You'll be just like them, Elena. There are days I spit on the morning I gave birth to you."

Elena squeezed her eyes shut. If only she could shout back, "Maria Petrovna is no whore. She is as brave as any Russian soldier at the front lines, maybe braver. But she herself wasn't brave enough to speak like that to her mother. Even Ernst, Walter and Freidrich stayed out of Mama's way when she was in a mood like this.

With trembling hands Elena placed the cooling iron on the stove surface and picked up the hot one. As she did, the petticoat slid from the ironing board to the floor. Elena instinctively reached for it, bending down to pick it up. When she stood, she felt the blood drain from her head and the room spun before her. She saw a look of alarm on Friedrich's face as she reached for the ironing board to support herself. She slid to the floor and fell on top of the freshly ironed fabric, thinking, "I'll have to iron it again," before the hot iron dropped on to her left hand.

She smelled the burning flesh and felt the searing pain at the same time. She screamed. In the next few minutes the men picked her up, her mother plunged her hand into cold water and then smoothed soft butter over the burn before wrapping her hand with a dish towel. Elena alternated between screaming and crying.

Someone must have sent for the colonel because he was there examining her hand. He barked orders and then her mother wrapped her in blankets before Freidrich picked her up and carried her out the door. He made soothing, hushing sounds as he rushed along a path.

Mama shouted, "That is your punishment for betraying your country! Whore!"

Freidrich shifted her body in his arms. He slowed down as he trudged through the snow, crossing toward a row of cottages. The only time she'd been away from the big house was the night she ran into the woods. Although Maria had told her the estate the Germans occupied was outside a village called Lvovsk, she still had no idea where they were. No idea where Freidrich might be taking her. She didn't care as long as it would be someplace where they'd make her hand stop hurting.

They reached a cottage at the end of the row. Freidrich had to set her down to open the door. A strong odor of disinfectant hit her nostrils as soon as she entered. Heavy curtains hung over the windows; a carved side table most likely from the big house served as a reception desk. It was situated in front of a roaring fireplace. An orderly who sat at the desk wrote down the information about her as Freidrich spoke. The overheated warmth of the room made her hand throb more.

"Hurry," she cried in Russian. "It hurts so badly." Tears ran down her face.

The clerk wrote precisely in a ledger as Freidrich continued to give him information. The clerk finally laid his pen on the makeshift desk and stood. He was a tall, thin man. He said a few words to Freidrich and then waved him away.

Freidrich smiled, exposing yellow, uneven teeth and then gave her a short salute before leaving her alone in the infirmary.

She wanted to run after him, to hold on to him, but the stern look on the orderly's face stopped her. She went as he directed her, entering a kitchen, and sat at the table. The room was spotless. Vials and medicines lined the shelves where once there were pots, pans, and dishes.

She found by holding her hand over her head the pain eased a little.

"So, *Fraulein* Federova . . ." She heard a booming voice behind her. "You have burned your hand," a man said in heavily accented Russian. He came into her line of vision, blocking her view of anything else in the room. The man was huge, like a bear. He smiled at her. He wore *pince nez* with a gold chain that disappeared inside his white lab coat. "It is problem with work in kitchen maid."

"I'm not a kitchen maid. I'm a pianist. Can you fix my hand?" she cried as she extended the wounded hand toward him.

"Ach. A pianist you are? I look." He turned his back to her and went to the stove where he picked up a kettle of steaming water and carried it to the sink. There he mixed it in a pot with soap and scrubbed his hands for several minutes. "You are playing hot piano?"

It took her a moment to realize he was joking. A short giggle erupted in spite of her pain. "No. No. I was pressing Miss Maria's clothing when I fainted."

"Fainted," he repeated as he dried his hands on a fresh white towel. "Faint-ed?"

"Faint," she repeated. "Fall down." She used her good hand to demonstrate, raising it above her head and then dropping it down toward the floor.

"*Ach. Ya znayou. Ohnmacht,*" he said in both German and Russian.

"Did you take care of my father, doctor?"

"Your father sick man. I did so take care until he was strong to send Germany. He is well-being, but he will have taken leave of his arm. I am sorry." She struggled to understand his fragmented Russian.

"Miss Maria shot him. She thought he would steal her chickens."

Ignoring her comment, the doctor sat at the table next to Elena and examined her hand. He then poked and prodded at her ears, nose, and throat. "Sitting on table, Miss Federova. I must to clean your hand and to examine you further for fainting."

Elena shifted to the tabletop while the doctor pulled bandages and other items from the cupboards. She eyed a large needle with trepidation.

"You will having much pain, young lady, and so I am shotting. Rest head on pillow." He helped her to lie back, gently placing a pillow beneath her head. "First, I listen at heart."

He hovered over her with a stethoscope. "Oh, please. My hand, doctor."

"I am called Dr. Maxwell Brandt. Not to move. I am to studied medicine in Hamburg and Massachusetts General Hospital in Boston, America," he continued in his heavily accented Russian.

"Then you speak English!" she replied in English. "I was learning English before we left Leningrad."

"Very good," he sighed in relief as he responded in English. "You must undo these clothes or I cannot examine you. Overall, you appear to be in much better health than most of the prisoners I have seen."

"I am not really a prisoner. My family was walking to Germany when Colonel Hüber found us. I work with Maria Petrovna. She is the mistress of the colonel." Elena tried to put a disapproving note in her voice. The doctor might not approve of her friendship with Maria.

"Miss Maria is an entertainment for the colonel," he said as he jabbed the large needle into her hip, surprising her. "By doing so, she is also providing food for her family. Do not be too harsh, Miss Federova. These are difficult times for everyone. Now you will rest and later when you awaken, you'll find yourself in a small room upstairs in the cottage. Your hand will be wrapped in petrolatum coated gauze. Though your hand may hurt, you must not remove the bandage. Do you understand?"

"I will not remove the bandage, doctor. Why are you looking at my stomach like that?" Elena raised her head to look down at her exposed skin. Her ribs and hip bones stood out, reminding her of an old mare she'd seen on a family outing in the country.

"I examine everyone who comes to the infirmary. It is my job."

"You must have examined Wilhelm," she said through a yawn.

"You sleep now. I work." He tugged her trousers up and placed the blanket over her.

She felt a warm glow and her head felt light and fuzzy. "Yes, Papa, I sleep. Did I tell you, Papa, about the nice boy I met? His name is Willie."

Twenty-four

Her stomach heaved. She felt someone hold her head as a cold metal pan was braced against her chin. She retched and then fell back against the pillow.

Pillow? She opened her eyes. A blond-haired soldier barely older than herself sat beside her on a wooden stool. White sheets and gray woolen blankets covered her. "I'm sick," she said in Russian.

"*Ya*," the boy answered. He rose from the chair and left the room with the metal bowl.

Elena looked about, trying to get her bearings. She was in a comfortable bed in a warm room. She started to push herself upright when a searing pain shot through her left hand. She cried out and the young man dashed back into the room.

"What's happened?" Her hand was wrapped in bandages that ran all the way up to her elbow. "It hurts. What happened?"

The boy put his hands on her shoulders and tried to gently press her back down on the bed. She struggled to get up. "S-s-s," he admonished her with a finger to his lips. "*Herr Brandt ...*"

Before he finished, the doctor entered the room. He had to duck through the doorway. "So, young lady, you're awake. I'm sorry about the sedative. It often makes people ill, but it also makes it much easier to work on the patient. So, you will remain here for a few days. No work. Albert is the orderly here, and he'll help you."

Elena eyed the sour faced young man who stood to attention as the doctor spoke. "Help me for what?" she asked.

"You'll need assistance to eat, to wash yourself. You may notice you are in a clean gown and have been thoroughly bathed."

She looked down to see a clean flannel nightdress. Albert stared straight ahead.

The doctor continued. "I will give orders when you return to your duties, that you are to be permitted to bathe regularly. It is vital to your good health." He paused and almost chuckled but caught himself. "In any case, I shall make the suggestion. Also, I shall check your hand in a few days. We must leave it wrapped and let it heal. I have used a new technique which I learned in Massachusetts. You're a fortunate young lady to have burned your hand in my jurisdiction." He patted her on the cheek and sat down on the edge of the bed. For a moment she feared the bed might tip over on its side with his weight.

"I burned my hand," she said, still feeling slightly disoriented.

"Keep it elevated on the pillows. That will help to reduce the swelling and lessen the pain."

"Please give me whatever medicine it was you gave me last night. It hurts so badly, doctor." Nausea still threatened and the pain was excruciating.

"That was this morning, Elena. It is still Sunday, though it's late in the evening. You must go back to sleep after you've had soup. Albert will feed you." He then gave orders to the boy in German. Albert scurried from the room.

The doctor waited until he heard the boy clatter down the stairs before he spoke again. "So, Little One, who is the Papa?"

"My father?" The question confused her. He spoke of something she didn't want to think about. Her head ached and she wanted him to give her more medicine to make all the pain go away, the pain in her hand and the pain in her head.

"Of your child. You do know you are going to have a baby, yes?"

She heard the words, but they didn't make sense. Her stomach lurched as she looked frantically about for the basin, but the boy had taken it away with him. "I'm going to be sick again."

Doctor Brandt reached across to a nearby bureau and picked up an empty bowl. He held it for her.

When she was finished, he wiped her face with a damp cloth and brushed her hair from her face. She fell back against the pillows, exhausted. "That can't be true. It cannot."

"How old are you, Elena?"

"Fourteen."

"And you have been intimate with a man?"

"No!" she tried to raise her head to protest, but it felt too heavy. She could only cry. "No. Never."

"Come, child. You're speaking with a doctor. I know how these things work. You must tell me if I am to help you."

"But I didn't."

"Is it the nice young man who brought you here?" He smoothed her blankets as he continued to question her in a soft voice.

Memories pressed in from the edges of darkness; memories crushed and buried. This man was trying to force her to remember something from the past, something ugly, painful.

"You're a Nazi doctor. Why should I trust or believe you?" she lashed out, eager to say anything that would keep her from thinking about what he'd just told her.

Instead of responding with anger, the doctor's face turned sad. "I returned home to Germany in order to avoid the Americans who would have me deported or confine me for being a German, but when I arrived home, I learned I was suspect because I had lived and worked in America. The worse they could think to do was to send me to this remote outpost where all my studies would mean little, if nothing. I see mostly frostbite and minor injuries." He paused briefly. "And too many dead bodies as they are brought back from the front – too late for my skills."

"Good," she grumbled, recalling her father's opinion. "My father says a good German is a dead German. Only he uses a different word for them."

And still she hadn't angered the man. Though his expression remained sad, he smiled. "Just think, if I had been one of your good Germans, then I would not have been here to save your hand so you can still play your piano in a concert hall someday.

The war will end, child, and with God's help, we shall once again have music and concerts."

She studied his face for a moment, wondering if he was joking with her. Maybe he was right and she had been lucky to have him here precisely when she needed him. "I like to play Chopin." She studied his face, the sad eyes magnified behind the spectacles. "Will I really be able to play again? It feels terrible right now. If you had cut it off, it might feel better."

"It will heal. With a burn, pain is a good sign. If there is no pain, there is more scarring. I'll give Albert a sleeping medicine for you to take after you've eaten. We can talk more tomorrow. The war won't end before then."

"When it does, the Russians will be the winners."

He stood to leave. "When it does, no one will be the winner. Good night, Little One."

"Wait!"

He paused at the doorway. "*Ya*? What is it?"

"Maria. She—she did something that night. She said it would keep me from—from this." Elena pointed toward her abdomen. "She said she . . ."

"Herbs and old wives' remedies often work. Unfortunately for you, that was not so this time. You can have the child or not. Whatever you decide, I shall help you however I can."

She watched him leave thinking she ought to get back to the big house and her work. She closed her eyes for a minute to think about something the doctor had just said.

When she opened them again, lantern cast shadows in the dark room. Her head rested on real pillows. She yawned. A chair scraped on the wooden floor startling her. The doctor's helper, Albert, emerged from the shadows of the room, his face a sinister mask in the shadowy light.

She placed her hands to either side in order to push herself upright and then screamed as the pain in her left hand hit her. She fell back against the pillows. "*Rouka maya! Rouka maya!*"

Albert smirked as he held out a glass half filled with water and a saucer with a pill.

"My hand. My hand is hurting." Tears streamed down her face. "I remember the doctor. He looks like a great bear. He said–he said I would play the piano after the war is ended. I don't see how, the pain is so bad." She held the heavily bandaged hand up for him to see.

He looked at it, shrugged and moved closer with the water and pills.

She eyed them suspiciously. "What are those?"

He didn't respond but moved the saucer to her lips so he could tilt the pills into her mouth. Hesitantly, she accepted them and took the glass of water herself. When she finished, she handed the glass back to Albert who turned and left the room. She watched him go down the stairs, not wanting to believe the hateful look on his face.

The doctor said the hand would heal. She hoped he was right and not just bragging about his ability as a physician. What could he care, anyway? He's a German doctor. He must be bad. He must be very, very bad. He said something else that was very, very bad. Her mind couldn't cope with the confusing messages coming at her in three languages. She slept again.

Between shots and pills she remained in the foggy haze of narcotics for several more days. Each time she awoke, Albert stood by ready to provide more pills or to shovel food and broth into her mouth. When necessary, he escorted her to the other side of the room where she used a portable commode. She didn't remember seeing her mother during her convalescence.

Ten days after the accident, Doctor Brandt brought her downstairs to the kitchen/exam room to change her bandages for the third time. Her hand still hurt and looked raw.

"I can barely move my fingers," she said.

"We shall begin therapy when you are ready for it. You must still heal. Have you thought any more about what you want to do about your child?" The doctor focused on his work as he rewrapped her hand.

"What child?" she asked, completely confused by his question.

"When you first came to me. It was obvious about your condition, young lady. I have asked you several times what you want to do. I understand you are not a Christian, so I am presuming you wouldn't object to a termination." He disposed of the old bandages into a stainless-steel container.

Elena focused on the garbage can. She didn't remember any conversations about a condition or about a child. "I don't know what you talk about."

"You're pregnant, Elena. I have not spoken to anyone else about this situation because it is none of my business. You are a prisoner of the Third Reich and legally entitled to medical care. I am offering medical care."

"You've been kind to me, Doctor, but you have to be mistaken. A woman has to be with a man to have a baby and I haven't." She looked straight at him, daring him to tell her different.

"The father of your child is not Wilhelm, the soldier with whom you were friendly?"

"Of course not! Willie was my friend. He was good to me. We played cards and chess together! You can't say he did anything to me!" Her head ached. She wanted this conversation to end.

"You haven't much time before you must make a decision."

She gasped. "You're telling me I have a baby in me and you want to kill it. Is that what you're telling me?"

Doctor Brandt patted her good hand. "Not at all. I asked you if that would be your choice. It wouldn't be my choice under ordinary circumstances, but these are not ordinary circumstances."

"I'm not pregnant." She spat out the word, angry that the doctor thought so little of her he would believe she'd been a bad girl.

"Elena, something happened to you. You are going to have a baby in about six months."

"No." As he tied the end of the bandage and cut off the excess, she stood. "I don't know why you're saying these things to me. Thank you for fixing my hand. I should go back to the house."

"Sit down!" The strength of his command sent her rushing back to the chair. "I took an oath to help people in need of medical care. The oath didn't state only Germans. It didn't say I mustn't help Russians or Americans. I am here and I can help you through this. You are under most difficult circumstances to be having a child. You're very young; you've suffered from malnutrition; you are in a poor mental state. I shall speak with your mother this afternoon unless you tell me who is the person responsible for your child."

She stared at him, still uncomprehending that she could be pregnant. "I told you, Doctor, I never did that thing that makes babies. I'm not even sure I truly understand what it is one does. A man and a woman must lie together, but after that, I don't know." She felt tears run down her cheeks.

"Then I shall talk to your mother." He heaved his large frame from the chair and moved to the sink where he washed his hands.

She watched his back as he stooped over the sink. Little doors opened and shut quickly in her mind. She saw fragments of a horrific picture. The dining room; a fork on a carpet. A girl screamed. She dropped her head onto her arm on the table. Tears puddled on the white enamel. "No. No. That wasn't me. Not me."

She felt a hand on her shoulder, and then she leaned against the soft cotton lab coat of the German officer/doctor and cried. She cried until she fell asleep.

She awoke in the bed again.

Though she'd been asleep, it had been a restless sleep, full of nightmares. She tried to focus on the cheerful room and crystal glasses on the table sparkling in the sunlight, but then those little doors opened and closed offering her fleeting glimpses into what had happened and then they suddenly became one large door that flew fully open. She saw Herman standing over her, his private parts all wet and slimy. She cowered in pain on the dining room carpet. Then she was stabbing him in the chest with a fork, but he laughed at her.

She'd stumbled into the forest in hopes of dying but Willie found her and carried her back to her mother.

"My mother didn't believe me. Do you know that? Did she tell you that? She said I flaunted myself at all of you just like Maria. I'm not like Maria, am I? And if I am, why is it that I'm going to have a child and she isn't?"

Willie's face turned bright red. "I don't know about these things so much, Elena. My father told me prostitutes and bad girls have ways of not getting that way. He warned me if I ever got a girl in the family way then I would have to marry her. Before I came into the army, he reminded me. He said, 'Would you want a Russian or an American soldier to rape your sisters? Then you behave honorably at all times.'"

Elena tried to digest what he was saying. "So, who did you kill? Herman?"

"Yes. Herman. When I found you in the woods, you had barely fixed your clothing. You sat under a tree staring at the darkness. When I asked you to come with me, you didn't answer. I picked you up. You didn't resist. You were like a limp bundle of rags."

"I remember, Willie. I remember what happened. How did you know it was Herman?"

She remembered. Herman. Willie. The fight. Herman is dead. Willie went home to Germany.

She thought she'd been awake, but when she woke again, this time she saw stern faced Albert sweeping the floor. The lantern lit the room. It was dark outside.

Twenty-five

Late February 1943

Elena sat at a small writing desk in the corner of a room in the hospital-cottage. The tall clerk no longer worked in the infirmary. The large table had been removed to be burned in a stove for heat. With her bandaged left hand elevated on cushions, she used her right hand to copy notes for the doctor. Even with the stove burning, she cloaked herself in a woolen blanket, and wondered if she'd ever be warm again.

"You cannot risk infection in the hand if you are to become a famous pianist, young lady. I have requested your services as a clerk in my office so you do not have to work as a scullery maid in the kitchens. What do you think of that?" Dr. Brandt had announced a week ago, once Elena was able to move about without too much pain. It had been three weeks since the accident and Elena had spent much of the time resting, enjoying the relative warmth in the upstairs bedroom, and eating hot broth and crusty bread. Even Albert's alternating belligerent and sullen attitude didn't bother her any longer. Now, the kindly doctor offered her an escape from her mother's verbal attacks and the smirks of the men in the kitchens. She missed conspiring with Maria but Maria had managed well without her before she arrived so she would be all right without her.

The smile on the doctor's face told her it pleased him to offer her the work. She felt secure for the first time in months.

Dr. Brandt showed her how to enter each patient's name in the books, to record dates, times, symptoms, diagnoses, and disposal of each case. With her mind occupied learning the German words and script, the time moved quickly. She was able to ignore her nausea in the mornings, blaming it on wood smoke, or being too cold or too hot.

One morning a man barged in with a bloodied cloth covering the right side of his face, reminding her of Willie after the fight. She must have turned pale at the sight of him because he smiled at her and said something in German. When he removed the cloth for the doctor, there was a large cut over his eyebrow. He'd hurt himself chopping wood for the fires. But the sight of him brought back memories of Willie – Willie and her playing chess on the cot in the little room behind the kitchen; Willie telling stories about his family in Germany. She missed him and hoped he was able to get his old job back as a clerk in the insurance company.

When war was over maybe she could go to a music conservatory in Germany. Surely, once the Russians conquered Germany, they would keep opera houses and conservatories open and she could find Willie.

Until that time she would write the doctor's notes into composition books. Even when he was short of medicine and other supplies for his patients, he had an endless supply of ink and notebooks.

"The Germans are an organized and ritualistic people. We must have three copies of everything. Everything. It could drive a man crazy to write so many things over and over again. Are you learning from your work?"

"Doctor Brandt, the only thing I'm learning is better English from you and a little German."

"In the copying of the notes I had hoped you would be learning something of medicine. Not so?" He sat and put his feet on a console that sat at right angles to his desk.

"Perhaps the German words for many medical implements and procedures, but I don't think I'm learning enough to be a doctor."

"I thought more of an assistant." He dropped his feet to the floor, folded his hands in front of him on the desk and peered at her over his glasses. "How are you feeling?"

"Mostly tired. I miss my family."

"Tired is normal. With any luck your father is making a nice recovery some place in Germany. As for your mother, the colonel has told me he will not permit her to visit you. When you are repatriated to the kitchens, you shall see your mother."

Elena put her pen down and scooted her chair around so she could face him squarely. "It's not exactly that, *Herr Doktor*. It's more because I miss what our family was before the war, before the siege, before everyone went crazy."

"I understand. During the first war my studies were interrupted when I was called up. I had to leave my family. While I was away, I lost many family members. My brother and my brother-in-law. My sweetheart married another man. It was no easy homecoming. No family is ever the same."

"You see my mother. Did she ask about me at dinner today?"

He didn't answer. She could tell the way he lowered his head and blinked his eyes whenever he spoke about how much her mother missed her. At the end of these conversations, he always admitted he made up the answers to make her feel better. It had become almost a game between them, first his gentle lies of her loving and concerned mother, but always followed by his own caring commentary on the difficulties her mother faced living as she did. Mother had become something of a harridan, he told her, shouting at the men in the kitchen morning, noon, and night. And still she always turned out excellent meals in spite of shortages so the colonel kept her working in the manor house.

"You're eating well; you're looking well," he said, "But you are not sounding well. I know you're frightened and lonely here. Albert treats you as he's been taught. You are, after all, a prisoner here."

"He's not so bad, doctor. He is more indifferent to me than mean. I don't think he considers me worth noticing." She turned back to her task. "He's right, you know. I'm beneath notice. Like a worm." She picked up her pen and began her meticulous script across the page. *Emil Gerhardt, Grippe,* followed by his official identification information.

"This is the way it will be, child, at least until the winter ends. When your baby comes in May, we shall see about transferring you. If the roads are passable, perhaps you can travel to Germany in a convoy. Last night we had a new arrival of Russian prisoners. They are in an enclosure on the edge of the hamlet. I will go there today to help examine them and make recommendations. Some will work, others…no."

She turned back to look at him as he stood. "You are also lonely here, doctor. Is it so terrible to have to take care of the prisoners?"

"Humph, now you're beginning to sound like me. Get on with your work. I do what I can, but nothing is ever enough. You bring a small spot of joy into my life, Elena. Do you know that?"

Her heart fluttered. Joy? How could she bring joy to anyone in her condition? The only joy she ever brought to anyone was when she played her piano. Even when they all lived together in Leningrad during the blockade, no one laughed or smiled unless she played the piano. "How can that be? I'm an ugly girl who is marred for life by this . . . this thing in me."

The doctor only needed one large step to reach her. His face reddened. She recoiled in fear. "You will not refer to yourself or your child in such a manner again. It is not a thing; it is either a boy or a girl. It will be your child." He grabbed his hat and overcoat from the rack by the door and stormed from the room.

"It is a boy or a girl." She mimicked the doctor. "Whatever it is, I hate it!" She put her head on the desk and cried, not caring when her tears blotched the notes she'd just made.

Twenty-six

April 1943

Elena reclined against the pillows in the bed with her fabric piano keyboard draped across the sheets. She could no longer deny her condition as the piano seemed to move of its own accord whenever the baby inside her shifted. Still resenting her situation, she concentrated on healing her hand so she could play again.

She'd been trying to remember a particular passage from the Chopin Etude in C major, Opus 10. "A simple exercise, you stupid child," she criticized herself as her instructor had done so many times when she was at school. She'd been secretly practicing and exercising her hand and wanted to play it for the doctor.

When Dr. Brandt removed the bandages from her hand six weeks after she'd burned it, he carefully snipped at the blistered skin to keep her fingers from fusing together. Then he cautioned her to be careful to keep it clean and dry. "I did not spend so much time and money at Massachusetts General Hospital learning these new techniques so a silly Russian girl can ruin my reputation by not following instruction. I have asked Colonel Hüber to allow you to remain here at the infirmary as my clerk. That way you can avoid further injury."

Her body ached. It had to be almost time for her next pain shot. The rain pounded relentlessly against the small window. Albert refused to light a lantern, claiming they were low on fuel. He insisted the doctor needed it for treating the German patients who were far more important than a Russian prisoner. In the beginning she believed she could win Albert over to her side. He might even be a replacement for Willie, but Albert showed no signs of understanding Russian or English. He treated her with barely concealed contempt.

She closed her eyes as she stretched her piano across her lap. Her fingers migrated automatically to the keys as she recalled the particular exercise she wanted to play for the doctor. The cramps came and went, generally mild, but sometimes so strong she was sure she'd be having the baby soon. With no one to ask, she focused on the music, always the music so she wouldn't have to think about a baby coming out of her body. She still wasn't even sure how it got out. The cramps had begun in the early morning two days ago as she sat at her desk copying Dr. Brandt's notes into the ledger. At first, they felt like hunger pangs and she ignored them. By noon when she went into the kitchen to have lunch with the doctor and Albert, her whole middle ached. She couldn't find a comfortable position to sit or stand. Dr. Brandt gave her permission to go upstairs and rest following the midday meal.

"These contractions are normal at seven months. I suggest you rest and wait for real developments."

Once upstairs, she tried to take her mind off the waves of pain by counting the tiny flowers in the bed curtains, but to no avail. If she were in a real Russian village, there would be a midwife, a woman with whom she could speak. Almost as quickly as it came, the thought flew out the window. She continued to focus on the flowers, lavender blue and white lilies. There must have been thousands of them but the wallpaper hung in ribbons, where the background was once white, it was now mostly yellowed with age. She hadn't thought peasants on an estate could afford a luxury such as wallpaper. The aching worsened until she clenched her teeth against the pain as much as the prospect of stupid Albert being in the room when she gave birth. If there had to be a man, then let it be Dr. Brandt.

Tears stung her eyes, overflowed, and ran down the sides of her face. "Papa, Papa," she moaned through gritted teeth. She wanted him nearby. She wished she could tell him he was right to want to walk to Germany; that the Germans would feed them and care for them, forgetting that rape by a German put her in this position in the first place. She didn't care that he was really wrong about the whole thing if only he could be here now, right this minute, everything would be all right. "Papa, come back to us. Papa, Papa."

And then she screamed out in pain. This must be the development the doctor had talked about. She heard someone clambering up the wooden staircase. It didn't matter who it was as long as she could get a shot. She wanted shots like the doctor had given her for her hand.

"Help!" she called to him in English as her fingers smashed notes. *"Bitte! Bitte, Doktor Brandt."*

Albert's face appeared briefly above her. She tried to focus on him, but he looked as frightened as she felt. He disappeared and she heard him scrambling back down the stairs calling for the doctor.

An hour or more passed when to her surprise, Maria appeared. "The doctor asked me to come, to keep you company so you would be calm. He is busy with wounded soldiers. He said it's too early for the baby. He wants you to rest."

"I don't want this baby. I don't care if it comes too soon because then it will die." Elena turned her face away from the judgment she saw in Maria's eyes. When Maria didn't speak, Elena said, "Anyway, I'm glad you came. The pain has eased. But I could have had this baby and no one would have been here with me."

"Elena," Maria began as she placed her hand on Elena's shoulder and gently turned her so she faced her. "I don't blame you for not wanting this baby. It was conceived in the most violent way, but every single life is precious. Too many people are dying. While we who are left are struggling to stay alive, you mustn't want your own child to die."

"You didn't care when Willie killed Herman."

Maria tensed and then frowned in thought. "You're right. What I cared about then was revenge. Revenge for you–and for me. Besides, they were still the enemy, and the more enemy we can kill, the more we are helping to win this war."

Unconvinced by Maria's argument, Elena ignored it. "Why are you here? Tell me," she said, "why isn't my own mother here? She wishes me dead—I know she does."

"Your mother doesn't want you dead! Where did you get that idea?" Maria sat up straight, pulling her hand away.

"You saw how she treated me! She hates me. She has not once come to visit me since I've been in the infirmary."

"Elena! You are prisoners. You don't have choices. Your mother is not permitted to come visit you. This isn't a holiday camp. She works like the lowest serf in the poorest farm. Do you think she has time to be correct and proper with a rude daughter? I don't know your mother well, but I wonder how much you have looked at her the past year and a half since the siege began. She is an old woman and not well. What was she like before the blockade, can you tell me?"

"She was a teacher and sometimes she was nice. Mostly she didn't pay any attention to me. My grandmother was more like my mother."

"'Sometimes she was nice to me,'" Maria repeated the words in a whining voice, imitating Elena.

Elena sulked but her cheeks burned. Mama was always bossy, but it was true she was happier before the war, before the starvation. She didn't like teaching the nursery school, but when she was called with all the other women to volunteer to help defend the city by digging trenches, she would come home exhausted, yet cheerful and talkative about the important work she'd been doing. "I didn't think."

"Of course, you didn't. It's not the job of a girl in ordinary times to worry about what her parents are thinking, but these are not ordinary times. You have to put away your petulant attitude, your secret desires and wishes. You must be brave. You must be a woman now."

Once again Elena chose to ignore Maria's comments as she glared at her, looking so healthy and strong in her military garb.

"What about you? You come and you go at will. You're free to do your spying…"

Maria struck her hard across her face. The slap stung. "Shut up! You stupid, stupid girl!" Maria's face was inches away as her voice turned to an angry whisper. "I trusted you. Don't you ever dare say another word about my work again. Ever! If I hear anything from you, I shall be the one to come kill you *and* your baby. Do you understand?"

Elena stared at her wide-eyed.

Maria gripped her wrist. "Do you understand?"

Elena winced as pain shot from her wrist to her injured hand. "I do. I understand."

Maria dropped her wrist and left the room without another word. While reflexively rubbing her wrist, Elena watched as Maria disappeared down the stairs. The front door slammed shut.

Elena slumped down in her bed, hands over her head as she cried, not noticing as her piano fell to the floor.

Doctor Brandt arrived late in the evening. He checked her eyes, took her pulse, listened to her heart, and then left without a word. Albert came in several minutes later with her supper, a bowl of watery porridge and a slice of black bread.

The next few days she spent much of her time crying and hating everyone in her life. She felt abandoned and totally alone in the world. Her one slim connection to anyone was the doctor. She was determined to play for him. He would smile when she played. At least *he* would like her.

She heard him come up the steps. Dr. Brandt stopped and looked down at her. His face had become gaunt. His uniform hung loosely about his frame. Their rations must have been cut just like hers had been in Leningrad.

Before he could examine her, she brushed the hair from her face and smiled at him. "I have been practicing so I can play music for you. I shall play the Etude in C major, Opus 10. It's Chopin. Just for you."

"Where did you get that?" He pointed to her keyboard.

"It's mine," she said as she pulled it up under her chin. "My family made it for me when our house was bombed. I keep it with me all the time. Everyone's been so mean to me, I wanted to do something nice so they'll like me again."

He scowled as he pulled a wooden chair up close to the bed. "So, you're thinking everyone is angry with you. Do you know why that would be?"

"They think I ought to be happy that I am about to have a baby. I'm not."

"It is more than that, my child. You have been working with me for nearly three months and what have you learned of my work? Have you taken any interest? You have watched me triage any number of patients, but yet you sigh and carry on as if you are the only person to suffer in this war. Do you know how many women and girls have been raped and died? Maybe they would not have liked to be carrying a child of their enemy, but perhaps it is better than being dead. If I can help you to keep from giving premature birth, then you should have a perfectly healthy normal baby in a few weeks. You will care for it, am I correct?"

Another lecture. She didn't want another lecture about how selfish and childish she was behaving. She opened her mouth to answer when an explosion rocked the room. Elena rolled to the floor, grabbing at blankets as she sought shelter under the metal framed bed. The doctor knocked his chair backward as he dashed from the room and raced down the stairs. Albert shouted from below. Other men's voices chimed in. Elena shivered in fear. For months now, she'd felt almost safe in the camp with the Germans.

She covered her head with a quilt and placed her hands over her ears. How easy it had been to forget a war raged all around them. She heard gunfire and intermittent shouting both from downstairs and outside. She perspired. The baby inside her kicked and rolled.

The sounds of war carried on through the night. No one came to see her safely in bed. She remained huddled beneath the bed praying the Russians would wipe out this ugly nest of Germans, but part of her prayed Dr. Brandt would remain safe.

She pulled more blankets and her pillows from the bed then fell asleep in her new nest. Rain beating on the window woke her during the night. It was still dark out, but light flashed periodically, like lightning. Instead of being followed by rolling thunder, though, the flashes were followed by the boom of artillery being fired. Russian or German fire, she didn't know which. She pulled herself to a sitting position against the wall, legs stretched out before her and listened for any sounds in the building but heard nothing. Albert wasn't downstairs rattling in the small kitchen making the ersatz coffee or cleaning as he always did shortly before dawn. Company, even the surly young soldier, would be most welcome just now.

Sliding herself, along with her nest of blankets under the steel framed bed, she waited for the shelling to stop and when it did, the silence roared in her ears. She pulled the covers over her head and waited for daylight.

She was a little girl again playing at the park. It was summertime and she wore a white pinafore over her blue dress. The trees along the avenue made a long shady tunnel as she and Tatiana walked to the park. They took turns pushing each other on the swing and then later Mama took them to buy a flavored ice. Her ice fell out of its paper cone and Mama came to comfort her and bought her a new one. She smiled at the memory until Mama's face melted into Grandmother's face. "Grandmama," she wept at the sound of her own voice.

Her heart raced. She wondered what the daylight would bring. Would it be Albert and Dr. Brandt, or Russian soldiers come to rescue her? Perhaps the Germans had fled? She had no idea how this house was situated in the hamlet. She remembered being carried to the infirmary, but she'd been in so much pain, she hadn't taken much notice of how they got here. If she wasn't too far from the manor house, maybe she ought to get there. Maybe that's where everyone went to hide.

Her body trembled uncontrollably. She decided to wait until daylight and then she would go in search of the doctor. Dr. Brandt never gave her a shot last night. She was afraid to go another whole day without one. Her hand ached. The baby hiccupped. She resettled herself in her nest, pulled the covers over her head and fell asleep counting the seconds between hiccups.

Twenty-seven

Sunlight streamed through the window awakening Elena. She covered her eyes with her hands and moaned. It took seconds for her to realize that she rested on a mess of blankets on the floor and then she remembered last night. The baby was still. Pulling herself to the window, she peered down on the muddy street glistening in the hazy sunshine. Horses stood harnessed to farm carts, loaded with bundles ready to move. German soldiers secured the bundles with ropes. Trucks with canvas covered beds stood in a line further down the street. Troop transports.

"They're leaving! They're leaving!" Her heart lifted as she believed the war to be over. She crawled to the top of the stairs and peered around so she could look down. Slowly creeping down, she finally drew up enough courage to call for Albert and Dr. Brandt.

Unsure what to think when she received no response, she grabbed her outer clothing from the pegs and pulled them on. She silently thanked the Germans for being such a tidy people. Her underclothing, as well as the clothing she wore when she arrived, were all clean. The trousers barely reached her ankles, but she was still able to tuck them into her boots and tie the waist with a piece of rope. She laced the boots. When her father had given them to her it seemed it would be years before they ever fit her properly, now her toes nearly reached the end with only two pairs of woolen socks. Her piano was safely tucked above her expanding middle.

She moved cautiously into the kitchen in search of food, anything to eat. A pot of cold coffee sat on the stove. The cupboard doors stood open. All the drugs and medical supplies were gone. She found a clean cup and poured coffee from the pot and then drank the cold coffee. Still no one came. A plate on the table still had a sizable piece of bread which she grabbed and ate as she headed for the front door. Albert's desk was cleaned of any papers. The Germans were definitely leaving.

She yanked open the door and crashed straight into Maria.

"So! You're dressed. I've come to collect you. How did you find out we're leaving? Everyone's been rushing about so this morning. It was only five minutes ago Colonel Hüber ordered me to come for you."

"I didn't know anything! Why are you here? Where are we going?"

"I don't know any more than you. The colonel ordered me to escort you to a truck and to remain with you." Maria led her down the front steps of the infirmary. Their boots squished in the mud as they trudged toward the trucks. The baby kicked violently as Elena gasped for breath in her effort to keep up with Maria.

"Is the war over? Is that why the Germans are leaving?"

"We're all leaving."

"But the colonel . . ."

Maria yanked at Elena's arm and turned her so they stood face to face. "The colonel and I do not see eye to eye about my future. He assures me my family is all dead and it is in my best interest to do as he orders." Maria's voice was cold, unemotional.

They continued walking. "Now we must survive together. Your mother and I have salvaged some food. You're lucky the colonel feels a responsibility for your condition. He is, after all, a family man. No matter that he can murder women and children in their beds, he won't murder someone he knows by name. We are to ride in a truck. The other prisoners and the soldiers will be lucky to sit atop the farm carts. Most of them will probably walk. Hurry, you ignorant child."

Elena stopped. "What do you mean? You think I'm receiving special privileges? Aren't you riding in the truck as well? What about my mother? You're friends with the colonel…"

"Shut up! I'm sent to help you. And I suppose he likes your mother's cooking. Perhaps he wants to keep her safe for the next camp." She grabbed Elena by the arm and dragged her along past half a dozen trucks. When they reached the first one in the line, a soldier reached out to haul her up.

Once inside the canvas covered truck, she looked around. German soldiers, hollow eyed, wrapped like mummies stared at her. On the bench across from her Anna sat.

Elena stared at her mother. She'd grown even thinner since she last saw her. Her face had dark circles under bulging eyes and lines and wrinkles she didn't remember. Her nose protruded like a beak.

"Mama," she said.

Anna looked up at her with the same hollow eyes as the soldiers. "Elena? Elena?" The older woman pushed herself up from the bench.

Now eye to eye, Elena realized she had grown taller. The thought of Maria's and the doctor's rebuke flashed through her mind.

"Hello, Mama. How are you?" Elena said, her heart racing, her knees weak. The baby protested all the moving about by kicking, punching, and rolling. Elena winced and grabbed at her middle.

Elena couldn't be sure, but she thought Mama reached out a hand toward her when Maria climbed into the truck and took Elena by the arm and pushed her all the way in. Elena stumbled onto the bench closest to the cab of the truck. Maria squeezed in next to her. Anna remained at the rear of the truck, near the opening. Elena leaned forward so she could see her mother, but Anna's eyes were downcast, her gloved hands folded in her lap.

Soldiers shuffled through the opening, quickly filling the benches, and then taking up all the floor space. The space was crowded to suffocation.

The truck lurched forward, bouncing through the ruts and over the rocks.

"Do you really not know where we're going?" Elena asked Maria.

"I'm a prisoner the same as you. I know nothing."

Her piano wrapped about her middle along with the several layers of clothing warmed her. In spite of the jolting movement of the truck, the jostling of the man who sat on the floor using her legs as a backrest and keeping her from sleeping, she felt snug and safe in her darkened corner. The steady patter of raindrops on canvas combined with her dark, cozy corner, lured her into a sense of safety. The baby even remained still throughout the ride.

Around noon the truck swayed, suddenly throwing everyone from her side onto the people in the middle. When the vehicle came to rest at a steep angle, men shouted at them to get out and push. No one took any notice of her or her condition. She was expected to help.

To her surprise, Freiderich, the ugly boy from the kitchen, spoke from behind as she leaned her shoulder into the back fender along with a dozen other prisoners spread out across the back of the truck. "You pretend to push. I will do your work," he whispered to her in Russian.

"*Danke,*" she whispered back. He stepped behind her, his body close to hers as he shoved at the truck. Elena had to use all her strength to keep from running away.

After half an hour the truck was freed and they all clambered inside, now soaking wet. Elena was hungry and needed to relieve herself. Her room in the infirmary was already a fond memory of luxury. She closed her eyes and imagined her piano but the notes were sour. Frightened by the off-key notes, she struggled to play the correct ones as she'd been taught. A sharps and B flats became muddled in her mind.

Rifle fire woke her. With no idea how long she'd been asleep, Elena looked around to see who was shooting and why. Her fellow passengers all looked out through the opening at the rear of the truck. She pushed herself to a standing position to see but the backs of heads blocked her view. Though the rain had stopped, the day remained gloomy and grey. Men muttered and grumbled as they squatted back to the floor. When she finally looked out in the fading light, she saw smoke rising from the chimney of a nearby small cottage. The naked bodies of three women hung from the bare branches of two trees, outlined in the stark relief of twilight, an etching in black and white. Her eyes remained fixed on the gently swaying corpses while her mind played Chopin's Prelude Number 4, Opus 28, a slow and funereal piece.

She played and stared until the bodies disappeared from sight.

"One day I will kill them all." Maria spoke. A tear formed in the corner of her eye, paused, and then slid down her face.

Elena reached out and placed a hand on Maria's knee to comfort her. "One day the war will be over and you won't have to."

Twenty-eight

"We need food in here!" a man shouted from the center of the crowded truck.

"Food!" another called out.

The man on the bench opposite banged on the cab of the truck. Two more men joined in. "Food. Food!"

Their cries went unheeded.

The man on the floor in front of Elena grumbled at length. Maria translated. "He says they fight a fucking war for their country and are repaid with no food. He suggests they refuse to fight any longer."

"Who can expect a man to fight when he has no strength?" Elena said. She was wedged between Maria and the cab of the truck and so able to remain upright. Pain shot up her back from sitting on the wooden bench, and her legs hurt from the soldier leaning against them on the floor. The baby rolled inside her, triggering periodic waves of nausea.

"It doesn't take so much strength to pull a trigger. Our own government not only has hungry soldiers, they have no bullets to give them. A Russian soldier must first kill a German soldier and then take his weapon so he can shoot more of the enemy."

Elena leaned her head against Maria's shoulder and spoke behind her hand so the others wouldn't hear. "Herman was evil, but the rest of the Germans at that camp seemed – well, seemed almost like normal people."

"Don't believe it. Now, rest." Maria patted Elena's head awkwardly.

Elena thought about Dr. Brandt; no one could ever convince her he was a bad man, enemy or not.

The trucks rolled on through the night, sometimes becoming stuck in mud. When they stopped Elena, Maria and Anna trekked as far as they could under the watch of a guard in order to relieve themselves.

Once during the night they stopped so everyone could clamber down an embankment to a creek for a drink of water. There was still no food offered and she wondered when Maria or Anna would give her a bit of what they'd salvaged.

As if reading her mind, a man at the rear of the truck said, "I smell bread."

Another spoke. "It's cheese. I've been thinking that I smelled cheese all day. That's what makes me so hungry."

A soldier banged his rifle on the floor. He spoke for a moment and then Mama's voice rose above his. "Get your filthy hands off me," she shouted. "I am under Colonel Hüber's protection!"

Although Elena was unable to understand all of the words, she understood the mood as more soldiers joined in the fray,

"He's saying she has food. They want to search her," Maria explained. "I will help her. You remain here." Maria shoved and pushed her way to the rear of the truck and reached Anna before the others could shred her clothing in search of food.

Maria spoke in Russian and then translated her words into German. "Leave her be. You must give her a chance to remove the food for herself. I, too, have food. Because Anna cooked for the officers and because I worked for the colonel…"

Several voices rose up in protest, but Maria silenced them.

"I can only beg you to trust me. I have done what I must. We didn't know where we would be going, nor for how long we'd be traveling. We also had no idea about provisions so we brought as much as we could hide in our clothing. Give us a moment and we shall share what we have with you."

Elena's heart sank. She didn't want to share anything with anyone, most importantly not with German soldiers. "We have bread and a bit of cheese and…"

"Stop talking about it. We don't want those in the other trucks to know, do we?" Anna scolded.

Maria helped Anna hand out crusts of bread and lumps of cheese. Germans and Russians shared and Elena was surprised when a whole boiled egg and a generous sized piece of bread found their way to her, the last one to receive food in the truck. No cheese, but she was grateful for the bit of food.

Part III

THE CONCENTRATION CAMP

Twenty-nine

For nine days and nights the trucks slid and plowed through muddy tracks as the slow procession wound its way across the flat countryside. From time to time they stopped to let the prisoners and their captors relieve themselves. Freidrich had found a tarpaulin the three women used as a screen. Elena and Maria slept close together in their corner near the cab, huddled for warmth on the hard wooden bench. Elena wasn't sure if the heat from the engine made this spot warmer or if she imagined it, but between them, she and Maria had convinced the others that the spot belonged to them. There had been no food for Mama to cook the past three days.

For a while, the soldiers had helped many of their comrades into the backs of trucks, but when there was no way to squeeze more in, the weakest were left behind to fend for themselves.

Remembering the chicken she had found in September, she wondered if they were the lucky ones.

They awoke on the morning of the tenth day to the smell of soot and smoke. "I smell a fire," Maria whispered as she prodded Elena to wake up. "A fire will mean food. Come along."

Elena's head bumped against the wooden railing, dislodging her cap. She pulled it off, scratched her scalp which felt alive with vermin, and then tugged the cap on again. "Let me sleep. If there is food, you can tell me. I'm tired."

She tried to curl her feet under her on the now empty bench, but the bench was too narrow. Her back ached. The baby had been still since yesterday morning, allowing Elena to sleep a little when the road was not too rough.

Elena shifted on the bench and tapped out Brahm's Lullaby on her temples in an effort to drown out the sounds of the voices outside the truck. Maria once again shook her. "You must come. It's a railroad crossing. They're giving out food. You and your baby need it. Come."

Elena let Maria help her shift out from the bed of the truck and onto the muddy ground. A chill gripped her as she stepped out into freezing rain. A crowd of gray, hunger driven soldiers huddled under a makeshift canopy. Steam and the fragrance of boiling onions and cabbage rose from the center of the canopy and spread under the canvas ceiling. Maria dragged her along the sloppy terrain until they stood at the edge of the starving mob. Slowly, persistently, Maria eased the two of them through the bodies until they emerged at the center, not three feet from the steaming cauldron of soup.

Mama had been called away to work with unfamiliar soldiers and now ladled soup into metal cups while someone else passed the welcome food to outstretched hands. Even the baby seemed to smell the food as it kicked and rolled violently in her belly. Her stomach remembered hunger and suddenly she wanted the food as desperately as the soldiers. She willingly joined Maria to inch around to the man who passed out the empty cups, and then waited impatiently to have it filled.

As she held it out toward her, she waited for Mama to say something, anything to her, but Anna ladled the soup without looking up.

The cup warmed her hands. The steam warmed her face as she closed her eyes and smiled in anticipation. A piece of carrot floated in the broth. She stuck close to Maria as they fought their way from the center of the crowd, starving people like themselves eager to reach the cauldron before the supply ran out. Broth splashed onto her gloved hand. Quickly, she brought the hand to her mouth to suck on the liquid.

"Stop, Maria. Let me drink my soup right here."

Maria paused only long enough for Elena to take a few sips, lowering the level so she wouldn't spill any more as they continued away from the group. Once free from everyone, the two of them gulped the rest of their meal.

As they finished, a soldier in a clean dark uniform pointed with his rifle, directing them to cross the railroad tracks. Elena turned, startled to see a long line of bedraggled men and women standing like passengers waiting for their train to arrive.

"Come on, Elena, that must be where we board a train. Say goodbye to Russia for a while," Maria said and Elena wondered at Maria's optimism. The object of leaving Leningrad in the first place, was to leave Russia and the war behind them. She had no intention of going back.

"A train. Luxury," Elena said. "Now, if only they have more food."

"We can only hope," Maria responded as she led her across the double set of railroad tracks.

A tall, lean officer dressed in a black uniform with gold buttons and a skull and crossbones on the hat, snapped his fingers and waved them toward him. "Name?" he demanded.

"Elena Grigoryovna Federova," she answered, her voice shaking.

"*Ach*. Colonel Hüber has told me about you and your little family. You will go stand there." He pointed toward the line which she now could see was guarded by soldiers, their bayonets attached.

"He wants us to go with them?" she asked in a weak voice.

"You go," he said as he snapped his fingers. A young soldier also dressed in black stepped up smartly and saluted. With another gesture from the officer, the younger man crowded her so she had no choice but to move.

She turned to Maria, who nodded, encouraging her. "I'll be with you in a minute."

Elena moved slowly, hesitantly toward the line. The people all looked so sad, so hungry. She didn't want to be near them.

"*Schnell!*"

Panic clutched at her heart. She jumped at the command and hurried, stopping a few feet from the end of the line. A man turned to watch her. His eyes, sunken in dark hollows, made him look like a skeleton. His teeth were too big for his face. She had no idea where these people came from, but from the appearance of the skeletal man before her, Elena was fast losing hope of finding more food.

She turned to watch for Maria. When her friend arrived, the two of them remained slightly apart from the main crowd.

The skeletal man turned and stared at her feet. His own were clad in sodden felt boots. Elena silently blessed her father for bringing home the too large army boots months ago. They now fit properly with two pairs of woolen socks.

"What's making you happy?" Maria asked.

"I'm not," she automatically responded. "What makes you think that?"

"You smiled."

"I'm not happy, but I'm glad for my boots. Where do you suppose the train will take us?"

"I have no idea, but anyplace will be better than out in the open like this. Colonel Hüber promised me we would be well treated."

"Colonel Hüber?" Elena thought about him for a moment and then shrugged. "He let me work in the infirmary with Dr. Brandt. That was good."

They both fell silent as a large group of grim-faced men and women shuffled by, herded by stern, armed guards. She continued to watch as the guards poked and prodded the prisoners until they were satisfied with the configuration of the line along the side of the railroad tracks.

"Why did you come with us? You could have gone back to your family," Elena said, not really caring about the answer, but wanting conversation, something she missed in the months at the infirmary.

"My husband was killed. My mother-in-law died. I'm tired of taking care of those two fat cows at the cottage. I stayed first for my husband, and then for his mother. I did my duty. Now, it is time to take care of Maria. I prefer to take my chances with the Germans."

"Like my father."

Maria's face clouded briefly. "Yes, like your father. But I have only myself to think of now."

"We can help each other."

"You forget, you'll soon have another being to concern yourself with. You won't be having time to worry about others."

The baby had been so quiet for the last hour that Elena had put it out of her mind. Though she'd long ago reconciled herself to the fact she'd be having a child, she still didn't want it. She sighed. The food had bolstered her for a little while, but now, once again, she wished to lie down and sleep until this war was over.

Time passed slowly as they were forced to remain on their feet, waiting in the gray, foggy day. Elena stuck close to Maria. At one point she had tried whispering but their guard turned his head and lifted his rifle.

"To speaking, no," the guard said in badly accented Russian.

The German soldiers they'd traveled with loaded the tents and tables back into the trucks, climbed in, and then the convoy bounced across the railroad tracks and disappeared into the drizzly evening.

Two cars and one truck remained along with two or three hundred sad-eyed strangers and a contingent of German guards.

"We're going to die here," Elena whispered to Maria.

"A train will come."

"*Madchen!*"

Elena turned to see who spoke.

An old man grabbed Elena's hat and pulled it off. Her blonde hair cascaded around her face. "Aha!" he shouted as he grabbed a fistful of hair and tried to pull her toward him.

She hardly had time to react when a guard stepped up and pulled him away from her and dragged him a short distance before making him walk ahead of him. When they were twenty yards away, the soldier shot him in the head. The man crumpled.

Elena watched, frozen with terror. Nobody moved to help or check on the fallen man. Elena watched the guard approach his comrade. The two men laughed briefly and then he turned to the crowd. "*Schweigen!*"

They were supposed to have left death behind in Leningrad. With trembling fingers, she bent down to retrieve her hat.

She wondered what had become of her mother since the soup line had closed and the tents taken down. Maybe Colonel Hüber intended to keep her as his personal cook and took her with them. Elena had mixed feelings about that. She hoped her mother had gone with the colonel to a place where she would be well fed so she could get better. The Mama of Leningrad grew kinder in Elena's mind as the months passed until now the old Mama was a saint. On the other hand, Mama was all she had left of family; they ought to stick together. Standing against Maria, Elena allowed her eyes to close, falling into a state of semi-sleep.

Men coughed and sneezed, their tin cups clanked against one another as Elena moved into the concert hall where the furnace ran full blast against the winter's cold and audience members silently filled the seats. What would she play tonight? Her fingers moved as if searching on their own for an appropriate piece of music.

The tremendous squeal of metal scraping on metal brought her out of her reverie. The ground beneath her feet rumbled. A locomotive, steam spewing, ashes flying, raced past followed by car after car, wheels clacking, brakes screeching. Elena joined the throng as everyone pushed back, away from the train. It seemed like it would never stop as the cars continued to pass, slowing, slowing, slowing until she recognized after the first few passenger cars, the rest were box cars filled with people. When it slid to a final halt with more clanging and chains rattling, and voices shouting from the cars, Elena felt a sense of foreboding worse than any she had experienced. Not even when Father said they would walk to Germany did she feel like this. The train loomed over her like death; then the baby squirmed and she thought briefly about life.

The guards became active, running to the last two cars to slide the doors open. Two men jumped inside the empty cars and slid out ramps. They then set up their tables at the base of the ramps, ledgers open.

A guard began calling family names from a list. Men and women responded to the name of Abramowitz, Bernstein, Levy, Rosenburg, Solomon. The names continued and the crowd beside the track dwindled as people boarded the train. Men to the last car, women in the next to last. Finally, there were only Anna, Maria and Elena left. Anna stood further down the track, a lone figure huddled in her long winter coat.

The clerk at the table glared at them. He barked an order in German. None of them understood.

Elena wondered what they should do. The train could leave without them and then they'd be stranded here with no one, no transportation, no food. Colonel Hüber and his troops had pulled out an hour ago. She marched over to the table. "Where do we go?" she asked in German.

She felt like a bug the way he glared at her over his wire rimmed spectacles.

"Full name," he replied.

"I don't understand you."

"Full name, I said!" the man at the table barked. "I am speaking to you. Full name!"

"Elena Federova from Leningrad," she answered.

He looked at her with a raised eyebrow before he flipped through the sheets of paper and then, giving up, turned to a new page. "Russian girl, you go there." He pointed at the train car. She hesitated. "Go! Now!"

She moved slowly, hoping to hear what Maria had to say, wondering how she would explain coming forward as a Federov.

"Full name."

"Maria Petrovna Federova," she heard her say in a strong voice.

"Relative of that girl?"

"She is my niece. That woman over there is my sister-in-law."

Maria is now my aunt, Elena thought as she moved slowly as possible toward the car.

"Your husband is here?"

"No. He is dead."

"Go."

Elena entered the cavernous train car that smelled of old straw and hay. And human waste. As her eyes adjusted to the darkness inside, she saw those who had entered before her standing on the straw lined floor. They were mashed together like sardines in a can.

"Come here, Anna," Maria said behind her.

Elena turned and saw her mother entering. How frail she looked now. How fragile, as if she'd break if anyone tried to touch her. Water streamed down her face, looking like tears. "Hello, Mama," Elena said uncomfortably, wishing desperately that they could be back in Leningrad before the war, before their house was bombed, before her piano was destroyed. "Will you stay with us? I think we Federov's should stick together."

Anna looked from Elena to Maria, halting, making a decision. Without speaking she shuffled toward them.

It was completely dark by the time the large doors slid shut. A chain rattled as it was pulled through the handle, followed by a solid thump. They were locked in.

The train's whistle came from far away. All those cars filled with so many people.

Men shouted along the rails outside. Then came a chain reaction of sound as the first cars began to roll. After a few minutes, their car jolted, and they were on their way.

But to where?

Thirty

Daylight poked through the cracks in the boards. The three of them clung to one another for balance as the train swayed. They'd been traveling all night and now dawn approached. Elena slept on her feet because there was no room for her or anyone to lie down.

"I need to use a toilet," she said, yawning. "What are the others doing?"

Maria looked at her as if trying to focus in the dim light. "Can't you smell what they do? You saw the bucket, didn't you? How long did they think that would last?" she spat in reference to their captors.

"We have to stop soon. We need food and they said they would take care of us." Elena shifted her weight on her feet, trying to keep her knees from buckling. During the night, she'd heard a commotion in another part of the car. One of the women had swooned and fallen. No one helped her to her feet.

If she fell, Elena wondered, would Maria and Mama help her up? She couldn't be sure. Although Mama stood with them, her face still had a pinched look of disapproval whenever her eyes landed on Elena. Maria would probably make an effort.

Elena realized if she needed to relieve herself, she had to do it where she stood. Thoroughly humiliated, she let the urine run down her legs. Relief flooded her body even as the stench of her own urine mingled with the already vile odors in the car. It was no comfort knowing Maria and her mother would have to do the same thing.

The sun heated the car to stifling, the air burned as she tried to breathe until Elena thought both she and her baby would die before they arrived at their destination.

In the early morning of what they believed was the third day, the train pulled onto a siding. No one came to unlock the doors. Everyone in the car was silent.

Elena, Maria, and Anna had worked their way to a corner of the car and huddled near a small opening in the boards where wisps of fresh air wafted in on a gentle breeze. It was hard to believe she would die that way, holding hands with her mother and friend while remembering the childhood prayers Grandma had taught her. She looked out on a green meadow where a line of trees cast long shadows. A stream reflected shards of sunlight as it bubbled its way out of sight. The entire scene misted as *Morning* from Peer Gynt floated through her head, and her fingers drummed lightly on the wall.

The baby hadn't moved for such a long time she wondered if it had died. Like those in the cattle car around her, perhaps it sensed where it would be and chose not to live. Elena placed her hand on the hard lump and pressed on it, wanting the baby to move at the same time hoping for no reaction. Would the women stack it on top of the corpses of those who had died? A tear slid down her cheek.

Unable to control her feelings, her thoughts overwhelmed her and she slid to the floor, curled in a heap, sobbing. Other women clucked in disapproval. She didn't care anymore; she would die with her unborn child. Heavy dry sobs wrenched themselves from her body. Maria stood over her like a wolf protecting its cub.

Night came and still no one came to open the door. Other women whimpered and moaned throughout the night. Elena drifted in and out of sleep as her stomach cramped. Mama slept, propped in the corner. Maria held Elena wrapped in her arms near the fresh air.

On the morning of the fourth day the doors opened. Elena watched in wonder as her fellow prisoners struggled from the car, down the ramp and into the green meadow surrounded by snow-capped mountains.

"They're saying this is Austria, Elena!" Maria said in wonder. "Who would have thought a country could be so beautiful?"

Though there were plenty of SS guards, they remained high on the hillside, watching, observing like starlings on a clothesline. Elena saw them through the opened door but couldn't bring herself move. Once there was enough space, she sank to the floor and continued to watch. The younger, healthier women tripped and staggered down to the stream that meandered in the shade of ancient trees untouched by the war. Sun glistened on the early morning dew and she wondered briefly if this was the heaven Grandma had told her about. Her mouth was dry and she craved water, but the dull, heavy ache in her back and belly gripped her. The thought of standing and then walking all the way down the ramp, across maybe fifty yards to the stream overwhelmed her.

By mid-morning Maria had fetched several cups of water for her.

"There are men at the other end of the train cleaning it. You must get out and come by the water. It's so pleasant over there. Believe me. Come with me."

Reluctantly Elena held her hand up so Maria could help her to stand up. Supported by Maria, she made it to the shade of a tree before the cramps that had begun earlier became unbearable. She let out a loud moan.

Mama sat apart in the sunshine. She never turned at the sound of Elena's distress.

One of the German women from the train separated herself from her group and approached Elena.

"I am Miriam," she began in halting Russian. She wore a heavy black overcoat, black opaque stockings, and tattered shoes. Eyes like little black dots peered at her from the shadows of her scarf.

"I speak German. What do you want with my daughter?" Anna said over her shoulder. She pushed herself to a standing position and lurched unsteadily toward them.

Why is Mama speaking so rudely to this woman, Elena thought, and why does she suddenly care what happens with me?

"I begin again. My name is Miriam. I'm a midwife in my village and came to help."

Elena looked from her to her mother.

"I see your distress. Your labor has begun, has it not? Soon you will need me."

Anna glared at Miriam as if she, Anna, were condescending to listen to one of the peasants. She then turned her head toward Elena without moving any other part of her body and translated in a sullen, dull voice. "You like Germans so much, here's one to take care of you. She's a midwife. And a Jewess." She turned to leave but Miriam stopped her with a hand on her arm.

Anna looked down at the hand and flicked it away as one would chase a fly.

Miriam said, "Please, madam, explain I am not a German. I am Polish but speak German. I will need your help for continuing translation."

Anna sniffed in disdain, but joined Elena, Maria, and the midwife under the tree.

Elena had watched this whole exchange, surprised she could understand most of what Miriam had said. She hadn't realized how much German she'd learned during her months in the infirmary. Dr. Brandt had scolded her for not paying attention. The thought of Dr. Brandt brought fresh tears to her eyes.

"More pain?" Maria asked.

"No. I was thinking of Dr. Brandt. Wouldn't it be nice if he could be here now? He has drugs for pain."

"Yes. And wouldn't it be nice if we could be in a clean room with fresh linens on the beds and icy cold water in crystal glasses, and boiled eggs and pickled beets. How about fish in aspic?"

Elena laughed in spite of the increasing pain of a fresh contraction. "At least we have the icy water," she said indicating the stream.

"Give me your clothes," Maria said suddenly as she removed her own jacket and sweater.

"What?" Elena clutched at her coat.

"You're going to have to remove them soon anyway unless you want the baby to drop into your filthy underpants. Now, hand them over!"

Elena's spine stiffened as another contraction, stronger than the others, took control of her body. "It – it won't go away. I feel like I'm going to burst."

Miriam placed a hand on Elena's belly. "It is good. Very good." She then began to untie the rope on Elena's trousers. "Almost ready."

When the contraction eased, Elena drew a deep breath. "How long is this going to go on?"

Anna spoke up from her spot on the other side of the tree. "With the devil's child, it could take days. You could die."

Elena gasped.

Miriam continued to help her remove her trousers and underclothing. When she came to the coat, Elena refused to let go.

Miriam looked puzzled.

"I'm cold," Elena complained.

Anna translated Miriam's next statement. "She says you can use the coat as a blanket to lie on. It's better it's out of the way when it's time for the delivery."

Reluctantly, Elena removed the coat. The piano bulged under her sweater. She lifted the sweater in order to unwrap the piano. Miriam watched, not understanding what the object of clothing was Elena removed. When Elena held it up, Miriam clapped her hands. "So good! Playing a piano you are!"

The last comment was made partly in German and partly in Russian, so it took Elena a moment to digest its meaning. "*Da! Yah!* I'm going to America after the war—" The next contraction seized her so suddenly it left her breathless.

Now nearly naked in the chilly mountain air, she curled on her side on the coat while the other three women surrounded her. Even her mother had stopped saying nasty things to her.

Could having this baby really kill her? Having babies wasn't a topic she and her mother or her grandmother ever talked about.

Even though she and Tatiana had talked about growing up and having babies, the concept had been abstract. Neither one of them had had any idea how it worked.

During the next few hours as the contractions increased in duration and frequency, Maria had gone to the stream and cleaned all their underclothing and laid them out in the sun to dry. Elena wished she could be cleaned and laid out in the sun as well. She wished she could be anyplace but on an Austrian mountainside having a baby.

Wagner, fierce and thunderous, roared in her head as the pain increased. Could the Valkyries lift her up and carry her away?

At one point during the long afternoon, Miriam handed her a large twig. "You bite on this stick when you can't bear it any longer. I'll tell you when it is time to push the baby out."

"My baby's dead," she gasped between ever increasing pains. "It hasn't moved in days and now it's stuck in me."

"Hush. It was resting up for this great event. Sit up and then get on your feet. You must squat like so."

Elena stared unbelieving at the little woman, who demonstrated how she wanted her to position herself. She then directed Maria to go behind Elena to support her.

"Trust me. It is the way it is done. Up you get." Maria said as she helped Miriam position Elena.

"How would you know, you never had a baby," Elena protested.

"Now breathe through your mouth," Miriam ordered while Elena gripped Maria's hand tightly, balancing herself with her other hand against a tree.

Surely, the pain couldn't go on much longer. Her body dripped with perspiration in the cool mountain air. The pains increased. Her stomach rolled. The urge to stand and the need to lie down pulled at her at the same time. She groaned and pushed as if for a bowel movement.

"Not yet. Don't push yet," the midwife cautioned in a calm voice.

"I have to!" Elena cried. "It hurts! Make it stop!"

"It will come in its time."

She hated the calm woman kneeling in front of her, looking at her private parts. What did she know?

As if reading her mind, Miriam said, "Elena, I have given birth to eleven children. I know what you're going through. Now breathe and stop pushing until I tell you. Baby will do the work."

Elena panted and gasped for breath as Maria wiped her forehead with a cool, wet cloth. The pain stopped and she relaxed. For a minute. The next pain began and built so that she clutched her belly with both hands and felt the mound increase until she thought she would burst. Maria supported her, preventing her from toppling over. And then Miriam shouted, "I see the head. It's coming. Push now. Push! Push! Push!"

Elena screamed and pushed and forgot to breathe until Miriam ordered, "Breathe! Deep breath and push again. Its head is coming now."

Her body would surely be split in two. "I can't," she groaned. And then a pain so bad, so unimaginable, tore at her. She screamed.

Miriam's voice joined hers. "It's coming. It's coming. It's almost over, Elena. Little mother. You have a baby. Keep pushing!"

Elena gasped, pressed her heels into the ground and pushed one more time. The baby slid out.

Through her own screams of agony she heard the women from the car cheering.

"A boy–no, a girl. You have a girl!"

A baby cried. Elena collapsed back onto the grass.

Once it was out and Miriam announced she'd had a girl, she believed it was over, but then a new pain wrenched her belly. "No more," she cried, exhausted. "I'm finished. This can't be another baby." She yelped as she felt a rush of hot gooey material spew from between her legs.

"This is good. Now you are finished," Miriam comforted her. "Your friend, Maria, is collecting water from the stream and then we'll wash you and your daughter. Here, have a sip from my cup."

While she talked, Miriam removed a shoestring from her own shoe and wrapped it tightly around the cord leading from the baby's stomach. Elena stared in awe, finally understanding what a belly button was. She and Tatiana had talked about belly buttons and their conclusion had been it was the special hole through which babies were born. They'd heard all the stories about storks and cabbage patches, but they weren't completely stupid; they knew babies came from the mothers' stomachs and they thought they knew how they came out. She wished she could tell Tatiana about it so Tatiana would have advance warning about giving birth.

Elena drank thirstily from the proffered cup and then collapsed back onto the grass. "Thank you. Thank you so much. Now, please, I need to sleep."

"You don't want to see your baby?" Miriam held up a bloody, naked, wailing infant.

"Oh, God. It's real. I really did it, didn't I?" She stared at the squirming infant in awe.

Maria struggled up the hill with a bucket looking suspiciously like the one from the cattle car, pulled out soaking rags and began swabbing down between Elena's legs while Miriam cleaned the squalling baby. When she was satisfied that Elena was clean and dry, she looked around and then picked up the piano.

"Leave that alone," Elena ordered.

Ignoring her, Miriam held it out as if to measure it and then slid it under Elena and wrapped it snugly around her belly, tucking it in on itself to secure it in place.

"What's that for?" Elena asked. "It's tight."

Maria answered. "It's to bind you. That's what's done after giving birth. Your piano finally has a practical use."

The baby squalled and Elena shuddered.

"She's strong, like her mother," Maria said proudly as she handed Elena a cup of water. "Rest for a little while. You are going to have to feed her soon."

"Feed her?"

Thirty-one

Miriam showed Elena how to nurse her infant. The red-faced infant suckled greedily from the start. While she leaned against a tree in the shade several women came to admire the new arrival. One woman, her front teeth broken, offered her berries.

Shocked by an obviously starving woman offering her food, she tried to reject it, but the woman insisted, pushing the berries toward Elena's mouth. "For your baby. You must eat."

"Take the damned berries," Maria ordered. "Her baby was murdered when they were taken from their village. She wants your baby to live."

Elena picked a few from the woman's hand and ate them. The sweet juice tingled as it slid down her throat. "Thank you. Now you eat some."

The woman held up a hand to protest. "I shall die. You and your child must live." She moved back a few yards and sat to watch Elena with her child.

"Why is she going to die and we're not?"

"They're Jews. They fear the Germans will either work them to death or kill them in gas chambers."

"That can't be possible." Elena stared at the woman.

"Those are the rumors."

Miriam sat smiling, as the baby nursed. Elena asked, "Is Miriam a Jew as well?"

"She is."

"Will they kill her?"

Maria shrugged. "They've been transferred from another camp. Miriam says their camp was overcrowded. She supposes if they wanted to kill them, they could have killed them there and saved themselves the trouble of transporting them to another one."

Elena didn't want to think about gas chambers or working to death. "The berries were good. Do you think we could find more?"

"I'll look. Looking at the numbers of people out here, I don't hold out much hope for finding much more to eat. You rest."

Elena slid down so she could curl up and sleep. Maria tucked the infant inside Elena's coat before she left. The baby might be outside of her but it still wriggled and disturbed her sleep.

She awoke in the twilight to see hundreds, maybe a thousand, people strewn about the meadow sleeping alone and in groups. Armed soldiers wandered singly amongst them, occasionally nudging someone with a boot. Still more soldiers remained high on the hillside sitting around a fire. A fire would be nice now.

Shifting her weight, she was startled when the baby mewled. She opened the coat and looked down. A pale white face with large black eyes stared up at her from the blackness. It hiccupped, then closed its eyes. Elena checked on a soldier walking close by, wondering if he'd been down in the copse near the stream where she, Maria and Miriam slept. There were other women by the stream as well. "Maria," she whispered to the sleeping form next to her. "Maria, wake up!"

She propped herself up on an elbow so she could reach Maria and, in the process, tipped over her metal cup. Berries spilled onto the grass. Looking around to make sure no one was ready to leap on her and claim them, she scooped a handful into her mouth and savored the texture and the tangy juice. Instead of waking Maria, she waited until she finished all the berries. After all, as the Jewish women told her, she had to live in order for her baby to live. Her stomach churned with the unfamiliar food, yet she wanted more.

A weak cry came from inside her coat. The baby wanted its turn at food. Elena sighed and tried to arrange herself so the baby could eat. She had no way of knowing if anything really came from her and filled the baby, but at least it was quiet while it nursed.

Strangely the sucking at her breast caused a tugging, pleasant sensation in her belly. She'd have to ask Miriam about that when she woke up.

Miriam had separated herself a little distance from Maria and Elena. Elena envied her her sound sleep.

Once the baby either had its fill, or tired of sucking, it went back to sleep. Elena thought for the first time that being a mother might not be so bad. You feed the baby and it sleeps.

"What are you thinking?" Maria asked.

She hadn't realized Maria was awake, she'd been lying on her back with her hands under her head. What had she been thinking? "I'm thinking it might not be so terrible to take care of it, especially once we get situated in a proper camp where we have food and a place to sleep."

"She needs a name."

"A name. I never considered a name. I was afraid it would be a boy and remind me . . ." she couldn't finish the sentence.

"Still needs a name."

"What about naming her after the woman who helped me, Miriam?" Elena suspected Miriam was also the one who delivered the berries.

"Too Jewish. Think of something else."

"It's a pretty name. Miriam."

"What about Tatiana?"

Elena didn't like to hear her best friend's name coming from Maria. It somehow felt like a betrayal of the friendship to have someone else speak of her. "You know Tatiana was my closest friend?"

"Then, what about Rebecca?"

"Where did you get Rebecca? Isn't that a Jewish name, too?"

"That was the name of the little girl in a book called *Rebecca of Sunnybrook Farm*. I read it when I was young."

"In American?"

"My mother translated it for us."

"Miriam is a good woman who believes she will die soon; what's so terrible about naming this baby for her?" Elena didn't care about either name, Tatiana or Rebecca, any more than any other name.

"Hah! I didn't know you knew about Jewish customs. They name their children after their dead relatives." Maria sat up and opened Elena's coat to peek at the baby.

"Don't wake her. She just fed and went back to sleep."

"Sounding like a little mother already!" Maria teased. "Do you think they'll ever bring us food? I'm going down to the stream. I'll bring you more water." She picked up the empty cup and looked into it.

Elena felt her face go red. She hadn't saved anything for Maria. As Maria headed down the hill toward the stream, Elena moved slowly so as not to disturb the sleeping infant and leaned against the tree. The baby wiggled, but then was quiet again. Elena breathed a sigh of relief, only then realizing that she'd dreaded the baby waking again and wanting to eat. The baby needs a name. A name. She drew her knees up, leaned her head against the tree and began to cry. "I can't, little baby. I can't do this."

"I've rinsed your cup for you. Have some water," Maria knelt down beside her. "Why are you crying now? Your baby is alive and we're in clean, fresh air."

Elena drank the spring water before answering. "I wish we could creep away. Leave this baby here and go. Look across the tracks. What do you see?"

"I see a field and further away hills. I see smoke rising as if from a factory." Maria stopped. "What do you mean, leave the baby here?"

"I'm so tired, Maria. What am I going to do with a baby? I never wanted a baby. I'm tired, so tired."

"Give her to me and you sleep. However long we'll be in this spot, we must take advantage to restore ourselves. Tatiana and I will go in search of more berries."

Elena drew the infant from the protection of her heavy coat and passed her over to Maria, who took her in both hands and held the little body close to her face. "She's precious, Elena. Precious. I shall name her both Tatiana and Rebecca. We can register her officially one day. You rest now and I'll return soon with something to eat."

Maria tucked the baby inside her own jacket and left Elena alone by the tree. Within moments Elena was fast asleep, dreaming not of her daughter but of herself in a flowing blue gown standing in a concert hall while the audience applauded.

Thirty-two

A baby cried.

Elena stirred in her sleep, shifting to ease the knot in her back. She smelled earth, damp earth. The baby continued to cry. Her breasts ached. A train whistle shrieked in the distance. She tried to move but something held her in place.

"The train is leaving without us," Maria whispered in her ear. "Baby's hungry. Turn over."

Maria slept right behind her, Anna on her other side.

"I'll go get more water while you feed her." Maria lifted Elena's shirt, placing the baby so it found the nipple and began sucking.

Elena eased back down with the baby at her side. By the time Maria returned, she was nearly back to sleep.

"Drink this. Drink as much as you can. We have no way of knowing what's going to happen next. You need lots of water for Tatiana."

The soldiers huddled on the hillside, silhouetted by the blazing fire. Elena wanted to close her eyes and be back at school, even with old Mrs. Uspenskaya scolding her when she hit a wrong key. Now other things occupied her mind. Diarrhea from all the berries kept her awake and constantly worrying about soiling herself. Every time she had to go, she also had to worry about the bleeding from having the baby. Maria and Miriam had torn her camisole into shreds and found other scraps of fabric to help stem the flow, but she was exhausted and pain rolled through her in waves, sharp, staccato, throbbing. She thought she would accept any way out even if someone told her she'd be shot in the next five minutes.

"I don't want any more water for Tatiana," she whined. "Why don't you just give her water directly from the stream?"

"Because she needs the nourishment from you, that's why." Maria's voice was harsh.

Miriam took Maria aside so Elena couldn't hear what they were saying. She glared at them, hoping to stare holes right through their backs, wishing them to disappear so she could fall back into her music. Music, soft and gentle, like lying in her featherbed at home.

When the two women returned, Maria studied her for a moment before speaking. "Miriam tells me women often act selfish and unreasonable following the birth of a child. They cry a great deal. Some even kill their babies."

"What does she know? She wasn't raped. She wasn't forced to have a baby she doesn't want. When this war is over, she and her friends can go back to their old lives. I'm stuck with a baby."

She wanted to shout at the two women, but she needed them. Maria was doing a lot to care for the baby. Maybe she would have even fed her if she could. And Miriam was so patient, working with Maria to find berries and helping her to keep clean. She took a deep breath and wiped her tears. "I'm sorry. You've both been so kind and helpful. I don't know what's going on. I'm so tired. It's as if someone has added a hundred-pound stone to my back. I don't feel like I can carry it."

Maria surprised her by grabbing her in a bear hug. "Don't be silly, we're your family now. We'll help you carry that big stone. Miriam says you'll be fine in a few days."

Elena cried again.

"Achtung!" The voice reverberated through the valley.

A truck had stopped at the top of the hill, black against the backdrop of the white mountains. The voice bellowed from a speaker on the truck.

Elena watched the soldiers spread out in a line and begin marching down the hill, herding the prisoners before them. A woman slipped and before she could recover, she was hit in the head with a rifle butt. She lay where she fell as the soldier stepped over her. The line of armed men continued their steady march as the women scrambled ahead of them.

Maria scooped up the baby and hid her inside her coat. Elena pulled herself up, trying to ignore her spinning head as she tied her clothes together. She must remain standing long enough to satisfy the guards.

"What's happening?" she asked Maria.

They were forced into a column, Elena between Maria and Anna. A stranger stood at the other end. Without Maria's support, Elena could barely hold herself upright. How long would they be made to wait? Was another train coming for them?

There were bodies left on the hillside. She saw the black spots as random musical notes. They danced on her bleary gaze as she tried to see them as a manuscript, sheet music for a familiar melody. She heard the notes in her head, but they were discordant and out of tune. She closed her eyes and leaned against Maria.

Startled by the sound of a truck's engine, she turned. It rolled slowly down the hill, through the meadow, crushing the wildflowers and anything else in its path. It didn't bother to avoid the bodies left lying on the hillside. Another truck appeared at the crest of the hill. Men climbed down from the back, not soldiers, but men wearing striped pajamas. They walked behind the truck as it too made its way down the grassy slope, though this one avoided the bodies. She could see why. The pajama clad men tossed them onto the back of the truck. Far ahead, across the stream, more trucks and more men cleaned the grassy hillside.

"Stand straight!" Maria pushed her away. "They're coming down the line, counting us. Counting us like sheep in a pen."

"Sheep in a pen wouldn't stand in lines with everyone facing in the same direction." Elena's shoulders ached. The baby in Maria's coat snuffled. Elena almost laughed when she saw the front of the coat moving, but the humor of the moment was quickly wiped away by the guards arriving at their row.

She hadn't paid any attention to how the count was done. Did the prisoners keep track of themselves? Was she number one in her line or number four? Maybe she was supposed to follow the number of the women in front. "Pay attention to what's in front of your eyes," Madame Uspenskaya had said to her so many times when she missed a note. Eyes forward, unblinking, she waited. The guard rattled off numbers in German and moved on to the next row. She breathed a sigh of relief.

The line began to walk forward once the count was completed. They trudged beside the railroad tracks toward the town where the factory chimneys loomed high over the landscape.

The baby began to cry and the Germans stopped them once more to be counted. With a guard every dozen feet or so, she couldn't imagine how anyone might have escaped. They had to stand still, no sitting, and be counted again. A group of guards moved to the side to smoke. Their voices sounded relaxed, maybe even telling jokes amongst themselves; joking when hundreds of starving prisoners stood in the bright Alpine day, getting steadily hotter as the sun climbed higher in the sky.

"You have to feed her or she won't stop crying," Maria said.

"How am I supposed to do that with the soldiers standing right there?"

Maria ignored her. "I'll pass her over. Slide her under your shirt. They didn't see anything when they did their first count. They don't recognize us as people. One sheep looks like another. Nothing will happen."

The guards moved down the line, counting again as if they'd never done it before. This time it seemed to go more quickly and they started walking again. Tatiana was once again tucked away under Maria's coat.

Toward mid-afternoon they passed through the village of Mauthausen. There was no one in the streets. The shop windows stood stark, shuttered or with their shades drawn. Once outside the village they climbed a hill along a winding, serpentine road. Above them stood a colossal granite wall, like the outer keep of a castle.

"A fortress," Maria gasped.

"A castle," Elena said, already imagining food and a bed.

Straight ahead, set into the stone were wooden doors at least twenty feet high. Above the doors hung a massive eagle clutching the Nazi emblem, a swastika. Turrets at either end of the long wall housed more guards. The structure was overwhelming. No one would create such a grand building just to house starving prisoners. The sight began to restore her faith in her father's decision.

Outside the gates they were counted again. Maria still supported her. Two women nearby collapsed. Their colleagues quickly helped them up. Looking back down the road they'd just climbed to this fortress, Elena saw a long snaking line of prisoners waiting.

"There are so many," she whispered in awe.

"Turn around. They're opening the gates." Maria nudged her to move forward.

The gates opened onto a broad empty square. The only sounds came from the boots of guards as they paced along the top of an arcade to the left. To the right a three story windowless brick wall loomed over the large central courtyard. Two old vans stood against the wall, looking like toy trucks against the massive wall.

"March!" The order was barked by an unseen guard. The prisoners shuffled in.

Though there were probably a thousand of them, they hardly filled the square.

Tears coursed down Maria's face.

"What's wrong? Look at this place; it has to be better than riding in a boxcar. They'll have food." Elena was alarmed at the tears. Maria never cried. "What is it, Maria?"

"This is the end for so many of these people. Miriam. The others." She nodded her head toward the surrounding crowds.

"What do you mean?"

"They are Jews coming from another camp. Miriam told me. She told me how they were treated there. Now that the Germans are pulling back, they're also consolidating the prisoners."

"Why are the Jews prisoners? What did they do?"

"They're Jews."

"And this is the end of them?"

"Many of them. They've heard the stories and they are sure."

Elena gazed at the women closest to them. No one appeared any more upset than she herself felt. "But they don't look frightened."

"They know they can't do anything about it. It's their fate. Some will work in the quarry or the factories and die or they will be put to death right away."

"What about us?" she asked in alarm. "Will they kill us, too?"

"We're Russians. I don't think so." Maria shrugged. "At least I haven't heard stories about Russians being murdered in prison camps."

Elena waited for her to say more. Instead, she rocked and hummed softly to the baby.

They stood and waited. After a while Elena nursed the baby and then passed her back to Maria. A metal gate banged at the far end of the yard and a line of black uniformed SS guards goose stepped in their jackboots toward the shade of the arcade. They pulled out tables and chairs along with boxes of files and ledgers. She watched in surprise as a disorganized group of men approached carrying musical instruments - two violins, a bass, a clarinet, and a trumpet. They disappeared into the shadows of the arcade and returned with chairs. One stood in front, raised a baton and they began to play. She recognized it as chamber music, but the piece was unfamiliar.

More standing, a little movement, but at least it felt like she was doing something. No matter how slowly, they had to be moving toward food and a bed. After registering, the women before her separated into new lines. Elderly women stood to one side, isolated in their black coats and scarves. Another group, a larger one, took its place along the far wall and continued to grow as the afternoon wore on.

The musicians were playing *Claire de Lune*, one of the first pieces she'd learned at school, when a guard shoved her forward and she stumbled to the table. Behind the men at the tables taking down information, stood others, some in the black uniforms, some in ordinary drab brown.

She gave her name. "Elena Grigoryovna Federova."

He rattled something too quickly for her to understand.

"He wants to know your home city," Mama spoke from behind her.

"Leningrad."

The soldier's eyebrows raised, his pen poised over the registration card on the table. He said something else.

"He doesn't believe you," Mama translated.

"I am a Russian citizen," Elena said.

A tall man in a brown uniform stepped forward and spoke to her in Russian. "Where are you from?"

"Leningrad. My family and I have come from Leningrad."

"Who is your family?"

Elena turned and pointed to her mother and Maria. "My mother and my aunt."

"What is your date of birth?" The man asked.

"Eight August nineteen twenty-eight," she lied, making herself two years older, thinking somehow it would be to her benefit.

"Religion?"

Religion? She'd never been asked that before. She glanced at her mother, but Anna wouldn't look at her. "I'm Russian Orthodox." The words felt strange coming from her lips.

"Occupation? Never mind. You are too young for . . ."

"I am a musician!" she blurted.

"A musician, indeed." He translated.

"A pianist," she added. "I could play with your orchestra."

The tall man laughed. "When we are finished with the processing, we shall see what work you will do. You are . . ." He consulted a ledger. "Three five two four. Next Russian?" He signaled to Maria.

A guard escorted her to a spot by herself in the large square. She watched as Maria went through the process and then was sent to join her.

"As long as we're here, Tatiana is officially mine," Maria told her.

Elena felt a pang, a little twitch in her heart as she looked at the infant sleeping in Maria's arms. She chose to ignore it.

Anna followed shortly after. And again they stood. The last woman left the tables. It was the men's turn.

Elena didn't object when Maria passed the baby to her for feeding. They had a smooth routine, though Elena still couldn't tell if the baby was getting any milk. Her breasts didn't feel much different after the feedings. When the baby fell asleep, she passed her back to Maria.

"You're quiet today, Elena," Maria said.

"I was listening to the orchestra. They're playing music I've never heard. I wonder how much music there is in the world that I haven't heard, yet."

"Hmm," Maria responded.

"Doesn't it bother you? To find there is so much in the world that you don't know about? Here I am, I can hardly stand my knees are so weak, but I want to see the world. I want to hear the music."

Maria gave her a wan smile. "I'll join you in seeing the world once we've had a bath, food and a night's sleep. Look, two men are coming to our little square."

Elena watched with little interest. One man, slightly taller than the other, used a crutch to limp across the yard. The other, shorter and thinner with a long, straggly beard, walked with unsteady steps beside him. "The short one looks like Rasputin. Why do you think he keeps his hands in his pockets like that?"

"Don't look at them," Maria instructed as she shifted her own position.

Elena followed suit but peeked one more time over her shoulder. She wrapped her arms around herself and listened to a new unfamiliar melody. "What is that odd, sweet smell, Maria?"

"I don't know. I've been noticing it, too. Never mind. What they want us to know, they'll do in their own good time."

"Oh my dear God is in Heaven and Jesus Christ is with us today," Anna gasped, stumbling forward, past Elena and Maria.

Elena watched in amazement as Anna threw herself at the Rasputin look-alike. Mama's cries could be heard echoing in the courtyard.

"Grisha? Is she saying Grisha?" Grisha is Papa's name. Why would she be calling that shrunken old man Grisha? Papa is dead. He has to be. Feeling faint, she grabbed onto Maria's jacket sleeve. Maria stumbled but caught herself. The jarring motion set the baby crying.

Mama half dragged the man to them. "It's Papa, Elena. Papa. Do you understand? All will be well now. He's back! He's returned to us." She fell to her knees with her arms about his legs.

The man who might be Papa pulled his left hand out of his pocket and reached up to remove the balaclava that hid half his face. Papa.

"Anna, is it really you? What has happened to our daughter? To my Little Rabbit?"

On hearing those words Elena couldn't stand it anymore. Without thinking about the guards, she rushed to her father and flung her arms around him. "Papa, Papa," she cried. "It's me, your Little Rabbit, but not so little. Oh, Papa. They took you away. I thought you were dead. We all thought you were dead."

He reached around her with his left hand and hugged her while Anna pulled herself up using his coat. "Not dead as you can plainly see. Many times I thought it might be better to be dead, but now, seeing you and your mother here, I am overwhelmed with life."

"*Achtung!* You Russians. You must stand to attention until you are given your orders to report to your barracks."

Elena slowly released her grip on her father, still not believing he was alive and with them. A few feet away from them Maria stood with the infant's muffled cries coming from under her coat. The top half of her body rocked gently forward and back, side to side.

"Who is this woman with you?" Papa asked as they formed two lines facing each other. The man with Papa stood next to him. Elena stood next to Maria.

"Papa, there is something you have to know…" she opened her mouth to warn him about Maria being the woman who'd shot him. She wanted to explain how good Maria had been to her ever since. She didn't want him to know about the baby.

"She had a baby," Anna interrupted.

She felt her heart sink.

"It was two days ago," Anna continued. "Elena has been helping her to care for it."

Why would Mama say something like that? It didn't make sense.

Grigory studied Maria's face. With dark circles under her eyes, her jacket collar turned up nearly covering her nose, Maria looked like she could be an undernourished new mother. He took a step closer and reached out with his left arm.

"Papa, what's wrong with that arm?" Elena pointed to his right arm, the hand still in the pocket. He hadn't used the arm since she'd seen him.

Distracted, he looked at her, his black, Rasputin eyes sad, as he used his left hand to pull the empty sleeve from the pocket. "Remember when I was shot? The infection? The good Doctor Brandt sent me to a field hospital."

Maria shuddered beside her.

A Samba? Could she be hearing right? The orchestra now played dance music, lively dance music. She wanted to think about the music. She'd never been permitted to play what Madame Uspenskaya called frivolous music. Of course, she remembered when Papa was shot. Maria did it. She looked at Maria to see how she'd reacted to Papa's statement. Except for the slight shudder, Maria showed no reaction, she continued to rock. The baby was quiet.

"Is it really gone? You're not fooling us and it's really in a splint under your coat?" she asked her father.

"This is no time for fooling," Anna admonished her. "Have you been in that hospital all this time?"

"Until the retreat. Then we were all sent to that railroad crossing and loaded onto the boxcar. Is that where you were also?"

"We were there," Anna said.

"And it all worked out, Papa," Elena said. "Here we are with the new baby and we survived. It was horrible. No food, no toilets. Horrible. But you were right, weren't you? Here we are in this fairytale fortress. We'll be fed and cared for until the end of the war."

"It should not be too long in coming, my Little Rabbit. It won't be such an easy time." He turned to the man beside him. "This is my friend from the field hospital. Yuri Ivanovich Kuznetsov. His left leg is made of wood." He continued with introductions that felt oddly formal in the circumstances. He paused when he reached Maria. "And you, the new mother, may we meet your baby?"

Maria hesitated a moment and then took a step closer to Grigory. She opened her coat enough for him to see the sleeping infant. "Your wife is correct, Comrade Federov, this child was born in a meadow two days ago. It's a girl and she is mine. Her name is Tatiana Federova. That is the name I have given her so that she won't bear the name of a Nazi SS ogre."

"Federova." Grigory smiled and then looked more closely at Maria. "I know you, don't I? You are the woman from the cottage! The woman who shot me!"

Elena closed her eyes. *Please don't start fighting right here in front of the Germans.*

"If you recall," Maria began in as cold a voice as Elena had ever heard in her life, "You pulled a gun first. Please don't create a scene; you must realize that your wife is unwell."

He turned to Anna. "Anna? Anna look at me."

Instead she looked at Elena. *Here we are all together and maybe we're all going to die, but still she looks at me with such hatred.* Elena wished for the last time that her mother would put her arms around her. Just one gentle hug.

Yuri Ivanovich stood red-faced a few feet away listening to the conversation.

"You're ill, Anna? Why don't you talk to me?"

Anna glared at Elena and then hid her face in Grigory's coat. "I am only happy to have you alive now, my Grisha."

The band was playing a waltz. The guards formed the largest group of prisoners into lines and marched them across the long parade ground toward massive iron doors at the far end. The doors rose up and the waltz continued as the people disappeared through the gates and out of sight. The gates slid shut.

That left two groups. The little Russian family and another sizable group of men and women who took up the space near the high wall. The larger group was formed into lines, men separated from women and then marched through the same iron gates. This time the orchestra played triumphant military tunes.

"There go the Jews," Maria said softly to Elena

"Miriam is in one of those groups."

"I'm sure she will be safe. She's smart and strong."

Thinking about the women who were separated earlier, she said, "She's old."

When the crowd had gone through the gates, the musicians put down their instruments, replaced their chairs under the arcade and walked away.

The tall soldier in the brown uniform approached Elena's group. "You will follow me to the Russian quarters."

And perhaps now, once in the Russian quarters, they, too, would get to eat. They followed the officer, Elena lost in thought about her mother's behavior about the baby, saying it was Maria's. Did her mother care for her after all? Maria must be wrong. Mama could not be out of her mind, or sick in her head. No. But then Maria claimed the baby for herself. Mama might call her a whore; Elena called her a friend.

Thirty-three

Elena, still in a state of shock at seeing her father alive, followed the guard. Her legs felt rubbery; she wondered if she was too young to die from heart failure. Instead of leading them to the large gate the others had gone through, he took them through an ordinary looking door in the right corner of the square. Before her, another huge square, but this one was lined with neat rows of buildings.

"This is where the Jews are quartered," the soldier offered.

"Where is everybody?" Elena dared ask. The officer didn't seem as rigid as the men in black uniforms, the SS.

"Many work. Many are inside waiting for the evening count."

"Slave labor," she heard Yuri mutter under his breath.

"Will we work?" She was relieved to hear the Jews would be working and not getting shot.

"You will be in the Russian sector. Your status is different than the Jews."

A Russian sector. She hoped it was as neat and tidy as this sector was for the Jews. The soldier marched on. Maria, Papa and Mama kept up with him. She and Yuri were falling behind. Blood still flowed and ran down her legs. Her head felt light, like when she stood too fast. Without thinking she grabbed on to Yuri to keep from falling. Instead, the two of them toppled to the ground.

"I'm sorry," he said.

"No, it's my fault. So long without food."

"You, too? They don't even feed women and children?" Yuri struggled to his knees and then helped Elena to her feet.

Her face burned with embarrassment at her condition. Bleeding, filthy and hungry. She held out her hand to help him up.

"You two! Come here immediately! You are not to be talking!" The officer pointed at them with a riding whip she hadn't noticed before.

"I fell. I knocked him over," she began to explain.

"You will be quiet and come here," he shouted.

"It's my fault," Yuri said quietly. He took her arm and together they rushed to catch up to the others.

Elena stumbled along the pavement, glad to have Maria's support when they reached her.

"Can you walk more slowly, please," Papa said. "You can see my family is in great distress."

"You will keep pace," the officer said, but Elena noticed he'd slowed his gait a bit. They reached another wall, another door.

The officer banged on it with his stick and it opened. After a quick flurry of words, Papa and Yuri were ordered through the door. It slammed shut. Elena watched with disbelief. She just found her father and now he was gone again.

"Where are they taking him?" she cried.

"He will be in the men's camp. You will be in the women's. Come." He walked downhill between two stone walls.

While the walking was easier, Elena still wasn't sure she'd make it all the way. This camp was enormous. They must have walked more than a mile since first entering the gate under the iron eagle. Finally he stopped and, using the handle of his riding crop, banged on another door. He stepped aside and let them enter before speaking with the guard on the inside.

"Quarantine," the guard said in fairly clear Russian. "This building. Three weeks. Tonight nothing. Tomorrow clean."

He led them to a large building and opened the door. Inside the dark room lit by a single light bulb, women with large, haunted eyes who a moment ago had been chattering amongst themselves, stopped to see who was coming in.

"Welcome," a tall, fairly large woman wearing a gray skirt, dark blue sweater and a traditional *babushka* said. "I am Svetlana, in charge of the quarantine. You will have the bunk in the back. Tomorrow many of these women will join the regular population and so you will have much luxury while you are here. That is, unless the Nazis find more of you to confine." She laughed, a fierce, grinding sound that made Elena shudder. Svetlana pointed to the other end of the long room. The room had a center aisle with a stove in the middle. The light bulbs, she saw there were actually two of them, hung between the wall and the stove. Women wearing civilian clothes lined the three-tiered bunks. No one else greeted them. They just stared in silence. Every one of them whose head she could see, had closely cropped hair. As they reached each bunk, the women in it moved slightly back as if not to be contaminated. When they arrived at the back of the room, it was clear this was a quarantine area separate from the rest of the quarantine building. Three sets of bunks were isolated by walls forming a nearly private room. No one else was in there.

"You take a bunk and supper will arrive shortly. Toilets are outside behind this building, but you must ask permission to use them. Do you have any questions?" Svetlana's expression dared them to say anything. "Good. Make yourselves comfortable."

She laughed as she returned to the front of the room. If a foot was in her way, she kicked it to the side. At the front of the room, she sat on a wooden chair, arms folded.

"Privacy," Maria said. "After these past weeks, this is like heaven."

"Are you crazy?" Mama said as she eased herself onto a bottom bunk. "At the estate I had a private room behind the kitchen where I was warm and well fed. This is not luxury."

"I like it," Elena said, taking another lower bunk for herself. She put her head down on the rag covered straw and closed her eyes. "I'm going to rest just until the food arrives. I'm happy Papa is alive." She fell asleep.

"Because we can't mix with anybody tonight," Maria was saying.

Elena shook her head. "What?"

"I've just been telling you why our food was brought to us. This Russian bulldog makes the rules for the quarantine building. She is afraid we have lice or maybe even diseases and so we're separated until we can be cleaned and examined.

"I fell asleep. What is the food?"

"Tonight we have a grand meal of bread, jam, a piece of sausage and hot tea," Maria announced. "If we continue to eat like this, we might even gain weight. In any case, it's good for Tatiana! Now come and sit up."

Elena took a piece of the black bread and dipped it in the jam then dipped both into the tin mug of tea. She held the bread in her mouth and let the tea trickle down her throat. Only then did she chew the bread and savor the taste of the sweet jam. Maria handed her a piece of sausage. The way she felt at that moment the meal could have been a holiday feast. When she'd eaten it all she licked her fingers. "Now I can truly sleep."

"First, Tatiana." Maria handed her the baby.

Elena resigned herself to feeding it, raised her shirt and let it suckle. This time when she sucked at the nipple, Elena felt a surge of fluids leaking from her breast. She looked down and saw white milk collecting around the baby's mouth. Milk. She was drinking real milk from the breast. She rested on her side and let the baby suckle. "Now I'm a real cow," she said as she put her head on the makeshift pillow and fell asleep. She couldn't think of any music for cows.

Thirty-four

"This room is for those who are obviously ill. They stay here until they get better or die," Svetlana explained as she clipped away at Mama's hair. "Usually people come in by the trainload but you three–four–are somehow special. Where did you come from?"

Elena exchanged glances with Maria who shrugged slightly. It didn't matter what they answered. "Leningrad."

"Yes, but since then?" Mama's waist length hair was now an inch long. Svetlana wrapped a towel around her neck and picked up the straight edged razor.

Elena stared, fascinated by how deft Svetlana was with the razor blade. "We were in Leningrad and then we left. In September we were in a hamlet with the Germans. Mama cooked; I worked in the infirmary after I burned my hand in the kitchen." She couldn't tell her or anyone about the rest of it.

"And you?" Svetlana said looking at Maria.

Elena waited to see how she'd explain being the colonel's mistress, spy or not.

"I was with them. I worked also."

"So, you all left Leningrad in September? Why are you here and not in Finland?" She scraped the razor across Anna's skull. The last of Anna's hair fell to the floor along with the lice.

A commotion broke out in the main part of the building. Svetlana dropped her razor into a basin, picked up her tools and headed out. "Clean up this mess. I'll finish with you two after breakfast. You will get your turn at the toilet after the others." She left.

"Breakfast! We get breakfast, too," Elena said. "It's not exactly as good as the camp, but better than Leningrad!"

Anna slapped her face. "It is not better than Leningrad. There we had family. There we knew what our daily ration would be. Here we have shaved heads and wooden pallets in a crowded bunkhouse. Here we have become attached to a bastard child of a whore. Don't tell me it is better here."

Stunned, Elena fell back onto her bunk. "Mama, in Leningrad we would be dead by now."

Anna spat, "But there would be no shame on the family."

Sitting in the shadows of the bunk, Elena looked at her mother. A small rivulet of blood ran down from the top of her bare skull and traced a path around behind her ear to disappear into the collar of her shirt. Sharp lines etched her face, deep dark canyons surrounding her nose. Her thin lips were pinched. Blue eyes, cold and unforgiving, turned away from her. There would never be any gentle hugs. She curled up in the bunk, pulled the thin cover over her chilled body and waited for breakfast.

When breakfast came, it turned out to be nothing more than a cup of tea. She had to remind herself that for days they'd had nothing, only then could she sip the hot liquid gratefully.

After breakfast, Svetlana gave them the rules as she shaved Maria's hair. When it came her turn, her eyes welled with tears. "They washed my hair only two or three days ago," she pleaded. "I don't have any lice." But while she spoke, she could feel a traitor crawling on her scalp. Reluctantly, with no other choice, she took her place in the chair.

"When we're finished here, you'll go to the latrine in the back and then we'll go to the showers. There you will wash your clothing. You have brought nothing else with you, so we will find other clothes. When the other prisoners are moved to regular housing, you can shift into the main part of the building. Now quickly, the latrine and then the morning count." Svetlana removed her apron, picked up her tools and left.

Halfway down the main room she stopped and looked back. Elena took the lead and followed Svetlana. The women in the main room stopped talking and stared as they marched through the aisle between the bunks.

Elena wanted to talk with them, to find out where they'd come from, how they got to be prisoners. Were they in Germany on purpose? Were they fighting in the war and captured? They didn't wear pajamas like the musicians had worn; they were in ordinary street clothes.

The latrines stank as badly as the toilet in the basement at home. Except the basement at home only held her own family's waste. She gagged when she entered but finished quickly and rushed out.

Shrill whistles sounded throughout the camp and women swarmed from the barracks into the central court to line up for counting. It was eerie, except for the sounds of shuffling feet, done in complete silence. Five hundred women lined up in units in front of their barracks. They were counted once, twice, and a third time. When their captors were finally satisfied no one had run away during the night, they were excused. Most of the women left for assigned jobs. The women who had been in the main room of the quarantine hut paraded off behind a German guard—Elena guessed to new barracks.

"You three, follow me!"

Svetlana marched them to a large bathhouse where they were to shower.

"You remove all clothing and shower. I bring you new, and then you'll wash your old things and so have two sets of clothing. You." She pointed to Elena,

"Yes, ma'am?" Elena wondered what she could do with her piano. She couldn't wash it.

"Do you want to continue wearing those ugly boy pants? I can bring you two dresses if you like."

Instantly on edge, Elena worried now what the price would be. There was nothing about Svetlana to indicate either a kind or generous nature.

Elena slowly unbuttoned her shirt. "It would be nice. Thank you very much." She turned her back as she removed the shirt. She glanced over her shoulder to see if Svetlana was paying attention. Svetlana leaned against the doorpost studying her fingernails. Unwrapping the piano, Elena carefully placed it on the shelf next to the baby. With her back to everyone she removed her underpants. With no towel to cover herself she stepped into the white tiled shower room, chose a shower head at the far end, and stood under it searching for a faucet.

"You wait until the others are ready and then I turn it on," Svetlana said.

Keeping her eyes forward she sensed rather than saw Maria and Anna take their places. Svetlana came in to hand them each a small piece of brown lye soap. "You scrub all over with this. I'll give you the towels and clothes when you are finished." Svetlana stepped out and almost instantly a blast of cold water surged over them. Elena shuddered and gasped. She quickly scrubbed her bald head, the soap stinging where her scalp had been scraped, and then worked her way down her shivering body. She couldn't count her ribs as easily as she had in Leningrad. Tiny red bites covered much of her body. She hoped this brown soap would kill the lice. She wondered how thin her mother had become, but shame kept her from glancing over at Anna. Maria had squealed at the blast of cold water, but now she hummed, sounding happy to be soaping and rinsing.

Elena stepped out of the shower shivering with cold. The baby cried and at that signal, her breasts began leaking. Still naked, she picked up the baby to feed it. She sat on a bench as it suckled for a few minutes from each breast and then went back to sleep. Elena returned her to the shelf, setting the rolled-up piano as a barrier to keep her from falling, although at three weeks, it didn't seem likely.

Mama and Anna remained in the chilling shower until Svetlana returned to turn off the water. She'd brought a bundle of clothing and a sack of shoes. Unlocking a cupboard, she tossed them each a small threadbare towel. "Dry yourselves. Then I spray you and then you can choose clothing. You'll be responsible for this clothing for the time you're here."

Spray us? Elena rubbed herself with the towel.

"Face me."

The three of them lined up and Svetlana brought out a Flit gun. Pumping the handle, she walked around each woman forcing a spray of foul-smelling powder over their heads, backs, and every crevice of their bodies. "Now you can dress."

Elena poked among the clothing and then chose a long woolen skirt and a white cotton blouse. While trying them on, she had a sudden urge to laugh. Maria stopped in the middle of dressing. "What's funny?"

"I am imagining what my friend, Tatiana, would have said seeing me with a bald head wearing these clothes with my heavy boots."

"They're clothes of dead people!" Anna buttoned a gray sweater. "Show a little respect." She turned to Svetlana. "Excuse me, Comrade Svetlana, but if I take a pair of leather shoes may I still keep my *valenki*?"

"Those filthy felt boots? Of course you can keep them. Give them to me and I'll de-louse them. What is that rag by the baby? It must be washed and disinfected also."

"It's not a rag," Elena answered, jumping to grab the piano before Svetlana could get to it. The action startled the baby, but Maria picked her up and held her over her shoulder, patting her on the back. The baby let out a burp making Maria laugh.

Svetlana sprayed the boots and then held her hand out for the piano. "Give me the rag."

"It's my piano. What are you going to do with it?" Elena held it close to her chest.

Svetlana's lips curled in a smirk. "This is your piano? Why don't you play a song for us?"

"Go on, play your piano," Mama said, her voice full of sarcasm. "Show her how you're going to be a famous piano player in America. Make your father proud."

Elena wished she could disappear beneath the floor. Why was Mama so ugly to her, so ugly about her piano? She and Grandma had made it with their own hands.

Svetlana stood with her arms crossed, waiting; Maria silently patted the baby; Mama had picked out a scarf and was tying it around her head. Elena held one end of the fabric and let the piano unroll onto the bench. Svetlana swooped in with her Flit gun and began pumping the powder over the keyboard. She laughed as the white powder coated the fabric.

"Turn it over."

Elena obeyed, praying she wouldn't now have to wash the piano.

"Comrade Svetlana," Mama said, "If we are to spend three weeks together, I wonder if you know how to play cards?"

"No cards, but I have backgammon."

Mama walked out of the building with Svetlana only turning back to say, "Elena, be a good girl and wash your mama's clothes."

Elena stood with her mouth agape.

"Don't mind her," Maria said. "She's like my mother-in-law. One minute she was kind, the next she was so terrified of losing everything she became mean and selfish. It's the war."

Elena sat on a bench and pulled on a pair of almost white socks. "I don't think it's the war, Maria. I think it's her life."

Maria shrugged into a pale blue dress with a white collar. Even with her bald head she could have been a film star. "We'd better hurry. I don't think Svetlana is happy about having to shepherd the three of us around as if we were important bureaucrats."

"First we have to wash the clothes." Elena gathered their old rags and threw them into a large tub by the wall.

Thirty-five

While Elena washed the clothes and Maria sang lullabies to the baby, Anna and Svetlana sat outside the washroom on wooden crates exchanging views on the German language. When she finished, her own new clothing thoroughly soaked, she carried the laundry outside. Svetlana led them back to the quarantine unit where they all helped drape the wet laundry over a clothesline strung across the room.

"The stove dries it quickly," Svetlana advised. "Now, you see, the men have cleaned this section to make it ready for another batch of prisoners. You can choose to sleep near the stove if you like. As you have seen, the nights are still cold."

"Now, what happens for three weeks?" Elena asked as Svetlana handed her a scarf to tie around her head. The warm stove felt good.

Svetlana shrugged and laughed. "Your hair grows a little. You eat. You sleep. You march out for counting three or more times a day. That's it. Your mama and I will play backgammon. She is helping me with my German and I'm trying help her to understand the life here."

"What's there to understand?" Maria asked while settling the baby in a nest of thin blankets on the lower bunk nearest the stove. "We're prisoners; you're a guard."

"I'm no guard. Not even a kapo[2]. The Germans leave us mostly on our own. They are convinced Communists are good

---

[2] A kapo was a prisoner who worked inside a German Nazi concentration camp during World War II in certain lower administrative positions. The official Nazi word was *Funktionshäftling*, or "prisoner functionary", but the Nazis commonly referred to them as kapos.

organizers. I was elected leader when we first arrived and have remained here in quarantine ever since. It's not good, but it's not so bad."

"Elected?" Elena found Svetlana too unbelievable.

"That's right. When you get to your barracks there will be an elected leader there also. We have meetings three times a week amongst ourselves, and one with a German liaison officer on Monday."

Elena shook her head, still disbelieving.

"Now you must be counted before lunch. You'll be alone today. All the other quarantine prisoners have gone on to regular barracks."

Maria raised a hand like a schoolgirl asking permission to speak. "May I leave Tatiana here? She's sleeping so soundly."

"No. Everyone must be counted."

"Please let her sleep. She's only just been born..."

"Stand up. Get ready to march out for counting!" Svetlana's face turned red as she pointed at the entrance.

"I didn't mean to upset you..."

Svetlana lunged toward Maria and grabbed her white collar in both hands. Elena flinched and took several steps back, bumping into a bunk. She caught herself and then held her breath to see what Svetlana would do next.

"Do you know," she said, her face only inches from Maria's, "Who runs this camp? Do you know?"

Maria shook her head.

"The SS Death's Head Squads. The worst of the Germans. The Jews, the Spaniards, they all have kapos in control of their units. We're fortunate here to be allowed to choose our own overseers. If we don't follow every rule, we will be executed. Just like that!" She snapped her fingers. "They will begin with the youngest, least able to work. Do you understand?" She let go of Maria so quickly Maria stumbled backward into Elena.

Elena scooped up the baby and handed her to Maria. Without a word, they all marched out for their pre-lunch count.

A reasonably thick potato soup served as lunch along with another cup of tea. Afterward Elena fed the baby, passed her back to Maria, and then settled in on her bunk for a nap until time for the evening count.

During the next two weeks Elena had time to recover from the birth, feeling stronger every day as they ate, never enough, but regularly. The skin rashes from the vermin disappeared. She played her piano when she could, lost in the worlds of Scheherazade, Romeo and Juliet, and old peasant Russia. The baby thrived. Maria scavenged for cloth to use for the baby's diapers and blankets.

Toward the end of the third week, Svetlana wakened them with, "Gather your things, you are being transferred to the main camp. We have more guests arriving." She laughed.

Thirty-six

With her piano rolled neatly around the few pieces of clothing Svetlana had provided, Elena stood in a formation with Maria and Anna, waiting to be transferred to her new quarters. Maria had created a sling for the baby who slept quietly.

After the morning count, they were ordered to remain on the parade ground to await further orders. Svetlana turned her back on them to instruct two male prisoners how to clean up the barracks for the incoming women.

Elena held her face up to the sun, savoring its warmth. A fly buzzed near her head. Her fingers began moving to "The Flight of the Bumblebee." She liked Rimsky-Korsakoff, mainly because he was Russian, but also because of the challenge he provided, but then all the composers were challenging. "L'Isle Joyeuse" by Debussy had taken many tedious hours, even with her school version of the music, before Madame accepted it and let her move on. Maybe after she finished the Bumblebee, she'd try that one again.

Mama thumped Elena on the back of her head when the German came for them. This one held a dog on a lead. When Mama had struck Elena, the dog's hackles rose. It snarled at Anna, prancing and pulling at its lead. The German ordered it to be still; it obeyed instantly.

They followed the guard and his dog across the empty parade ground, passing building after building until they came to the last one.

He continued beyond to a gate in the wall she hadn't noticed before. It sprung open when he tapped a signal. After a brief exchange he stepped aside and pointed, "*Hier.*" He handed them over to another guard. "*Heil Hitler,*" the guards saluted one another before the gate closed.

The new guard, also in the black SS uniform, shoved Elena with the butt of his rifle. She stumbled, caught her footing, and walked hesitantly into the compound. Instead of pristine brick barrack buildings, this compound housed two rows of wooden huts, appearing half-heartedly hammered together. The guard continued to shove her until she felt like turning on him. Instead she reminded herself to take one step at a time, to follow his instructions. She didn't want to be shot after all their efforts to get to Germany in the first place. And now that Papa was alive, she felt more confident than ever she would make it to America and be able to play her piano at Carnegie Hall.

About two thirds of the way down the row, six maybe seven huts, she'd lost count, he pulled her right shoulder which turned her toward a doorway and then he gave her yet another shove, this time hitting her in the left kidney, sending her sprawling to the ground.

Sharp pain shot through her entire body. With the wind knocked out of her and the pain in her side, she remained on the ground, hoping for Maria or her mother to help her up.

He shouted at her in German. "Get up, Russian whore!"

Gasping for air, she tried to collect herself to push up. Apparently, she was too slow. He kicked her in the ribs. "Up! Now!"

She closed her eyes and remembered Grandma in their basement home as she handed her the fabric piano. "There is a God, child, and He will not give you any more than you can handle. You must assume the responsibility to be what he intended. Whatever happens, you must concentrate on your music. Think of the music, Elena."

"The music," she said. Before he could strike again, she heaved herself to her feet and stumbled into the room clutching her piano to her chest.

No Svetlana greeted her. The long narrow room was like the one they'd vacated, but far smaller. It stank of too many unwashed bodies in too small a space. She waited until her eyes adjusted to the darkness and then moved along the rows of bunks in search of an empty one.

The three of them, left to their own devices, searched but found no bunk completely free of personal possessions. The pain in her back and side forced her to quit looking. She sat on an upended crate, one of several surrounding a cold stove.

"We wait until everyone returns from their work," Maria said. "Feed Tatiana while it's quiet." She passed the baby to Elena. "Are you all right?"

Elena nodded. "We'll have to work, won't we?"

"Would you rather sit in this room with nothing to do? I'm ready to work," Maria said. "I thought I'd go mad in quarantine. I hear they are creating an arms factory here. Maybe I can sabotage bomb parts."

"Don't even make a joke about such a thing," Anna criticized. "If you work in a factory, you do your best work, no matter what or who it's for."

"So they can kill more Russians? I won't. I wonder if the Geneva Convention allows us to refuse to work."

"I wouldn't want to test the Geneva Convention right now," Elena chimed in. She placed the baby on her shoulder, sending a spasm of pain down her side. She winced but continued patting its back until it burped. She then handed it back to Maria.

Maria placed the baby in her sling. "This is one person who isn't going to starve while we're here, right my little Tatiana?"

Elena watched Maria with the baby, her eyes tearing for no reason she could explain. "Someday Tatiana will be proud to call you Mama."

Anna sneered. "And who would want a German bastard to be proud of her?"

Elena suspected if Maria hadn't been holding the baby at that moment, she would have attacked Anna. Instead, Maria turned her back and rocked the baby to sleep. The fierceness with which she rocked made Elena seasick. She wondered what it was doing to the baby.

As the sun lowered behind the mountains, women returned from their jobs. They chattered and squabbled like a gaggle of agitated geese. The three of them stood aside while the workers found their bunks and flung their bodies down. Two or three women to each bunk on all three levels. Elena looked around the room, watching for a bunk with an empty space. She couldn't detect one. All she wanted to do was to lie down and sleep away the pains in her body.

"So, you are the new ones. I understand you're special." The fittest appearing woman of the group approached them. "I am the head of this building. Agrafina Mikhailovna Zosimoffna. When everyone is settled, we'll find your place."

"What do you mean by saying we're special?" Anna said.

"You walked into captivity yourselves. We have just three spaces. I will move the others about so you can be together, that is, if you want to be together."

Although Svetlana had never asked for any favors in return for being reasonably kind, this one had a mean look about her. She had a jowly, ruddy face with a permanent scowl mark between her heavy brows.

"We do want to be together, if it's possible," Elena spoke up, concerned because she needed to be near Maria and the baby.

Agrafina Mikhailovna smiled exposing her crooked, broken teeth. "That's settled then. For one week, you will give the women who are to be displaced one half of your bread allowance. Follow me." She lumbered down the long aisle toward the rear of the building, stopping about two thirds of the way back and then turned back to them. "Top or bottom or middle bunk?"

"What will that cost us?" Elena asked, almost afraid to hear the answer.

"One half of your soup from lunch."

That's what made her the healthiest in the place. She made sure she was the only well-fed person. Elena looked at Maria and Mama. Neither one of them said a word.

"One third," Elena said.

"Elena…" Mama began.

"One third. We need food for the baby."

Agrafina folded her arms and smirked. "So, we have a little hooligan in our midst." She reached out a beefy hand and before

Elena could react, slapped her heartily on the shoulder. "One third it is."

"The bottom bunk," Elena said.

Agrafina gave orders to the three women who sat glaring on the lower bunk. None of them said a word, but by their looks, Elena knew they hadn't made friends of them. The displaced women picked up their few possessions and moved to the bunks assigned to them. Their possessions included the blankets.

"How much for the blankets?" Maria asked.

"Blankets are free," Agrafina laughed. "We can't have you starve and freeze to death. I will bring them before lights out. Now you must prepare to go out to be counted. After that, supper, and then lights out. Work tomorrow."

They lined up for the interminable counting. Elena was hungry and questioning her judgment about giving up half their bread to be together, but she couldn't think of any other way the baby could be fed without disrupting everyone unless they were together.

"You were smart to jump in like that," Maria said as they waited for the whistle to silence them so the counting could begin.

"I hope I didn't make enemies of the women who had to move."

"Why should they be angry? They'll have extra bread for a full week."

"Do you believe Agrafina Mikhailovna really gives it all to them? They didn't look so pleased about it."

The whistle blew and everyone stood to attention in straight lines.

The officer in charge took note of the four new residents of his compound. Elena watched his expression as Agrafina reported to him. His eyes moved back and forth between Agrafina and them as they spoke. A slap of his crop against his boot indicated the end of the conversation. Agrafina took her place at the front of their formation.

Almost as quickly as they returned to their bunks, the food arrived. No one jumped up or swarmed the large pot of sausages and boxes of bread. Elena watched as the women in the first row of bunks carried their metal plates and cups to Agrafina and the young German who had remained to help serve. She passed out precisely measured portions of food to everyone, not forgetting when Elena and her family arrived, to give them half a ration of bread. The German youth raised his eyebrows a fraction but didn't say anything. Elena had forgotten which of the women were the displaced ones so she couldn't tell if they received their extra portions.

That night, the three of them slept in the lower bunk, huddled together for warmth. The baby slept between Maria and Elena. Anna slept on the far side, away from Elena.

Her first night in the overcrowded room left her miserable the next morning. Between the coughing, snoring, moans, and groans, and then feeding the baby, she felt she hadn't slept at all. Her ribs and back hurt worse than the night before. Her eyes were gritty when the morning tea arrived.

"A treat today. Strawberry jam for the tea," Elena looked over to see who had spoken. A young woman with thick brown shoulder length hair sat on the neighboring bunk smiling at her. "We get that every Sunday."

"We had jam some nights with our bread when we were in quarantine," Elena told her.

"Couple of times a week. We get that. I'm Lydia," she said. She rested her head against the back of the bunk. "Count, work, count, eat, count, sleep. Someone ought to write a poem."

"I'm Elena. Nobody's told me what work I'll be doing."

Lydia snickered. "Don't worry and don't ask. Be sure they'll be here soon enough to tell you."

"What do you do?"

"I make rifle barrels, at least that's what they look like. We work in an underground factory. It's noisy." She yawned. "At least it's not in the quarry where the men work. Lifting heavy stones day after day until they drop."

"Drop?"

"Dead. They work them until they die. Then they bring in more to replace them. They don't feed them enough to keep them alive; only enough to pretend they're feeding them in case the Red Cross should come for a visit."

"But why? That doesn't make any sense. If they want the men to continue working, they must feed them. That's the way they did the ration cards at home; the factory workers had more food than those who did nothing."

"But here, they don't care if the men die. There are always more to take their places and that makes more food for us."

"That's not right." Elena couldn't believe what she was hearing.

Lydia shrugged. "They're Jews mostly. The Germans are trying to rid the world of all the Jews. Do you have any cigarettes?"

Elena shook her head. "My father only has one arm. He wouldn't be able to work in a quarry."

"Be sure they'll find something for him to do. What regiment was he with?"

Elena paused. Regiment? Ah, Lydia thinks Papa was injured in battle. "No, he wasn't in combat. He was the supervisor at the shoe factory. My friend – aunt – shot him. Accidentally."

Lydia raised herself enough to look at Maria who sipped her tea pretending not to listen to the conversation. "You have a lovely baby."

Elena opened her mouth to respond when she remembered Maria was the one who'd claimed it and registered it with the camp authorities. She watched Maria's eyes light up with pride. "She is a beautiful baby and someday she'll make her Mama proud."

"This tea is so much better with the jam. You could almost feel like you're at home, couldn't you?" Elena said to Lydia.

"Not likely. Of course, I don't know what your home was like, but even in our village we had bread and eggs and sausages and *blini*." She stopped as she became lost in her reminisces.

"Our housekeeper made the best bread and cookies in the whole world." Elena let the preserves roll around in her mouth before swallowing.

"My grandmother made sausages from our own pigs. There's nothing better in the world than a grandmother's homemade sausages. No butcher shops for us. My mother and grandmother grew all our own vegetables. We had chickens and cows." Lydia now had her hands behind her head.

Elena sighed.

"Time for counting. Everybody out. Now!"

Maria picked up Tatiana. Elena followed her out onto the parade ground. Count. Count. And count again. Once the guards were again satisfied no one had either escaped or snuck into the camp overnight, the guard who had kicked her stepped forward.

"We have work for thirty women."

No one moved. Elena whispered to Maria, "Should we do something? Step forward?"

Lydia, who stood directly behind Elena, hissed at her. "Hush. Never, never volunteer in this place. You don't know if this is for real work or for medical experiments or for gassing. Look at the ground."

When no one stepped forward, the guard paced in front of them for a moment, his eyes searching amongst the women. He then began pointing. "You! You! You!" he commanded as he walked along the front of the lines.

"Whatever happens, I pray we're together." Elena closed her eyes and took Maria's hand.

"Me, too."

Thirty-seven

Thirty women, including Elena, Maria, and Lydia, but not Mama, followed a guard all the way to the main square. Mama had gone on to her regular job in the factory. Elena pulled her coat more snugly against the chill morning air, dreading and curious at the same time about their destination. Her ribs sent a jolt of pain through her body with every step.

The guard stopped at a parked truck. The driver, a grizzled old man, appeared to be asleep behind the wheel.

"Everyone in the truck," the guard ordered.

Slowly, reluctantly, they helped one another into the back of the truck. Elena held the baby while Maria climbed aboard, then passed her up. While trying to scramble aboard, a pain shot through her ribs. "I – I can't breathe," she gasped.

"Don't let them see you like this. Give me your hand," Lydia said. She reached down along with Maria to pull her up and packed her in the crowd.

There were no seats. The crush of standing bodies supported those in the middle. Those at the edge rested their arms on the wood slats that made up the walls of the truck bed.

Once in with the rest of the prisoners, Lydia said, "They execute the sick. Don't ever let them know anything is wrong with you."

"They can't do that," Elena said.

"They have the guns."

Billows of smoke puffed out of the exhaust as the engine roared to life. Elena and Lydia stood on either side of Maria to protect Tatiana from the jostling crowd. The truck rumbled down the hill they'd climbed barely a month ago. As it crossed the railroad tracks, Elena's eyes scanned the landscape for the spot where the baby had been born, but she couldn't tell one tree from another. They turned off the main road and bounced and swayed up a dirt path to a broad valley.

"They could be taking us to one of their sub-camps. I've heard there are two or three of them because ours is overcrowded," Lydia said.

"I don't see anything that looks like a camp. There. Look at that charming old farmhouse!" Elena was cheered by the sight of the house with its gingerbread decorations. Her eyes glistened as she absorbed the sight of the colors: bright yellows, red, green. They looked horribly gaudy, like a gypsy's wagon, but still, somehow, pleasing.

To her astonishment, the truck pulled up the lane, rolled past the house, and stopped several yards beyond it. A farmer dressed in a plaid flannel shirt, overalls, and high rubber boots, came from a barn behind the house. He and the driver removed the tail gate and helped the women down. The German guard riding in the cab stayed in place.

When it was Elena's turn, she held out her hand to avoid having the farmer lift her down bodily as he had the other women. In spite of her caution, the leap to the ground shot another spasm of pain through her. The farmer and the driver stepped back and allowed her to find her own way to the line of women who awaited further instructions.

"Don't be so trusting, Elena," Lydia whispered.

"What do you mean?"

"It shows on your face. You look happy to be here. Remember, to them we're slave labor. For me, I'm delighted to be outdoors in the sunshine, but I won't ever let them know it."

The women milled about waiting in a loosely formed line murmuring amongst themselves about what would come next. Dozens of chickens scratched in the dirt around the farmyard. A young, towheaded boy led a herd of cows from the barn into a fenced lane and headed upward toward a meadow. A horse whinnied.

"Your attention!"

They fell quiet and looked toward the voice.

It was the farmer who spoke. "I have contracted with the government for your services," he began. "You'll work here until the middle of September. If you cause no trouble you will be permitted to continue your work here. My wife and I will be supervising. Right now I need ten of you to follow my wife to the orchard. There she will explain what to do."

No one moved. The farmer, a hearty fellow with a ruddy complexion placed his hands on his hips and tilted his head sideways, looking perplexed.

"Come along. No one is going to bite you. You just go with Frau Zimmer and she will show you. You can have a drink of water from the stream over there."

Three women took hesitant steps forward. The farmer smiled. "Good. Now, seven more. Did you ever want to climb into an apple tree? This will be good work."

Two more joined the others.

The farmer shook his head and then approached the group. The women nearest him flinched as he held out a welcoming arm. "Go. You go there." After he chose five more women the group followed Frau Zimmer toward the orchard.

"The rest of you will work in the garden. There is much work to catch up on. Since the Army has taken my sons, Frau Zimmer and I have struggled to keep up with our quotas alone. But now with your help, we will all be able to eat." He began walking as he spoke.

"Come on," Elena said. "We're going to work in a garden. How difficult can that be?"

"How old are you?" Lydia said as she grabbed her arm to stop her.

"I told them I'm sixteen. I didn't want to be separated as a child."

Lydia shook her head. Her straight brown hair had been tied back, giving her the illusion of a young housewife. "Sixteen. What are you really? Twelve?" She smiled.

"Almost fifteen." Elena didn't know what Lydia was getting at, but she didn't like it. Shrugging free of her grasp, Elena started out to follow the farmer.

On seeing her take the lead, the rest of the women followed. Maria caught up with her. "Remember, we need to stick together for Tatiana."

"Ah, yes. Tatiana." Elena ignored the pain in her side and hobbled forward.

They stopped by a large, fenced patch of ground, bare of any plants. "You start here," the farmer pointed to four women. 'Use the hoe to make furrows."

When no one appeared to understand him, he demonstrated then passed the hoe to one of the women. He left three women at the next patch weeding between cucumber plants and then led Maria, Elena, and Lydia to another bare patch.

"With the potatoes, we are late this year. I show you. You plant."

Maria and Lydia appointed Elena be the one to carry and drop the seed potatoes into the furrows Maria created, while Lydia moved behind them to cover them with soil. Elena wouldn't hurt her back further by bending or crawling on the ground.

At first the sun felt good, but toward noon, Elena found herself tiring and perspiring from the heat. The three of them began taking turns to refresh themselves at the stream without being stopped. They could not decide if the farmer was too busy to worry about them or if he was kind and didn't mind them getting drinks at random.

At lunch, Frau Zimmer gave them chicken with dumplings, a meal such as they could never imagine having again. Frau Zimmer explained quietly to the prisoners that the German contract said they didn't have to feed them because they brought their own lunch, but when she saw their small lumps of bread, she couldn't help herself. "I have fed all my boys from this farm; I can feed a few women." The portions were small but felt like a huge feast to Elena. After lunch they were invited to rest in the shade of the orchard by the stream for twenty minutes.

"Did I upset you earlier?" Lydia asked as they rested under an apple tree after lunch.

"Why?"

"When I asked your age, you seemed offended. You're lucky to be chosen for this work before the men in charge of the brothel came around."

"What are you talking about?"

"For the convenience of the German officers. A brothel."

"What's my age got to do with it?"

"As horrible as they are, they seem to have areas of morality. They don't use young girls for the brothels. Had you said you were fourteen, you would have been safe."

Elena sighed. Tatiana nursed comfortably at her breast. "It seems like I'm safe now. We're here working on the farm."

"Of course," Lydia said. "I'm going to rest for a few minutes before we have to go back to work. How's your back?"

"It's my ribs mostly. I'll be all right." Elena closed her eyes and listened to the hum of bees and the distant chatter of the other women.

The summer passed far too quickly. Elena's ribs healed and her strength returned. Although they worked long hours, she learned to enjoy the labor, the friendly hausfrau's dumplings and noodles, and mostly the fresh air and sunshine. They worked until the middle of September when the farmer said he didn't need them any longer. He dismissed them with a "fond hope" they would be back in the spring. During the summer Elena had avoided everyone except Maria and Lydia, now a fast friend. Each evening between their meager supper and lights out, Elena played the piano, her fingers happily dancing over the keyboard as she hummed the melodies. The women enjoyed her playing.

In late September Olga Andreeva received a package from family members in the United States. She offered a piece of her candy to Elena as payment for "those brief moments of joy you bring into my life." Elena felt like she could survive this kind imprisonment as long as it didn't last forever.

Tatiana grew. By September she had enough hair to tie a ribbon in a sparse top-not and could hold herself upright with a little support. Though Elena watched anxiously for evidence, nothing about her reminded her of the baby's father. Tatiana's bright blue eyes reminded her of Grandma.

Anna had been working in the underground munitions factory. By September, her skin and hair had turned as gray as the gathering fall sky. If Elena didn't know her mother was only forty-one years old, she would have put her age closer to sixty, or maybe even seventy.

Elena's hair grew into a short blonde curly mess which Lydia and Maria told her was a flattering look. "When you get to Carnegie Hall, that is the way you should wear it," Lydia teased.

Thirty-eight

In September of 1943, one year since leaving her home in Leningrad, Elena and Maria were assigned to work in the aircraft assembly plant. Lydia was sent to the munitions factory with Mama. The days were shorter, the nights colder. When prisoners died, the women collected their clothing to protect themselves in the oncoming winter.

As Tatiana thrived, Elena grew thin.

"I think we should begin feeding Tatiana soup. We can soak the bread in it for her. At least for supper. You need to keep up your strength," Maria said one night as they lay in bed, Elena holding the baby to her breast. Mama already slept soundly on the other side of her.

"She's too young," Elena whispered, not wanting to wake her mother.

"She's almost six months old. She can have cow's milk and cereal and mashed vegetables."

"Where do you think we'll find those?"

"We can soak the bread in the broth for her. She already teethes on the stale bread. She would get more nourishment from the stale bread than she's getting from you right now."

"How would you know, you've never been a mother." Elena closed her shirt and tucked the baby between her and Maria.

"Neither have you," Maria said. She pulled Tatiana to her and snuggled down with the cooing infant.

Elena felt her face turn red. "I know. I'm just the cow who gives the milk. You're the mother. Do what you want." She didn't understand why her eyes stung with tears as she stretched out in an effort to get comfortable.

"Shut up and be still. I have to work in the morning," Anna said.

Elena lay back and folded her hands over her chest as if she was in her coffin. Tears slid down the sides of her face. *I'm not hungry. I'm not sad. I'm not weary. I'll be still and get up in the morning and drink my tea.* Her mind drifted to "Little Bells," the saddest Russian folk song she'd ever heard. The music came alive in her head, as vivid as the time she'd heard it in a church with her grandmother so long ago. A lifetime ago. The baby twitched in its sleep next to her. Elena's hand reached out, she turned and fell asleep holding Tatiana in her arms.

Each morning after the roll call, throughout the bitterly cold winter, they climbed into the back of a truck which took them to the tunnel where Elena and Maria assembled airplane parts. Maria claimed for every ten screws she tightened properly, she left one unnoticeably loose. "It probably won't make much difference," she told Elena, "but I feel better knowing I've done a little something for Mother Russia."

Elena didn't have the nerve when Maria suggested she do the same. "Who would feed Tatiana if I were caught?"

"As if you cared." Maria said.

Elena shrugged, ignoring the implied insult. "Someone has to do it. I'm the only one who can."

Over the noise of the machinery, Elena heard Maria humming "Kalinka Malinka," an old Russian folk song. Though the words spoke of junipers and raspberries, in the end the singer asks for love. Elena joined her and sang the words as well.

Soon the women working nearby also joined in. Pretty soon they were dancing at their workstations, bodies swaying, toes tapping. A young woman down the line climbed onto her workbench at the part where the long "Ahhh" precedes the chorus. She had a good, strong voice clearly heard over the noise of the machinery.

Women dropped their rivet guns and tools to applaud. A stronger voice hailed from the back of the tunnel. Though in German, there was no question what he said. The applause stopped as everyone turned their attention to their tasks. Elena picked up a piece of metal, not bothering to check what it was.

She heard the blow strike the workbench singer. The scream pierced the air. Elena focused on the piece of metal, wondering what she ought to be doing with it. Tatiana cried in her sling on Maria's back. When Elena dared to look, she saw even Maria had been touched by the event. Tears ran down her cheeks as she continued her work.

One morning in December Maria removed Tatiana from her sling just before worked started and passed her over to Elena. "You carry her at least for the morning?" Maria said. "My shoulders and back ache every night from holding her all day."

After lunch Tatiana cooed and smiled at Elena as she was being lifted into the sling on Maria's back. Elena studied the baby's eyes, felt her heart lurch, and paused briefly. She settled the baby in the sling and said, "Maybe tomorrow morning."

"M-m-m, mum, mum, mum." Tatiana gurgled as she reached out for Elena. Unable to deal with the overwhelming emotion, Elena turned back to her workstation. She never wanted this baby and yet now, here she was, alive and completely dependent on Elena for survival, able to giggle and laugh even in this place of horrors. For a few minutes Elena had trouble seeing the half-inch screws she was meant to be inserting into the panels.

That evening, when she unrolled her piano, Elena watched Maria change Tatiana's diaper and bundle her up for the night. She wrapped her in three layers of flannel gowns, topped by a bunting one of the women had made for her, then propped her against the head of the bed so that she could watch the activities before falling asleep.

"Play '*Kalinka Malinka*' again. Tonight we can all sing it."

A moment passed while Elena's eyes remained fixed on Tatiana. This time when the feeling overtook her, she recognized it for what it was. She was jealous of Maria. She forced herself to focus on her piano keys, the burgundy velvet now more black than red, the white a dingy gray. Knowing her shoulders slumped and her posture poor, she used two fingers to start the song as the women began to sing. Once they were in full voice, she joined in and played properly, her back now straight, her hands level as they ran up and down the keyboard. Madame. Uspenskaya would be proud of her now.

Everyone cheered when they finished. She played more folk songs until lights out. Tatiana was sound asleep next to Mama, who had not joined in the singing. She had her back to the baby. Elena moved Tatiana so she could slide in between her and Mama. Maria joined them a few minutes later, smelling of tobacco.

"Where did you find cigarettes?" Elena whispered.

"Why? You want one?"

"No."

"Then, it's none of your business, is it." Maria turned over. Soon her snores joined the rest of the night noises in the hut.

By February of 1944 six of the women in their hut had died from the cold. Elena used their blankets to insulate the outer wall behind their bunk and to create a softer and warmer padding. Between her quilted coat and Mama's fur, they managed to keep warm during the nights. Elena's hands were too cold to play the piano. No one had the heart to sing. All they wanted was to eat their supper and crawl into their bunks in an effort to keep warm.

Every day Elena looked forward to going to work in the underground tunnels. She didn't know the temperature in there, but it was warmer than the camp. Tatiana remained snug in her sling. Elena and Maria alternated carrying the baby during the long workdays. They could no longer put her down any place because she had started to crawl. In the mornings while dressing her, they would hold her hands and help her to totter from one end of the bunk to the other. Tatiana could now say "Mama," which she called both Maria and Elena. She waved "bye-bye" whenever a worker walked past them in the factory. And she had learned to like black bread soaked in the flavorless soup they were served for dinner.

Elena suspected the cooks were adding sawdust to the bread and using maybe one chicken for the entire Russian sector. No more jam appeared.

Early in April a sudden influx of new prisoners overwhelmed their hut. They brought mixed messages about the state of the war. Some said the Americans would arrive soon; others said it would be the Russians; some claimed the war was over, others said the Third Reich now controlled nearly all of Europe.

Bodies filled every bunk, three or four in everyone. Male prisoners came every morning to build new huts under the watchful eyes of guards and their dogs. Maria left the building every night after supper. She returned just before lights out reeking of cigarettes. She and Elena rarely spoke any more but they continued to share the burden of caring for Tatiana who now toddled about when set down on the floor. She had to be watched carefully so she wouldn't burn herself on the stove or wander out of sight. Mama had befriended a group of women her own age. Their 'club' met nightly at a corner bunk to complain about the state of affairs in the camp.

Elena taught Lydia how to play scales on the piano. By teaching, she refreshed her own playing. The girls grew closer.

Lydia came from a large family. Her parents, two brothers and four sisters had all been killed early in the war. She'd struggled to survive until picked up nearly two years ago and sent to this camp. At the beginning of the war she had nearly completed high school and was looking forward to university where she'd hoped to study medicine like her mother before her.

On Friday, April fourteenth, the two of them planned a special Easter program for Sunday when the entire Russian camp would be permitted to celebrate their holy day. Although they had no chaplain, the women had pieced together as much of the Orthodox mass as they could remember. No one had any eggs to decorate, but two women in hut number four had carved wooden eggs from scraps of lumber. Instead of painting designs, they etched patterns on them.

"We have to lead them in chants," Lydia said.

Elena looked at her friend. Her gray eyes had sunk deeper in her face. Her brown hair seemed wispier and thinner even pulled back into a single braid. "I only went to church with my grandmother a few times," Elena said. "I don't know chants. I was thinking there ought to be joyful music."

Lydia smiled. "I'll lead them in *Thy Resurrection* and *The Body of Christ* and then you can play Beethoven's *Ode to Joy*."

Elena giggled. "Not very religious though."

"It won't be a proper mass. No priest, no church."

"All right, but I'll have to think about it. I'm not sure I remember the entire piece."

Lydia turned her back and coughed, covering her mouth with a handkerchief. "Good. I think I'll turn in now. You practice. I'll sing at work in the morning and you can tell me if it sounds right." Without waiting for a response, she crawled into her bed and pulled her covers up over her head. Her bedmates sat with a group playing cards crafted from paper scraps.

Elena watched her silently and then rolled her piano and placed it under her coat. She had used it as a pillow since the weather had warmed a bit.

On Sunday, dozens of women gathered in the yard. Some sat on crates and boxes scrounged from the huts. Two women said the Orthodox mass as best they could remember it, stepping aside for Elena and Lydia to lead the singing portions. Elena hadn't brought her keyboard with her, so she closed her eyes and imagined the keys as she hummed the notes. The plan was for Lydia to sing the words and for everyone to join in. When it was her turn, nothing happened. Elena looked at her. Lydia's face was flushed, her cheeks bright red. Everyone stood in anticipation of the hymn.

"Can you sing at all?" Elena said in a soft voice.

"I can't breathe," Lydia answered. The effort to speak sent her into a spasm of coughing.

"Go back to bed. I'll finish here," Elena told her, feeling terrible because she couldn't stop and help her friend to the hut. The women shifted restlessly. Elena began the chant again, this time singing the words instead of imagining the keyboard. As she sang, she also prayed no one would laugh. The area remained silent, the women's eyes all on her. When she finished, she heard a collective sigh as they all sat down.

When the short service ended, people she didn't know surrounded her. They praised her voice. All she wanted to do was go to her friend.

In the afternoon Lydia coughed so badly that Agrafina personally helped her to the infirmary where she was diagnosed with pneumonia. She died two days later.

No one took any notice of her death. Elena privately played "Little Bells" for her.

Elena felt the emptiness of loss without Lydia. An older woman missing most of her upper teeth moved into the empty bunk. Anya Ivanovna brought stories of such horror that no one wanted to listen to her. "But it's true," she said. "At first they put me in with the Jews. I had to fight them all the way until someone finally believed me and had me transferred here. They have the men working in the granite quarry. Thousands and thousands of them. They carry the heavy stones up the steps, The Death Stairway, because so many die there. If a man collapses, he falls backwards. Like dominoes they fall, one after the other. If they don't die, they are shot because they are injured and no longer useful. They don't feed them enough to keep a dog alive."

"How can you know all this?" Mama asked.

"I was there. I told you. Look at me. You think I spent my life looking like a skeleton? No. I was a hefty woman. Here, you eat like kings. Look at yourselves. You have meat on your bones. Over there, they might kill you and cook you!" She cackled like an old woman, though she claimed to be only thirty-six. "They feed them potatoes you wouldn't feed your hogs. Bread is more sawdust than flour. Not even ersatz coffee. Trust me, I am happy to be here."

In May they came once more for the farm workers and she and Maria climbed into the truck. It was Elena's turn to carry Tatiana, who now spoke a few words. She clapped her hands when the truck began moving and waved "bye-bye" to the women being left behind.

Grateful to be going back to the farm, Elena leaned her arms along the top of the truck side and watched the landscape pass by. She smiled at the feel of sunlight once again on her face. "Do you believe what Anya Ivanovna says?"

Maria rested her chin on her hands as she stood next to Elena. "You didn't hear her last night when she told us what they did about the overcrowding. They shot Jews, gassed others, and put them in furnaces. She said some of them weren't even dead. There were naked corpses stacked like lumber along the brick walls waiting to be burned."

Elena shuddered. "That can't be true."

"Remember the smell? When we first arrived?"

"A strange, sweet odor." She was still imagining the stacks of corpses like firewood.

"We've become used to it. Pay attention when we come back tonight. I hate to say, but she is right."

Elena wiped her eyes. "It may be odd to say but a part of me feels that I want to be a Jew to share their noble suffering while another part is relieved to be a Russian and a Christian." She watched the trees for a moment. "Some days I want to die. Does that make me bad?"

"Bad is a word that doesn't seem to fit into our language any longer."

Thirty-nine

On their arrival at the farm, they learned the generous dinners they'd received the previous year would no longer be available. The farmers had been ordered to supply the army with far more food than before. There would be nothing to spare for workers.

"He means slaves," Maria said to Elena, but Elena wasn't listening. She stared at the garden. The seedling potatoes had already been planted by other hands. That had been her job. Hers and Maria's and Lydia's. Biting her lower lip to keep from crying, she wiped her eyes with her sleeve and turned to the farmer, Herr Zimmer, to await new orders.

Zimmer waited until the guards were out of earshot. "We can no longer provide you with good fresh food," he said, "but no one has told us you cannot pick out the dregs from the garden. I'm sure there are many potatoes and carrots left behind in the fall. The carrots might be tough and stringy, but they will flavor a stew. Take what you find. As for work, we have our son, Wilhelm, returned from the front during the winter after he was injured. He and the boy have been a great help. Now, here are your assignments . . ."

Elena didn't hear anything beyond the words, "our son, Wilhelm," and "injured." An image of *her* Wilhelm filled her mind and she had to be led by Maria to their new work. The two of them would be in charge of the chicken coops. They had to clean the nests, collect the eggs, sort them by size and then box them, nestled in sawdust, for delivery to the German Army.

Unlike last year when there had been only one lazy guard, this year guards stood watch all over the farm. There was no hope of slipping an egg or two into her pockets.

A guard caught one of the women taking vegetables for herself. He began berating her until Herr Zimmer stepped in to explain. From her vantage point in the chicken house, Elena watched the argument. If they came to blows it would be the end of their summer work. She held her breath and watched as both men flailed their arms in the air and shouted. In the end, the soldier stepped aside and the farmer signaled the women to continue their work. Herr Zimmer turned when a young man in farming clothes ran up to him.

She froze at the cloudy window and had to use the hem of her sweater to wipe it clean enough to get a good look. This had to be his son, Wilhelm. Willie. They stood together. Willie was slightly taller than his father, taller than she remember her friend. He had to stoop when they talked. Finally, Willie nodded and turned toward the farmhouse. He would walk right past her in a minute.

"Mama! Mama!" Tatiana called.

"Hush. Mama is busy," Elena replied without looking. She heard Maria's laughter and chickens' squawks, but her eyes remained fixed on the man approaching the house. He was slim, just like her Willie had been. Blond hair peeked from under his cap. She smiled. *Willie.* He even walked like him.

He paused and looked straight at the chicken house. She ducked away from the window and when she peeked out again, he was nearly at the door. Chickens skittered out of his way, clucking and complaining. From that angle she could only see the side of him. He was coming in. She grabbed her basket and chased hens from their roosts and made herself busy collecting eggs.

"*Dobra ootra.*" Good morning, Tatiana said in Russian.

There was no response. The only sounds were chickens clucking and scratching, bickering over their water or food dishes.

Elena dared a look. Without thinking, she turned away and cried aloud, "No!"

Willie Zimmer uttered a brief word she didn't understand. Trying to conceal her movement, she turned her head enough to see him kick at a chicken. He left without another word. Crawling to the entrance, she watched as he walked away, shoulders slumped and then turned the corner to enter the farmhouse. She sat with a thud the floor of the henhouse. Tatiana toddled over and placed two eggs on her lap. "No cry, Mama."

"Pretty horrible, eh? Poor man," Maria said from her corner where she was scooping out old straw from nests and replenishing them with fresh, clean straw.

"Did you hear? His name is Willie." Still stunned, Elena let Tatiana continue to pile eggs on her lap.

"At least yours only lost an eye."

"I know. Sometimes I think about Willie Becker at night, wondering if he ever went back to work as an insurance clerk." Elena gently placed the eggs in a basket and stood to brush the straw from her clothes. "And I only burned the back of my hand. How can he go on living like that?"

"If all the women he meets react the way you did, he'll most likely hang himself before the war is over."

"But his face. It's not even like a human being. Why wasn't Tatiana afraid?"

"Because, unlike us, she's a sweet soul, I suppose. Come on. We have to work."

Maria hustled through her job but Elena couldn't help but compare the back of her hand to the disfigured face she'd just seen. "Too bad he couldn't have had Doctor Brandt." She carried a full basket of eggs out to the small hut where she rinsed and sized them before putting them in their boxes. Tatiana helped by filling boxes with sawdust, dropping more back into the bin than into boxes, but it kept her busy.

She didn't see Wilhelm for the rest of the summer.

Elena's sixteenth birthday passed unnoticed.

"You will confine the baby or it will be taken away from you!" the supervisor at the airplane factory warned her when they returned in October.

"We'll work it out," Maria answered before Elena could respond. "She's a good little girl, my Tatiana."

"My cousin is well behaved," Elena agreed, her voice cold. She watched Maria hike Tatiana onto her hip. There seemed to be no point in any longer pretending Tatiana belonged to Maria. All the women in the hut knew, and if they didn't, they suspected. She wanted the charade to end.

Tatiana reached out for Elena. "*Moloko, moloko*, Mama."

"What is it she wants?" the guard asked.

"She wants to play now, but I'll explain we can play in a little while."

Maria and Elena headed to their posts at the work bench. Maria sat Tatiana on the bench. "We need a different arrangement. Tatiana is too big to ride in a sling all day."

Elena hesitated before answering. "Agrafina Mikhailovna has asked me if she could tell the officers about my singing. She said maybe we could get more food for the hut."

Maria's eyes grew large. "Why haven't you taken her up on that?"

"Sing for those pigs? You joke!"

"For food I don't joke. There could be more for us, for your mother, for Tatiana. You know she's not getting enough milk anymore. Why do you think I go out every night? You think it's because I like them?" Maria slammed her tools on the bench as she organized her workspace.

"What are you talking about? You mean for your cigarettes? What have you been doing?" Elena wasn't sure she wanted to know. Maria had been her hero, a brave woman who would do anything to save her country, but for a cigarette? She covered her ears. "No. Don't tell me. I don't want to know."

"What a fool you are, Elena. I agree they're pigs. All men are pigs, so what difference does it make who gives you the cigarettes or the bracelets? A little kiss, a touch, you do things for him and then you get presents. The pigs are the fools."

"Colonel Hüber?" Elena couldn't face Maria.

"What about him?"

"You said you slept with him to get information for your husband."

Maria snickered, but there was no humor in her voice. "I did say that, didn't I? You were so young, so hurt. I – I didn't want to look bad in your eyes."

Elena stared at the screwdrivers in front of her. The fingers of her right hand crept toward the longest one and then she grabbed it up and began stabbing the work surface. "You said you were a spy!" Stab. "You said you worked to save Mother Russia!" Stab. "You said you were my friend!" She threw the screwdriver onto the workbench.

Tatiana screamed as she reached out to Elena. "Mama. No, Mama. No cry, Mama." Her face turned red and tears dropped onto her sweater, a gift from Frau Zimmer.

Maria leaned toward Tatiana to take her by the arms, but before she could pick her up, Elena plucked the baby from her. "She needs to eat. I'll take her."

Elena tucked Tatiana under her arm and marched toward the exit. The guard, already familiar with her routine, let her pass. Elena took the baby to the wash house where she sat on a bench and let Tatiana nurse. Her mind raced with confusion. Dunya, Tatiana, Grandma and Grandpa all gone from her life. Her parents might as well not exist. Then Lydia and now Maria. What did she have left?

"Mama. Bye-bye. Ta-ta," Tatiana cooed in her sweet voice.

Elena grabbed her baby so tightly that Tatiana squeaked. The sound made Elena laugh and seeing her mother laugh, Tatiana laughed with her. "It's you and I together now, Tatiana. You and I and no one else. Did you know you're named after my best friend from school? Tatiana and I did everything together. That was before the war..." Elena rocked as the baby nursed. When she returned to work, she ignored Maria, not ready to confront Maria about her behavior. Maria didn't try to speak to her.

After that Elena kept to herself. She still sang in the evenings, but only when Maria was out.

Shortly before Christmas a guard came into the factory and ordered her to follow him. Knowing better than to argue, Elena began dressing Tatiana in her heavy winter clothing.

"No baby. Baby stays with the mother. Elena Federova is the only one ordered."

"But . . ."

"*Schnell!*" Hurry.

With her heart in her throat, she silently passed Tatiana to Maria and followed the guard, grabbing her coat from the hook on the way out. *Leave the baby with its mother.* Whatever became of her, she hoped Maria would take care of Tatiana. She'd been so good when the baby had been born, caring for her when Elena wouldn't. Shuddering from the cold, she trundled obediently behind the guard through the snow as they trudged uphill, climbed stairs into the compound and then onto the parapet. The guard hurried to the far side of the large open parade ground and then down the steps, beyond the arcaded wall. He stopped at a steel reinforced gate and banged on it with his fist. After exchanging passwords through a small opening, the gate opened. They stepped into a garden, bereft of grass and flowers, but still holding trellises and lawn furniture. He led her along a graveled path slowly filling with snow, to the entrance of a large stone house.

They waited on the steps of a broad verandah. A robust, rosy-cheeked woman wearing a large white apron over a dark blue dress opened the door to let them in. The guard stepped aside and indicated Elena should enter.

"*Herein!*" the woman barked.

"*Ya, meine Dame,*" she said, hoping she'd responded correctly. Elena stepped quickly across the threshold into a dream. The house couldn't be real.

Warm lighting glowed over highly polished hardwood floors and elegant deep burgundy draperies tied back with gold ropes. Matching velvet covered benches lined the dark, wood paneled walls. A puddle from her snow-covered clothing formed on the red marble floor. She thought one of the old czar's homes must have looked just like this at the same time she worried what to do about her wet boots.

The woman draped the outer clothing over a newel post and then knelt before Elena to untie the laces and help her remove the boots. When she finished, she pointed at a closed door to the right.

Elena pointed at the door and then to herself. "*Ich?*"

The woman smiled and nodded. "*Ya.*" When Elena didn't move, the woman crossed to the door and tapped on it and then opened it.

Elena entered the room. A uniformed officer, thin faced with a pencil mustache sat behind an oak desk, surrounded by shelves full of books. The last time she'd seen so many books had been in a library in Leningrad. She walked to the desk, hands folded in front like a schoolgirl.

"Sit," the officer said in a soft voice. "I don't bite."

She backed up to a high-backed wing chair and sat on the edge of the seat.

"You are Elena Federova?" he said in Russian.

"I am."

"You sing."

She cleared her throat, hoping he wouldn't ask her to sing then and there. "I do."

"Good. Is it true you also play the piano?" He leaned forward, eager for her answer, as if he'd just asked the most important question in the world.

"I used to. At home."

"I hear you practice on a make-believe keyboard every day." He picked up a silver case and offered her a cigarette.

"No thank you. I don't smoke."

"Do you mind?" he asked as he removed one for himself.

He was asking her? "No. Go right ahead, sir."

He took a moment to light his cigarette. "I am, I think you would say, the entertainment officer. I have other responsibilities as well, but at the moment I am most concerned about Christmas. If I take you to a piano, will you demonstrate your playing ability and sing a song for me?"

She felt her eyes go wide with surprise. Unable to answer for a moment, she shrugged. After swallowing twice, she stammered out, "I'll do my best, sir."

"I am Captain Albert Alexander Schulz, Miss Federova."

"Yes, sir. Captain, sir."

She stood on weak, trembling legs as he rose from his chair. Albert Schulz was her height, a slender man, emphasized by the black leather belt that nipped his waist. His brown uniform was neatly pressed with sharp creases in the trousers. His boots shone as though they'd never seen a front line or a muddy battlefield. The overall impression was of a toy soldier. He clicked his heels before stepping smartly in front of her to lead the way across the hall to the parlor where a baby grand piano stood as the focal point of the room.

"Oh my," she gasped. "It's beautiful." She ran her hands over the polished wood, seeing her reflection for the first time in years. A mass of blonde curls haloed her head. Her grey sweater hung loosely over the woolen skirt. Glistening ivory drew her eyes to the keys where she tentatively touched middle C with her right index finger.

"Play, if you please," Schulz said.

"If I please?" She turned to him. He relaxed on a Victorian settee, smiling at her. "It's been a long time since I've been near a real piano, sir. I'm afraid I may not be able to play." Her hands trembled, as eager to caress the keys as she was terrified to attempt to play.

"You have two weeks before our Christmas party. If all goes well, you will play for our New Year's gala. If I make you nervous, I shall leave you to practice in peace for two hours. First, I must hear your voice. Sing a Christmas tune."

"What Christmas tune? Silent Night? *Adeste Fidelis*?"

"Silent Night is good." He continued to smile, his thick lips too pink.

After clearing her throat, she steeled herself to ask, "Is it possible to have a drink of water?"

Without blinking, he reached behind him and pulled on a gold cord. The door on the opposite side of the room opened almost immediately and the plump woman entered.

"Hannah, water for our guest. Bring tea and cake as well."

Hannah dipped a quick curtsy and left.

Elena sat on the piano bench and ran her hands up and down the keyboard without pressing on any of the keys. She closed her eyes and imagined playing Silent Night, fortunately a simple song, originally composed for the guitar.

"I'm waiting."

Both hands now in place above the keys, she took a deep breath.

"I said to sing first."

She shuddered; her fingers trembled. The keys begged to be played. She struck a chord. The sound went straight to her heart. Cautiously, she played another chord. And another. The fingers on her left hand stretched the scarred skin. After several chords she whirled around on the bench to face Schulz. "Thank you, *Mein Herr,* it will be good. My voice will be good now I am playing the piano," she said, hoping her German made sense. Her head felt light, whether from the long walk, the lack of lunch or the joy of playing a real piano again, she didn't know. All she knew at the moment was Albert Alexander Schulz had given her life back to her. She smiled.

"Here is your water. Now sing."

Hannah placed a clean glass of water on a small table near the piano, then set a tray containing a delicate teapot, a single cup and saucer, and little pieces of cake nested in a bowl, on the table next to Schulz. He picked up a linen napkin from the tray, shook it out and placed it under his chin while Hannah poured his tea.

Elena watched, mouth-watering at the sight of cake. She ran her fingers over her mouth, and then chewed on her thumbnail while he ate.

He waved impatiently at her. "Drink your water and sing. I have other work to do."

As she swallowed the water, she imagined the flavor of tea with real sugar.

Turning her back to him, she cleared her throat and then sang scales to warm her voice. When she was ready, she once again faced him and began. "O, holy night…"

Schulz didn't comment on her singing a different song. With eyes closed, she saw the words before her and her voice followed the notes. Her voice wavered as she attempted a lower register and she opened her eyes to see if he noticed. A large piece of chocolate cake balanced on the end of a silver fork hovered before his mouth. Her voice cracked.

"Finish," he said just before the cake disappeared between the pink lips. Closing her eyes once again, she sang to the end and then waited.

"So. Something is wrong with Silent Night? It is a German song, is it not?

"I – I think so, sir. I hoped to save it so I might accompany myself on the piano. It is such a lovely song."

Schulz uncrossed his legs, wiped his fingers and mouth with the linen napkin and then stood. With an outstretched arm he shouted, "*Heil Hitler!*"

Elena's hands had been clasped in front of her. She released her right hand long enough to provide a minimal parting wave as he left the room.

He called for Hannah, but after that she could understand nothing from the hurried voices in the hallway. While she waited for further instructions, she sat at the piano and caressed the keys, stroking them, yet fearing to press her luck and strike them. If Grandma was right, if Elena remembered the music, it would come.

Forty

As they crossed the parapet leading back to the Russian gate, Elena wanted to hurry the guard, while at the same time she wanted the moment to last. Fresh snow falling two weeks before Christmas, the German Christmas on December 25th, not the Orthodox one in January, but Christmas in any form would bring new hope to everyone. And she would sing and play for them. Movement in the parade ground caught her eye. As they walked, she made her way closer to the edge. Her guard took no notice. She stopped to watch the swarms passing in through the gates.

The registration tables would be set up directly under where she now stood. As this mass of humanity entered, men in overcoats stood nearby directing individuals left and right. Men and women, parents and children reached out to one another. Guards and their dogs-maintained order. No musicians welcomed them.

The halt, the lame, the elderly lined the high wall opposite. "*Juden.*" She whispered the German word.

Her escort stood at the door leading to the stairs and waited for her. With her head bowed low, her arms wrapped around her middle, she walked past him into the stairwell.

"*Juden?*" she asked.

"*Ja. Juden.*"

With only a few yards to cover from the stairwell to the gate in the parade ground, Elena hesitated as her eyes connected with a girl who might be her own age. The girl, encumbered by two crutches, offered a weak smile. Elena offered a weak smile in return. The guard grabbed her by the arm and dragged her through the open gate.

"*Juden,*" he reminded her in a voice devoid of emotion.

They trudged side by side through the compound, she thinking about her opportunity to help the people in her building. She hadn't observed any "stacks" of corpses, but the weakest of the new prisoners had been lined up along that wall. With so little food available, obvious from their own reduced rations, there was little doubt in her mind what would become of the Jews—they'd die. But how?

All that was forgotten when she entered her hut. Everyone looked up, their eyes scanning her for evidence of what had happened this afternoon.

Mama sat amongst her cronies near the stove. Maria slept on their bunk with Tatiana asleep across her belly.

When she made her announcement, at last Mama would stand up and say, "That's my daughter." She'd say it with pride.

After checking to make sure the guard had secured the door behind him when he left, Elena removed her gloves, stuffed them in her pockets and then opened her coat, careful not to disturb the bundle hidden inside. She huddled over her package as she carried it to the center of the room. All eyes remained fixed on her and she enjoyed the suspense and anticipation.

"Agrafina Mikhailovna, will you please distribute this equally?" She lifted an edge of the package exposing pieces of cake. "We have pastries, cake and bread. A taste for everybody. And if I'm good, there will be more."

Agrafina hefted her bulk from the best seat in the house and reached for the booty. "Whom did you kill for this?"

Elena laughed. "I sang and played a real piano! I'm to go back there every day to practice for Christmas and then again for a New Year's party!"

Agrafina busily explored the gift of bread and pastries. By now, those few who'd been resting in their bunks had risen and crawled to the end of the beds so they could see what great event was taking place.

"And, I have even more news. My Mama will have the honor to cook for that entire week with their cook. There are to be parties and dinners and Hannah says I can bring all the leftover food back with me. For nearly a month, in the middle of winter in the middle of war, we, The Russian Prisoners of Hut Number Seven, will be the best fed prisoners in the world." She spread her arms as she had done so many times after a recital and waited for the applause.

A few women exchanged tentative smiles. A young woman on a top bunk called down, "Couldn't you get us any cigarettes?"

"What about shampoo?" another asked.

Bewildered, Elena looked for her mother's response. Anna glowered. The deep line between her brows, the downturned grimace on her lips didn't bode well. "Mama?" Elena said.

"So, you sing a song and bring us crumbs. You want us to kiss your feet?"

Meanwhile, others held out their hands for Agrafina to fill them with the treats.

"Anna Fedorova, if your daughter has found a position for you that can benefit the group, it is your duty to accept it and to accept it graciously," Agrafina scolded.

General laughter in the dimly lit room didn't help Mama's mood. "Gracious?" she screeched, silencing the room. "You, you peasant, are telling me about gracious? Do you know who I am?" Anna stood, the shadows around her face deepened by the single light bulb above.

Agrafina dropped the remnants of food onto her nearest neighbor's lap then stood, hands on hips.

Tatiana whimpered.

Maria, who'd been asleep, moaned and sat up.

"I know," Agrafina began, "you are one amongst thousands in this camp who are labeled and numbered prisoners. We are equals, but because we are Russians, we are not going to die like sheep led to a slaughter. If there is a single opportunity to extend our lives even for a few days, to aid in the survival of our own kind, it is our duty to do so."

Anna took a step forward toward her daughter. A gasp filled the room. Agrafina raised her arm and swung at Anna, striking her, open handed, on the side of her face, sending her crashing onto the stove. Women scrambled to pull her away to safety.

Elena watched all of this open-mouthed. Two bird-like women sitting next to her, continued picking bread and cake crumbs from their skirts, ignoring the activity around them. Maria held Tatiana over her shoulder so the baby wouldn't see what was going on.

The odor of burning hair and blood filled Elena's nostrils. She raised her hand to her face and was surprised to find it wet with tears.

Someone placed a comforting arm around her shoulder and led her to her bunk where she sat beside Maria. Other women tended to Anna who continued to grouse about her disrespectful daughter.

Tatiana slid from Maria's hold and toddled to Elena where Elena undid her clothing sufficiently for Tatiana to nurse.

"Did you have your cake?" Maria asked.

"No. No lunch either."

"You've missed supper."

"I know. I was so happy for a few minutes, Maria. I thought I was doing something good for everyone."

"You are. I'll be right back." Maria slipped away as Elena cuddled Tatiana. The women had already gathered into their regular groups and chattered. Elena wondered what would become of her new singing career now that her mother had refused to cook.

"That was brave of you, Elena," Agrafina's voice startled her.

"I'm not brave. I thought Mama would like to be in a warm kitchen in the winter and the housekeeper promised us food. I'm receiving more than anybody from this bargain. I'm going to be able to play a real piano."

"I have your cake and bread for the baby. Your mother doesn't understand the position she's in."

"How can she not know? We're at their mercy and must do what we're told. What else is there to understand?"

"You feed your baby. When the time comes . . ."

"I'll do it," Maria interrupted. When Agrafina looked at her in surprise, she added, "It's not fair to Elena to make her work side by side with her mother."

Agrafina studied them for a moment and then patted Maria on the shoulder. She left the small package of food on the blanket for Elena.

The following afternoon the guard waited for her after work at the factory to escort her to the house once again. This time she was brought to a side door that opened into a warm, snug kitchen where Hannah worked at the stove, stirring something heavenly in a large iron pot. Elena felt faint at the fragrance. As soon as they were in the room, she collapsed onto a chair.

Her guard remained at attention near the door.

"You are here for piano, Miss," Hannah said. "You leave your coat and boots here," she added, pointing to the wall near the door where a line of hooks held other coats and scarves. On the floor, an assortment of boots stood in line as if awaiting further orders.

After removing the boots and coat, Elena returned to the table, and then, overwhelmed with the warmth of the room, the fragrance of the soup, she slumped over the table. With her head buried in her arms, she wept.

"What? What is wrong? You don't cry; you play piano." Elena's hat was yanked from her head followed by Hannah jerking her body upright. "Why cry? Here is good!"

Elena wiped her eyes with the back of her gloved hands. "Forgive me. The soup. Your soup is so good." She inhaled deeply to emphasize her statement.

Hannah thumped her on the back of her head. "Bah! You Jews. I give you cake, you want soup. The Germans are right. Greedy Jew." Another thump.

Bewildered by Hannah's reaction, Elena struggled to keep up with her words. "Jew?" she questioned, not understanding immediately. "I'm not a Jew; I'm a Russian. A Russian prisoner. Ask him." She pointed to the stony-faced guard as Hannah hefted her from the chair and shoved her toward the door. Elena stumbled through the swinging door into the dining room where the table was already set for dinner. Dinner for six, she noted. Linen. Crystal. Sugar lumps in a bowl with little tongs.

"Herr Captain Schulz tells me for you to play." Hannah watched from the doorway until Elena moved into the parlor with the grand piano.

Keeping an eye on Hannah, Elena crossed to the piano, reached down for the edge of the bench and eased onto it. Hannah harrumphed and shut the door.

The fireplace warmed the room. Soft lights lent an air of unreality. Someone had left sheaves of music on the bench. On top of the music folders stood a tray with a glass of milk, a chunk of black bread, a square of cheese and a cup of cabbage and potato soup.

She turned, checking all around the room for the person for whom the food was served. Cautiously, she lifted the tray onto the piano so she could reach the music. The sight of the food was too much for her to resist. With one more glance around, she sipped at the milk, nibbled at the bread and then, when no one dashed into the room to stop her, she picked up the cup and drank the soup. For the whole time she ate, no one came into the room. When everything was gone and the glass empty, she smiled and picked up the first piece of music. Something she'd never seen, but something she'd learn to play if this is the way they would be treating her.

First, scales. She warmed up for nearly half an hour playing the scales from the simplest to the most complex. Her left hand resisted but by the end of her self-imposed exercise time, it moved more freely. Then she tried the music. The unfamiliar German script defeated her so she chose the only familiar musical score in the stack, *"Stille Nacht,"* the most popular German Christmas song she knew. After playing through it several times, she made an attempt to sing along with her playing. So wrapped up in the music, she was shocked when Hannah came into the room with her coat, hat, and a bundle of leftover scraps from dinner.

"You go now. The officials are pleased to hear you play. Tomorrow they ask if you will play and sing something different?"

Elena looked from the food bundle to Hannah. "Why…?"

"It's not good to be kind to Jews. I wait until no one left in house to see. Men are all in library with cognac now. You go. Come again tomorrow."

This time Elena was sure she understood all the words but instead of correcting Hannah, she nodded, bundled herself up against the weather and then waited for her escort to take her back.

She sang to Tatiana during the day at work and was eager for her escort every evening so she could play, sing and eat. The women in her hut waited up for her to see what surprises she might have for them.

A few days before Christmas, Elena informed Maria it was time to accompany her to the house to work as an assistant in the kitchen.

"What about Tatiana?"

"She'll be quiet. You'll see. Hannah won't mind." She hoped she was right.

The Austrian housekeeper welcomed the help and even enjoyed having the baby in the kitchen, although she remained apprehensive the Germans might think she was being too kind to the prisoners. "We do not have a choice, you understand," she tried to explain to Elena and Maria.

When Elena realized Maria was about to respond, she kicked her ankle. Hannah had never been inside the walls of the prison, so had no concept of their lives. "We understand, Hannah," Elena replied before leaving Maria and Tatiana in the kitchen. She didn't really understand, but then she'd been bewildered since the beginning of the war.

Everything worked smoothly through Christmas. Hannah had even provided a yellow silk dress for Elena to wear for her performances. Though she had no stockings or pretty shoes, the dress was long enough to cover her bare feet. Schulz had brought a tree into the parlor and decorated it on Christmas Eve. To Elena the entire experience was unreal. Night after night she played music by Germans for Germans, and then carried food to her hut. Everyone's spirits lifted and even the lack of Red Cross packages for Christmas didn't keep the others from enjoying the day. They ate scraps of roast pork, roast goose, potatoes and dumplings. The pleasure of her fellow prisoners more than made up for the guilt and shame she felt at playing for the Germans.

Maria shared cigarettes for Christmas and even provided a minute sip of cognac for anyone who wanted it on New Year's Eve.

Mama rejected the cognac and turned on Elena. "You! You think you're such a big shot now because of these miserable reminders of better days? There isn't enough for a mouthful for so many people. You come back with your breads and cakes and tidbits of meat to taunt us. That's the only reason the German let you sneak it away. You think we're supposed to feel like royalty eating this shit?"

"Royalty? I know the scraps I bring aren't enough to feed one whole person. They only provide a bit more nourishment, but mostly they provide hope," Elena replied, weary of her mother's antagonistic behavior. "It's not the Germans who give me the food, it's the housekeeper; she's an Austrian."

Anna turned her back. "Same thing. You have become exactly like that whore, Maria."

"I notice you don't refuse the food when I bring it," Elena shouted at her. "Don't accept it; that makes more for the others."

She handed her mother's portion to an old woman who slept in a bunk at the other end of the room. Not knowing her name, she placed the small bundle in her hands and said, "Here you are, Grandmother."

"Bless you, child," the old woman said as she hobbled back toward her bunk with her small treasure.

Mama grumbled to her cronies, but by now Elena didn't care what she said.

They returned to the routine of frozen nights huddled under Mama's fur coat, bitter cold morning roll calls, and never enough food to satisfy their hunger. Two more women in their hut died during January, whether it was from the cold or starvation, no one questioned. It no longer mattered. For the few days it would take to replace them, there would be more for the rest of them.

The underground airplane assembly plant was far warmer than the bunk house. Their lunch consisted of butter to go with their bread, and lumps of unidentifiable meat in their soup. Elena was grateful for her job. Elena and Maria partnered every day to produce the worst work they thought would manage to pass inspection. The guards stood inside the factory to keep warm. Maria no longer disappeared in the evenings and Agrafina, with no favors to dispense, became morose. She sat in her favorite spot by the stove, pretending it was warm enough.

Elena's clothes hung so loosely she had to tie her skirts and work trousers with rope to keep them from slipping down. Even Tatiana lost her chubby cheeks. Knowing no other life the toddler sat happily on the work bench. She pounded on pieces of scrap metal with wrenches and "worked" with Maria and Elena. At night she snuggled between the two of them. Sometimes she cried for more food, though usually exhausted like the rest of them, fell quickly into a sound sleep.

Throughout the horrific winter, rumors about the war filtered through the camp. As the food rations dropped to half and then half again, they feared Germany must be losing the war. Elena prayed she would be able to work in the Austrian family's garden again in the spring.

The first week in March of 1945 Elena was summoned from her job to the house where she'd played the piano during the Christmas season. Not aware of any special holidays in March, Easter was on April 11th this year, she speculated as she walked with her gloved hands stuffed in her coat pockets, shoulders hunched against the morning chilled air, through the overcrowded camp, about what type of music they would want. Perhaps a spring concert?

The long walk through the compounds sapped her strength as she struggled, short of breath, to keep up with the guard. The formerly neat and tidy façade of the prison had become a nightmare of swarming humanity struggling to survive under desperate conditions. She stared– the prisoners were working skeletons. Afraid to be caught looking at them and ashamed of her own relatively good health, she lowered her head and followed her guard, glad the transport that took her to the factory every day left the camp through a nearby gate and she didn't have to see what was really happening.

This time she was taken straight to an outside stairwell. It led to the basement where a group of male prisoners huddled, their eyes wide with fear. They were clothed in filthy trousers and tattered shirts. Once her eyes adjusted to the dim light from the single overhead light bulb, she realized she was the only female in the group, terror overwhelmed her. She whirled about but the guard slammed the door behind him as he left. She heard the latch drop. With her back to the door she searched the space for any means of escape. An interior stairwell rose on the far side of the room. The men didn't move, but all eyes remained focused on her. Before she could formulate any plan, a door at the top of the stairs opened sending down a stream of light. Gestapo boots came into view, followed by uniformed legs and then the rest of the man.

Elena recognized Schulz and nearly collapsed with relief.

He made no acknowledgement of her. He didn't even look her way. His face was grim and then, without introduction, he pulled a sheet of paper from a manila file and began reading. As he read out numbers, the men responded by holding up a hand. There were eight of them. When he called, "Three five two four," no hands went up.

"Three five two four!" Schulz repeated.

Elena remembered. "That's me. I am here, Captain Schulz. Elena Federova." She took a step forward.

Schulz snapped his ever-present riding crop against his boot. "Did I ask you to address me? You will remain silent."

Still recalling the pleasant evenings during the Christmas and New Year season, Elena spoke up again. "Excuse me, Captain, sir. I only wanted—"

His crop hit the side of the stairwell next to her head. She flinched. "I said to be quiet," he shrieked. "I will give you orders and you will obey them. Do you understand?" He addressed everyone in the room.

The only sound was the shuffling of feet on the dirt floor. The men stood with their hands folded in front of them, their eyes downcast.

"Good. You are here because you have been identified as accomplished musicians. Tomorrow we will have special guests here for the day. You will provide music for a reception to begin at four o'clock, after which you will play dinner music from six until eight and then chamber music until you are dismissed. All music will be of German origin. Your instruments will be delivered here to this room tonight. You will appear, clean and ready to practice immediately following the morning roll call. Clothing will be provided here. You are to discuss this with no one. Any questions?" His glare dared them to ask anything, as his crop slapped against his boot.

She ached to ask who the special visitors might be; it could make a big difference in the type of music they should play. Schulz's angry and cold manner kept her from speaking. All the way back to her building, while workers continued sweeping and mending the barracks, guards shouted orders, and prisoners scurried to obey them, she only heard Handel's "Hallelujah Chorus" loudly and clearly as if an entire choir followed her through the grounds of the camp.

That night as she cuddled Tatiana in her arms, her mind raced with possibilities.

Forty-one

On Thursday, March 8th, 1945 Elena stood in line for roll call, still unsure of the songs she might play for the special guests. The weather was crisp, the sun shone and the air smelled of wood smoke. Chimneys spewed fluffy clouds of gray into the clear blue sky.

She waited until the others left for work, having told Tatiana she'd be gone all day.

"Maybe tonight I can tell you," she said to Maria.

"Whatever is going on," Maria said, "It's big. All the huts have wood to burn. We had bread and cheese this morning, and the guards only counted us once. They're being too nice. Watch yourself, whatever it is you're doing."

Elena studied Maria's face for a moment as she wrested Tatiana's hands from her arms and handed her to Maria. "I can tell you this much. It's only music."

Resigning herself to the separation, Tatiana blew a kiss to Elena as the truck carried her and Maria away to the airplane factory.

Her guard collected her and marched her through the camp to the house. Maria had been right. Something big certainly was going on. She saw the Death's Head soldiers carrying Red Cross boxes into the barracks. The fragrant aroma of baked bread wafted from the food truck as it passed.

The men were already in the basement, dressed in plain trousers and white shirts. Nothing could disguise their gaunt features, but cleanly shaved and in regular clothes instead of their prison rags, they could almost pass for starving musicians. How would her own appearance affect anyone?

She was given the same yellow dress she wore in December. It was far too big, more than in December, but with the sash wrapped three times around her middle, it would be acceptable. She blinked back tears at having a clean dress against her skin again.

The men had their own ideas about what music would be appropriate for each segment of the evening, assuming she would be able to play whatever they wanted. She hoped Schulz would arrive soon and let them into the parlor so she could practice at the piano.

When they passed through the kitchen, she counted four cooks. The dining room table had been expanded to seat at least fourteen people. It had been set with an ecru lace tablecloth, gold rimmed china, gold flatware and three fine pieces of crystal stemware at each place. A bowl of flowers stood in the center of the table.

The music stands were to the left of the piano. Extra chairs had been brought into the room, set out in comfortable conversation groupings. Sheet music rested on the stands and on top of the piano. She glanced at the music and rolled her eyes in dismay; it was arranged for an orchestra. With shaking fingers, she picked up the first piece and tried to isolate her part.

The men sat in front of the fireplace and tuned their instruments. She fingered the piano keys and then, oblivious to the musicians' cacophony, began running scales, still trying to figure how she'd fit in with the group.

Thrilled to have her hands on a real piano again, she lost track of time. During the afternoon, Ivan, the violinist helped her and they all worked together to become a small orchestra. The violinist took the lead as conductor. By the time the first guests arrived, Elena, still nervous, felt ready to play for them.

Three women arrived first, greeted by Schulz. Two of them spoke English. The third, dressed in a severe gray suit with her brown hair pulled back in a tight bun, translated almost simultaneously for the other two. From the little bits of what Elena could hear, these women represented the International Red Cross, although they were gushing over *"Herr Captain Schulz."* They praised him for his openness and honesty in dealing with the Red Cross even to the point of blessing him for the wonderful care and treatment of the prisoners.

The tallest of the three, dressed in an expensive plaid suit with a matching hat said in American accented English, "I've heard rumors and gossip about atrocities but didn't believe it for a minute. I told my husband, I told him, I know war is war, but there's no reason to be brutal to non-combatants."

Schulz blushed as he smiled and accepted the praise. "Very kind, ladies, however you will meet the camp commandant at dinner and you may tell him of your findings. For now, shall we have cocktails? I hear the gentlemen arriving."

Soon two civilian men with Red Cross armbands entered with the SS officers. Schulz signaled the orchestra to play.

Elena struck a chord. The violinist raised his bow. The lady in plaid let out a sharp yelp.

"Oh, dear God, child. What in heaven's name happened to your hand?"

Elena's hands froze in position. She looked down at them. It took her a moment to realize the woman was talking about her scarred left hand. She looked up at the woman's alarmed face, puzzled by her apparent alarm. Elena raised her hand and said, "I dropped a hot iron on it a long time ago. It's all right now."

"That is an unacceptable explanation, young lady." She hesitated for a moment. "But you speak English. How wonderful. Perhaps after dinner we can have a little chat."

Schulz took the woman by the arm and led her to a seat across the room, speaking in German too rapid for Elena to understand. One of the men came to glance at her hand and then walked away to pick a glass of champagne from the tray held by a white-gloved waiter.

They worked their way through the evening as they'd been instructed by Schulz. After the American woman's comment about her hand, no one else had taken any notice of them. Although she wanted to listen to their conversations, she was too focused on the unfamiliar music and playing with an orchestra.

By the end of the dinner service, she'd forgotten about her hunger, joyous because her playing had achieved a new level of competency. While the guests refreshed themselves following dinner, the waiter advised them to go to the kitchen for their supper.

Schulz entered the kitchen and headed directly to her. She put down her dinner roll with a fragment of chicken in it. "You! You were told not to speak to the guests. What was it you said to that woman?" He leaned down so his face was two inches from hers.

The alcohol on his breath made her cringe. "I told her I dropped a hot iron on my hand. That's all." She finished chewing her food and tried to swallow when he grabbed her arm and pulled her to her feet.

"You will show respect when I speak to you." He spoke in a tightly controlled voice, his teeth clenched, his lips barely moving.

"I beg your pardon, sir," she said as humbly as possible without choking on the food still in her mouth.

"These people will be reporting to the world about your condition. It is imperative they send out a good report." Perspiration covered his brow.

He's frightened, she thought. He's afraid that they'll tell the truth, except it sounds like they have no idea of the truth. "Please forgive me, sir," she said, keeping her eyes downcast. "If anyone speaks to me later, what shall I do?"

"You will not reply." He stood straight and tugged at the hem of his uniform jacket.

"Begging your pardon, sir, won't they think I'm being rude?" She was aware that the rest of the musicians had stopped eating to listen to their conversation. They watched, gape-mouthed at her bold behavior.

Schulz seemed to be considering his response. He picked up a bottle of cognac and poured a tumbler full and then took a sip. "If those busy bodies try to worm information out of you again, you will ask for me to attend the conversation. Is that clear?"

"Yes, sir."

He slammed the glass on the table, clicked his heels and left the kitchen. The men scrambled to grab the glass still nearly full of the golden liquid. Elena chewed thoughtfully on her roll.

When they returned to the parlor, the guests had already drunk a considerable amount of alcohol. A Red Cross lady giggled in the corner while a German soldier was either kissing her ear or whispering something funny to her. Two of the Nazis spoke in raised voices, arms waving as if they were in a tennis match.

Elena crossed to the piano and began a piece by Mozart only to be stopped almost immediately by one of the Red Cross men.

"Say, little girl, don't you know something contemporary? How about a little Harry James?" His words slurred. She didn't know of any Harry James.

"Excuse me, sir. I must speak with Captain Schulz," Elena said. She scanned the room but Schulz was nowhere to be seen.

"Aw, go on. Ya don't know old Harry? Here, let me play a little bit for you." He sat down, pushing her aside with his hip and began fingering the keys.

She searched the room. Two of the SS officers stopped their conversations to stare at her. Her only hope was that they would come and remove this man.

"Here we go," he said. "I'll get by as long as I have you," he sang although his fingers on the keys didn't match the notes he sang. Sitting stiffly beside him, her hands clenched in terror lest Schulz return and see her with this drunken pianist.

"Wait a minute. I know a fun one. Here we go," he said. "Mairzie doats and does eat oats and little lambsie divey," he crooned, sputtering and laughing as he tried to play and sing simultaneously. "Well, they're a hell of a lot more fun than what you've been playing. Bunch of amateurs. You ought to try attending real concert halls and you'd find out what real musicians are playing."

He might have gone on except the woman in gray came to the rescue. She handed him a cup of ersatz coffee. "Come along, Frank," she said. "We've had a long day and now we have to write our reports. This child needs to get back to her room to sleep. Thank you, sweetheart for a very nice performance."

Elena nodded and then turned to the musicians, unsure what to do next. Ivan led the way by packing his instrument in its case. Elena stacked the sheet music, both relieved and sorry she hadn't had more of an opportunity to mix with the foreigners. As she carefully smoothed the papers and evened the stack by tapping it on the surface of the piano someone sat on the bench next to her.

"You spoke English earlier," the newcomer whispered out of the side of her mouth. It was the Plaid Suit Lady. "What really happened to your hand? Don't worry about the Germans. By law they are forbidden to punish you for talking to representatives from the Red Cross."

Panicked by the woman's approach, Elena again desperately searched the room for Schulz. *Summon him. Don't speak to this woman.* She continued tapping the papers on the piano.

"Speak to me. I'll make sure the truth gets out," the woman whispered, her whiskey breath making Elena feel ill.

"I told you the truth," she whispered, trying to keep her lips from moving. "I fainted and dropped an iron on my hand. A very kind doctor helped me."

"Here in this camp?"

"No. When my family was still in Russia. We spent the winter in a German encampment. They let us work for them." She felt perspiration on her brow and wished the woman would go away.

"They 'let' you?" Plaid Suit snickered. "Is your family in the camp, too?" She asked as if they might all be staying at the same resort.

Elena closed her eyes, desperately wanting to be in her bunk. "My mother and father," she said, afraid to mention Tatiana. "I have to leave now. Excuse me."

Before she could stand, the woman responded in a cold voice, "We're here to help you, young lady. You shouldn't dismiss us so casually. We can make things better for you."

Elena opened her eyes and looked directly at the woman. "Can you make the war stop? Can you kill all the Germans and rebuild my home? Can you make my friends Tatiana and Dunya come alive again? Go away!" she cried.

The room became quiet. The officers and visitors turned to stare. Even the musicians ceased packing up their instruments and stood straight, watching her.

Captain Schulz stormed into the room, followed by a large officer whose uniform was decorated with more ribbons than she had ever seen. Schulz' face was a mask of rage. He paused before reaching her at the piano and forced a smile. In a calm, but strained tone, he said, "I think this has been a tiring day for our young pianist. Hermann, you will please escort her back to her quarters?" His eyes dared her to open her mouth again.

Hermann, the waiter, set his drinks tray on a nearby sideboard and approached. "Very well, Captain. Come along. We'll go now."

"Not a single word," Schulz cautioned as he bent close to her at the piano.

The American woman wouldn't let it go, however. As Elena tried to move past her toward the exit, she stood in her way. "I don't for a minute believe the story you told about your hand. I think there is much more you could tell us."

A tall, graying man, speaking accented German took the plaid suited woman by the arm. "Come along, Janet. We've seen all we need to see, had a delightful dinner and perhaps a little too much to drink. We must get to Linz for transport back to Switzerland."

Elena kept her eyes downcast as she stepped around Janet and the man. Hermann kept close by her side while she changed.

Everyone in the barracks waited up, expecting leftovers as previously. She opened her hands and then her coat to show them she had nothing. "I made them angry," she muttered to their questions.

After snuggling into bed between Mama and Tatiana, Maria whispered, "You have to tell me, how did you upset them? It can't be so terrible or you wouldn't be here."

Elena thought about it. Her family starved while she ate rolls and chicken at the house. How could she have refused to speak to the visitors? She wrapped her arm around Tatiana and felt her soft breath on her cheek. "The Red Cross people were there and I answered a lady's questions," she finally answered.

Maria squeaked. "But that's good! That means they've seen the food we're being fed. Potatoes suitable for animals. Watery soup. They've seen how thin everyone is. Starvation. That's what they'll tell the world."

"Not so good," Elena sighed. "Not so good at all. I don't know what they were shown, but they think we're fortunate to be here. They heard rumors about all the bad things and they talked about being glad no such things happened here at Mauthausen. I need to sleep."

The next morning Elena was singled out to not receive hot tea. Instead of Agrafina, a German woman in uniform passed out meager portions of bread to everyone except her.

Following roll call Elena was told to remain in position while the others went to their jobs.

She stood in the middle of the open space on a bright March morning, at first enjoying the sunshine. The new guard sat on a wooden crate in the shade to watch her. Within an hour she felt herself sway and had to shake her body to remain standing. By evening she'd fallen four times, each time roughly dragged upright with the admonition, "You follow orders and stand as you were told."

When the others returned from work she was permitted inside the hut, but once the watery soup was passed out, the nameless guard handed her a cup of tepid water. "You made someone angry."

Elena looked at her in silence then listlessly moved to her bed where Maria slipped a small crust of bread to her under the covers. She chewed on it, savoring each scrap, not knowing if she'd ever eat again.

Life became a mist that wouldn't rise. Elena remained on punishment rations. Maria continued to try to share with her, but Tatiana needed more nourishment than she was receiving, so Elena encouraged Maria to give what she could to the active two-year-old.

No music arrived unbidden in the night.

By April Elena was too weak to work in the factory. She sipped the foul-smelling broth and clung to the crusts of bread until she could work up the energy to try to chew them.

Night and day mingled. Vaguely aware of the others crawling in and out of bed, nothing mattered any more. During one dream Madame Uspenskaya stood by her bed and demanded she play "Night on Bald Mountain." She wanted her to play all the parts of the orchestra and when she couldn't move fast enough, Madame hit the bottom of her feet with wooden sticks. She turned on her side, her hip protesting in pain against the planks.

"I'm too tired," she croaked through parched lips.

Now Madame shook her more gently by her exposed shoulder, a shoulder too bony to hold up the itchy woolen sweater.

"Wake up," a voice said.

Not Madame's light, lyrical voice, this was the voice of an ogre, deep and gruff. She closed her eyes more firmly, aware now she was not dreaming. Or was she?

"This one's alive. Give me a hand," the ogre voice said.

She opened one eye and gasped. A clean shaved man's face smiled at her. "Hello, Sweetheart. I brought you a present." He held something toward her. She smelled it above all the stench from the hut, a chocolate bar. She closed her eye, happy to remain in the dream of chocolate bars and smiling men.

He shook her again. "Come along. Help me get you out of here. We'll take you to a hospital."

"Hospital?" she managed to whisper. "Why?"

"Say, that's swell. This one speaks English. Come on. You're sick and we're going to get you better."

She opened both eyes. "Who are you?"

"Corporal Kevin Wanamaker, United States Army, 41st Calvary Reconnaissance Squadron of the 11th Armored Division at your service. Can you sit up?"

She studied the face before her. Green eyes. A round helmet, not like the Germans wore, covered his head. Even white teeth. A smile tried to reach her lips but she could only sigh. "It's over?"

"It's over."

Part IV

EUROPE

Forty-two

Elena awoke in unfamiliar surroundings. Her eyes caked with a crust that hurt to scrape away, she tried to figure out through the blur where she might be. It smelled of antiseptic, like the clinic where she worked with Dr. Brandt. She turned her head. To her right stood an endless row of bunks filled with patients. She lay on a mid-level bunk at the end of a room, a real room, not in the barracks. Uniformed men moved between the beds. So, the war wasn't over. She was still at Mauthausen. The American soldier with the big smile and nice teeth had lied to her. Or he was a wonderful dream. Tears welled, burning her eyes, but the moisture helped loosen the scab-like matter. She tried to wipe her eyes with the edge of the bed sheet but her left arm was restricted. She rolled her head to the left. Green wallpaper with a fleur-de-lis pattern. Looking down, she discovered her arm was secured with bandages to a board and a needle attached to a plastic tube that led up to a bottle hanging from beneath the bunk above her. Clear fluid dripped from the bottle through the tube and into her arm.

She closed her eyes. Sheets. She was resting between two cotton sheets. Maybe it wasn't a dream. Voices moved closer. When they reached her, she felt the heat of their bodies as they clustered around the beds. Whoever was beneath her was "coming along well."

Then it was her turn. What could they tell her? That she was starved because she spoke up to the International Red Cross people? Because she disobeyed Captain Schulz?

"Hello, Miss Federova. Time to wake up," a woman said in English.

Elena moaned. She didn't want to wake up. The clean sheets, the clean odors, the comforting voices soothed her. Awakening and reality were too harsh. She kept her eyes shut.

"We're hoping to move you to a different location tomorrow. Can you open your eyes, please?" a man's deep voice spoke in Russian.

She considered it for a moment. Move her? What about Tatiana and Maria? Where were they? She opened one eye. A man with thick bushy eyebrows above dark blue eyes smiled at her. He wore an American uniform. A stethoscope hung around his neck.

"You're Russian?" she asked.

"American," he answered. "Dr. John Peters. You don't have to talk. We've been treating you for several days and we're ready to upgrade you. You don't require intensive care any longer. Do you want to try to sit up now?"

The thought exhausted her. "No, I want to sleep."

"Nurse."

Next thing she knew arms reached under her pillow and helped her upright. Her head swam as the nurse fluffed and propped more pillows behind her. "Why?" she tried to speak again but her throat felt raspy and sore.

"Your child needs you. As soon as you can keep food down, we'll move you to be with her. Ready to try a little broth?"

Elena couldn't remember the last time she was hungry. Maybe it was at that disastrous dinner? No. It was the morning after. And the afternoon and evening. She closed her eyes again and rested her head against the pillows. "Broth. Tea. Both would be good."

By early evening she'd managed to keep down the richly flavored beef bouillon and two cups of sweetened tea. Moans filled the air punctuated by occasional screams as doctors worked on patients. She remembered something the doctor had said in the morning. Something about her daughter needing her. How did he know she had a daughter? Was Tatiana sick? What happened to Maria? She pushed back the covers and rolled to the edge of the bunk, but the IV attached to her arm stopped her from getting out of the bed. She fell back and examined the tube that disappeared beneath the bandages.

She slid back against the pillows and awoke when the doctor and nurse came to examine her again. This time she felt more alert and was eager for the broth and tea.

"What happened to the man with the chocolate bar?" she asked in English.

The nurse answered as she fussed with the bottle. "You can have chocolate once you're able to eat solid food. Right now it would be toxic."

"I don't understand toxic," Elena answered.

"Poison. Okay, upsy daisy. We're going for a ride."

Two orderlies stood in the center aisle holding a stretcher while the nurse and Dr. Peters lifted her onto it. The nurse held the IV bottle and followed as the men carried her out of the building into the cool air. She took a deep breath and smiled when the warmth of the late afternoon sun struck her face. With her eyes closed she left herself to the care of the strangers and drifted into a semi-awake state where she performed once again in a concert hall. This time a young girl in a blue gown sat beside her to turn the pages as she played. But what was she playing?

Her fingers moved; the girl turned the pages. She listened for the music but heard nothing.

The stretcher tilted, lowering her feet and then it was like she floated in the air as she was lifted into the back of a van. And then she slept again.

Jostling of the stretcher woke her as men carried her into a brick building. Another hospital atmosphere greeted her. This time she heard cheerful voices and the sounds of busy people moving through the rooms mingled with children's laughter.

Children? No, a single child's laughter. Opening her eyes she saw Tatiana dressed in an oversized white cotton shirt sitting on a bed playing a clapping game with Maria. When Tatiana saw Elena, she tried to jump off the bed into her arms but Maria caught her.

Elena's bones felt like rubber when she made the effort to sit up. "Tatiana," she said, holding her right arm toward her. The orderlies and the nurse shifted Elena to a bed close to Tatiana's. Her body sank into a real mattress, not a thin pad over wooden planks. She looked around. The bed was one of four crowded into a wallpapered room. Late afternoon sun streaked across the room and spotlighted golden-haired Tatiana. Tatiana coughed when she laughed. Blue circles ringed her daughter's eyes; her skin looked delicate, like parchment.

"Mama! I sick. Doctor makes me better. Are you sick?"

"A little bit. I'll be strong soon."

"Tatiana," Maria scolded. "It's time for your supper and then you have to rest. Enough playing for today." Maria fussed with Tatiana, settling her into her cot and propping her up against her pillows. She then raised planks to keep her from falling out of the small bed.

A soldier with the darkest skin she'd ever seen stepped into the room through a wide archway carrying a tray overloaded with cups and glasses. Beyond him was another room similar to this one. Heavy green velvet draperies hung by the full-length windows. The Americans had brought them to someone's house. He passed out cups, bowls and glasses to two other women on the opposite side of the room, then stopped at Tatiana's bed.

"And for the princess we have creamy chicken soup, chocolate milk and pudding for dessert."

Tatiana peered over the tray and wrinkled her nose. "No soup." She crossed her arms.

"Okey dokey, princess. But the general says I have to take away the chocolate milk and pudding. It all comes together." He turned away from her bed. Elena caught a hint of a smile on his face.

Tatiana couldn't possibly understand the English words, but she definitely understood the meaning of his gestures. She scowled and held out her hand imperiously. The soldier swooped the tray onto a table near the bed and deposited Tatiana's dinner.

Elena smiled, her heart warmed by her daughter. A similar supper was set on the table next to her own bed. She eyed it, trying to decide if she was hungry. As she pondered, Dr. Peters strode into the room.

"All settled?" he asked her as he studied a clipboard in his hand.

"Thank you," she croaked.

Maria moved to her bed and helped prop her into a sitting position. The nurse who'd entered with the doctor went to feed Tatiana. "I would feed her, you know," Maria said to Elena, "but they want to measure everything she eats."

"What's wrong with her?" Elena whispered to Maria, afraid to let Tatiana hear.

"They don't tell me. My guess would be tuberculosis because of the coughing. But what do I know?"

"Doctor?" she reached out and grabbed his writing arm. "Is it true? Does she have tuberculosis?"

Dr. Peters glared at Maria before answering. He sat on the edge of the bed and shooed Maria away. "Her aunt is being dramatic. Tatiana was very ill. The fact that most of you were starving and suffering from malnutrition doesn't help your recovery. She thinks a healthy supply of food for a few days and you'll become strong, just like that." He snapped his fingers.

"It's only two days. But what about Tatiana?"

"It's been four days, Mrs. Federova."

"I don't have a husband. My name is Elena."

"What happened to him?"

"He died," Elena and Maria spoke at the same time.

He appeared confused by their joint comment. "So. You're a widow."

Maria popped up from the foot of the bed where she'd been sitting on the floor. "Not much of a widow. She was only married long enough to have a baby."

"Don't you have a bed or a room where you're supposed to be, young woman?" Dr. Peters snapped at Maria.

"No. Sadly I'm neither sick enough to be treated for anything nor strong enough to help anyone. I like to keep Tatiana entertained."

"Tatiana needs to rest. If she's to get strong enough to leave with her mother, you must stop getting her so excited with your games. Can't you read her stories?"

"Fine." Maria folded her arms. "Bring me Russian children's books and I'll read them to her."

Dr. Peters chuckled. "Is she always like this?"

Elena didn't care at the moment what Maria was like. She wanted to know more about Tatiana's health and when she'd be well enough to care for her.

When she didn't respond, the doctor moved closer to her so Maria couldn't eavesdrop. "I'm only here for a few days. There are so many camps we have to liberate; so many people we have to help. Before I go, I want to make sure I've helped you and Tatiana. We've been supplied with a new drug called penicillin. Once I determined that your daughter was suffering from pneumonia, I decided to try it on her. It appears to be working."

Without warning, emotion overwhelmed Elena. She fell back against the pillows and began sobbing. Doctor Peters reached out and touched her shoulder. She turned her face so her cheek rested against the back of his hand. "Dr. Brandt was good, too. He fixed my hand." She raised her left arm slightly from the bed. It was still encumbered by the board and bandages.

He took it in both his hands, tears forming in his eyes and then, astonishingly, leaned over and kissed the back of her hand.

"Elena, you have no idea what I've seen these past few days. Not just the bodies, hundreds, thousands of dead people. Starving people. Living skeletons. The children were the worst— toothpicks for legs, swollen bellies, the lice! So many of them dead; so many of them beyond help."

The hair at the crown of his head was thinning. He would soon be bald. How different he was from Dr. Brandt. Though both men were kind, Dr. Brandt had been strong. This man seemed broken. She wondered if she ought to stroke his head like her grandmother used to do to her when she was upset. Thoughts of her grandmother brought fresh tears to her own eyes.

He pulled a khaki colored handkerchief from his trouser pocket to wipe his eyes and blow his nose. He patted her hand. "I'm sorry. I had no business becoming emotional. You've suffered enough without having me burden you further. The fact is, I am happy with your daughter's status. It will still be another six weeks or longer before she is restored to full health, but she won't die."

Elena used the corner of the sheet to wipe her eyes. "Thank you, doctor. Thank you so much."

He smiled again. "She's such a sweet child, I couldn't resist her. It was my pleasure to help. But now I have to move on. Work on getting stronger and then I have arranged for you and Tatiana to be on a priority list for accommodations in Vienna. There are several international relief organizations throughout the area, but I spoke with Mary Parker, an English woman with the International Red Cross. You'll like her."

"You're so kind, Dr. Peters. So kind." The move from the other facility to the house and then the conversations had sapped her strength. "One more question. What about my parents? Did you see them?"

Dr. Peters' face remained blank. He blinked once. "All I know of your family is Tatiana and your aunt, Maria. I didn't realize . . ."

"She didn't tell you?"

"She didn't tell me. I know nothing. You can talk to Mrs. Parker about them. I really have to go." He stood to emphasize the words. "I have orders. We're being dispatched to another location."

"You're leaving?" She looked up at him, astonished. There were so many questions she wanted to ask him. Why did he speak Russian so well? Why did he choose Tatiana above all the others for his precious medicine? How long before they could go to Vienna?

He frowned as if trying to decide what to tell her. "In spite of your condition, the condition of the women in your compound," he held up a hand like a stop sign, "I know things have been terrible for you, but the others…"

"The Jews?"

"The Jews. Not only the children, but all the people. This isn't the only camp. There are so many. Too many. You're young. You'll grow strong in a few weeks and one day you'll marry again and have more children. You'll see, life can be good."

Not understanding why, his speech offended her. "I'm going to play the piano at Carnegie Hall. Beautiful music will make the people smile. I won't marry and have more children."

With a faint smile and a salute, he said, "Sure you will. Goodbye, Elena Fedorova."

She slid down in her bed as she watched him leave the room without glancing left or right. That was it. Dr. Peters, whom she hoped would become a friend like Dr. Brandt, was gone.

She turned her face away from Tatiana and Maria as tears slid down her cheeks. *Mary Parker of the International Red Cross. The same people who caused trouble in the first place. Not while I'm alive.*

"One, two, three, four, five,

"Little rabbit…"

As she began to drift off to sleep it came to her where she was. Sitting up, heart thumping wildly in her chest, her eyes raced about the room, searching for familiar objects. The wallpaper. The draperies. She was at the piano house. But there was no piano.

"Maria!"

Maria had fallen asleep next to Tatiana who lay in her cot, wide-eyed, holding a rag doll, speaking softly to it. Maria, startled, jumped up at the sound of her name. "What?" she answered in Russian. "Who is it?"

"Only I," Elena said. "Where's my piano? What happened to it?"

"Your piano? I have it under my pillow. They were going to throw it away with all the lice ridden rags in the barracks."

Elena breathed a deep sigh of relief. "Thank you. Huge thank yous. I'll never forget you for the favor."

Forty-three

Thanks to the new drug, Tatiana recovered rapidly, becoming the favorite of the nurses and doctors who had taken over the house-hospital. Elena found herself a close second with her ability to speak several languages. While it took nearly two weeks for her to regain enough strength to move amongst the rooms to translate for the nurses, she felt useful and almost happy. Maria acted as Tatiana's personal nanny, taking her outdoors for the sunshine on good days and then reading to her and playing games when it rained.

Besides translating for the American medical teams, she also helped the various members of the international organizations who had arrived to begin sorting out the survivors. It was their job to determine who would return to their home cities and who would become a "displaced person."

In the evenings she played her piano, humming the notes as she done for her parents and grandparents. Her fellow patients wanted happy songs, sad songs, even Russian patriotic music. Some nights the staff of military medics joined in the festivities and taught her American tunes.

During that time she learned more about the liberation of their camp. Right after the Allies had liberated it, the American leader, General Eisenhower, had ordered the villagers of Mauthausen to dress in their Sunday suits and then made them come to the camp to bury the dead. The villagers claimed they had no idea what was happening. The officials from Vienna told them that over seventy-eight thousand men, women and children lived in the main camp as well as at least two subsidiary camps. Depending on whom she was listening to, anywhere from eighty thousand to nearly a million people died since the camps opened. She listened to the news and heard the numbers, but none of it connected to her life. For the time being her world was in the house with Tatiana and Maria. The Americans took care of them. Nothing else mattered.

She awoke one morning with Tatiana still asleep in her arms, smelling soft and baby-sweet. The windows stood open, birds sang, and the air was fresh. Elena felt contented, happy to remain exactly where she was forever.

The staff appeared to be in an unusual hurry to rush through their rounds, not once stopping to chat with a single patient. Elena sat up after someone took her pulse and declared her "recovered."

Maria's bed was empty. Careful not to wake Tatiana, Elena slipped out of her own bed, pulled a cotton dress over her nightgown and then headed to the opened front door. Across the way, the familiar gate to the main camp stood open. The gate she'd passed through so many times to play for Herr Captain Schulz. Hesitantly, she stepped through the opening and watched the activity in the large courtyard as if in a dream.

People scampered from place to place – ants at random. Trucks rolled by sending up clouds of dust that blocked the sun. The activity frightened her. Could the Americans be leaving already? Dr. Peters had left two weeks ago, but no one said anything about the rest of the Americans leaving. She bit her lower lip and watched wide-eyed as a truck stopped near the arched walkway. Soldiers, the doctors and nurses, emerged from the shadows and climbed into the back of the truck. It edged its way forward and stopped before Elena.

"Excuse me, miss, can we get through?" a man spoke from behind her.

She stepped aside and watched as the men and women she'd come to rely on as friends climbed into the truck without a word. Unable to bear it any longer, she grabbed a nurse before the woman could get by.

"Where are you going? Why are you deserting us?"

The woman brushed her aside. "You don't have to worry. The Russians and the Austrians have control of this camp now.

You'll be home in a matter of months. Good luck, dear," the woman said as she eyed the truck. "I have to run. You'll be fine."

"But," Elena began. She didn't want them to leave. "Where are you going? We still need you." She jogged behind the slow-moving vehicle, arms outstretched, as if by her own will she could stop them from leaving.

"We're going to another camp that needs us. You'll be in good hands."

Russians and Austrians? The words sank in. Not Russians. She didn't want to be under the control of the Russians. What if they found out about her father? He was a deserter. They'd shoot him on the spot. Her skin crawled. She began to perspire. She had to find her parents and get away before the Russians found them. First, she needed Maria.

"I left a present for Tatiana!" the nurse shouted as the truck slipped through the main gates. Elena watched for a moment. Something was different about the gates, besides the fact that they were open. The enormous eagle with the swastika in its claws had been replaced by a long banner written in Spanish. The best she could interpret was, "Antifascist Spaniards greet the forces of liberation." Spaniards, a group of people she'd been unaware of. She wiped her eyes, unaware she'd been crying, and headed back to the house. Who would take care of them now? Not the Russians. At that thought she began to run.

Maria was tugging Tatiana's right arm into a pale pink sweater. The toddler already wore a matching pink hat tied with a deep mauve ribbon under her chin. Underneath the sweater she was dressed in dark green corduroy pants and a gray cotton shirt, clothing donated by Frau Zimmer.

"Look," Maria said, smiling brightly. "These were on her cot with a note for you. Aren't they darling?"

Elena stopped in the doorway. An American soldier sat on the white enameled stool smoking a cigarette. Rusty brown hair fell over his forehead, stopping just short of his eyebrows. A smile lingered on his pale, freckled face.

Maria picked up the baby. "Kenny, this is my sister by marriage, Elena," she said in carefully precise English.

Except she had said it wrong. Elena wasn't a sister by marriage. She wasn't a sister by anything. Maria had passed herself off as the wife of Papa's youngest brother. That would make her an aunt by marriage. Elena stepped into the room.

"How do you do?" she said to Kenny as she reached for Tatiana.

Maria clung to the baby, turning her back to Elena. "Auntie Elena has an appointment with Mrs. Parker at the Red Cross office," she cooed in a childish voice to Tatiana and then said, "Kenny and Mama are going to take wittle Yana for a ride into the town."

Elena's heart felt like it dropped to her feet. She froze, her hand still stretching out for Tatiana. "Yana? Since when do you call her that?" she said in Russian.

Maria swayed as she held the baby. "Kenny likes that for a nickname for her. I think it's sweet. Why are you being rude in front of my friend?"

"You're not taking my baby out of this camp. Give her to me so I can carry her with me to see Mrs. Parker. Do you know if they've found my parents?"

Kenny stood, his eyes going from woman to woman. He was a tall, lanky young man. Elena nearly laughed at the thought of this innocent looking boy in the clutches of Maria, the seductress. "If you all will excuse me, I'll just wait out back in the Jeep. Keep in mind, I got my orders. I can't wait long to give you a ride, Maria." He replaced his peaked cap, which made him look like a little boy playing at soldier, and stepped gingerly around Elena, who glared at him until he'd exited the building.

"What is that all about? How am I now your sister-in-law and what do you mean by calling Tatiana your baby?"

Maria easily relinquished the baby this time. "I like Kenny. I didn't want him thinking I was so old; he thinks I'm twenty-two. He's twenty-one." She reached under the mattress and pulled out several packs of Lucky Strike cigarettes. "Look what he gave me!"

"Where were you planning to go with that American?"

"He wants to marry me and take us to America."

Elena put her hands on her hips. "Who is 'us'?" she asked, a suspicion forming in her mind.

"Tatiana and I." Maria leaned across the bed and pleaded, almost convincingly, "You do want your daughter raised in America, don't you?"

"I do," she answered, knowing Maria rarely did anything for anyone else unless there was something in it for her.

"So, part of your prayers is answered. I'll take Tatiana and then, later, when you get there, we can all be together again." She made the statement with such conviction Elena was tempted to accept the premise, but then she thought of Kenny.

"That boy can't want to marry you. He's only known you a few days," Elena pointed out.

"Two weeks."

"It doesn't matter. I won't give you permission to take my daughter away from me. We all go together or she doesn't go at all." Elena crossed her arms.

"Kenny has many little brothers and sisters. He loves children! His family lives on a farm in a place called Arkansas. A farm, Elena. Tatiana could grow up on a farm with all the fresh food she could ever want."

"No."

"Think about the Zimmer farm. The fresh air, all the food waiting to be pulled from the ground or plucked from the trees. Tatiana can have all that if you let her. Think about Tatiana for a change."

Elena felt as if her face had been slapped. The feeling was so strong, she reached up to touch her cheek. "I always think about her."

"When you're not thinking about your musical fantasies," Maria spat at her.

"Why are you so anxious for Tatiana to go with you? Why don't you go with your Kenny and make your own babies?" As Elena said it, she understood. Kenny was more interested in rescuing Tatiana than marrying Maria.

Maria squared her shoulders, prepared to argue.

"You needn't say anything. Maria, you'll find another American who wants you just for you. Give it another week. For now, we have to make plans to get out of here quickly before the Russians find us. Do you think your Kenny will drive all of us into the village?"

Maria wouldn't let her opportunity go so easily. She tried one more time. "Maybe you forget, but Tatiana is registered here as my daughter. You didn't want her."

Elena sucked in her breath.

Forty-four

"You're not taking Tatiana from me. She is my daughter. After what we've been through? Think again," Elena shouted.

"Who do you think they'll believe? You, a sixteen-year-old?"

Kenny stood in the entrance. "Hey, y'all want a ride or what? We're moving out and I gotta get this here Jeep into town."

Elena realized with the chaos at the camp and the thousands of refugees in need of resettlement, she didn't have time to consider. She made her decision. "May I come as well?" she asked Kenny.

"What about your parents?" Maria scoffed at her. "Don't you want to find them?"

"You know what it's like. We need to get away from the Russians, don't you understand?"

Tatiana sucked her thumb, her eyes going from Maria to Elena.

"Two minutes ago you were so worried about them, about your father. What happened?"

Elena felt Tatiana's warm breath on her cheek and knew what happened; she understood finally—she was a mother. Tatiana needed her. Though the moment had come to her in a flash, it had taken a long time for her to reach this point. The past months she'd grown closer to her baby, taking more control over her care, especially after learning about Tatiana's close escape from death. She would be forever grateful to Dr. Peters. Now she had to get her two-year-old away from this camp, away from the Russians whom she feared; Russians who would deliver them right back to the old ways. Instead of answering Maria, she lifted the edge of the mattress.

"Pick up your cigarettes, Maria, they'll be useful to us," Elena said.

Maria glared, but picked up the four packs and stuffed them into her pockets. "Let's go."

Elena grabbed a small cloth bag that held all her possessions, including the piano.

They followed Kenny along the path to the American Jeep and climbed in. Elena looked back at the stone and brick house, leaving it with feelings of relief and longing. She'd been able to play a real piano for a short while. Now, with her baby and a fabric piano, she was going to a new life. All she had were the tattered clothes she wore and the still sturdy boots her father had provided. Maria carried a small bag with Tatiana's clothes.

Trying to ignore the sight of the massive camp walls, Elena stared straight ahead. As they crossed the railroad tracks her eyes searched the fields for the tree next to the stream where Tatiana had been born. When the turn-off to the Zimmer farm caught her eye, she wondered briefly how that family had fared, but understood she would never know. She was in the hands of the American, Kenny, and hoped he wouldn't be the last one she would meet.

Two years ago she'd arrived at Mauthausen, one day after giving birth to Tatiana, but she could not remember the exact date. She had an idea. "Kenny! What's today's date?"

"May 30th, Ma'am," he shouted over the roar of the engine.

"Today is Tatiana's birthday. May 30."

"Actually, it's May--" Maria began.

"I said it's May 30th," Elena said, cutting her off.

The Jeep stopped at the edge of a town to allow a large group of people to cross the road. Men and women dressed in rags similar to Elena's, their faces grim, eyes fearful, huddled close together as they walked in unison. Her heart leapt as she heard Russian words. She stood up in the back of the Jeep and scanned the small crowd for a sign of her parents.

"Hello, comrades!" she shouted. "Does anyone know of Anna or Grigory Federov?"

Their heads turned as one toward the sound of her voice, but no one seemed to understand her.

"Anna and Grigory Federov," she repeated.

The group continued on until they had all crossed the road.

"Can you wait a minute?" she asked Kenny in English.

"Barely," he grumbled. "I really gotta get this Jeep back."

She passed Tatiana over to Maria and leapt to the ground. At the first person she approached, an old woman, she looked directly into the vacant eyes and spoke again. "I am searching for my mother and father, Anna and Grigory Federov. He has one arm."

The woman stared as if she hadn't heard. Elena grabbed the front of her dress. "Speak to me, at least, old woman!"

The woman cringed but the group closed around her, facing Elena.

She gave the woman a shove. "Never mind. I'll find them myself later."

"What was that about?" Kenny asked as he shifted into gear and drove into the village proper. American soldiers bustled around assorted military trucks, cars and open Jeeps like the one they rode in.

"I asked about my parents, that's all," she said, annoyed the old woman had cowered away from her.

"You were pretty rough on that old lady," he said as he swerved to avoid a pair of local children skipping across the street. Their ruddy cheeks made her Tatiana look so pale and delicate by comparison. She hated them. "If you think I was rough it was only because those people are too stupid to know they are free. They can go where they want. They can create new lives."

"I don't think it's as easy as all that, ma'am. It's one of the reasons I want to help Miss Maria and Yana to get to America where people really are free. She told me about all the red tape and complications." He gave a quick smile to Maria, who responded with a shy smile of her own before turning forward again.

"She did, did she?" Elena studied the back of Maria's head. She switched to Russian, "Let's see how complicated it becomes when you try to bring your sister-in-law and her parents with you."

"That won't happen. We have our plans in place."

"You're not taking Tatiana with you."

Maria shifted Tatiana on her lap. "Mommy's little girl is going to be so happy living on the great big farm, aren't you?"

"Stop calling her your little girl. She's mine. I can prove I've had a baby; you can't."

"What makes you think that?" Maria answered, turning her head just enough so Elena could see the smile on her face.

"Would you two please speak English? If Yana's going to become an American, she might as well start learning right now."

"Now!" Tatiana shouted in English, throwing her hands in the air. "Eat now!"

In spite of her anger, Elena managed to laugh at her daughter's exuberance. "You see, Kenny, she is speaking it already."

"Okay, ma'am, this is where we part company for a while." He leaned over and kissed Maria quickly before dropping them off in front of a closed bakery. "Wait at the coffee shop on that corner and I'll be back in an hour," he advised Maria.

"One hour. Coffee shop," she repeated.

"That's what I said, baby." He blew her a kiss and headed down the street.

"I hope you had your fun with him because that's the last you'll see of that fellow," Elena said.

"What would you know about it? Don't think you're going to move in on my plans. Tatiana and I are going to America with Kenny. He can be her Papa. Come on, let's get coffee or whatever they're serving down there. You can take time to say goodbye to Tatiana. But don't worry, you'll be able to see her once you get to America. I'm sure it won't take you long."

"I'll come to your coffee shop with you, but don't think it's because I plan to say any farewells. I'm hungry." Her heart lifted, momentarily forgetting about their disagreement. They had the choice to go for food at any time of the day or night. There was no one to tell them what to do and when to do it.

"What about money?" Maria asked.

"You have cigarettes."

Maria nodded as she rushed to keep up with Elena.

"That's what they're for. They're not for you to smoke."

A mob of foreigners filled the café, pouring out onto the sidewalk where a dozen or more tables were set– Americans, Russians, Finns, French, and others speaking languages Elena had never heard. She sat down abruptly at a table as two large Russians stood to leave. The older of the two frowned at her.

"Pardon me, sir. It's so crowded, my friend needs to sit for a while and I didn't want to miss the chance to take this table."

He smiled at Maria who still held Tatiana. "It's not a problem, young lady. I hope they have food left. They have been running out in the afternoons. He tipped his hat and moved off.

Elena sat across from Maria. Tatiana reached out for her. Maria didn't stop her. The toddler crawled across the table to Elena and settled herself on her lap. "Now eat," she said in English.

"In a minute. We have to wait for the man," she answered in Russian.

Maria drummed her fingers on the tabletop. Tatiana tried to imitate her. Elena then began running her own hands over the tabletop, practicing imaginary scales. Tatiana rested her hands on her mother's and laughed as they moved back and forth across the small table. Involved with Tatiana, Elena forgot about food and began singing the notes. Tatiana followed suit, singing out of tune in a sweet baby voice. Maria pushed away from the table. "I'm going to find someone to serve us. Keep an eye out for Kenny."

Elena had forgotten about him in her delight at sitting in a public place with no one to tell her what to do. "I'll watch," she replied, still not convinced he'd return.

"Here's an easy one. It's a student piece. *Marche Militaire.* Ready?" Elena held her hands several inches above the table. Tatiana did the same. "Here we go."

She hummed the tune as she fingered the music over the tabletop. Tatiana was delighted to be playing, giggling when her hands didn't keep up with her mother's and slapping the table happily when she recognized the melody repeating itself.

There was no letup in the trucks churning through the street. Men and women came and went at the tables and still neither Kenny nor Maria returned. Tatiana yawned and curled up in her mother's arms. Elena shifted in order to be more comfortable with the baby on her lap, but continued to play more melodies, humming or singing as she played.

"Say, Miss, wouldn't it be easier if you had a piano in front of you?" a man's voice came from behind her. Not Kenny's.

She turned to look up. A good-looking American soldier smiled at her. They all have the nicest teeth, she thought. "Of course, it would. There do not seem to be any available."

He removed his cap revealing a shock of hair as blond as her own. "Would you mind if I sat across from you? Not only are there no pianos, there aren't many places to sit."

She hesitated. "I have a friend…" Maria had been gone for at least half an hour. "Of course. Please sit. After what you Americans have done for us, the least we can do is let you sit down for a little while."

"My name is Myles Hall." He held out a hand.

"Elena Federova."

"Russian?"

"Yes, Russian, but I am going to America soon."

"Good for you! You're one of the lucky ones. What are you having?" He folded his arms on the table, making himself comfortable.

She looked at the table and then back at his face. He had laughing brown eyes. "I am having nothing."

"Eating. I meant what did you order to eat? Sorry about that. Your English is very good. A he…heck of a sight better than my Russian."

"My friend went to get the food. I do not know what we'll be eating." Tatiana squirmed and Elena had to shift again to try to get comfortable. She wasn't used to having to hold her for so long at one time. "Do you speak Russian?"

"Not a bit. Learned some German during the war, but nothing I could say in front of a lady." He leaned across the table. "Will your friend be upset if he sees me sitting here?"

It took a moment to realize what he meant. "No! My friend is Maria. We have been together since two years."

"Prisoners?"

His questioning made her uncomfortable. She wished either Maria or Kenny would show up. "Yes, prisoners. Up there on the hill," she nodded in the direction of the camp.

His eyes widened. "Wow! And you survived?"

She tilted her head to the right. "Look at me. I sit here. I am alive. My baby is alive."

"You Jewish?"

The way he said it added to her discomfort. "And if I am? Will you stop talking with me?"

"No, no." He hurried his words. "Nothing like that. I was up there, helping to liberate the camp. I didn't see anyone who looked like they could last more'n a day or two. You look pretty fit for being in there."

"We were fortunate to be Russians, I suppose. We were simple prisoners, not a race of people dedicated for extinction."

Myles leaned back in his chair. "I'm sorry. I guess it's been bad for a lot of people."

"Yes. It was bad and I am very hungry. Would you have any money so we could get a little food? I do not know what is keeping Maria for so long. Perhaps they do not accept cigarettes for payment."

"Uh. Sure, kid." His eyes became wary. "Let me go get the food. If your friend comes back, tell her I'm bringing more." He jumped up from his chair as if he couldn't get away fast enough, but he did go inside the café where the noise spilling out onto the sidewalk was deafening.

She leaned back and sighed. Living outside the prison was going to take getting used to.

"Miss Elena, isn't it? I wasn't sure I got your name right. Maria's English is pretty bad," Kenny said as he dropped down onto the chair vacated by Myles. "Where's Maria? We need to go if we're going."

Elena laughed. "Yes, I am Elena and Maria went to get food about an hour ago. You might find her if you go in there."

He looked at the entrance where people were lined up, waiting to get in. "I'm serious about us marrying, you know. We have an appointment to talk to my chaplain. There's a lot of paperwork, but I think I can convince them we'll have a good life together on the farm. Especially with Yana. She's so precious, it would be a shame for her to live here as a displaced person. No home. Nothing."

"There's something you ought to know, Kenny." Elena took a breath, knowing she would be betraying her friend, but what had Maria done to her? "Tatiana is my daughter, not Maria's. And I am not ready to marry anyone. I am going to America to work and study so I can play the piano at Carnegie Hall. That is my dream."

Kenny's face was blank. It was if he she hadn't spoken.

"Did you hear me?"

He shook his head. "Um, I don't understand. Are you sure?"

Elena pinched her lips.

"Why would she say Yana is hers?"

"She is my closest friend now, Kenny, but Maria is anxious to get away from here and I think she cares not much who she hurts doing it. She was prepared to take my baby away from me."

"But she said she has papers!"

"Papers that are lies."

Kenny's eyes filled with tears. "That just don't make any kind of sense."

"You are too soft in the heart, Kenny. Maria understands. She knew you would marry her if it meant that would save Tatiana."

Kenny cleared his throat. "Geez. This can't be real. I did offer to take her baby home with me if I was allowed. I hadn't thought about marrying her at all until she mentioned it. Tell Maria I'll see her in a couple of days. Um—I'll come here at noon day after tomorrow. I have to think about this." Saying that, he reached across the small table and gently patted Tatiana on the head.

"It will work out for you, Kenny. My father brought us to Germany so we wouldn't starve in Leningrad. Sometimes I didn't trust or believe him, but here we are. The war is over; the Germans have surrendered to you…"

"To the Allies," he corrected.

"Yes. He was right. We didn't starve. Sometimes I thought we would. It was not always good, but we did not die."

He looked so sad, she wanted to hug him. "Go home, Kenny and be happy in America. Someday you will come see me in a concert. If you want to give me your information, then I can send you letters and pictures of Tatiana."

He took two sticks of chewing gum from his shirt pocket and passed one to Elena. "This should help until your food arrives." He unwrapped it for her and she stuck it in her mouth, unsure what to do. She watched him chewing. The gum was sweet. Another American thing to like. She smiled at him. "Thank you, Kenny."

Kenny pulled out a small notebook and wrote on a page, tore it out and handed it to her. "And when you get to America, if Tatiana ever needs anything, you be sure to let me know."

"I will do that, Kenny." He weaved between the crowded tables and disappeared in the crowd. She'd known him for a few hours and missed him. Was she always going to become attached so quickly to every new person she met? She closed her eyes, grateful to be alone for a few minutes with no one who knew her.

"Here you go."

She opened her eyes to a platter full of potato pancakes and a bowl of applesauce. Myles stood there holding plates and utensils.

Tatiana woke up, rubbing her eyes. "Eat. Now."

"That's what I like to hear, little girl," he said as he seated himself. "Chow time. Can you say that? Chow time."

"Chow time," she repeated like a little parrot. "Now eat."

"She's cute. How old is she?"

"Two today."

"Happy birthday. For that you get an extra pancake, little girl." He loaded the plates with food.

Elena bristled at the way he spoke. These Americans were all so friendly, she didn't know what to make of them. "Her name is Tatiana."

"Tatiana." He frowned in thought. "Wasn't that the name of one of the Russian princesses who was killed?"

She flinched at the reference. "They were grand duchesses. Yes, the same name, but my daughter is named after my best friend who died in Leningrad."

"Didn't mean to offend. Go on. Eat. These are good!"

Tatiana had no trouble wolfing down her pancakes and making a mess of getting the applesauce into her mouth.

They'd been eating for a few minutes when Maria returned with a tray bearing drinks, bread, and a pot of honey. Her face fell when she realized the soldier at the table wasn't Kenny.

"This is Lieutenant Myles Hall." Elena introduced them in English.

Myles stood and offered his chair to Maria.

Maria scanned the tables. "Have you seen Kenny?"

Elena looked directly at her. "No."

"Kenny, bye-bye," Tatiana said through a mouthful of pancake.

"I have tea." She set the tray on the table amidst the mess Tatiana had created. "Where did all this come from?"

"Myles brought it for us." Elena smiled at him, but Myles was busy searching for an empty chair.

Maria shrugged. "This is all I could get. It's been over an hour. Are you sure you haven't seen him? Have you been watching? Or have you been too busy eating?"

Elena smiled at her. "Eating is one of my new favorite things to do. Taste these. They're delicious. The applesauce is fresh as if it's from Frau Zimmer's farm."

Maria picked up a pancake in her hand and dipped it in the applesauce. "It's good," she said in Russian. "What's this fellow's game?" She nodded toward Myles, who was now dragging a chair to their table.

Elena shrugged. "Nothing. I asked him for money for food and he went and bought it for us."

Maria's eyes grew wide. "You begged?" she shouted at Elena.

"It wasn't begging. He's an American. They have lots of money. And they can't stand to see hungry babies. You had that one figured out already."

"Let's not fight, girls. There's plenty of food to go around." Myles licked his fingers and used a napkin to wipe his mouth. "What are your plans? Will you go back to Leningrad?"

Maria looked alarmed. "What makes him think we're from Leningrad?" she asked Elena in Russian.

"I told him about Tatiana's name." She then translated for Myles and added, "We want to stay from Russia because my father might be killed for being a deserter. We are going to America."

"Right." Myles nodded. "I'm working on logistics. Displaced persons. Finding homes. We're fixing up an office across the street. Maybe I can find something for you."

"Dr. Peters, that is Captain Dr. Peters, said he would put Tatiana and me high on the Red Cross list for a room in Vienna."

Myles laughed. "Sorry. I have no control over what the Red Cross does. You can go see them if you prefer. I thank you for the company, but now I have to get back to work. Remember, I'm across the street."

Both girls watched him leave before speaking.

"So. If Kenny doesn't come back shall we get to America with his help?" Maria asked.

"Why not? But not your way," Elena answered as she stared at the building across the street.

Forty-five

"We need a place to sleep tonight." Maria gazed around the bustling village center.

Elena's legs turned rubbery as she staggered to a nearby bench at the edge of a small park. "This has been too much for me today. I thought I was ready to meet the world." She let out a half-laugh and then drew a deep breath.

Maria remained on the sidewalk, hands on hips surveying the area. Even in her tattered dress and scruffy black jacket she looked haughty and beautiful.

Elena watched her for a moment considering what they should do next. Ever-resourceful Maria probably could find them a place to sleep in this suddenly overcrowded town. That would be the first step. She had an idea forming about the next one.

"Maria! Why don't you go in search of a room while I stay here with Tatiana? The idea of sitting in the sunshine with no guards, no doctors, no nurses is too appealing."

"Are you sure you're well enough to take care of her? You're looking terribly pale."

"Don't worry. She'll be fine. Remember, I'm her mother; I'll protect her."

Elena turned to see Tatiana had removed her woolen booties and was stepping gingerly on the grass behind the bench, giggling with delight as the grass tickled her feet. An acorn caught her eye, but before she could pop it into her mouth, Elena scooped it away from her.

"Chow time!" Tatiana shouted with her arms outstretched toward Elena.

Elena and Maria exchanged glances, both smiling.

"We must go to America," Elena said as she gathered Tatiana in her arms. Tatiana wrapped her arms around Elena's neck and squeezed.

Maria agreed. "I'll see about rooms. Meet you here in time to look for supper."

"Leave me some cigarettes."

"For what?" Maria clutched her pockets protectively.

"An emergency. If Tatiana gets hungry before you return. I don't know." Elena watched Maria reluctantly pull four cigarettes from a pack, passing them to her as if they were solid gold. Probably more useful than gold at this moment, she thought. "Thank you."

Once Maria was out of sight, Elena picked up Tatiana, replaced her booties, hiked the strap of Tatiana's small suitcase and her bag over her shoulder and headed back to the street where they'd eaten earlier. Tatiana announced their arrival before Elena caught sight of the café. "Chow time!" she cried out, clapping her hands.

Elena shifted her in her arms and turned her attention to the building across the street.

"Chow time later," she told her baby. "America time now."

Autos and trucks still crammed the street, the noise overwhelming, the fumes nauseating. She stepped off the curb between two parked cars and edged her way into the traffic. No driver took any notice of her and her baby. Elena's lower lip quivered as she tried to calculate how to cross to the other side. Horns honked to her left, adding to her confusion. A man crossing to the left of her raised his fists and shouted obscenities at the vehicles, forcing them to stop, allowing him to pass.

That took courage. Step out and pray.

Inching her way forward into traffic, she hugged Tatiana tightly, and then took a giant step into a gap between two trucks. The horn blared from the oncoming truck but it stopped. She crossed in front of it, giving a little wave of thanks as she then maneuvered the rest of the way across the busy avenue. She gasped once she reached the curb and leaned against the side of the building to catch her breath.

She set Tatiana on the sidewalk. "Tatiana wants to walk, yes?"

"Chow time!"

Elena looked where Tatiana pointed. The shop window behind her displayed new and used furniture along with an arrangement of children's toys. She didn't see the connection to food, but Tatiana insisted. Elena scanned the furniture again. Her eyes stopped at a child's highchair where a baby doll sat with a small bowl and spoon on the tray before it.

Smiling and shaking her head at the simple wonder of her child, Elena said, "Baby is having chow time. We'll eat again later. Now we'll go to see Mr. Hall."

She opened the glass door with the hand printed sign taped on it, "Temporary HQ – Allied Expeditionary Forces, Central Tracking Services," written in English, Russian, French, and German. "Up we go."

Tatiana's eyes grew huge as she stared upwards toward the light at the top of the stairs. Without hesitation, she climbed the first few steps, hands first followed by feet. When she was four steps up, Elena followed, ready to catch her if she slipped.

They made it successfully to the top. Tatiana announced her arrival by clapping her hands and reaching up for Elena.

Exhausted by the steep climb, Elena took Tatiana's hand and led her to the first of several doors in the long hallway. She read each sign on the doors until she arrived at the one that announced, "Lt. Myles Hall, U. S. Army, Central Tracking Services." She knocked and waited. Tatiana copied her action even to folding her arms and tapping her foot.

Raised voices on the other side of the door didn't bode well. Elena eyed the empty hallway and wondered which other door she ought to try to get away. Across the hall from Myles' office a sign announced, UNRRA, with no other explanation. As she considered knocking on that door instead, Myles' door flew open. A short, stout woman brushed past them as she stormed her way out, muttering in unintelligible German.

The American who had opened the door signaled for her to enter. His appraising glance suggested he considered her less threatening than his last visitor. "Speak English?" he said.

"Yes. Is this where I can find Lt. Myles Hall?"

"Chow time," Tatiana said.

"Do you have an appointment?"

"An appointment?" She never considered needing an appointment. "No, but he asked me to come see him only an hour ago."

The soldier peered over his eyeglasses, making him look like an old man. "Did he really?"

"He really did. May I see him?"

"He's – um – not available at the moment."

The inner door swung open and Myles stepped into the small reception room. "Clark!"

Clark pulled himself to attention. "Yes, sir!"

"Have you checked—?" He stopped when he saw Elena and Tatiana. "Excuse me, I didn't expect to see you so soon."

"You said to come if I need help. I need help."

"Sir, you told me not to…" Clark stopped speaking as Tatiana jumped into Myles' arms.

"Chow time!" she shouted gleefully. Myles tossed her in the air and caught her. Tatiana snuggled contentedly in his arm while Elena followed them into his office.

"I'll need a new file, Clark."

"Yes, sir," Clark answered as the door closed.

"Coffee?" Myles asked Elena.

"Coffee?"

"It's almost real. It comes with cookies." After offering her a chair, he went around behind his desk and sat with Tatiana on his lap.

"In that case, yes," she smiled at him wondering what Maria would do next. Maria never took Tatiana with her when collecting favors from men.

"Clark!" he shouted. When the aide popped his head around the door, Myles ordered coffee, cookies and then added milk for Tatiana.

"What's your problem?" he asked Elena when Clark was gone.

"You told that man to get a new clerk. Does the clerk have to be an American?"

"Clark? No, I meant a folder in which I put information. I assume you're here like everyone else who wants to go to America. I can't promise anything, but we can start the paperwork. You'd be better off if you wanted to go to Brazil. They've already got a boatload set to leave."

"Brazil? Why would I want to go to Brazil?"

He shrugged. "It would get you away from this." His free hand waved toward the right of his desk. It faced onto the street she'd just left.

"But I don't speak Brazilian. How could I survive?"

"I think they speak Portuguese." He gave Tatiana a pencil and showed her how to make marks on his desk calendar.

"I don't speak that either. I came because Maria is looking for a room for us to spend the night."

The blank stare on his face suggested she hadn't explained herself well.

"Maria is usually the one who can get things done."

"An admirable trait."

"Yes," she answered. With her hands folded in her lap, she felt like a schoolgirl called up before one of her teachers. She chewed her bottom lip.

"What do you want, Miss Federova?"

"It is true I came here to ask for help to go to America, but when that other lady left so angry, I thought perhaps today is not a good day to ask for favors."

"But you still knocked on the door, so you do want something." Tatiana threw the pencil onto the floor. He picked it up. This began a game.

Elena told her story as Myles continued to entertain Tatiana. She began by pulling her tattered piano from her bag and spreading it on the edge of his desk.

"What in God's name is that?" he said.

Clark stepped in and handed a manila folder to Myles, glanced once at the piano, and then left.

"It was a gift to replace my destroyed piano, but that's not what is important." The thread used to seal in the paper her grandmother had given her proved to be stronger than the fabric – it shredded as Elena tried to undo the stitches. When the fabric tore, her hands flew and she knocked a stack of files from the corner of his desk.

"I have it," she said, dropping to the floor and collecting the scattered papers.

"This is the information about our American relatives. I know they will take us in. These are my father's brothers." She passed the paper covered in Grandmama's penciled scrawl to Myles.

"It's in Russian."

"I'll translate it all for you. Look. They live in Flatbush Avenue in Brooklyn on Long Island in the state of New York. Can you write all that down? I can give you their full names and everything I know about them."

Myles set Tatiana on the floor with blank paper and pencils and began writing. When he was done, he inserted the information into a fresh file. "I'll see what I can do. Is there anything else?"

"I want work. When I heard that last lady leaving, I thought perhaps I could work for you."

"What could you do for me?"

Tatiana shouted, "Chow time."

Elena laughed. "I believe she thinks that is your name."

He picked Tatiana up and said, "No, that's her name. Chow Time!"

Clark tapped on the door and stepped in with a tray laden with a coffee pot, cups, saucers, creamer, sugar, and a plate stacked with cookies. After placing it on the desk out of reach of Tatiana, he poured the coffee.

"Milk for the little girl?" Myles asked.

"It's coming, sir. The UN ladies are warming it."

Tatiana eyed the cookies. Her arms couldn't reach them and she quickly stood up on Myles' knees and began to crawl across the desk, knocking the telephone from its cradle, and a pile of papers to the floor. Elena jumped up to stop her, but Myles beat her to it.

"No grabbing, Chow Time. Let me get one for you." He handed her one cookie and she held out her other hand for another. He gave it to her. She leaned back against his chest and happily spread crumbs all over her face, sweater and dribbled them down his uniform.

While this had been going on, Elena's mind raced around the possibilities. What could she do for him? Then she remembered he'd said at lunch that he couldn't speak Russian and not very much German. He probably didn't speak French either. "I could be your translator."

"You?"

"Yes. I speak English, and of course, Russian. Also very good French and fairly good German, so I could be many persons for you."

"You are talented. What else do you do?" He handed two more cookies to Tatiana.

Elena studied his face for a moment to see what he meant. She decided the question was an innocent one. "I am good at playing the piano, although the opportunities have been rare because of being in the prison camp."

"I would imagine they were nonexistent. How old are you, Miss Federova?"

How old? At the prison camp she pretended to be two years older than her real age. The Nazis hadn't cared one way or the other. "Almost nineteen."

He nodded. "Do you have family here besides Maria?"

"My parents are someplace. My mother and I were together. Papa was separated from us. He has one arm."

Myles picked up a pencil and wrote on a sheet of lined paper.

For the next half hour she answered his questions about herself and her family. Elena managed to rescue two cookies for herself while Tatiana mashed the rest of them into her mouth.

The UN ladies had sent in a baby bottle full of warmed milk which Tatiana sucked down.

"Go look for Maria. If she hasn't found a room for you, come back. There are a couple of schools and a convent where we've been putting up people."

"If possible, I would not want to return to a crowded camp," Elena said as she stood.

He passed Tatiana across the desk to her and then reached into his trousers' pocket, pulling out an odd-looking currency. "Use this for your dinner. It's occupation money. The vendors have been advised that this is the legitimate currency."

"And my job?" she asked while grabbing the money and stuffing it in her skirt pocket. Tatiana reached for it, but Elena brushed her hand away.

"I'll have to see about that. Let me know where you're staying and I'll notify you if I can work something out."

Feeling rejected by Myles when she left the office, she led Tatiana slowly along the hallway, wondering what her next step should be. On her way down the stairs, an elderly couple worked their way up. They were speaking Russian.

"Don't bother. You need an appointment and they don't speak anything but English up there," she grumbled at them.

"They didn't help you and your child?"

"Oh, yes. They helped me, but I speak English." She turned to continue down the stairs.

"Can we pay you to translate for us?" the old man asked.

"What have you got?"

Forty-six

Elena stared at the small, gold medal depicting St. George the couple had handed her. She pocketed it.

"They usually require an appointment, but I may be able to convince them to see you now," she said, sounding more confident than she felt. The medal probably wouldn't buy much food, but she accompanied them up the stairs anyway.

Clark redirected her to the UN office across the hall where dozens of people lined the walls on benches, awaiting their opportunity to find a new home, a family, temporary shelter, or food. Elena translated for the couple as they wove their way through the maze of official paperwork which only resulted in them being assigned to a nearby convent for temporary housing. Tatiana grew impatient from time to time but was easily distracted by strangers who caught her attention and played games with her.

As they left the building hours later, they thanked Elena again. "St. George will be as good to you as he has been to us," the woman promised. "Bless you and your child."

Elena watched the two of them totter down the street, papers in hand; the man kept his arm around his wife to support her. The vision of the elderly couple reminded her of her own parents. A young woman stopped them. After a brief discussion, the man pointed to where Elena stood in front of the entrance to the building.

As the woman approached, Tatiana took that moment to be shy and hid behind Elena's skirt. Elena wanted to hide as well. The emaciated woman's skeletal face and flat, black eyes gave her the appearance of a hollowed-out crone. A tattered scarf covered her head, where only tufts of short, wispy hair stood between her scalp and baldness. Afraid the girl would surely die in front of her, Elena shuddered.

"My name is Barbara Horowitz," she began in German. "They said you could translate."

Barbara stood so close her foul breath made Elena take a step back. "It's my job," Elena said, hoping the talking corpse wouldn't pursue the matter further.

"I have nothing to pay but I could perhaps care for your child."

Barbara couldn't care for a fallen sparrow in her condition. Elena wanted to walk away.

"I'm trying to find my family. I was told the Americans might be able to help me. Do you know anything about them?"

"A little."

"Does anyone speak Yiddish? I can speak German and Yiddish."

"I don't know." Elena sighed. "Follow me. It's a long flight of stairs. Can you climb them?"

Barbara stepped through the entrance and looked upward. "If that is what I must do to find my family, I will climb them."

By the time they reached the third step Tatiana begged to be carried. Elena picked her up, slung her onto her right hip so she could pull herself up the stairs with her left hand on the railing.

She led Barbara directly to Myles' office instead of to the UN ladies. Clark smiled when she entered.

"Lieutenant Hall asked me where you were living and I had to tell him that I forgot to take your address."

"This girl wants you to find her family. I am her translator. Will you please tell the lieutenant that we are here?"

"He'll be available shortly. If you'll give me your address?" His pen poised over a piece of paper, he waited.

"I don't have an address."

"How will we reach you?"

"I will be here. I have a new business."

Myles entered the reception office from the hall a few minutes later, dropped a heap of files on Clark's desk and then signaled Elena to come in.

"Chow time!" Tatiana cheered.

Elena led Barbara into the office. Myles handed Tatiana blank papers and a pencil before opening a new file. As he questioned Barbara in English, Elena translated into German.

Tatiana grew weary of drawing pictures, climbed onto Elena's lap, curled up and went to sleep.

With Tatiana now sleeping over her shoulder, she found her way back to the park hoping Maria had found a room.

Streetlights were on by the time Maria returned stinking of cigarettes and whiskey. "We have a room for a week. Share a kitchen and toilet," she said as she sank onto the bench next to Elena.

"Is it at least clean?"

"What do you want? It has a roof and a bed. Where did you go? I returned for you ages ago. When you were gone, I went to see what's in this village."

"I went to the American's office to meet with Lieutenant Hall. He might be able to help find my parents."

"And what else did your GI do for you?"

"He's not my GI. Nothing. I'm going back in the morning to offer to work for him. I translated for people today so he could see how useful I can be." Elena smiled, proud of her accomplishment. "Oh, and he gave me some currency for food. He's very nice."

"Fine. Let's find some supper and then I'll show you our new home."

"Not for long, I hope." Elena scooped up the sleeping child.

"No, not for long. I, too, have a plan." Maria's walk seemed a little too jaunty, but maybe that was the whiskey. They returned to the café where they'd had lunch.

Elena stood in the doorway on the third floor of a large old house on the outskirts of the village. The room turned out to be more squalid than the prison camp. The building already had the smell of poverty and despair with the odors of urine and cabbage permeating the air. The mattress on the double bed pushed against the corner of the room sank in the center. Cigarette burns and moth holes decorated the worn woolen blanket. Shoved into the opposite corner were a small kitchen table and three metal chairs. An incongruously grand armoire stood to the right of the entrance. A single light bulb threw feeble, sour light into the tiny room. Elena stepped onto the faded linoleum, wondering how long it would take to make the place clean enough for her and Tatiana.

"Don't frown, Elena. It's better than some of the rooms in here. Remember, it won't be for long. Come on, I'll show you the bathroom and water closet. They're one flight down next to the kitchen."

Too tired to argue, Elena followed Maria down the stairs, used the water closet which had a real flushing toilet, and then washed Tatiana and herself, preparing to sleep.

As they shifted on the bed, trying to get comfortable, Elena told Maria about the convent. "I think the sisters would keep it very clean. Perhaps we should ask Myles about it tomorrow."

Maria laughed. "Perhaps you should come with me to the club I found. There are a lot of GI's that would appreciate your singing voice. Then we would be able to afford our own better room."

"It might be something to consider." Elena yawned, convinced she'd never fall asleep, what with the lumps and the moldy odor of the bedding. Tatiana snored quietly, curled under Elena's arm. "At a convent, the nuns could look after Tatiana while we work."

"Forget the convent," Maria said. "I don't think nuns and I would get along."

Elena was surprised to wake up to sunlight streaming across the floor, brightening the room. She'd slept soundly all night. Maria and Tatiana still slept next to her on the musty mattress. She eased herself off the bed, slipped her dress over her head and found her way down to the kitchen where two old men, both clothed in dark trousers and graying white shirts with suspenders, sat smoking in silence.

"Good morning," she said in Russian.

One of them grunted. "Good."

"Do you mind if I look around?"

"Look," the other one said.

After a cursory inspection, she decided that at least for today she and Tatiana would eat at the café across from Myles' office. She would watch for people who required a translator until either the UN ladies or Myles recognized her value and hired her officially. In the evening she could check on the nightclub with Maria.

With Tatiana freshly bathed and her hair sparkling, Elena stood on the sidewalk waiting and watching for potential clients. Tatiana sat on the sidewalk, her legs splayed, the piano draped across them. For an hour she "played" the piano and sang songs only she could understand. The sight charmed the GI's who walked by. The first one who offered Elena money received a stern reproach, "We are not beggars. We are waiting for people in need of translation. That is my job."

He laughed. "Good for you. But you don't mind taking it for the little girl. You can use it for her food. Go on, it's not that much," he said, pushing the money into her hand.

He was right, it wasn't much, but it covered lunch. She'd had two customers in the morning, both of whom offered her religious medallions. If she kept collecting Russian saints, she and Tatiana would still be poor, but blessed for the rest of their lives.

In the evening, she told Maria she'd earned the money from translating.

"Now we go earn *real* money. Supper at the club and then work." Maria brushed her hair, styling it as she had the first night Elena saw her in the cottage. A blonde movie star.

Elena brushed her own hair, unconvinced that singing in an American nightclub was the right thing to do, but Maria promised there was a room where Tatiana could sleep. It had to be cleaner and nicer than their room.

The club turned out to be a smoke-filled bar, crowded with GIs and plenty of women with too much lipstick. Elena's heart pounded as she followed Maria through the room.

"What are you trying to prove?" a red head with a large chest cawed at her. Elena had to look down to see the woman who spoke.

"Hello, Baby," a GI crooned to Elena. "What's the game with the kid?"

By the time they reached the stage, where a middle-aged man with armbands holding up his shirtsleeves, played honky-tonk music, Elena was ready to run, except she was afraid to fight the crowd to get out of the room. Maria dragged her beyond the piano, between green brocade curtains and into a relatively quiet hallway.

"You have to meet the owner. I told him about you. You'll go on at ten o'clock."

"Ten o'clock! How does he even know I can play?"

"He trusts me. It's already after eight. Come on. They have costumes. Let's see if we can make you look more like a showgirl."

Elena had her doubts about being a showgirl, especially if it meant looking like the floozies in the bar.

The dressing room consisted of one long table against the wall with several small mirrors tilted at various angles, leaning against the wall. Tubes of lipstick, pots of powder and rouge littered the tabletop along with used cotton balls and water glasses containing various levels of liquids, none looking much like water. A single bed stood at one end of the room covered in coats and dresses. Maria quickly shoved them aside to make a nest for Tatiana, who at first refused to sit there, but relented when Elena unrolled the piano for her.

"You play in here while Mama plays over there." Elena pointed to the doorway. Tatiana had rarely been alone since being born; she hoped her child wouldn't feel abandoned.

Tatiana laughed at her own music while Maria helped Elena change into a pale yellow evening gown. She combed her hair for her and added a fake flower over her right ear. By the time

Elena was ready to make her first appearance, Tatiana had fallen asleep with the piano clutched in her fist next to her face. Maria pulled a jacket over her.

"You look like a damned virgin, kid. The GIs are going to want to buy you hot chocolate, not champagne," Egbert, the owner of the club said when Maria introduced them. "You better sing good and play better!"

Elena's heart was in her throat and her mouth was dry as she waited her turn to go on. Why had she let Maria talk her into this? She'd had so little time to think about it or to make any plans.

The pianist had finished his gig and now, after a fifteen-minute break, she would make her stage debut, playing—what?

Forty-seven

The piano player whistled to catch the attention of the audience. Elena stood in the darkness behind the curtain, her left hand hurting; she could feel perspiration staining the pale yellow gown. No music or songs came into her mind. Nothing.

"And now to entertain you until the early hours of the morning, we have talent straight from–from the Moscow Conservatory, Miss Ellen–Ellen Russky!"

Face burning with embarrassment, Elena stepped through the curtains into the spotlight. A smattering of applause and a few wolf whistles greeted her. The piano player took her hand and led her to the piano to the right of the small stage.

"Whatcha gonna play, kid?" he whispered, as he helped her get seated. He smelled like perspiration and whiskey.

Voice croaking, she said, "I don't know. I didn't expect to be doing this."

"Your friend says you entertained in the camp every night. What'd ya play there?"

"Russian songs, mostly."

He patted her on the back. "Start with one of those. This crowd ain't gonna care a whole hell of a lot what you play anyways."

Placing her hands on the keyboard, she closed her eyes. Madame Uspenskaya told her to always sit up straight, hands level. She'd even had to balance coins on the backs of her hands when she practiced. *Strike a chord*. The keys were stiff. She struck another chord. "*Ochi chorniye*," came to mind. Another chord in the right key. The music began. She attempted to play it in the blues style the GIs at the hospital had tried to teach her.

The piano player edged onto the seat. "Let me take over, kid. You go to that mike and sing."

"What is a mike, please?" Her fingers continued to move along the keys.

"Microphone. Over there." He tilted his head.

His hands replaced hers as she stood and walked on shaky legs to the "mike." She smiled at the crowd, who ignored her. After listening to the music for a few bars, she found a spot to join in.

"*Óchi chórniye, óchi zhgúchiye*
Óchi strásniye i prikrásniye."

She sang it through to the end, hands gripped tightly to the microphone stand. When she stopped, the room was silent.

The piano player began to applaud loudly, and within seconds the smoke-filled room reverberated with cheers. Elena stood petrified, tears welling, lips trembling as she received the approval of the audience.

"Hey, sing it in English, girlie!" someone shouted. "Yeah, what's it mean?" another added. "Are you married?" a third voice followed. "Who cares?" "I saw her first." The noise overwhelmed Elena.

A tall, dark-haired woman stepped onto the stage and came to her side. "You're good, sweetheart. One more like that and they'll be throwing money and marriage proposals at you like confetti. Keep it up." With a slap on the backside, the woman disappeared through the curtains into the backstage.

Two hours later, the piano player brought out a stool for her and a glass of watered-down whiskey. With only two short breaks, she sang until nearly three in the morning.

By the time they stopped performing, Roger's tip jar on the piano had been emptied several times. He handed Elena a wad of bills. "Your share, kiddo. Them's U. S. dollars. Can you be here again tonight?"

"Tonight?"

"Yeah, go get some sleep and then get your pretty little backside back here by seven."

"Thank you. Thank you so very much. Will Mr. Egbert mind if I bring my little girl with me again?"

"You have a kid?"

"I do. We're going to America soon. I'm going to play in Carnegie Hall."

"The piano? You're going to play the piano in Carnegie Hall? The one in New York City?"

"Yes, that is the one. Do you know it?"

He scratched his head. "Sure, I know it. Maybe you'll sing there, but you sure ain't gonna play no piano there. Change your clothes and get outta here. Bert needs to close up."

Stunned by his comment, she turned to leave. When she reached the curtains, she faced him again. "My name is Elena – Elena Federova."

"Right, kid. Oh, one more thing. See if you can find some gloves to go with the dress. That hand is one ugly mess."

She awoke at nine in the morning, dressed Tatiana, left Maria sleeping and headed back to the sidewalk café where she paid for their breakfast. She then took up her station next to the entrance to the Central Tracking Service and UNRRA, as noted by a new, professional looking sign mounted on the brick wall to the side of the door.

After a day of translations and donations, she carried Tatiana to the nightclub where she took her place at the piano and began to practice. Tatiana sat next to Elena for an hour before it was time for supper. To her surprise the dark-haired woman from last night invited her to join the rest of the group for the evening meal. Pleased with the invitation, she waited politely while the dark-haired woman served the food and they passed the plates around. Elena watched as she handed them one after the other until finally, she gave Tatiana hers and the next one belonged to Elena. She studied the odd-looking pinkish rectangle of food on the plate. The others made fun of it, calling it SPAM. Elena cut a small piece and tasted it. Though it was salty, she liked it. Tatiana enjoyed it along with the mashed potatoes and even ate the unfamiliar greens.

"So. Ellen, I am Janina,' the dark-haired woman said, "wife to Egbert."

The American piano player chain smoked while he ate. Maria arrived shortly before seven, having already eaten with the GI she came in with. Elena learned that her job was to encourage the GIs to drink. Elena didn't think they needed much encouragement, but if Maria could earn money that way, it was fine with her.

With American songs added to her repertoire, Elena gained popularity with the GIs in the area. She sang "Besamé Mucho," "I'll Get By," "Don't Fence Me In," "Chickery Chick," and dozens of other songs. Though she understood the words, the meanings of many of them were lost on her.

After her humiliation the first night in the club, she always wore long black gloves with her gowns when performing. Men shouted proposals from the audience; they asked her out after hours, but she refused any advances. Surviving with Tatiana had become the focus of her life.

Maria went her own way, but periodically showed up in their bed. Nicer furnishings also showed up. Elena wouldn't spend money on a room she planned to leave as soon as possible, but Maria believed they should be comfortable wherever they lived.

"What's the point of being alive if one can't have some pleasures," she argued one night when she came home with two GI's tagging along behind carrying a cot with a mattress for Tatiana and three new woolen blankets.

Another night Elena discovered four crystal tumblers with a bottle of single malt Scotch on their table. She helped herself to a shot and found she liked the taste. That became her drink of choice.

At the club when a customer offered to buy her a drink and she asked for a single malt Scotch, they rarely bought her two, claiming she was too rich for their tastes.

Egbert didn't pressure her like he did the other girls. If they didn't sell their quota of drinks for the night, they were threatened with banishment.

"Here is your reward. Very good tips tonight in the glass," Roger told her nearly every evening. "You're a lady of discerning taste." He would salute her as they lifted their glasses.

After the show, Elena put her cash, much of it in American dollars, in a box she kept under a floorboard beside the monstrous armoire.

They celebrated Tatiana's third birthday at the club. Janina and Egbert gave her a dress ordered from Paris. Tatiana twirled and danced before climbing onto the piano bench and playing "Happy Birthday" to herself. "I am happy, happy, happy. I'm free!"

Elena laughed. "You're not free, you're three. Say three."

"I am free," Tatiana insisted.

"I suppose you are at that. You're three *and* free. And a happy, happy girl."

"Dance with me, Mama!"

Myles came to the party, having provided Hershey bars, cocoa and evaporated milk earlier which Janina used to make a chocolate cake.

After dinner and cake, Elena sat at the bar, Scotch in hand, observing her daughter's ability to charm the adults, admiring and envying her joyful innocence.

"Why so unhappy?" Myles asked when he came to the bar for a fresh drink.

"I am not unhappy. Tatiana is happy; that makes me happy." She turned to look at him, how his green eyes focused on her, his beautiful even white teeth when he smiled, and wished once more that he wasn't married. "Are you happy?"

He laughed. "I'd be a lot happier if I could be home, but for now, yes, I'm reasonably content."

"I too, would be happier if I could be in America."

He shrugged. "Bureaucracy. What can I tell you?"

"You could tell me when you think of any plan that would work to get me there." After swallowing the rest of her drink, she wandered back to the piano and sat next to Tatiana who now regaled her audience with Russian and American nursery rhymes.

Tatiana jumped from the bench and twirled, showing off her new dress to latecomers. "Look. Me pretty!"

Myles joined Elena on the bench. "Wouldn't it be nice if her father could see her now?"

Elena's body stiffened. "What do you mean by that?" She dropped her gaze and turned away. Her eyes burned.

"Relax. I didn't mean to upset you. You said he died before you left Leningrad. I was just thinking of my own children and how much I'm missing them. She's adorable; he'd be so proud."

Her scalp crawled. The liquid in her glass rippled like a storm at sea. "I do not *ever* speak of him. Not *ever.*"

"I'm sorry. You'd better drink that before you dump it all over your dress." Myles stood to leave.

"He was an ugly, ugly man," she said under her breath, just loud enough for him to hear.

Roger took Tatiana's hands and spun her round in circles. Her laughter contrasted sharply to the raw emotion that threatened to overwhelm Elena. She finished her drink and stood up, hoping to escape the room that now felt overcrowded. Her breath came in short gasps.

"I have to get out of here. I must to be leaving." Pushing blindly past Myles, she stumbled into the hall. The noise followed her as she made her way to the dressing room. She slammed the door and flung herself onto the cot, burying her head under a pillow. Her hands clawed at the blankets as if to dig a hole for her to escape.

A knock at the door. She forced her breathing to slow and waited for whoever it was to go away. She couldn't think of a single English word to make them leave.

"Elena," Myles called. "May I come in?"

She bit her lips and remained silent. If she stayed there long enough, she might meld into the coats strewn over the bed and disappear. No one would find her. She could die.

The door opened.

"I planned to wait until tomorrow to tell you my surprise, but perhaps we ought to talk now."

Forty-eight

Elena moved her head slightly so she could better hear him.

"Do you want to come out from under there and talk? I think you'll like what I'm about to tell you."

"No."

"Hiding for the rest of your life won't work. Besides, people are going to want their jackets soon. Tatiana will need to go to bed. And you need to pack."

Unsure of what she heard, she shifted again. "What did you say?"

"We're going to Munich."

She shoved the clothing aside and sat up, wiping her eyes. "Who's going to Munich?"

Myles grinned. "My unit is transferred. I have papers for you, Tatiana and Maria to travel to Munich as well."

In shock, she went to him. "You are having us come to Munich with you?"

"Not exactly *with*, but yes. You'll find life easier there and certainly more opportunities for earning a living, more food, more housing." He held up his hands. "The city's not without its own concerns, but you'll be that much closer to America. And I'll be able to keep an eye on you."

Unable to contain herself, she flung her arms around his neck. He smelled so good, aftershave and perhaps a little cologne. His arms encircled her and he gave her a short squeeze before easing her away from him.

He loves me. For the first time in nearly three years, she felt cared for and loved. She grabbed his right hand in both of hers and led him to the chairs at the makeup table. "I think I should tell you about Tatiana's father."

"It isn't necessary."

"It is if we are to be friends; friends don't keep secrets. But please don't look at me while I explain. I'm ashamed and embarrassed to tell you." She knew she had to tell him if they were going to plan a life together. The story of Hermann and Willie was far too important a part of her life to keep it from the man who loved her.

Myles looked into the mirror. She knew he would cheat and watch her face in the glass. That would be all right with her. Tonight love filled her heart with happiness.

"My family had been at the German encampment for only a few days. I was disguised as a boy to keep the men from noticing me, but it wasn't long before they discovered me to be a girl. Wilhelm Becker befriended me. We played checkers in our off times and talked about our lives. I thought my father had been correct in bringing us to Germany because in the camp we had plenty of food and a warm place to sleep. The colonel and Willie treated me well. Then one day while I was preparing the dining room table for the next meal, Hermann caught me. I was alone. Defenseless. He was a large man. A mean and ugly man. He would not let me leave. He – my clothing." Her voice trembled.

"You don't have to say anything else, Elena. I can imagine."

"You cannot imagine the pain, the humiliation. Maria helped me. Willie and Hermann fought in a terrible boxing match. Hermann died." Elena studied her hands in her lap as she waited for her love's reaction.

His hand covered hers. "My heart goes out to you, Elena, but your official paperwork states that Tatiana's father is a deceased Russian soldier. Let's leave it that way. No point in complicating your emigration papers. Now, are you ready to get back to your daughter's party?"

Her eyes met his. There was no doubt in her mind of his sincerity, his love for her. Why would he become so abrupt, so cold? No, she didn't want to return to Tatiana's party; she wanted him to hold her and love her; she wanted her body close to his. Not like it was with Hermann, but gently, lovingly close.

Myles leaned toward her and kissed her lightly on the forehead. His lips were soft, like Tatiana's. Savoring the love, she closed her eyes and smiled. "I will be most happy to be going to Munich with you, Myles Hall."

"Good. Now, there's a little girl who's going to be missing her mother."

He pulled her to her feet before she could say another word. Next thing she knew they were in the hallway and then back to the party. Smoke floated in layers from the ceiling halfway down to the middle of the room. People shouted stories at one another. Tatiana danced like a dervish as Roger played his honky-tonk piano. Elena recalled reading about Dante's inferno; this is what it would look like. Garishly made up women and drunken men.

Munich. It would be better in Munich. "Come, Tatiana. Birthday's over. We'll go home now. Tomorrow is a special day for all of us."

After thanking Roger and Janina for the wonderful party, she caught Maria before she could disappear with her latest beau and explained about Munich. "…and he's arranged for you to go with me," she finished.

"Of course he's arranged for me to be with you. I'm the only one listed legally as Tatiana's mother. Where you go, I go. Besides, who would be your agent? Together we make good money. You let your GI take you home. I'll be there later."

Elena listened as Maria switched from Russian to speak to her GI friend in English. "We are to traveling to Munich tomorrow, Al. I am to be leaving. Tonight we shall be good with one together, yes?"

Elena smiled to herself. She would have to work on Maria's English if they would be traveling to America any time soon. With Myles now her official sweetheart, it could happen any day. She had a fleeting thought that he had a wife in America, but dismissed it—if he loved her, Myles would work it all out. Maybe his wife had already become tired of waiting for him to come home and found someone else to love.

Elena felt truly happy for the first time in years.

Forty-nine

Munich, August 1946

Elena hesitated before leaving the two-room apartment they'd shared for the past two and a half months. "You will stay in all night, won't you? Myles is taking me for a late dinner after the show."

"You look nice," Maria said, lighting a cigarette with a gold lighter.

Elena felt more than *nice* in a new dress Myles had helped her buy. In the last couple of months she'd gained weight and filled out. When she walked along the streets, the sight of a young woman striding along beside her, looking smart, shapely and sophisticated still surprised her when she realized she was looking at herself in shop windows. She was proud of her unruly blonde hair, which she kept immaculately clean, brushing it a hundred times a night so it would glisten in the spotlight. The blue sateen dress with its full skirt and sweetheart neckline accentuated her figure. She wore costume jewelry she'd bought from a street vendor. After slipping her stockinged feet into low heeled black pumps she picked up a light jacket, prepared to leave.

She'd taken to wearing a thin gold band on her left ring finger, European style, to keep men at bay and head off a lot of questions when she was out with Tatiana. When she and Myles took her to the park, people assumed they were husband and wife. They didn't know Myles already had a wife and children in Vermont in America. He shared their letters with Elena. The wife's letters spoke of loneliness and visits to a country club and the need for new appliances. She found them curiously impersonal.

Myles believed today was Elena's twentieth birthday. They'd become good friends. While disapproving of Maria's behavior, Myles tolerated her because he believed she was Elena's family. Myles gave Elena's business card to anyone requiring a translator so she managed to keep her small family fed and housed. Food was still hard to come by, but when it existed, they could afford it.

"Myles says it won't be long before it will be our turn to go to America."

"He says that every month. The only news I hear from my friends is that the American president hasn't approved a special quota for displaced persons. We could have been in England by now, living a good life."

"What makes you think life in England would be any better than here? They were bombed also. They still have rationing. It doesn't sound any better than Germany. America wasn't attacked."

"Neither was Argentina. Why don't we go there?"

"For myself, I don't even know where it is. Promise you'll stay in until I return."

Maria blew a smoke ring. "The minute you get home . . ."

"Thank you."

"Be careful."

Elena stepped out into the rubble strewn street and worked her way down the three blocks to the underground nightclub where Maria had found her a job singing. This would be the first time she'd left Tatiana at home. Her child loved playing the piano before the bar became crowded and the Russian manager enjoyed teaching her the scales and simple pieces to play. Tatiana quickly learned each song and was eager to know more. Elena couldn't remember if she'd been that eager when she was that age. Certainly she'd shown enough talent that she was able to enroll in the special school for musically talented students. When they finally reached America, she would find such a school for Tatiana.

"Achtung, Fraulein!" a man's voice called out.

Before she could react, she felt something brush past her shoulders. That was followed by a loud crash with dust flying up around her. Pieces of stone struck her back and legs and she stumbled to her knees. Her first thought was that she'd torn her stockings, a rare gift from Myles; then she worried that her dress had been ripped.

The stranger who'd tried to warn her crossed the street to help her up.

"Are you hurt?" he asked in German.

"I don't think so but look at my stockings." She turned her back to him. "Is my dress all right?"

"Pardon me," he said before he began brushing the dirt away. "It appears to be only very dusty from the falling bricks. May I escort you to your destination?"

"Thank you, no. It is only a short distance. I am fine." Eager to be away from the stranger and even more anxious to examine her dress, she hurried toward the building that housed the club.

The man scurried right along beside her. "It was not always such as this, the shells of buildings. The scaffolding that tries to hold the remaining buildings upright. Munich was a beautiful city until the Allies saw fit to drop bombs on it. Goddamned Americans and Brits, that's what I say."

"Leningrad was also a beautiful city," she managed to huff out.

"Ach, so. You are a Russian! I spit on them, too. And I am sorry I helped you."

She stopped. The man bumped into her. Taking a moment to look him over and catch her breath, she finally said to the hatless, toady little man, "Are you really?"

His small mouth pinched, his eyes bulged. "What do you mean? Of course I regret helping a Russian—no matter how beautiful she is."

He turned to go, but she caught him by his jacket sleeve. "I am alive today because there were two very kind Germans who helped me during the war. For the rest of you, I say, 'bastards.'" She spit at his feet, gave him a shove, and then ran from him to the safety of the nightclub.

After removing her dress, she found that a damp cloth dispensed with most of the dust. A fresh pair of stockings, after washing the scrapes on her knees, and she was ready to go out with Myles. First, she had to sing for at least four hours. "Please, God, don't let anybody remain after eleven o'clock. I want so much to be alone with Myles." There was more she wanted to pray for, but God would probably not approve. She blessed herself and went to find her accompanist. No one could guess which mood he'd be in on any night. When he chose to be Freddie, he oozed charm; when he was Frieda, his make-up and attire fooled the patrons. The regulars figured Freddie and Frieda were twins, brother and sister. He'd taught Elena some bawdy songs for the wee hours of the morning and lovely romantic songs for when couples came in. Her repertoire grew and as it grew, so did her income. As soon as Myles told her she could apply for a Visa to the U.S., she'd have the money to cover everything.

Maybe, if tonight went well, she wouldn't need all that money. Maybe she could use it to help buy them a new home in America. Glowing with happiness about her prospects, she pulled on her gloves and took the stage. Her joy must have shown because they cheered every song, laughed at every joke she and her piano player, Frieda tonight, exchanged.

She was a star.

When Myles arrived at midnight, the place was full of smoke, but that was left over from the crowd. A lone woman sat at the bar while two men each tried to convince her he was the best choice to leave the bar with.

Myles handed her a corsage of violets, tied with a white ribbon. "Happy birthday, Elena." He kissed her on the cheek. How much she loved him for his kindness and respect toward her. Tatiana adored him. They would make such a happy family.

With downcast eyes, she took his hand and bade goodnight to Frieda.

"What'd you do with Chow Time?"

"Maria agreed to stay in for one night. It's good for both of them."

"She's an amazing kid, the way she's picked up playing the piano. We ought to find her a private tutor."

We. "We should, but not until we reach America. I don't think it would be good to start her here and then change her suddenly. She likes what she's doing now."

He led her across a broad avenue where pedestrians strolled even at this late hour. The weather remained warm. "I have some news about that as well. I'm saving it as a birthday gift for you."

Her heart jumped. She grabbed his forearm in both her hands. "News? Tell me! Tell me now! I can't wait!"

He laughed and pried her hands from his arm. "Of course you can wait. It is a kind of good news. Anyway, I think you'll like it. Come on. We're dining here."

"Here?"

Disappointment must have shown on her face. Myles put on a hurt face, his lower lip sticking out the same as when Tatiana was upset with her. She laughed at him. "I will love whatever you are doing for my birthday."

"Your twentieth birthday?" he shouted over the noise in the room.

"Yes, of course." She swerved to avoid a serving girl who carried a large tray laden with at least a dozen steins of beer. The girl carried it with one arm, balancing it above her head.

They reached a pair of large double carved wooden doors. A man dressed in local attire pulled one side open for them.

Now she walked behind him as they wove their way between crowded tables, long tables with half a dozen or more people sitting on benches on either side of them. In spite of the hour, men, women and children filled the tables.

Lights twinkled in the trees spotted throughout the garden.

Myles stopped and turned toward her. His face was inches from hers. "Close your eyes now."

She closed them, her heart thumping. Would he really kiss her in the middle of such a crowd? He picked up her hand in his and led her further along between tables. "No peeking," he ordered.

"Now open them."

He placed his hands on her shoulders and moved her in front of him. She felt a table in front of her and placed her hands on it. Eyes open, it took a moment to focus on the faces at the table.

Tatiana helped by shouting, "Mama! Happy Birthday." Her fabric piano was the centerpiece of the table. In the center of it stood a porcelain vase filled with pink roses. Maria sat beside Tatiana to Elena's right. To her left, two old people watched her expectantly. Elena smiled politely, confused.

"Aren't you going to say hello to your mother and father," Myles spoke softly into her ear.

"Mama? Papa?" She staggered back and Myles caught her.

Fifty

Papa stood. Normally thin, he resembled a clothed skeleton, like the people from the camps. He held out his good arm and Elena broke free from Myles to run around the table and hug her father. "Papa," she cried into the rough cloth of his shirt. His ribs beneath the shirt protruded like a fragile model of a human. She released him, fearing that she might hurt him.

"You've become a beautiful woman, Elena, my daughter," Papa said, his voice choked with tears.

"I told you, young man, she is not caring about her mother," Anna's voice cackled from the old woman, who did not appear to have been starving.

Elena turned to her mother. "Oh, Mama, how I prayed for your safety. I hoped you and Papa had managed to find a new home and happiness."

"We've been sharing a room with eight other people in an old school building. Your father is the one who spent all his time searching for you instead of seeking a way to America." She slurped her tea, ignoring the rest of the party.

"Myles, how did you find them?"

"I heard about a couple searching for their daughter, 'Elena– the girl with the piano.' I thought of you, but the description didn't quite fit. Theirs was a sixteen, then seventeen-year-old girl who carried a cloth piano around like a child's security blanket. The girl they described was a brilliant pianist." He stopped, his face turning red. "Not that you aren't good, Elena, but you are a far better singer than pianist. You do know that?"

Insulted and pleased at the same time, Elena wasn't sure how to respond to Myles' comment. "They called me a brilliant pianist?" She looked at her parents, warmth flushing her cheeks in the glow of their approval and love.

"That's what was written in the report."

"Your father was searching everyplace he could be finding a displaced persons office. The United Nations, the Red Cross, all the churches." Mama waved a hand showing her disregard for such organizations. "Tonight we eat good. I am to be ordering the *schnitzel.*"

"Papa! Are you ill? Why are you so thin?"

Papa shrugged off her questions. He spoke in Russian. "I'm more interested in knowing how you have fared on your own. Have you been with this woman all this time?" He indicated Maria who was helping Tatiana drink a warm soda without soiling her dress.

"Maria and I have become like sisters," Elena replied.

Tea spurted from Mama's mouth. "Sisters? You and the whore?"

"Don't say that, Mama. Not in front of Tatiana, please. She calls her 'Auntie' and loves her."

Mama glared at Tatiana as if she were a poisonous snake about to strike. "You know what I think of all of you."

Elena sank onto the chair at the head of the table. Myles held it for her and then rested his hand on Elena's shoulder while he spoke. "I don't pretend to understand what was just said amongst yourselves, but I do know that it wasn't pleasant. We're not here to settle old scores or differences tonight. We're here to celebrate Elena's *eighteenth* birthday and the reuniting of a family unit."

"How did you know? How long have you known?"

Myles laughed. "Your parents told me. That was one of the big discrepancies. They searched for a younger girl. When I thought about it, it made sense. Because of all you've been through, you could be any age from sixteen to twenty-five. I have your photo in my files and showed it to them. They immediately recognized you. You should have seen your father's face. I've never seen a happier man."

Papa's attention was on Tatiana. "He does look happy," she said, feeling an overwhelming sadness at this reunion. If only her mother had been happy as well. "What happens now?" she asked in a leaden voice.

"Now we order beer, more tea for your mother, and food for everybody. For tonight, let's all be happy. Tomorrow, we begin on new paperwork." Myles signaled the waiter.

"New paperwork? For what?"

"We've changed the family arrangement and now we can begin anew to apply for a visa to America. Your father has brothers there. We need to locate them. But that's for tomorrow. Here comes the soup!"

"Chow time!" Tatiana laughed and clapped her hands.

The beer, when it arrived, turned out to be a mixture of beer and lemonade.

"The first time I encountered this drink, I wondered how anyone could drink such a horrible concoction," Myles said. "Then I asked them where they found lemons, when nobody in the country has access to fresh fruit, not even juice. Was I surprised to find out that, one, it tasted good, and two, that what Europeans call lemonade, we call soda or Seven-Up?"

Even in this restaurant, suspected of black-market activities to secure food, the scarcity of supplies was evident. The platters delivered to their table evidenced that as well, each plate and bowl holding a sparse portion of potatoes, cabbage, and schnitzel.

Both Mama and Papa dove into their food as if they hadn't eaten in months, though Myles assured Elena they were being fed at least two meals a day at the school. When she thought about it, she could have said the same thing about the prison camp; they received two meals a day. The schnitzel had arrived, hot and crispy. Though Elena couldn't identify the meat, she savored each mouthful along with the noodles, gravy, and red cabbage. When everyone had eaten, Myles stood. "I have a birthday gift for Elena and a late one for little Chow Time."

After pushing back his plates to make room for it, he placed his briefcase on the table. He removed two small packages wrapped in festive paper, both tied with pink ribbons. He passed one to Tatiana who sweetly said, "Thank you," and then tore the ribbon and paper from a book. "I have a book, Mama!" She held it up for everyone to see. "Will you read it to me? Can I keep it forever?"

"Let me see." Elena reached for the book. On the cover was a little mouse dressed in shorts and a sleeveless shirt, paddling a canoe. The canoe had a name on its side, "Summer Memories." The book title was *Stuart Little*, by E. B. White. She opened the book as if it was precious gold. Inside were pen and ink drawings of the adventures of the little mouse.

"How sweet," she said to Myles. "Where did you ever find it?"

"I asked my wife last November or December to send a children's book for Tatiana for her birthday. It took this long for it to arrive. But it worked out nicely. She says our children love Stuart and she enjoys the lessons in the book. Now open your gift."

His wife had chosen the gift. She probably also picked out the one for her. Elena flinched at the thought of a present that Myles' wife had sent, but to be polite, she told herself, she ought to open it. The package was about two inches square and eight inches long. She hefted it and was struck by its weight. She untied the ribbon, curious about what Myles' wife would think a homeless Russian girl might want for a birthday gift. Nothing came to mind. The colorful tissue wrapping fell away to reveal a plain white box. She looked up at Myles to see if there was a clue in his eyes, but he only smiled at her. Lifting the lid she peeked under the edge and was confused by what she saw. Waxed paper covered brown wrapping paper. She overturned the box onto the table to let the contents drop out. It looked like a loaf of something.

Myles cleared his throat. "It's a fruitcake."

Her heart dropped to her toes. "A fruitcake?"

He shrugged. "I told her about the food shortages. She makes these every year for Christmas. They're really very good. Would you like to have some now for dessert?"

She slid the cake toward him. "Will you please serve it? I've never seen a fruitcake before. It's been in the mail…."

"Six months, but don't worry. These are made a couple of months ahead of time and soaked in sherry. That keeps them fresh and moist." He raised his arm to signal a waiter to bring them a knife and dessert plates.

She sank back onto her seat and watched him unwrap the solid looking cake. When the knife and plates arrived, he cut thin slices for everyone, leaving half the cake for her to take home. The sweetness made her mouth tingle. Taking tiny bites, she nibbled her way through her portion unsure whether she liked it or not. Mama eyed the closed box next to Elena's plate.

When they were finished, Myles stood once more to get their attention. "I have one more small gift for Elena on her birthday. He pulled a small package from his jacket pocket.

Her heart warmed with joy. Hands trembling with happiness, she took a small jeweler's box from his hands.

"I found this quite by chance in a shop last week. It reminded me of you." He smiled a sheepish, boyish grin and sat down.

More in love with him than ever, Elena lifted the lid. Inside rested a small, enameled pin set in gold. It was of a grand piano with the lid raised. Tears welled. She didn't know what to say.

"Now you really are the girl with the piano."

"Two pianos!" Tatiana said. "Let me see, Mama."

Elena held it out for everyone to see. After the ooh's and ahh's she removed it from the box and held it out for Myles to pin it to her dress.

"I'm not very good at that sort of thing," he said. "Maybe your mother would like to do the honors."

Elena looked at her mother and then to Maria. "Would you, please?"

"Yes, why not? These days it would seem more appropriate to give it to Tatiana. She plays the piano more than you do since we left the camp," Maria said under her breath so only Elena could hear.

"Tomorrow morning we start early," Myles announced, "so, let's call it a night."

"What do we start?" Elena asked.

"A new round of paperwork to get you and your family to America. We'll be working through The Intergovernmental Committee on Refugees. You come under a special heading of displaced persons who are unable to be repatriated to their home country." He raised his hands in surrender. "Don't ask. I fill out the papers. The UNRRA is still involved, as is the Red Cross. Your parents have been living on CARE packages from another new organization." He gathered up Elena's gifts and handed them to her. "Put them in your purse; keep them safe. I'll see your parents home and then we'll meet again in my office bright and early." He leaned over and kissed her on the cheek. "Happy Birthday."

"Stuart rose from the ditch, climbed into his car, and started up the road that led toward the north. The sun was just coming up over the hills on his right. As he peered ahead into the great land that stretched before him, the way seemed long. But the sky was bright, and he somehow felt he was headed in the right direction." From Stuart Little *by E. B. White*

Epilogue

New York City
May 1957

Elena waited in the wings for the music to stop. Her heart pounded so loudly she was sure the audience could hear it over the piano and orchestra. The girl with the golden hair wearing a blue dress stood, faced the audience, and bowed. She acknowledged the orchestra and then held out her right hand toward Elena.

Walking out onto the stage, Elena took Tatiana's hand as she stepped to a microphone. When the applause died down, Tatiana spoke. "Thank you for coming to Carnegie Hall to hear me play. Today is my fourteenth birthday and I must thank my mother, Elena Federova and my aunt, Maria Federova, for making my dream come true."

Tears ran down Elena's face, her lips trembled as she smiled, but she managed to applaud when Maria stood up in the front row. Papa also stood with his brothers, Alexander and Paul. Papa had only recently stopped wearing the black armband in memory of Anna, who'd died two years before.

She took the hand of the golden-haired girl in the blue dress and escorted her off the stage. With her left hand she wiped her tears with a well-worn lace handkerchief.

The End

About the Author

Veronica Helen Hart

Born in New York City, a graduate of Miami Edison Senior High School, Florida, Ms. Hart attended university in several states and two countries. Her studies focused on Russian Language, Literature and Culture. As described in the Foreword, it was at university when she met Lydia N., her Russian opera-singing friend, who told her the story of walking when a child from besieged Leningrad to Germany.

Ms. Hart has lived in several states, visited most of them, and has traveled extensively throughout the world. She spent four years living in Tehran during the 70s. London and Paris are two of her favorite cities.

She writes about historical, humorous, adventurous, and always, strong women. The book awards have been for humor, (*The Prince of Keegan Bay*), historical (*Elena-the Girl with the Piano*), science fiction (*Silent Autumn*), paranormal murder mystery (*The Knife*), and a young adult adventure (*Escape from Iran*).

Ms. Hart is married to veterinarian, Dr. Robert Hart, also an author. They have six daughters and eleven grandchildren. They make their home in Ormond Beach.

Other Titles by Veronica H. Hart

<u>From Paranormalice Press, LLC</u>
The Knife
Storey's Orphans (speculative fiction)
Annie Karenina (speculative fiction)
Recovery (a short sci-fi story)
<u>Uppity Women Press</u>
The Reluctant Daughters
Escape from Iran
<u>Champagne Books</u>
<u>The Blenders Series:</u>
The Prince of Keegan Bay
Swimming Corpse
Safari Stew
Midnight in Mongolia

Silent Autumn
Coming in January 2021: Boy comes Home

All books available on Amazon, Kindle, and at Uppity Woman Press.com or Paranormalice.com

Readers are an author's lifeline. If you enjoyed this book, we'd appreciate a review.

www.ingramcontent.com/pod-product-compliance
Lightning Source LLC
Chambersburg PA
CBHW051234260626
47162CB00002B/427